D0391518

NO LONGER PROPERTY O
SEATTLE PUBLIC LIBRARY

A PAIR
OF WINGS

A NOVEL INSPIRED BY PIONEER AVIATRIX BESSIE COLEMAN

CAROLE HOPSON

Copyright © 2021 Carole Hopson

All rights reserved. No part of this publication may be
reproduced, distributed, or transmitted in any form or by any
means, including photocopying, recording, or other electronic
or mechanical methods, without the prior written permission
of the publisher, except in the case of brief quotations embodied
in critical reviews and certain other non-commercial uses
permitted by copyright law. For permission requests,
write to Permissions at info@jetblack.press

Jet Black Press
69 Montgomery Street
P.O. Box 465
Jersey City, NJ 07303
www.jetblack.press

Design and Layout: Ute Kraidy
www.utekraidy.com

Print, hardcover ISBN: 978-1-7355111-7-7
Print, softcover ISBN: 978-1-7355111-6-0
eBook ISBN: 978-1-7355111-8-4

Printed in the United States of America

Second Edition

For
Michael,
Joshua,
and
Coleman

You were born with potential.
You were born with goodness and trust.
You were born with ideals and dreams.
You were born with greatness.
You were born with wings.
You are not meant for crawling, so don't.
You have wings.
Learn to use them and fly.

Jalal al-Din Muhammad Rumi
30 September 1207 – 17 December 1273

CONTENTS

CHAPTER 1

So, this was death.
No engine growl, no propeller beating the air,
no wind in my face, no sun on my neck.
My eyelids felt weighted and wouldn't budge.
My arms and legs felt heavy when I tried to move them.
I forced myself to be still and to remember,
but memory was elusive, each thought slipped
out of my grasp just as I tried to capture it.
Fuel—acrid, pungent, vital. That I could feel it burning
the back of my throat meant I must not be dead.
Images began to flicker—a still propeller that should have been spinning,
voices calling from below me,
the earth rushing up.
Sky land, sky land, sky land ...

My altimeter had been reading a comfortable two thousand feet before its long hand began a vicious counterclockwise spiral, counting down the feet I was rapidly descending. Instinctively, I yanked the stick back into my chest, causing an abrupt upward pitch that heaved the nose of my aeroplane towards the sky, speed bleeding off as it rose. Since altitude gain was lost for good without any power, the only thing left was to reach a glide that would cover the most ground. I thrust the stick forward to regain the speed I needed.

The plane rattled, as if with fever. The engine spit once, and then, like a ruptured heart, my Curtiss OX-5 engine burst, spewing hot oil from both sides of its chest. My heart pounded in unison, as a square of tin sheet metal peeled back, shearing off like ripped skin from a wound. As what now amounted to a giant razor blade hurtled past my head, I ducked and said a silent prayer that it would land far away from any living thing.

Through my oil-spattered goggles I could see nothing but hills in every direction, but in the distance, I thought I could make out what looked to be a level field, and with a plan to put her down gently—engine out, no big deal—at the glide speed of fifty miles per hour, I felt confident that I could make it. I'd just set her down nice and easy like, directly into a headwind to give myself maximum lift.

Alone in the cockpit, with only myself to rely on, I began speaking directions aloud and counting on the science I knew by heart: Because of the wing's humped shape, it cuts through the air in a way that produces a positive—or upward—pressure under the flat bottom of the wing and a negative—or reduced—downward pressure on the hump on the top of the wing. This relative difference in pressure, while small, is big enough to produce lift.

With less than a thousand feet to go, my scientific meditations stopped abruptly. The field I had been aiming for no longer appeared static. As I descended, I could see that it wasn't a field at all. It was a playground; the doors of the building attached to it were flung wide, as dozens of children fanned out in every direction, their barrettes and brass buttons flashing in the sun.

I ruled out what not to do. Any turn I made would be disastrous. A slow-speed turn would mean one wing awkwardly pointed downward and the other wing up. A deadly spiral would come next. I would strike the ground wingtip first, and a wicked cartwheel would splinter the plane, grinding everything below me to bits. At five hundred feet, distance, gravity, and the inescapable laws of nature added up to hard facts and a set of desperate calculations. There were only two things I could think of that would give me enough distance to glide past the schoolyard. Next to me, I had strapped body-sized rucksacks filled with

Coast Tire leaflets. The heavy weight of the paper was dragging my speed, and so I unbuckled my seatbelt, unbuckled the sacks, and heaved them over the side, providing a couple knots of airspeed and adding a fraction of a minute to the time I had left in the air.

The milliseconds clapped by in my head. Only two hundred feet to go, and I was descending fast, close enough to the ground to see the plaid pattern on a boy's cap, the plaits bouncing atop a redheaded little girl. I could see light glinting from another girl's spectacles as she bent and scooped up a fallen child—a slighter girl in a blue-and-white gingham sailor-dress. A nun in a habit was trying to herd the children back into the building, but to no avail, the little ones were scrambling everywhere, scattering like billiard balls. At a hundred feet above them, I was now near enough for the plane to eclipse their view of the sun, and for the howl of the wind from my wings to drown out the sound of their screams.

In my peripheral vision, I saw a schoolhouse flag waving gently in the breeze, indicating the direction of the wind. If I could land with the wind at my back, I might add a couple of yards to my landing distance. In a normal situation, a tailwind is the least desirable wind with which to land. A tailwind pushes, forcing the plane to roll, sometimes past the end of an air strip. A tailwind can push you into a chicken coop, pigpen or, worse yet, into a grain silo, or even off a cliff. But I was already smack dab in the middle of a worst-case scenario, so I snatched the last opportunity I had. Every foot counted. At this point, every inch counted. Cartwheel be damned, I threw my boot into the rudder and sliced right. A gust of wind obliged.

Within seconds, there were no more choices. At fifty feet, I tugged on the stick, pulling it back as far into my body as it could go, but it was exhausted. There was no more air left between me and the ground, and the earth rushed up at me before it swallowed both me and my aeroplane whole.

CHAPTER 2

T he day had not begun in peril. The cool morning of February 4, 1923 promised to give way to sun and fair skies, not at all like the bleak Chicago winters I had escaped. Here in Santa Monica, the streets were lined with palm trees and blooming hibiscus all year-round, and the Pacific Ocean lapped miles of warm powdered-sugar beaches.

Arriving at the airfield before dawn, I rolled the hangar door. It squealed, peeling back with a tangerine-like tease, revealing inch by squeaky inch, my very own biplane with its propeller pointed due east. The smell of the hangar greeted me as well—machine parts freshly bathed in lung-coating petrol.

Using a footstool, I hoisted myself into the open cockpit, where I settled onto the pine bench. Draping a tattered old windsock that doubled as a shawl around my shoulders, I drew it in tightly against the predawn chill. Dust from cloth wings settled around me as I waited reptile-like for the warmth of sunrise.

A giant ball of blood orange pierced, then splashed itself across half-darkness, erasing a canvas of navy sky. Our brightest star radiated throughout my body. Like youth and beauty, the great intensity of the sun climbing above the horizon proved to be fleeting. And soon the world turned on its axis just enough so that the afterglow and wonder of sunrise melted, vanishing into the ether of a new day.

My plane's maiden voyage was going to be a short hop, a forty-five-mile jog east to the fairgrounds at Palomar Park. Like any good aviator, I had checked the weather, and the *Santa Monica Evening Outlook* promised blue skies and fair winds. Over the course of the next three days, that pure California sunshine would yield twenty thousand people, all gathering to catch a glimpse of me—the first Negro aviatrix in the world. After three grueling years of training and performing, I now had the skills to become a barnstormer, and I planned to dazzle my audience, treating them to daredevil stunts and trick flying the likes of which they had never seen nor even imagined.

I would make my audience dizzy with loops, tingling and terrifying them with the thrill of my spinning so close above their heads that they felt the danger above them was more theirs than mine. But the orchestrated stunts are not the scary part; I could do these tricks in my sleep. What gave me pause was flying these old relics, some of which had no business being in the air. Up until now, all of my shows had been performed in borrowed aeroplanes. I had been lucky, real lucky. Only sixteen years after the Wright Brothers had flung themselves into the firmament, I had too. And since then, many aviators had paid in blood for our lessons. I had trained in France, Berlin, and Amsterdam, and I credited the dogfighters of the Great War with what I learned early on— they taught me that many flyers will encounter the test before they learn the lesson. If one survives the test, the lesson has been learned. If one does not, whatever knowledge they have gained dies with them.

Although assembled only the week before, this aeroplane was already six years old, its parts having come in an unopened crate from a Great War surplus graveyard. When given the chance, I had chosen it myself—a 1917 Curtiss JN-4. Nicknamed "Jenny" by lonely soldiers, this aeroplane was the best of a pitiful lot. My camouflage-painted biplane was mine, but I didn't own it. It was almost a gift from the Coast Tire and Rubber Company, who had hired me to use the Jenny to shower the public with Coast advertising leaflets, floating them from the sky down onto the beachcombers below.

A Mr. Robert Paul Sachs, the President of Coast Tire and Rubber held the aircraft registration and title. In a quest to fulfill his boyhood dream to fly, he and I had formed an old-fashioned quid-pro-quo partnership. I had promised to fly him around old oil rigs and empty fields and, in exchange, I could use the plane when I wanted. No matter how generous this arrangement appeared, I was under no illusions about it, for although I alone could operate the aeroplane, it was Mr. Sachs who controlled the comings and goings of the plane itself. I hadn't forked over a single Indian-head nickel of my own, yet that bucket-of-bolts was the extent of the company's investment in me until I proved myself. I was nearly destitute, and this new job was the promise of hope itself.

The enormity of what I was about to do was epic. Here I was, one thousand, five hundred miles away from where I had been born and raised as a Texas cotton picker, flying an aeroplane in order to sell tires to Pacific sunbathers who were wealthy enough to drive motor cars! While the thrill of it was breathtaking, my extreme good fortune was fragile at best. The "new" Jenny was flying upon old cloth wings, which I prayed had not suffered from dry rot in that crate.

But it is hope, then and now, that remains my life's currency. Although the aeroplane and much of my life felt tenuous, I considered that glorious morning the best day of my life, and I was brimming with anticipation of the great things to come. I hopped out of the Jenny and began my preflight examination. These old clunkers always needed something. I checked the engine oil and tightened nuts on the cowling, the engine's tin fender. Then, a final walk around her forty-two-foot, double-decker wings and I was as satisfied as I could be.

"Mornin', Bessie!" Brock called. The depot mechanics always arrived early. I heard the chafing of his freshly laundered overalls, his long strides headed my way. "Need anything?"

"Just a hand-prop," I called back.

Brock, who had assembled the plane, nodded that he would oblige. We dragged it out and pointed its nose into the wind, and I hoisted myself into the cockpit again.

With a mass of glossy black hair and periwinkle eyes, Brock was like many of the white men I'd met here at the depot in Santa Monica. He was a puzzle of neutrality—neither friendly nor unfriendly—and unlike his one-syllable name, he was opaquely uncomplicated.

After my seatbelt was secured and my handmade charts were stowed, I took one last look at the sky and shoved my goggles into place. With the ease of a magician, Brock threw my plane alive with a hard spin of the propeller and dove out of the way. We exchanged a thumbs-up followed by a salute, and he sauntered back along the path leading to the hangar.

Over the objection of my stomach's jitters, I pushed the throttle forward. At the same time, I drove the delicate cherry-red mixture knob to its most forward position. The mixture control regulated the amount of fuel and air that blended and flowed through a valve into the carburetor. During takeoff, I needed the aeroplane's maximum performance, so I opened the mixture valve wide.

The plane rumbled. In one sweep I ran my fingers through my hair and then the palm of my hand over the dash to soothe my machine. I took note as I did so of my own shabby condition. Dark engine oil ringed the cuticles on hands that were neither smooth like a southern belle's nor manicured like a debutante's, the overall effect a confirmation that I'd never find a home in either of those worlds. But it didn't matter. Here my heart raced, pulsating to the beat of the aeroplane's cylinders. This was the only place where I'd ever really felt that I belonged. As prop-wash swirled about the plane, a sense of awe washed over me. I was overcome with gratitude, for I had made my own improbable place in this world, and it was right here on this flat pine bench. I didn't care who the documents claimed as its owner, this ship was under my command, and that made her mine.

I pushed the throttle forward and the engine grumbled in response. Then the rudder pedals sprang to life beneath my feet. When I had first learned to fly, steering the plane with my feet had been a revelation. Push the right foot pedal, and the plane veered to the right. Push the left foot control, and the machine slewed left. By now, using the balls of my feet to steer on the ground, or to lead the stick in the air had become second nature. I didn't have to think at all. To keep the aeroplane going straight, my boots danced on the rudder pedals, right, right, right, right, then a little left, then right. I sat so low in the seat that I could only peer over the glare-shield. At twenty-five miles per hour, there were enough aerodynamic forces to lift the tail skid off the ground. Before that, I couldn't see a thing—it was all feel.

As I gathered speed, a sea of tall grass and short shoots whizzed by. I straddled the stick, cradling the length of it between my legs. The stick commanded two axes of flight—roll right or left and pitch up and down. During takeoff, I needed the stick to operate the control lever of the tail assembly, the elevator. To do that, the tip of the stick would rest squarely between my knees. The width and feel of the thing was like the handle of a broomstick. With just the slightest squeeze of its shaft into my torso, I felt my aeroplane climbing, and for a breathtaking moment, I felt both great peace and invincibility. It did indeed feel as though I was riding upon a witch's broomstick, gliding upon the breath of the supernatural, carried by the anxious whispers of my ancestors.

Perhaps those ancestors had chanted warnings but, like Icarus, I wasn't listening. Traveling east into the stunning sunlight and leaving the coastline behind, I headed inland toward Palomar Park. As I climbed higher, trees grew smaller, cows became the size of dogs, a barn looked like a shed, and clusters of buildings became bumpy alligator skin; a winding road carved an S deep into the land, and the tufts of tree tops reminded me of my youngest sister's curly head when she was just a tot.

With increasing altitude, all things change. While objects shrink, perspective grows. Everything was as it should be. Or at least it was for a tantalizing moment, in which flying felt pure and I was fearless. But in the time it took to blink, something had gone wrong, gravely wrong.

CHAPTER 3

I heard their footsteps before I saw them.

My lids and lashes batted away dirt and blades of saw grass, and my eyes opened on a sky so blue and a sun so bright that it hurt to look up. Flat on my back in a pool of gasoline, somehow all I could smell was strawberries. I twisted a bit, thinking that if I could only free my right leg I would be able to crawl away, although to where I had no idea. But like my aeroplane, I had been spiked into the ground, unable to move, let alone feel any sensation in my useless limb.

It took every effort to lift my head in order to see who or what was approaching, and when I raised my arm to wipe away what I thought was sweat clouding my vision, my hand came away dripping with blood. This new discovery meant that I now had one working leg and one working eye, through which I could see a woman approaching where I lay. As she got closer, I recognized her as the nun I'd seen on the playground. Her flowing robes were black as crude, and under her white wimple her face was a cameo of distress. I had been raised a Southern Baptist deep in Texas, and nuns like this woman were frightening to me, completely foreign in their look and having unknowable power. On her heels, bobbing up and down and holding some sort of brown bag, was a man shorter than she, in a black priest's robe. Atop his Roman collar and slung around his neck, was a glossy stethoscope that at first I had taken for a snake. Beads of perspiration glistened on both their brows as they knelt down in a black-and-white heap next to where I lay trapped and buried under debris. Wood spars had snapped into spiked stakes, and flying wires were tangled in the grass, forming a dozen fox noose-traps that caught feet and fingers. Fuel leaked. They panted from their efforts and from what they now saw. There was dread in their eyes.

They began removing shards, working together to pull and remove the heavy OX-5 engine that had pinned my leg deep into the ground. When they finally cleared the debris, I could see my mangled leg, twisted grotesquely and pointed in an entirely unnatural direction, like a half-ripped off ragdoll's. The toe of my right boot was buried in soil up to the arch of my foot, while my heel saluted the sky.

What was revealed beneath the heavy metal was a thigh that had been sliced nearly in half. The bone had ripped the skin wide open, and surrounding the wicked wound was a flap of brown skin, filleted back and badly frayed at the edges; flesh hung down like a banana peel. No longer staunched by the heavy engine, plumes of blood pulsated in a red fountain.

Prying me out of the wreckage, with what remained of a shattered leg, did not appear to be a straightforward undertaking. But the priest fashioned two tourniquets from the fabric that he ripped from the petticoat beneath the nun's skirts. He tied one around my upper thigh, the other he knotted tightly above my knee where, even so, blood stubbornly continued to seep through the cloth. Above the knob of my knee, the priest used his collar to create a strap to secure the bandage. Finally, the blood hydrant stopped, but the gaping wounds still leaked. We were all three covered in blood—their robes, their hands, and my own.

At first, they worked gingerly, methodically, to break through the wreckage. But as I began to lose more blood, their work became more urgent. The only thing that was clear from their conversation was that they did not want me to understand what they were saying. They spoke in code.

The priest was soft spoken and whispered something inaudible, but the response from the nun made it clear she had had enough. Tiring of their discretion and sounding more like a man's, the nun's harsh, deep voice rose as if from a well, somewhere far below her throat.

"Should we just sever it?" she breathed heavily.

With every minute the situation worsened. In the time it might take to dig me out with their bare hands and carve me away from the wreckage,

I could bleed to death. But if they amputated my leg in order to free my body, it would not necessarily improve the chances for my survival. If they sacrificed my limb, the doctor whispered to the nun, "She may still bleed to death right here in the dirt."

They made a choice. The latter was the best course. The doctor rooted around in his dusty old medicine bag that, up close, looked like a boxer's glove, scratched and worn. From it, he tossed bottles of pills to the ground, followed by vials of liquids, some of which shattered into more shards. Finally, he drew out a hideous instrument, whose steel handle glinted in the sunlight. The wicked blade was curved like a minia-ture scythe. "I don't have everything I need," he confessed to the nun. "Holy Mary Mother of God," he pleaded, "What I need is a bone saw, and I don't even have any way to cauterize the stump." His staccato whisper now came in a series of hoarse commands, "Run! Hurry! Fetch the largest costotome."

I learned to fly aeroplanes from ace dogfighters in the Great War. During the teens, the newspapers were chock full of atrocities and medics' confessions—barbarities in their methods of cauterizing battle-field amputations. The enemy of infection set in after mud, bone, and blood mixed. Medics became creative as salvage mercenaries. They sealed gaping wounds with hydrochloric acid, smelting skin into liquid glue; packed the stump with salt, and dunked the limb into boiling oil. They'd use a wicked fishhook device to snag arteries out of the stump and tediously tie them into knots to stop the bleeding, or they would burn the wound shut by simply dousing the offending stub with fuel and setting it on fire.

"Fetch the tenaculum," he barked, adding this to his list of mutila-tion gadgets.

"Anything else?" she pressed.

"We should pray," he whispered.

I didn't know what in the world they were going to pray about, but I myself was praying for a miracle.

The nun snatched one of the discarded bottles from his medicine bag. In large, block lettering its label read CHLOROFORM. She doused another blood-soaked strip of her petticoat until the rag was dripping garnet droplets, and in one swift motion passed it to the priest. Then she took off running. There it was again, the whiff of strawberries, I thought, as she disappeared from view. Here we were in a strawberry patch, the ground littered with smashed berries, their juices joining in pinker swirls with pools of blood. But soon, the chemical odors obscured all else; the gasoline and impending chloroform masked the berries' perfume and pushed me further towards darkness.

I needed to stay awake. These strangers intended to amputate my leg, and I needed to keep them from doing it. But I had no power to fight them in the condition I was in, and the priest shoved that bloody cloth over my nose and mouth, holding it down so hard that I thought he would surely suffocate me. I gagged then struggled. Everything hushed, and even the blinding sun began to dim. Blackness closed in around me, and it was as dark as the folds of the priest's cassock.

CHAPTER 4

S nares. Thunder rolling around, deep inside an old copper kettle. My good eye unhinged, Cyclops-like, flung itself open, and then closed again in reaction to the bright spotlights that bounced off bleached subway tiles lining the walls from floor to ceiling. The throbbing percussed again deep in my skull, but it was nothing compared to the clatter and clangs of a modern hospital emergency ward. With a more careful squint, I saw the indigo tattoo of St. Catherine's Hospital stamped on the crisp white sheet covering my upper half. Everything below was caked in blood, dirt, and oil. What looked to be an entire convent of stern nuns huddled around me, nurses scurried, a white man in a pristine lab coat fussed over a tray of bone saws, which did nothing to still my heart. Everything was confusion, mayhem, a roiling timpani cluster of sounds.

What is happening?

A nurse came closer, holding a huge syringe up above her head. It looked big enough to baste a turkey. I had seen quite a few tire gauges that big, but surely this wasn't meant to enter a human vein.

"You will only feel a little pinch," a thinning smile smeared itself across the face of the pretty brunette, as cloyingly sweet as it was condescending. Eager to complete her duties before I could protest, her free hand patted the back of mine. It was an action that was practiced and emotionless, the way a weary adult might comfort a frightened child. She flicked the glass vial and plunger apparatus with her middle finger. Like a balloon on the point of a lance, the tiniest liquid-filled bead balanced. That liquid bead steadied itself until she thumped the syringe again. This time, she forced it to break off and slither down the tip of the harpoon. I watched it splash, forming a tiny crown as it burst open on the tile floor. Seeing my distraction, the nurse plunged her spike of a bayonet deep into my arm.

"Wait! I need to be somewhere!" I objected.

I had never been in a hospital before, not even to be born. I'd had twelve siblings, and each one of us had come into this world within the confines of my parents' bedroom. Behind the heavily bolted door, a stoic team of female neighbors, led by one matriarch we all called Aunt Ruth, had made blood, muck, and rags disappear, leaving nothing but a freshly scrubbed baby behind. And still, four babies, the siblings I would never know, did not make it out of that room alive. And when the women's work was over, burying those tiny bodies under the Texas pecan tree in the garden had been Daddy's grim task alone.

Instinctively, I knew that this lance carried drugs that were meant to silence me.

"Listen, I have to be in Palomar Park," I said as loudly as I could manage. My bloody fingers circled her freckled wrist, and she looked down archly at my grip.

"I am expected to do an airshow in a couple of hours," I pleaded.

"My dear, we will be lucky if you ever walk again, not to mention fly," said the doctor-priest, who had returned to the side of my gurney. I tried to concentrate on the meaning of the last words I had heard him say, before the chloroform took over, *if you ever walk again*. I tried to look down at my leg, but I couldn't raise my head. The medicine in my veins had left me, noodle-like, unable to command any part of my body to do what I wanted.

"Did you do it? I heard you and the nun. Did you cut off my leg?"

I felt my hold on consciousness fading again. The doctor-priest was speaking; he was answering me directly, moving his lips and making words, but not in a way that made sense to me. What I did hear was music—Beethoven's *Moonlight Sonata*, specifically; it soared above the sound where there had been only the chatter of nurses just a moment before. As the music swelled, it seemed less and less important how many legs I now had. There was only the music.

I had heard this music before, and it bore me back to the day I arrived by rail at Oakland's 16th Street Station. Sliding through the leaded glass doors, I had made my way across the elegant grand hall and down to the labyrinth below, where I had found a line of wire-cage lockers to stow my cheap cardboard suitcases. The metal boxes were surrounded by Samson-like fluted pillars, and although it may have looked like a dungeon, this was the home-away-from-home resting quarters for the Pullman Porters, who made the railroad run.

My eldest brother was one of them. He and many other Negro men were at home in this underground world—laughing, joking, eating. In this subterranean maze they could take off the masks they wore in the world above and be their own selves, in their own brown skins. On the day I first arrived, one of these men had drawn a fiddle from its tiny black casket and had played the sonata. Echoing off the limestone pillars, swirling over stacked suitcases, and sliding down staircases, it seemed to flow right through me. I was captivated. So too were the fifty porters gathered around him. We circled the fiddler, mesmerized and silent, watching this man, and afloat on the magic he could draw forth from his instrument. His eyes were closed, he hugged the fiddle lightly, as if it had grown straight out of his arm.

And here was that same music again, only this time, instead of letting it flow over me, I flew into it. Instead of my uniform, I was now wearing a red chiffon flapper's gown. Violin strings collided; the resonant cries of the cellos seemed to be at war. I grew camouflage wings and fought to stay in the roiling atmosphere between bleating flutes and crashing timpani. Suspended in their cloud-like midst, updrafts and downdrafts dragged me along on a rope of unstable air that undulated between stormy firmament and murky ocean. As the music grew to a roar, my wings stalled between sky and water, and my propeller became ensnared in chiffon, while unforgiving riptides of current ate up the sky.

As if in the tumultuous space between heaven and sea, I waded somewhere between this world and the hazy hereafter for more than a week, suspended in a drugged waking-slumber. I heard the sonata again, only this time, slowed and blurry.

I somehow wrenched myself free from the murkiness. There was silence and darkness. It was night. I thought that I was alone. But just in case I wasn't, I played possum—I wanted no more sleeping potions.

My mind reeled on moving pictures. Jumpy images flashed by in the

17

dark—grimaces, my ghost ship looming over a playground, children running, my crushed wings, smashed berries, the razor-sharp scalpel, fuel, a nun and a priest in black gowns, blood congealing on dirt. I remembered bringing my hand up to my face and lowering it again sticky with blood. I did the same now and felt a taught patch over a bandaged eye.

A groaning hinge gave way to a squeal from the other side of the room. Slowly, the door opened, and light flooded the entryway and spilled into the room. The cone-shaped beam cast ghastly shadows around the unfamiliar surroundings but provided just enough light for me to steel myself to take a terrified look.

My leg.

I lifted my head a few inches from the pillow and saw a hideous cast encasing my leg from hip to ankle. Although it must have belonged to me, it was hard to recognize. Strung up with metal spiked pins and connected to heavy chains and leather straps, my limb dangled precariously from the ceiling.

But somehow, that leg was still attached to me.

I recalled reading a *New York Times* headline that boasted of The Hospital for the Ruptured and Crippled in Manhattan being able to make Great War soldiers whole again by knitting bones with steel pins and such. But I was three thousand miles and a whole world away from those new techniques and pioneering surgeons.

"You're awake," said a voice that sounded vaguely familiar. As I moved to find the owner of the voice, the chains hanging from the ceiling rattled against each other, and the clanging breathed life into a memory of the ghost in *A Christmas Carol*, which I used to read to my three younger sisters every year. Maybe the ghost had stopped by to taunt me instead this year. My visitor yanked a cord and there was more light.

But this spirit bearing light appeared as flesh, and I recognized him. It was the priest from the strawberry field. Here, in this sterile hospital room, his dark eyes seemed kinder than I remembered, a welcome contrast to what haunted me—his flashing scalpel and the look of blessed domination as he was smothering me to sleep.

"Yes, I'm awake. And thanks to you, I am alive," I responded warily.

"The thanks go to you." He stepped closer to my bed and reached for my bandaged hand.

"How is that?" I asked, flinching, although I didn't want him to see my fear.

"We came running the moment we heard the commotion in the schoolyard," he said.

"Oh, God! The children ..." My throat felt as if I were swallowing gravel.

"Thanks to your skill and quick thinking, they are all fine. We consider it a miracle. In our line of work, we still believe in them, you know," he smiled. "And although I may have tended to you, it was God who helped you land just beyond the schoolyard. The children at our orphanage came away without a scratch."

"My name is Bessie Coleman," I said, the gravel only slightly starting to recede. The doctor-priest filled a cup from the pitcher by my bed and handed it to me. I considered it holy water.

"We know. You are quite famous. It is not every day that we get a celebrated barnstormer in our sleepy little hospital," he said. "When I learned who you were, we did everything we could to save your leg. I have repaired many broken bones in my time, but yours was the worst I have ever seen. Did you know that the femur is the longest and strongest bone in the human body, and yours had snapped in half? You've got a good deal of mending to do, but we will get you out of that bed soon. You will need to exercise to regain your strength."

I was to discover that in addition to a broken femur, I had suffered broken ribs, internal bleeding, and a series of lacerations that covered most of my body. More than that, and almost more painfully, the realization of what had taken place plunged me into a terminal case of gloom. Not only had I deserted more than twenty thousand fans, but also my aeroplane was ruined in a heap of twisted metal, wires, and rags and, with it, my sponsorship from Coast Tires, too, was gone. I had lost everything.

There on my nightstand was a stack of newspapers. "Flies all over Europe!" shouted *The California Eagle* headline; "Makes Demonstrations in New York and Chicago—Meets Waterloo in California. Fall Laid to Defective Plane." Just like that, my entire life had been summed up—a succinct tombstone epitaph in black and white. The only thing missing was the added note: Born a cotton picker, struggled to attain big dreams, fell to earth on vainglorious pride.

Another headline echoed the first, "Plane Falls; Woman Hurt"—this one was from the *Los Angeles Times*! Unable to focus fully, I skimmed the article—"shaken and bruised ... smash-up ... engaged to give an exhibition ... nosedive, and crashed to the ground ... demolished, but did not catch fire ... wreckage ... the cause of the plane's sudden failure could not be learned."

Failure—

Not long before these headlines, *The Daily Examiner* of San Francisco had said, "Miss Coleman is the only American flyer who has ever flown over the ex-Kaiser's palaces at Berlin and Potsdam, and the only woman possessing an international license entitling her to make flights anywhere on the globe. She has the distinction of flying the largest plane flown by any woman in the world. She made exhibition flights at the American Legion convention in Kansas City, in the presence of Lloyd George of England, Prime Minister Briand of France, and other world notables— enviable recognition among flyers of both sexes throughout the world."

Back in 1921 Robert Abbott, my good friend and the publisher of *The Chicago Defender*, my favorite newspaper in the whole world, had had an article written about me, "Aviatrix Must Sign Away Life to Learn Trade." And it seemed he had gotten it right.

The *Examiner* article quoted Mr. Sachs, of Coast Tires, as being complimentary, but he had also said that my crash was merely a "mishap," and that it "delays his advertising work temporarily," making it clear that Mr. Sachs would continue with his advertising campaign. He would just allow someone else the opportunity to do it for him. It was at this moment that I understood my own sudden powerlessness. I could not move an inch, let alone fly and, more than that, my good name and reputation lay crumpled in that strawberry patch along with my aeroplane.

I began to do what in the past had always served me well, both on the ground and in the air. I made a long hard assessment of the facts as they presented themselves at that moment, a moment that seemed insurmountable from where I now lay.

Later that day, the nurses somehow poured me into a wheelchair so that I could use the privy instead of the bedpan. As we entered the stalls, we passed a looking glass attached to the bleached subway tiles of the bathroom walls, and I was startled by my own reflection. A weary old woman, who looked like me, but with dark circles and a sallow complexion, peered back from the cloudy glass. Beneath the eye patch, yellow pus oozed onto my swollen cheek. My hair sprang from my head in an unkempt mass—elastic and wild, a halo of tangled wires; I wore the crown of the insane. In an effort to hide from myself, I sank down deeply into the wood and wicker wheelchair.

A brisk knock on the door provided a grateful distraction. The pretty brunette nurse who had wielded the syringe had come to fetch me. Kneeling at my side, she announced gruffly, "You have visitors."

"Oh, dear God, I'd rather that you stab me again with another one of your bayonets than let anyone see me like this," I muttered. "Who are they?"

"A Mrs. Bass and a Mr. Luther Ramsay," she said. At her answer, I sank further in the wheelchair, hoping that eventually I could melt into the lavatory floor.

"Bessie," Mrs. Charlotta Bass had said only weeks before, "I am going to have the carpenters erect the grandstands right alongside the air strip, so that all twenty thousand people can see you when you hop out of your aeroplane contraption!" Her smile had been wide with pride. As the first female publisher of a newspaper in California—and the largest Negro paper, at that—Mrs. Bass had promoted the airshow by putting both her name and her money on the line for me.

"Only Colored Aviatrix in the World a Los Angeles Vision," proclaimed Mrs. Bass's *California Eagle*. And I had been that. But now what? What could I say to her? I knew she hadn't received word of my accident in time to share the news with the throngs of people who had planned to attend. How much had I cost her wallet and her reputation?

"Come, let's wash your face and make you presentable. Your visitors said they will not leave until they lay eyes upon you," said Nurse Bayonet. Although freckles wriggled on her nose when she smiled, I saw pity beneath her cheer, and that pity cast an infinite pall over me. She had the look of someone who knew all the layered components of her field, from fixing broken bones to mending broken spirits. Her understanding gaze undoubtedly indicated a long and difficult recovery ahead for me.

At the rumble of my rickety wheelchair, Mrs. Bass and Luther turned to look as Nurse Bayonet and I entered my room. Next to the bed, Mrs. Bass had discovered the pile of newspapers proclaiming my destruction that I had read earlier in the day. They dangled from her fingertips now like evidence in a crime scene. For an uncomfortable moment, no one spoke but everyone stared.

I greeted them with the titles of affection reserved for church members. "You, my dear sister, will never be a poker player. Your face betrays your every thought. Luther, you too are crystal clear."

Mrs. Bass bent down, threw her arms around my neck, and cried like a mother upon seeing her child's spilled blood, while Luther backed himself into the hanging hospital curtain encircling my bed, curling his body into it as if he might disappear. My wounds hurt him too much for him to meet my eye.

While they waited, Nurse Bayonet got me settled into bed, returning my leg to traction, attaching the hulking mass to the leather straps, like a ham suspended from an abattoir ceiling. Chains, rods, leather straps, and pulleys made up the device that was attached to a long line of pins going through my leg. Blood, both dried and fresh, pooled at the connectors, staining the plaster cast. Luther winced as the nurse cranked a winch to turn clicking gears that hoisted my leg back into midair.

"I'm sorry," Mrs. Bass whispered. "As a rule, I try not to cry." Tears streamed down her cheeks, and I instinctively reached out and touched her hand. Although we were ordinarily the same caramel brown, I was struck now by the difference in our skin. While Mrs. Bass's body glowed with her usual rosy complexion, my blue-green pallor looked dead against her vibrant arm.

A decade older than I, Mrs. Bass was a well-dressed, dignified sort. The newspaper she ran proudly celebrated and defended the Negro race, especially those members of it who had launched their careers in this rugged western frontier called California. Yet Mrs. Bass looked, and her southern lilt sounded, more like the South Carolina church lady that her mother must have been than the militant West Coast journalist she herself had become.

"It is I who should be begging your forgiveness," I said, forcing myself not to look away from her stare. She had pulled herself together and was regarding me now with the knowing gaze of a warrior who had gone to battle for our people. Her arsenal was made up of provocative headlines that chronicled the massive movement of Negroes from the South to the West, heralding their struggles for meaningful work, housing, and education—all after having survived the journey of their lives. Mrs. Bass's cherubic features disarmed many a foe who had underestimated her, and her innocent, ladylike demeanor was yet another weapon she wielded to attain her goals.

"I am so sorry about Palomar Park," I managed to whisper. "I am so ashamed."

"Our people acted most disgracefully. When they heard you weren't coming, they rushed the ticket booth. I heard more than one story about people saying they knew you couldn't be real. I got a telegram from St. Catherine's the next day explaining what had happened. But even before then, I knew something must have gone terribly wrong for you not to be there." She glanced at the square cut-out on my thigh and at the six inches of bubbling stitches that bulged up through the plaster.

"As a race, we too often suffer from self-loathing. Your good intentions confuse our sense of trust. If *The California Eagle* had been a white newspaper sponsoring the event, our people would have accepted an explanation, any explanation," Mrs. Bass declared.

"Who in the world let you see this garbage, Bessie?" Luther interrupted. He had been standing over the nightstand, glancing at the stack of papers there. As was common in that day, a regular helping of violence against us was chronicled in gruesome detail on many a page. The *Bakersfield Morning Echo* that very day had published the headline demanding that the city "Lynch Two Negroes."

Luther pitched the entire stack into the metal trashcan next to my bed. "Read this instead," he said, and handed me the current *California Eagle*. On the front page was an article he himself had written, "Other Race Appreciates Girl Flyer. Miss Coleman Spoken of Most Highly" in which he challenged all the *Eagle*'s readers to dedicate themselves to the effort of helping me defray the cost of my hospital stay. "I hope that you will allow yourself time to heal because I need you back."

Luther, five years my senior, was as protective as one of my brothers. A dapper, hazelnut-colored fellow, Luther and I had met in Chicago. I was teaching flying classes out of a storefront, and although I had a full class, Luther was my only paying student. After a couple of loops and spins in my borrowed plane, Luther convinced his bosses at the Oakland headquarters that I should become a flying advertiser. He was the best salesman I'd ever met, for he, a Negro, had persuaded his white bosses to buy me an aeroplane "to fling advertising flyers from heaven." Luther became my biggest cheerleader. All he asked in return was for a few thrills for himself in the sky.

Luther had started out as a salesman for Coast Tire and Rubber and had soon become the first Negro promoted to lead the entire mid-western team of salesmen. Up from the Deep South, Negroes had thought that the Midwest and the North were all opportunity, and in some respects they were. There was work in abundance but being frozen out of unions kept Negros from being able to protect themselves from poor conditions and low wages, and they soon discovered that getting a home loan was nearly impossible too.

From Detroit to Gary, no one would lend a Negro a down payment to buy a picket fence around his dreams. So instead, Negroes bought fancy automobiles to proclaim their new city slicker status. But rugged dirt roads and bumpy cobblestones meant that all automobiles would one day soon need new tires. So, Luther sold more tires than his white counterparts on the East Coast and in the South combined.

"You are both generous and kind," I said, dabbing the puss that leaked beneath my eye patch. "I'm not a down-in-the-dumps sort. But I feel real low right now," I said to Luther. "I have lost everything, the aeroplane and that sponsorship you gift-wrapped for me. I feel like I've lost my ability to keep moving forward. I just keep replaying the moments before the crash over and over."

"Bessie," Mrs. Bass said quietly, watching me with growing concern. "We can't change the past; we can only learn from it. You have no choice but to keep going."

"You know there are people out there right now saying, 'See, I told you so, a colored woman flying an aeroplane—too big for her britches!'"

I wept.

"What you feel right now is perfectly normal, Bessie," Mrs. Bass offered. "Loss forces mourning, and you must mourn. But since you have the time, you must simultaneously reflect and heal. Use this time you have been given to teach others what you know. I want you to recall your memories, and when I say memories, I mean all of them. Force your most intimate thoughts onto paper; record your bold desires for the future. Because you do have a future."

"I couldn't possibly."

"You can. And you must!" Mrs. Bass said.

"What's this?" she asked, fingering some scrap papers on my tray. Each paper was stained with coffee rings and dotted with food smudges.

"That's just scribble-scrabble, just the stuff I could remember after I woke up," I mumbled.

Mrs. Bass must have already been prepared for this moment. She dropped the papers and dug deep into her large pocketbook, producing five beautifully bound leather notebooks. She then drew out a gray felt box. A tiny piano hinge along one side squeaked as she opened it to reveal a black and gold pen with a small snowy star on top. Delicate gold filigree danced on its clip, and an internal hose-like bladder supplied a steady flow of ink to the gold nib. On the felt, the word Montblanc was elegantly stitched.

Mrs. Bass christened the first book, her sweeping hand wrote in one fluid motion before passing it to me.

Be strong and of a good courage. Joshua 1:6
Bessie, you must leave a trail.
Let my faith in you spark your belief in yourself once again.

The first tear stung. The stitches below my eye twitched. For the first time in my life, I felt afraid of absolutely everything I used to do without so much as a second thought. How could I ever find the strength to climb back into an aeroplane again? Hell, and even if I could, where would I get the money for one?

Jumbled recollections on scratch paper were one thing, but what Mrs. Bass was challenging me to do was a much bigger task. I was rattled by her assignment—she meant for me to tell the whole truth about my humble beginnings, and she clearly meant for me to include my most intimate entanglements, those that I had worked so hard and for so long to obscure. I had spent a lifetime hiding my real self from the public, shielding my vulnerabilities in order to convince the world that I was a fearless swashbuckler. I wanted my spectators to see a stunt flyer, not an ordinary loner, broken by the very thing that had made her so audacious. Telling the truth meant exposing the most basic facts about my life. Not even my good friend Luther knew how old I was. He had described me as "a spirited twenty-three-year-old" in his newspaper plea on my behalf. This was a bald-faced lie! But I made sure not to mention it.

I was thirty-one.

With all these busted bones, I felt older still.

"How can I write about my life? Where would I even start?"

"You must begin at the beginning, my child," was all that Mrs. Bass would say before leaving me alone with my notebooks and elegant pen.

I started to walk again. I had weaned myself off of the murky tincture that lessened the pain but kept my mind too foggy to think. The doctors insisted I exercise outdoors, and Nurse Bayonet, in all her freckled beauty, had turned cruel, insisting that the doctors' orders meant wheeling me to the beach on a pitted road where I was bumped and bounced the entire way. She would watch from afar, as I strengthened my muscles by hobbling over shifting berms of sand, a daunting challenge for my fragile mending limb and ribs.

Late one morning, while draggling myself up and over a piece of driftwood, I caught my foot on a mound of seaweed, stumbled, and fell. Before I could right myself and pull myself up again, the wind took a turn and a sandy gust hit me full in the face. But in that same gust of wind, I somehow thought I heard the plaintive voice of the Italian opera tenor Enrico Caruso.

And I had. Caruso's longing was floating up from some unseen Victrola needle and through an open window of a beach hut across the inlet from where I lay. And as his voice soared and plunged through *The Pearl Fishers*, I allowed myself to let it flow over me as I stared up into the sky.

I had seen the opera in Paris. I knew the story about a love so great that not even the threat of death could destroy it. And it was that love that called up the greatest emotional response in me. As I lay there listening, I felt again the unshakable love I had for flying. I loved it as much as Leila loved Nadir, and in the same way, even the threat of my own death had not been enough to deter me and it never would. Mrs. Bass knew this about me before I knew it about myself. Today, I limped along the beach, but one day I would soar in the firmament again. Waves crashed, Caruso mourned, I was somehow back in my wheelchair, and then somehow back in my room.

I flipped open one of the journals that had been set on my nightstand in a perfect stack. The spine of the book cracked as I opened it wide, and the smell of glue from the binding filled the air. I stared down at the blank page for a long time before I finally took up the fountain pen in my hand. It was cool to the touch—unused.

Tuesday, February 20, 1923
Santa Monica, California

On January 26, 1892, nearly thirty years after the Emancipation Proclamation was signed by President Abraham Lincoln, I was born in a tiny shotgun shack in Atlanta, Texas. My birth was just a quarter-century after the Thirteenth Amendment was ratified. My Mother, Susan Coleman, was born before all of these laws. She was born a slave. My Daddy, George Coleman, was both Negro and Choctaw Indian. Neither my mother nor my father could read or write. And while their literary skills were underdeveloped because of their circumstance, my parents were resourceful, intelligent, and resilient.

Daddy built our house with his bare hands. We were all hardworking laborers. My parents believed that laziness was sloth and punishable by caning. By age ten, I picked cotton with my sisters and brothers. My tiny fingers bled from the pincers on the bolls. The old men and women who had picked all their lives had an unmistakable humpback that came from season after season of stooping, bending one's back till the bones folded. When I could, I switched jobs to washing clothes and carved out my own laundry route. It's an irony that today I am called Queen Bess, or Queen B, for only a short time ago I was just another faceless, nameless, black drone, a worker bee of the southern economic exploitation that was, and remains, modern slavery—the cotton fields of Texas.

Although my desires were at first undefined, from the earliest age I was convinced that much better had to exist. I craved a better life. No matter how dangerous it was for me to dream of rescue, no matter how vague the pursuit, I knew my survival depended on wishing and, more importantly, striving for greatness.

During the year of my birth, Benjamin Harrison, a Civil War General who had fought for the Union, was President. And while immigrants were welcomed through a brand-new castle built on Ellis Island in New York Harbor, a U.S.-born shoemaker named Homer Plessy, an octoroon, with one-eighth drop of African blood, was thrown off a train because he sat in a Whites Only car.

At the same time, technological wonders were mushrooming. The ticker-tape machine tapped out stock prices and got rid of messenger boys. Thomas Edison, a celebrated inventor with hundreds of patents, was perfecting the telegraph; Alexander Graham Bell, the telephone. Lewis Latimer, a Negro draftsman who worked for both men, was a silent but brilliant ingredient in both of their success stories.

During the next two decades, the Wright Brothers would sweep the world with their wings, and Henry Ford would make the Model T. By 1908, Ford had not only re-invented his automobile, making it more durable, but he had designed a production line that would turn out 10,000 autos that year! This new mass-produced automobile was not more expensive but, in fact, it was cheaper. Ford's assembly line and less expensive automobiles would change how Americans moved about the country—forever.

To "leave a trail," was a provocation for me to organize my thoughts, along with the dozens of newspaper clippings I had squirreled away, and to make sense of this unlikely peripatetic life that I have led.

Peripatetic, now there was a two-dollar word, if ever I had heard one. I thought Mrs. Bass was accusing me of something when she hurled that charge at me once. "Bessie you are a nomad, you have become peripatetic," she blasted. My face must have betrayed confusion as well as offense. For she quickly followed with, "You have become Aristotle's disciple."

As I saw things, Mrs. Bass was an intellect. If she followed the scientific teachings of Aristotle, who taught as he wandered through ancient Athens then I, likewise, had become a disciple of hers. Yes, I had become a journey-woman just like her. Mrs. Bass traversed the country to speak the truth; I crisscrossed two continents to learn to fly. Cotton picker turned aviator—yes, I agreed—at first glance my life defied explanation. If anyone should tell my story—Mrs. Bass was right—it should be me.

After that, the pages just flowed, and so did the tears. So did the laughter—even though our life was hard and our struggles harsh, a great deal of merriment could be found in a house full of Colemans. As I worked my way through my memories, reflecting became an integral part of my healing. I began to bleed the chapters of my life onto the blank pages of the journals that Mrs. Bass had given me. And before long, I would fill one, then another, and then another.

I was going to need a lot more ink.

PART ONE

THE EARLY YEARS

CHICAGO
1915

CHAPTER 5

I n the last letter from my brother, Walter told me that he would meet me inside the LaSalle Street Station. He said I should look for the giant clock above a dozen brass doors and that he would be under it. He said I couldn't miss it. Walter had left home in 1900 at just sixteen years old. In the fifteen years in between, he had become a Pullman Porter, had married, and now lived with his wife in an apartment he shared with our brother John and his wife, Elizabeth. I would be yet another dependent.

There had been plenty of time to think about how long it had been since I had seen him and how his life had changed in that time. The ride from Dallas to Chicago, which had cost a twenty-seven-dollar fortune, had lasted twenty-three hours, with two hundred and fifty of us crowded into a car built for one hundred occupants. Stuffed in between seats, children fussed and cried. I tried not to drink a drop, so as not to have to use the toilet—the air coming from it was putrid, little more than a weeping pot teetering on wooden planks that had deteriorated into squishy pulp. The smell inside that outhouse-like closet was strong enough to stick to taste buds.

Many riders clutched hobo sacks full of hidden treasure—pecan pie, fried up yardbird, biscuits—traveling food. We read *The Chicago Defender* or had it read to us. While it couldn't guarantee dignity, *The Defender* had promised us a shot at a job and housing up north. Every one of us on this train would put up with overcrowding and any other discomfort we had to endure, having convinced ourselves that life itself pulsed in each breath of northern air. We braved the unknown today for the freedom that we hoped to breathe tomorrow.

The men and women on this train were not just taking a trip. It had been only fifty years since slavery had bound us to the South, to cotton fields like the one in which I had labored. Our parents were slaves, then sharecroppers, and now here we were—travelers, dragging our threadbare possessions, with our heads filled with dreams of owning a home, modern conveniences like indoor plumbing, and a layer of fat we'd call prosperity. Even old age loomed as a luxurious possibility. Nikola Tesla was lighting up the world with his alternating current as we left our dark shacks to flood into electric-lit apartments, comfort, work of our own choosing, children—a real future.

The Carolinas and Virginia brought many of us to Washington, DC, Philadelphia, Newark, New York City, and Boston, while Mississippi, Alabama, and Georgia Negroes flooded into Chicago, Gary, and Detroit. Texas was split up the middle, many of us traveled due north to Chicago, while others went north to Oklahoma. If a family's stamina could hold out, some of them made it all the way to California. But whether we settled in Philadelphia, Chicago, or Los Angeles, most Negroes started in the Deep South and took the trains north. The web of the train lines determined our path of escape.

While the Hebrews had Moses, we Negroes had Robert Sengstacke Abbott, the founder and publisher of *The Chicago Defender*. Abbott was our defender and guide out of the wilderness, and in a 1916 headline he christened the Negro departure from the South, "The Exodus." Mr. Abbott believed that we would, we could, and we definitely should, grow exponentially in northern cities, especially in Chicago. Mr. Abbott led us north with articles, encouragement, and enticements. *The Defender* created a path for Negro migrants by offering a special advertising rate for those Chicagoans who had apartments and rooms to rent—thirty-five cents for one week and fifty cents for two weeks of listings in the classifieds. Living in our own neighborhoods had a great side-benefit—we could pool our spending and keep our dollars circulating among our own Chicago grocers, barbershops, tailors, and funeral directors. Mr. Abbott even gave us a new name. He called us "Race Men and Women"—a modern name for those who made a bold, new start. All we had to do was believe and pull against gravity while hauling ourselves north, where promise waited.

Over the years, I collected many clippings from *The Defender*, and one of my prized articles was from way back on February 13, 1915, the day I arrived in Chicago. The headline read, "Railroad Men Great Help to *The Chicago Defender*." The Pullman Porters were those "railroad men [who] circle the globe, and [take] *The Chicago Defender* ... with them." There was a photo of two brand-new auto trucks, with signs painted on each, "*The Chicago Defender*, the World's Greatest Weekly at all stands, 5 cents a copy." The caption boasted further, "Four men, eight hours to supply newsstands, which are networked throughout Chicago." That early caption said there were already "42,000 readers in Chicago"!

Yes, Pullman Porters like my brother were essential to moving us modern Hebrews north. If *The Defender* was our sheet music, the Porters were the choir. We were six cars full on this trip—fifteen hundred deep. If every week brought us north in the same number, we would swell this city by seventy-eight thousand a year. We surely would need every room, cold-water flat, and pitched tent in mecca. More newspapers on newsstands were needed, and so too was a biblical-sized army to settle us.

Our passage may have been rapture, but only one car away I could see what transcendence looked like. White passengers in a separate compartment sat in lavish comfort, but only when someone flicked the blue velvet curtains could I sneak a peek inside their civilized world. Their seats were plump and roomy, upholstered in a tartan plaid of blue and green. There were several functioning toilets and there was leg-room to spare. "Resentment never filled an empty belly," was one of the many truisms my Mama had taught us. Right, as always. I heard her counsel in my head, and told myself that this part of the journey would be over soon.

And it was. Finally, the Rock Island train rolled into the station. I may have stepped off a train, but I felt as though I had stumbled into an icebox. The sky was gray, and it hung menacingly low, as if the clouds held stones. The wind hit me next. We had plenty of gales in Texas, but I had never imagined wind like this—so cold it felt as if shards of glass were cutting your skin.

Amid the crush of passengers, I searched the faces in the crowded station. Would I recognize the grown-up brother I once knew as a child. How to age him? Sprinkle his temples salty? Add lines where my mind could recall only flawlessness?

Walter had left Texas with a rucksack full of ambition. He was convinced that a better life existed up north, declaring, "A colored man just can't walk upright here. If he don't bend his back under the Texas sun, he's gonna be lynched."

Journalist Ida B. Wells proved my brother's point. Mrs. Wells, in Chicago now, hailed from Holly Springs, Mississippi—the place that inspired her to write, *The Red Record, Tabulated Statistics and Alleged Causes of Lynching in the United States*. In order to be safe from "the charge of exaggeration," she said that she had used *The Chicago Tribune* as her source in order to detail the frequency, as well as the horrors of lynching. I owned a copy of Mrs. Wells's book, and I held onto it as if it were a precious copy of the New Testament.

Mrs. Wells reported that in 1892, the year of my birth, two hundred and forty-one persons had been lynched, one hundred and sixty were Negro, the others, it seems, were Indians or of a Negro mix or, as the *Cairo Evening Telegram* described, were "Colored," but they were "neither yellow nor black."

That is twenty people each month! Where was the outrage? In twenty-six states, "Lawlessness and mob violence ... encouraged this state of anarchy," Mrs. Wells reported. These murders were carried out by way of live cremations, shootings, or mob beatings. Whether they were yellow, black, brown, or red, most of those human beings were tortured and ended up dangling from a noose in a public execution.

Mrs. Wells wrote that the "offenses charged for lynching" included: "arson, stealing, political causes, murder, train wrecking, enticing [a] servant away, kidnapping, writing letters to a white woman, insulting whites, well-poisoning, self-defense, asking a white woman to marry, introducing smallpox, conjuring, alleged murder, rape, or no offense at all."

Mrs. Wells didn't just report the grisly facts, she gave flesh and bone and names—humanity—to the two hundred and forty-one people who were murdered. On February 11 she published a story in Little Rock's *Arkansas Democrat* reporting on the obliteration of an entire family. According to the article, first a farmer husband was shot to death in his own home over a disputed one-hundred-dollar debt. His pregnant wife, nursing an infant, was made to watch her husband's wasting. Then she was shot to death. Their thirteen-year-old boy was witness to both his parents' murders; then he was shot twice, including once "in the bowels." The boy watched as the murderers robbed $220 from his dead mother's socks. The infant at her breast "had a slight wound across the upper lip." But where was this orphan now, I asked myself? Father, mother, brother, baby in her body, all murdered in England, Arkansas. Lingering for hours, the thirteen-year-old recounted his family's tragedy, and then he too died of his wounds.

Mrs. Wells wrote about two men in Tennessee who were lynched because they "were saucy to white people." And then there was the wagon-dragging and burning of a man in a pile of brushwood drenched with coal oil in Roanoke, Virginia. There seemed no end to the stories of these atrocities. I felt sickened with outrage as I tried to comprehend her meticulous way of detailing such horrifying finality. There was no reckoning. And there would never be.

My brother Walter had been part of the southern exodus of Negroes who had faced down the fear of the unknown in order to avoid the viciousness they knew. In Waxahachie, Walter's independence and his enterprising nature could easily have cost him his life. I wondered, as I made my way through the crowds, whether he was the same now, whether he had retained that brave spirit he had shown when he was young. Although we were siblings, Walter had become a stranger to me. There were a few letters, but I hadn't laid eyes on him since he had headed North. And now I was searching for my long-lost brother in a sea of strangers.

Thank goodness, I spotted the clock.

As I approached it, a tall copper-colored man said, "Hi, ya, miss." I thought his chin looked a little soft, but could this be Walter?

"Walter? Walter Coleman?" I asked.

"You can call me Walter if it makes you happy, baby."

"What? I ..."

"Beat it, buster! My sister don't need no fast-talkin' hustle!" a voice rumbled behind me, deep and gravely. I recognized it at once. Walter sounded just like my father.

"Sorry, man, she's a real looker. If she was my sister, I would keep her under lock 'n' key!" With that, the stranger moseyed off, blending back into the crowd.

I turned and became confused all over again. The simple act of recognition made me question whether this was my brother or my father. Walter was thirty-one, about the same age as Daddy had been when he left us to go to Oklahoma. Staring into my brother's face, I felt as though

I were peering through an old-fashioned kaleidoscope. The swarm of people, the train whistle, the ticking clock, were all part of a swirling color-wash of background, yet my brother was clear and in sharp focus.

"Walter? Is it really you?"

I was staring so intently that he asked, "Bessie, are you alright? You look like you seen a ghost." Walter reached forward to relieve me of my satchels, but he dropped them when I threw my arms around his neck and held on for dear life. Walter hugged me back. In that embrace, my brother represented life, new life. Here in Chicago, where everything was cold and unfamiliar, Walter became the bridge from my family roots to my undefined, but optimistic future.

"Forgive me, Walter. It's just that you are a dead ringer for Daddy."

Indeed, I felt my Daddy's ghostly presence, as an image of my father churned up from memory— slender, redboned, with black curls, each the size and shape of a berry.

"John tells me the same thing. Now, John looks a lot like Mama," Walter laughed.

"You even laugh like Daddy," I smiled. "Now, that's a sound I long for often, Daddy's laughter … " I felt my own smile dissolve. The loss of our father felt like a deprivation we both shared—the loss of our protector, our family compass, the man who guided our lives and who had gone missing for so long. We Colemans were loath to admit the truth, but without Daddy we had become rudderless, each one of us breaking out, trying to forge a way forward. The only counsel we had was our own individual set of experiences, since we were not able to benefit from the meager assets, nor the priceless wisdom, earned by our father. Perhaps, right here, right now, together, we could combine the shattered pieces of our family to find our way in this world.

"You even walk like Daddy," I breathed to myself as we headed for big glass doors that were framed in shiny brass. We were on our way, together we charged ahead.

Once we got outside, I was distracted again. Snow! The sky that had menaced so, now appeared less ominous, as it sprinkled tiny white flakes. Swirling in air, small flecks of winter melted on my fingertips. I had heard about snow, but the tingling sensation was like nothing else that I had ever experienced.

My brother laughed—it was a big and hearty happiness that summoned my father again. "You southern belle!" he said as people rushed by. "This is your first snow! Welcome to Chicago, baby! There's plenty more where that came from." He ushered me to the curb, "Our streetcar is coming."

The streets of Chicago were chaotic, filled with horseless carriages, Ford and Studebaker automobiles, electric streetcars, and an elevated train called the "L." A race-track shaped loop of iron lace, the L encircled downtown above the ground, appearing to whisk people away in midair.

A shiny cream-and-red streetcar glided to a stop right in front of us. We threw my satchels in and hopped aboard. A moment later we were floating down the street, lurching to a full stop at what seemed like every intersection. Entering passengers would climb the rear stairs, while riders, carrying their bundles, exited by the front. To signal a stop, a rider pushed back an ivory-colored porcelain button just above the seat. A bell tinkled to let the conductor know to stop.

Heading south on State, we arrived at Twenty-sixth Street. Over just those few miles, the entire landscape had changed. While passing the tall buildings downtown, the streets and the streetcar had been filled with white people. By the time we reached our stop, the passengers were nearly all colored folks.

"The Stroll" sparkled. An oasis that I had read about in *The Defender*, State Street from Twenty-sixth to Thirty-ninth was where Negro dentists, doctors, intellectuals, shop owners, and restaurateurs had created their own glittering world, and electric lamps stood ready to light up the night. Cruising State at a glacial pace, I was struck by a finely polished Patterson horseless carriage. With great enthusiasm my brother informed me, "That automobile was built by a Negro!" Everywhere I looked, the flagstone sidewalks were crowded with well-to-do brown people. I had arrived in Chicago, but I thought I had landed in heaven.

Here, Negro women dressed divinely. Bell-shaped cloche hats matched sturdy coats with fur trim, and beneath the protection from winter peeked beaded dresses—tassels, fringed hems, lavish frills, dripping extras. The men looked like they had leapt off the pages of a Sears and Roebuck catalogue. Their Norfolk jackets and spiffy knickers were perfectly pressed. Garters kept socks from rolling, spit-shined Oxfords glued peg-legged trouser-cuffs into place. Spatterdashes, or spats, were a fashion throwback; unlike the dirt roads we hailed from, no backwoods mud threatened these finely laid streets. The cobblestones that lined State Street were as neat as a row of dentures.

My brother's apartment building loomed. Compared to what I was accustomed to—cramped lean-to shacks and shotgun hovels—these buildings were gargantuan. Walter's was four stories high. The tile floor of the entrance vestibule had a maze of black-and-white flowers, forming dizzying marble octagons. Down a corridor, a second glass door opened into a darkened hallway. There were no windows.

Walter sensed my unease, "It's kind of dark here, but inside our place, it's plenty bright."

Two at a time he climbed the steps, worn wood groaning beneath his weight. At the top, I could hear him fish his keys from his pocket. As promised, light reappeared when he opened the door.

The flat was roomy and flooded with gray light from the frosty clouds. Shaped like a barbell, his apartment opened on a tiny vestibule that flowed into a front room that had three large windows facing the street. Two doors lining a long corridor led to my brothers' rooms. At the far end of the apartment was a kitchen with wide, oak-plank floors.

It was clear that I would not have my own room, and I wasn't really expecting to; I was grateful to make my bed anywhere at all. And when we got to the kitchen, Walter opened a final door to let me peek inside. The bathroom was a nice-sized room with a sink, water closet, and a small claw foot tub.

I was accustomed to walking out back to pump water, heat it, and then take a sparrow's bath. But here, I could just turn on a tap! I had never lived in a place with a private bathroom. My Mama and I had cleaned Mrs. Jones's every day, and no matter how much kinder she was than most white folks in Texas, her maids would never be permitted to use a bathroom in the house.

"Ummmmmm, a hot bath." I cooed.

Walter flashed a big, toothy grin at me. "Yep, hot as you want it."

Our revelry was interrupted by the thunder of a slamming door down the hall. Padded feet drummed our way. I held my breath. In seconds I would be face to face with Walter's wife, my sister-in-law. Mama had warned me to mind myself, "because Wilhelmina Coleman is as possessive with your brother as a dog is with his bone." I was overwhelmed by sudden dread at the thought of finally meeting this stranger who claimed my brother as her own.

Willie, as she liked to be called, appeared in the kitchen doorway, and for the first time ever I felt my brother cower. He withered beneath her penetrating glare. Yet, she was not at all what I had expected. From my mother's warnings, I had figured Willie to be dumpy and homely, but Willie was anything but that. She was a striking woman and closer to my own early twenties than to Walter's thirties. Although her face was eye-catching, it was not as fetching as her body, which must have been a relentless provocation to my brother. She had slender hips and a high pocket-behind that was small and tight. Willie was cedar brown, and her hair was a thick, raven mop barely restrained by a starched blue-and-white bandana. Her eyes were big and pretty, but were ringed by inky semicircles, which hung like shadowy slivers of blood moon above her sharp cheekbones.

Her mouth was terrifyingly beautiful. Her fine white teeth were a stiff fringe, but years of curling her lips into a scowl had led to a pouty moue. She slinked my way and circled around me where I stood. Like a cat, she stalked then pivoted to address my brother. In a thick Texas drawl she purred, "Walter, she really is very pretty." Well, I thought to myself, maybe she's not all that bad.

Almost on cue, my brother John and his wife Elizabeth appeared in the doorway. Disheveled, and adjusting their clothes, whatever they had been doing, they had obviously hurried.

"She don't look dumb, so I hope she don't try and bring no dumb-assed Niggas 'round here. This ain't no ho-house, and we don't want no nappy-headed little basta'ds up in y'ere. If she bring that shit up in this house, she outta here!" Willie spat at my brother.

I was more stunned and embarrassed than hurt. I just stood there with my mouth wide open.

"Willie, don't you go insultin' my baby sister. She just got here. Sometimes it's a mystery to me why I keeps you. Tame your tongue, girl," Walter warned. His growl was fearsome, at least to me. But Willie was undeterred. "Now you look-a here, gal," this time moving in close enough to me so that I could smell her breath, although it was she who flared her nostrils, as though she smelled rot on me.

"I don't say nothing behind your back that I don't say in front of yo' face. So at least you know what I'm thinking. I'm from Tyler, Texas, the same dirt-poor, shit-kickin' place as that Waxahachie stank hole that you just slithered outta. I know your kind. I don't give a shit if you is my husband's sister. The instant you step outta your place, I'm gonna enjoy throwin' yo' red ass on the trash heap where you belongs. I can't stand no lowlife free-fucking-loaders. You best be getting a job, cause we ain't feeding yo' ass fo' free neither. We clear?"

"Now you look a-here, Willie," Walter rumbled before I had a chance to respond. "You got a nasty mouth. You talk to my sister that way again and you gonna be the one lookin' for a new place to stay."

Walter seemed tough. But then she turned on him.

"Who you threatnin'?" she hissed. "You musta lost yo' goddamn' mind!"

"Hey, little Sis. See you met Bud's better half," my brother John piped up, employing Walter's childhood nickname.

John slid past Willie with a laugh and took me into his arms for a hug. I hadn't seen him in over ten years, and Walter was right. As much as Walter looked like Daddy, John favored Mama. I held on to his wide shoulders, not wanting the hug to end. Right about now, it was comforting to be reminded of Mama's calm and kindness.

"Her bark is worse than her bite," John said. "She means well. That's her version of giving you sound sisterly job advice."

"I'm just gettin' warmed up," Willie spat.

"Damn, Bud, that woman of yours gots some mouth on her. She fine, but it's a awful lot to put up with for a little bit a ass. I always thought you was the Cat Daddy, but I think she wears the pants 'round here, brotha." John was talking to Walter now as if none of us women were even there.

Walter didn't reply. He wrenched Willie by the arm and all but dragged her down the hallway. She was still able to get off another round before the bedroom door slammed, "John, you stank-assed piece of shit, you need to shut the hell up! You ain't nothing but a drunk yo' damn self! I can't imagine that the rest of yo' family is gonna amount to nothing more than a stank pile of shit!"

The bedroom door crashed hard and rattled on its hinges. Then the screaming commenced in earnest. Walter yelled at her, but mostly we could hear her hoarse voice, every fifth word squeaking and breaking over top of my brother's. Insults flying, they splattered each other with a host of curse words and foul names, the likes of which I had never heard before—cock-sucker, goon, cake-eater, sap, skank—and every new smear had the f-word in front of it, behind it, or as Willie liked to place it, squarely in the middle of each word in a string of affronts.

I must have been staring bug-eyed, mouth wide open still, because Elizabeth, my other sister-in-law, seized the moment. "Come on Bessie, let's blouse. High time for twenty-three skiddoo!" Steering me to the entry, she grabbed a coat and lent me her spare. Gaining my elbow, and my confidence, too, Elizabeth announced to no one in particular, "See y'all later." After the big metal door slammed shut, I could still hear Walter and Willie. I was glad now to be back in that dark corridor. Not even the dark unknown seemed as formidable as Willie.

"Wow, Wil*hel*mina—at least now I know what the middle part of her name means," I joked.

"Never mind hell-on-wheels; she's a twist," Elizabeth laughed. "I like the word play on her name, though. There aren't many names that you can think of that Willie hasn't been called or, worse, that she hasn't called everybody else. Just so that we are ready for the next Willie rumble, what do you plan to do for work now that you are here in big, bad Chicago?"

I finally took stock of my other sister-in-law. Elizabeth was a kewpie doll—short, shorter than I was, with skin the color of warm cocoa. She seemed sassy and fun, with pretty, naturally curly hair that she wore short and bobbed. She wasn't fat, so much as she was perfectly round. Everything about her was round; her face, her eyes, her smile, her nose— all were a series of connected circles. She had large round breasts and large round hips. A small circle in the middle for her waist melted into biscuit bottoms and slid down to round thighs and round calves.

"So, what are your job plans? If I can help you, I will, snookums." Elizabeth offered.

What I wanted more than anything was to learn how to fly a plane, but that wasn't the sort of thing I could blurt out just then.

"I sure enough didn't come all this way to clean and cook for white folks. I could do that well enough in Waxahachie. I was thinking of going to hairdressing school. I have a little tuition money saved, but I don't want a long, drawn-out course," I reasoned.

"I may have just the solution for you," Elizabeth said.

"Really?" I somehow trusted my new sister-in-law implicitly.

"Yep, that's what I do, I'm a hairdresser. I went to the E. Burnham School of Beauty Culture on State Street." Elizabeth pulled me over to a newsstand. She flipped the newsie a nickel and from the top of the stack picked up a crisp copy of *The Chicago Defender*. Looking through the pages for the classifieds, she folded the paper to reveal an ad for the E. Burnham School of Beauty Culture. Elizabeth seemed to think that this school and its licenses held entrepreneurial magic. "I love my work. The tea they spill is better than the gossip pages, the tips are swell, the school is bunny-easy and, speaking of which, it's just a hop away," Elizabeth smiled roundly.

It seemed almost too good to be true that on my first night in Chicago opportunities were already opening up for me. And it felt good to have an ally in Elizabeth.

"You can pick your courses too," she added, sensing my enthusiasm. "You can get your hair license, your cosmetic products ticket, or your nail technician certification."

"Stop right there. 'Nail technician certification'—what's that?" I asked.

"Why, a nail technician is a fancy, citified way of saying a manicurist. It's a nifty situation, 'cause you go to school for a week, then take your exam on the Friday of the same week. Now if'n it were me, I would be a saw-girl for men only."

"Why?" I asked.

"Here's the square, Bess. Colored dames 'round here get their nails done, but in a day or two, they're back to sportin' hooks," Elizabeth informed me. "Besides, some of these dumb Doras wanna give you the high hat, all jazzed up in their glad rags, off to the juice joints on Saturday nights. They go to a dive and think it's a palace. But I got 'em made, Sis. Come Monday morning, they are back to scrubbin' floors. Truth is, they really don't wanna waste much cabbage on doing their paws. But, on the other hand, no pun intended," Elizabeth said, winking at me exaggeratedly, "the men who gets their mitts buffed are willing to fork over plenty scratch to make it appear as though they do plush office work."

My new sister-in-law loved to talk. Her Alabama accent was as sweet as Karo syrup and layered thick with city-slicker slang. Elizabeth became my tour guide, job counselor, and interpreter all in one. A meat-wagon was an ambulance, a ten-cent box was a cab, spilling tea meant talking gossip, a moll was a gangster's girl, an ofay was code for a white person, and a floozy was a loose woman.

"Since it takes a month of Sundays to scrub oxblood off the Stockyard knuckles of butchers, men are willing to pay a lotta jack. When you work in a barbershop it's real cushy, your marks are already right there, getting their haircuts and trims. I have to slum outside my hen coup scrounging for every red cent, so I'm thinking about adding nail technician to my license, too," Elizabeth said.

"Why you are just the cat's meow," I declared. "It'll take the bum's rush and ten sawbucks to drive me away!" We laughed as I tried on my new slang, "It's all jake with me! I'll start nail technician school lickety-split."

The idea of manicuring nails was infinitely more attractive than being a maid or working in the Stockyards, where there were always openings to turn bone into buttons, scrub chitterlings, convert albumin into printer's ink, sack lard, or scavenge floor scraps to shove into hog casings for sausage.

While the *Chicago Tribune* had chronicled the deaths of dozens of firefighters and workers in the last big Stockyard fire, *The Defender* advocated moving the meat-packing plants far from the South Side, where Negros had begun to form neighborhoods. Slaughterhouse conditions were deplorable, with the South Fork of the Chicago River becoming known as Bubbly Creek—it literally gurgled with the carcasses of decomposing animals. The Stockyard was filthy mayhem, a constant threat to Chicago's hardscrabble South Side, the fragile Negro settlement that was fast becoming known as "The Black Belt."

Butchery, disemboweling, and flaying, with their tripe, offal, maws, hides, tails, bristles, fur, innards, ears and, over all, maggots—call it charcuterie or sausage as you choose, but to me it was all blood, bone, and formaldehyde. Women didn't work the "kill floor," but every foot of the Stockyard was too close for my taste—angry men with their razors and sabers, mallets, knives, axes, chisels, hatchets, machetes, and saws, eviscerating ten thousand hogs, sheep, and steer every day made me taste bile.

In my mind, the word *Stockyard* was synonymous with pestilence, slaughter, rage. Yes, it was steady work, but I wouldn't last a week in that place. I planned to follow Elizabeth's advice and chisel away at men's nails till the cows came home.

CHAPTER 6

Late that afternoon, Chicago's wind chomped at our fingers and toes, and then chased us back inside for shelter. We settled into the front room, thawing our freezing hands on the radiator. Walter emerged from his bedroom and headed toward the kitchen. Seeing my eagerness to talk to him, Elizabeth rose to her feet. "Come on, let's join them before they drink too much coffin varnish."

My brothers were already hunched over the kitchen table, drinking strong-smelling hooch out of jelly jars. Elizabeth plopped herself right onto John's lap and kissed him fully on the lips. I was embarrassed at their open affection, and while I thought it rude to stare, I couldn't help myself.

"How is it that my little brother gets more action than anybody I know?" Walter said. John winked knowingly. Turning his attention to his bride, John whispered something into Elizabeth's ear. It made her smile. Then, after sending her off with a firm tap on her bottom, Elizabeth slithered from his lap.

"It's because I am da' Man!" he slurred. No sooner than his lap was empty, his glass was empty, too. John went about pursuing another drink with as much lust as he had shown for Elizabeth.

"It's okay, honey," Elizabeth said as she passed me on the way to the cupboard and the stove. "It's all natural." The smile this time was rounder still. She laughed and hummed while rustling up supper.

"While I'm chopping, tell me about your family, Bessie. Walter and John are men, who by definition, never recall details. I can't wait to meet your Mama. How many of your kin still live down in Waxahachie?"

With that invite, I told Elizabeth our family saga. We believed that my mother was ten years old when she was freed from bondage on Juneteenth in 1865. By the time I was born in January of 1892, my mother was already thirty-seven years old. Between the ages of twenty-one and forty-three, she gave birth to thirteen of us, starting with Lillah, the firstborn, in 1876. Nine of us survived, and our births grouped us sequentially, two girls, three boys, then four more girls. Our parents gave a few of us names that were biblical, hopeful or even wistful, but mine carried none of those lofty pretenses. My name was downright utilitarian—the name of a nag or an old jalopy. Anyway, we were: Lillah, Alberta—Walter, Isaiah, John—Bessie, Elois, Nilus, and Georgia.

"In 1901," I began, "when I was nine years old, my Daddy left Texas in search of open land as an Oklahoma homesteader. By this time, Walter and my older siblings had all left, too. Only Mama, my three youngest sisters, and I stayed behind in Waxahachie. Mama said she just couldn't go to Oklahoma.

"Daddy's departure," I told her, "was one of the greatest heartbreaks of my life." Elizabeth listened attentively, and in as much time as it took for me to draw our family tree, she prepared a meal large enough to feed us all. Eggs were whipped into a fluffy omelet with bits of cubed ham. A diced onion and withered potatoes were transformed into savory home fries. Steaming-hot green beans, with a mound of butter sliding down the poles appeared in a big white bowl—and everything smelled delicious.

"Dinner's ready!" Elizabeth called over her shoulder. "Want me to go rouse sleeping beauty?" she asked Walter.

"Nah, I'll get her." Walter swallowed hard; a gulp passed his Adam's apple. He headed down the hallway as if he was headed to war.

In a few minutes he and Willie emerged from the bedroom. They sat, and everyone began chatting. Everyone, that is, except Willie, who sneered openly at me without touching anything on her plate. Finally, she began to eat, and when she had finished two full helpings of eggs and green beans, she got up from the table, bumping my chair with her hip on her way to the sink, where she washed her plate and then headed back to her bedroom. As she sauntered down the hallway, she belched loudly as a final punctuation and then slammed the door.

Willie was out of earshot when John breathed, "Man, brotha! What you dealin' wit'?"

"Shut up man! Look a-here, Bessie, it will take Willie a couple of days to warm up. Don't pay her no never-mind. She's going through a tough spell. You're welcome in my home," Walter reassured.

"Thanks, Walter. I appreciate that," I said, and then, quickly changing the subject, I announced, "Elizabeth and I think we've found my new job. Tomorrow, I am going to the beauty school to start a course on manicuring men's nails."

"Working with all men?" Walter objected. I somehow knew my brother might not approve.

"Yes. You don't think it's a good plan?" I could feel myself getting ready to mount a defense, but to what, I wasn't sure.

"It's a great plan. You gonna make a lot of dough. You're pretty, smart, and single. Men are going to come on to you, but I won't be able to watch over you, 'cause my work keeps me away," Walter explained.

And he sure did work. According to *The Chicago Defender*, my brother Walter was one of six thousand Pullman Porters who traveled the country by rail. Day and night they carried bags, served food, shined shoes, and cleaned the train cars while each answering to the name "George." They provided flawless service to the white passengers who roamed the country in luxury by train. These Porters had fought their boss, Todd Lincoln, who happened to be Abraham Lincoln's son, for better wages. In '15, each porter earned twenty-seven dollars a month for four hundred hours, or eleven thousand miles per month, whichever came first. While this money was steady, it was meager. Porters like my brother got little rest, and as there were no sleeping accommodations for them, they napped on short breaks in the blue haze of the men's smoking car. Denied membership in white unions, the Porters had begun to whisper union amongst themselves—fair wages and rest were worth the fight.

Walter rose from his chair and pushed his glass forward, but before his fingertips could let go, Elizabeth took it to the sink. She floated across the floor, and in no time her soapy hands were washing the glass squeaky clean. "I gotta assign you to John," Walter whispered as Elizabeth hummed and John slipped into the bathroom. "But he drinks too much, and he don't always show up."

"You don't have to worry about me. I'm a big girl," I winked. "Besides, all I have to do is mention Willie's name. That oughta scare 'em," I smiled.

He smiled back and gave me a big bear hug. "It's been a long day, and morning comes fast. Bessie, we are going to set you up on the davenport," Walter said, before leaving the kitchen. I heard him shut his bedroom door.

Elizabeth continued cleaning until the kitchen was spotless. She offered me a towel and sheets, but I told her that I had brought my own. I did not want to be a burden. "Prepared for the big city, are you?" she smiled. "Let me help you make up the davenport."

"You have done enough for me already. Go on, now. Thank you for making me feel welcome. You are going to be a real sister to me," I said.

She kissed me on my forehead, and she and John headed off to bed. Hissing pipes pumped hot water, forcing the ornate cast-iron radiators to knock and bang. I dug out my towel, sheets, soap, and toothbrush from my suitcase then shoved the case back into the closet.

I crept down the hallway to the bathroom, being as quiet as I could. Pulling the chain of the light overhead, I studied the handles atop the tub—C for cold and H for hot, I assumed.

I turned the valve, and the water came gurgling out—first a trickle, then a torrent. Hanging from one of the spigots was a dangling chain with a white rubber stopper attached at its end. I quickly grabbed it and shoved it into the drain hole.

When an inch of water had accumulated, I put my bare toe in the water and yelped. It was hotter than I had expected. I added a little cold water, turning the handle of the spigot with a C on it.

At this pace, it would take several minutes before the tub filled, so I stripped off my clothing and then turned to make sure that the door was closed tightly. I fastened the hook at the top of the door. As I released the doorknob, I came face to face with my own image, reflected in a full-length mirror on the back of the bathroom door. We had never owned a looking glass this big, so as I waited for the tub to fill, I used it to take a long look at my full naked body. I was twenty-three years old, and I had never seen my entire naked form before. I stared at my own image, taking in the whole body, before studying my individual parts.

I was aware that I'd lost quite a bit of weight since heading north. I had not been eating well nor, for that matter, had I been eating enough, and my neck showed the signs—not much more than skin clung to bone. My breasts were small, and because of my wet foot in contact with the cold floor, my nipples had hardened stiff as could be.

My stomach was flat, and my wiry arms were long. My forearms looked bigger than I had imagined and forced the cartoon character Olive Oyl into my head. All that scrubbing on the washboard from my laundry-work, pumping that heavy wooden dolly stick, had made my arms knotty and hard. I allowed my eyes to slowly study the rest of my body.

My legs were long for my height. They were muscle-knotted, too, from the miles I had walked to complete my laundry route each day. My thighs plunged into strong knees and my muscled calves narrowed into ankles that seemed a little too scrawny to support my frame.

The bottom half of the bathroom window was opaque glass to deter peeping neighbors. The top half was clear. I turned off the meat-market light overhead and allowed my eyes to adjust to the darkened bathroom. A full moon shone in, casting a glow on the steamy bath. When it was half full, I plunged my entire body into the slipper tub, my weight making the lion claws grab the floorboards.

The water was hot and dreamy. I thought Willie undeserving, so I selected one of the lavender soaps that I had brought for her and used it myself, soaping my entire body. I wondered how often John and Elizabeth would emerge from their bedroom tousled. I thought about back home in the deep woods of Texas. People had plenty of sex, but no one ever talked about it, nor shared affection in public—more than a hint of which I had already witnessed in my brothers' apartment.

Even in all my sexual immaturity, I could see that Chicago was full of pretty women and handsome men, and that everyone seemed to pay attention to their appearance. My new surroundings left me charged and alert in ways that had been dormant. So many images floated through my head as I scrubbed my privates, the soft piece of fleshy skin beneath my hairy bush grew thick with pleasure the more I stroked it. I was rubbing myself harder and faster with more force and speed than I knew how to command—until the spell was broken by a noise coming from the kitchen.

Startled, I froze. I listened to the sound of footsteps, followed by the clinking of a bottle against a glass. I was terrified of being discovered. What I was doing to myself felt good, but it certainly didn't seem like anything I should share. What if it was Willie about to peep through the keyhole?

And just like one of the steamy curls that rose above my bath, the moment of pleasure evaporated. Whoever was in the kitchen had left, so I climbed quietly out of the tub and began wiping the bath clean. Although my body was still wet, I used my towel to shine and buff the porcelain clean as new. I wanted to leave no evidence of my pleasure.

The circular polishing movements made me recall cleaning Mrs. Jones's bathroom, which Mama and I had done back in Waxahachie. And it was during this routine chore that I had first learned of a news story that would affect me more profoundly than any other in my entire young life. We had been preparing for Mrs. Jones to host a Christmas party and were told to make the whole house sparkle. While I was buffing the porcelain on the tub and tiles, the normally placid Dr. Jones rushed into the parlor and began speaking to his wife in such animated tones that I hurried to the doorway to hear what he was saying. In order to eavesdrop for as long as possible, I intentionally upset a basket of towels that Mama and I had meticulously folded, hoping that she would be distracted by having to fold them again, giving me enough time to listen to the doctor's story. Dr. Jones was a man of science. Everyone knew he was keen. If he was intrigued by some development, I was eager to learn what on earth had spiked him so.

It was the week before Christmas, in December of '03 that Dr. Jones read aloud from *The Dallas Morning News*, and I learned from my hiding spot in the doorway that in a place called Kitty Hawk, North Carolina, two brothers, both bicycle mechanics, had successfully flown a contraption that the newspaper called a "Flying Machine."

"Two men climbed into the air and manipulated a powered machine with wings. It had a motor, and that flying machine took a man into thin air! It flew at thirty-one miles per hour and stayed aloft for twelve seconds. Seconds today, an hour tomorrow! What will they think of next?" Dr. Jones exclaimed.

My eleven-year-old mind was abuzz with wonder.

A machine that flew.

"Two men climbed into thin air?"

How on earth could one climb into, or onto, air?

I scurried to finish my work and then waited for Mama outside on West Main Street. There, in the dried mud of a Waxahachie ditch, I used a hickory stick to sketch what I thought a flying machine might look like. Was it like an insect, or a bird of prey? "Powered," he had said. By what? Where would such power come from? I was so spellbound, that I didn't even hear the ice truck barreling towards me.

Just in time, Mama snatched me out of the way. "Damned Niggas!" The ice-man yelled from his perch above the rig; he rocked unsteadily as the horses rumbled down the dirt road. They had trampled my drawing into dust, but they hadn't put a scratch on my imagination.

Weeks later, Mama returned from the Joneses with her own surprise. "Here," she said triumphantly, tossing me a copy of *The Dallas Morning News*, as well as a picture cut out from another newspaper. Spilled across the page was the Wright Brothers' flying contraption.

Connecting the top and bottom wing, the craft was held together by a spider's web of poles and wires, and a propeller and giant tail fin also belonged to this marvelous contraption. I took note of *The Dallas Morning News* commentary: "The machine is driven by a pair of screw-propellers placed just behind the wings. The power is supplied by a gasoline motor, designed and built for Messrs. Wright. It is of the four-cycle type and has four cylinders. The pistons are four inches in diameter and have a four-inch stroke … At the speed of 1,200 revolutions a minute, the engine develops sixteen brake horsepower with a consumption of a little less than ten pounds of gasoline an hour."

I read the article over and over and over, taking care not to smudge the printer's ink with my sweaty fingers. When I had consumed it all, memorizing nearly every word, I folded the newspaper and placed it reverently inside Mama's metal strong box. Mama's gift was what would launch me on a lifelong scrapbook-chronicling, building a journal of mankind's quest to fly. Because the Wright Brothers did it first, America's race to grasp a fistful of sky before other nations could do the same was now a part of history.

It was not lost on me that I was coming of age in a time of great technical progress. It was also a time of great tumult, and I was an eyewitness to both the dawn of the country's magnificence as well as the depths of its malevolence. For on that wintery day in December, a week before we celebrated the birth of Christ, man had triumphed, solving the mystery of the physics of a winged machine, and at the very same time, lynchings were taking place unrelentingly across the land.

Yet, despite injustice, or maybe because of it, the Wrights had given all of us a moment of brilliance, a moment when all of humanity, all over the world, could rejoice in what I came to believe was the greatest Christmas gift of all time—flight.

Something in my bones spoke to me about that moment. An aeroplane understood the rules of physics, not the laws of men. An aeroplane couldn't possibly care who flew it. The Wright Brothers were white men, but their invention didn't know that. When the contraption flew for a longer period of time, with more predictable outcomes, would they not make more of these crafts for others to fly? Could I even dream of escaping this world in one of these modern marvels? Surely, their brilliance would not stop here. This flying machine was being touted as the greatest invention of the century, maybe even of all time. The Wrights were being hailed in papers all around the world as "Birdmen." Years ago, their airship had been just a dream, so why couldn't I myself dream of flying one day?

Although my towel was now thoroughly damp, I used it to dry the rest of my body while filling the sink with water to splash my face clean. After brushing my teeth, I tugged at the rubber stopper in the drain and as the water made a whirlpool, a loud sucking sound followed when the last of the water funneled out. "Shhhh!" I whispered, as if I could silence the phenomenon of a whirlpool in the same way that the Wright Brothers had commanded elemental wind.

Creeping by my brothers' rooms, I settled onto the davenport and burrowed deep beneath the one luxury item that I had brought with me—an exquisite patchwork quilt, fashioned for me out of fragments of my own old clothing, and made for me by my best, best friend and college roommate, Norma Rae Pope.

Protected from the Chicago cold by Norma's gift and by my brothers' nearness, I had a dream. I dreamt that it was I, and not the Wright Brothers, who had climbed into a magic machine, left the earth, and gone flying. And the air up there held a completely different kind of pleasure.

CHAPTER 7

I awakened, as I often did, before dawn. I dressed quietly, and by burying my folded linens deep within the front-room closet, hid all evidence that I had invaded the couples' home. Elizabeth had kindly offered me winter protection, so I borrowed her coat, a woolen newsboy's cap, gloves, and sturdy leather boots. My shabby coat and thin shoes would clearly be no match for Chicago winters.

Not wanting to wake my brothers, nor their wives, I set out before anyone stirred. At the foot of the first-floor hallway, I spotted a copy of *The Chicago Defender* folded discretely on top of a pile of cardboard boxes. Copies of the paper routinely made their way down to Mississippi and Texas, carried by Pullman Porters like my brother Walter, who passed them on like contraband to segregated riders. Shared a few dozen times before it was shed, *The Defender* was a must-read for southerners like me. I snatched the paper up and stowed it covertly beneath Elizabeth's overcoat.

At the corner of Twenty-seventh and State, I found a hole-in-the-wall diner, with high stools at a counter, and ventured in for coffee, scrambled eggs, bacon, biscuits, and grits. The meal was an extravagance, but this was a rare morning, and my appetite matched my enthusiasm for my newly found treasure—a fresh Saturday morning copy of *The Defender*. Published every Saturday and sold at a price of five cents, or one dollar fifty cents for a yearly subscription, every edition was splashed with a bold crest of arms—wings, laurel leaves, the eyes of an owl, stripes and stars, all were symbols of strength embedded in the crest—and a boastful promise, *The Defender* proclaimed itself: "The World's Greatest Weekly."

And to me and tens of thousands of others, this claim was the truth—eight pages back to back, chock full of political headline news, reports of social unrest, world events, Great War warnings, advice columns, church information, theater and book reviews, education news, housekeeping tips, quotations from famous people, sports results, social-club gatherings, death announcements, voter registration guides, rooms-for-rent and job classifieds, and loads of advertisements for products you didn't even know you needed until *The Defender* let you know you couldn't possibly live without them. This was more than a newspaper. It was an essential guide for living, learning, and surviving in Chicago.

Perched high upon my stool like a real sophisticate, I left no crumb on my plate, and I left no page unread. The paper boasted at the top left-hand corner of every edition: "Latest News: If You See It in *The Defender* It Is So." What I saw was that the E. Burnham School of Beauty Culture advertised itself as the greatest beauty school in town, and so I believed it. When their doors opened that day, I planned to be waiting.

Although first in line, I discovered that the next nail-technician class was already oversubscribed. Undaunted, I offered to pay cash in full, as Elizabeth had suggested. That seemed to magically free up a spot. One week later, and just as my sister-in-law had promised, I finished my training and was ready to go. With the ink still drying on my certificate, I paraded up and down the Stroll, hunting for a position in the busiest shop, where I could make the most tips.

In the window of the *White Sox* barbershop, I saw a Help Wanted sign. Just past the entrance, a tiny manicurist table with two chairs graced an elevated platform in a fishbowl-like picture window—one for the nail girl, and the other for her patron. I wandered in and was hired on the spot.

That night at dinner, Elizabeth set the table while I whipped up my favorite dish—chicken fried steak, collards, fried okra, and biscuits—just like Mama used to make. While I put the finishing touches on our meal, I announced my new good fortune to my relatives. "I got a job as a manicurist at the White Sox today," I gloated. My brothers and Elizabeth cheered, as Willie sat sulking. We sat and everyone filled their plates. We ate and chatted. Then, because I couldn't help myself and because I felt a keen sense of my new position of power, I called to Willie over my shoulder from the kitchen as I cleaned up, "Maybe you should stop by sometime. Looks like bagging sausage entrails at the Stockyards has you in need of my new services."

I ducked and just in time, too. Willie threw her plate across the room and straight at the back of my head. Okra splattered across the upper cabinets as glass shattered into pieces all over the butcher block counter. John howled in laughter, Elizabeth ran to see if I had been hurt and, once again, Walter hauled his bride down the dark hallway. She cursed me as she went.

With my new job lined up, I sought my own apartment, knowing that if I stayed on the davenport much longer, Willie would poison me when it came her turn to make her favorite rabbit stew. A few weeks later, I found a place where I could continue to see my brothers and Elizabeth, but where Willie would never come. I had bought only one extravagance—a bed with an ornate brass headboard, under which I spread Norma's quilt. My apartment was not elaborate. It was tiny, but it was sunny, close to work and family, and more than anything, it was all mine.

Meanwhile, I began to settle in at the picture-window perch of my new job. From there I would watch the traffic along the Stroll and try to entice customers by making eye contact as they passed. More often, someone in for a smooth taper cut or a beard trim would finish with the barbers and then join me for a buff and shine. Many of these men were good tippers, and I squirreled away the extras for my flying war-chest.

I threw myself into my new job and was there from the moment the saloon-style doors swung open until the last customer walked out. Often, after a little meaningless flirtation, my clients forgot all about me, and I became a fly on the wall in a den of men. With their nails buffed to a mirror shine, they would move on to the barber's chair, where they would listen to, or share, a juicy story. Until this time, I had never known how much men gossiped and now, from my little roost, I got to listen to plenty of it.

The White Sox barbershop was owned by Mr. Maynard Duncan, a kindly, sage, father figure, as well as a savvy entrepreneur who owned its three-story building and rented out the three flats above it. An ebony-hued and girthy man of about fifty, Mr. Duncan wore a long, black-leather barber's apron, and in contrast to his bountiful mustache, he had a completely bald head that shone like an eight ball.

His employees were Bishop, Hash, and Squeeze, all of whom were top-notch barbers. Together they were gritty, jovial, roguish, earnest, hardworking hustlers who had life stories worth retelling a thousand times over. And that's what they did. They told stories for hours and listened to those of the men who, day after day, sat in their blood-red leather barber chairs.

Mr. Duncan had been a fine shortstop in his youth, and the shop got its name from the baseball team he loved. Because he was a Negro, Mr. Duncan could never play for the White Sox, but they had known enough to hire him as a trainer and so, during the season, he would join the team, leaving the well-organized business to practically run itself. Only when the season ended, did Mr. Duncan return to us and don his leather apron again.

Like other barbershops, the White Sox was an institution. It was where men came to get a haircut, to hear about a job, or learn about a vacant flat. It was where they came to unwind, to read *The Defender*, to hear a breaking scandal, or spread one with juicy add-ons. But unlike other shops, the White Sox was neat and orderly, and there was no hodgepodge of homemade signs or junk cluttering up the joint. At each man's station there was a thick, porcelain, shaving mug with no handle, adorned with a baseball on the front and the words White Sox emblazoned in black script on the other side. It was tasteful and boasted of a high-class establishment. The walls were freshly painted bright white, and the decorations were spartan. An identical series of pen-and-ink drawings of haircut styles floated above each station, and next to them, a simple but elegant silver frame held a price list: twenty-five cents for a shave and a cut, fifty cents for a shampoo—either oil or egg, customer's selection. And other services were listed too—mustache and beard trimming, or children's cut for ten cents. A plaque over Mr. Duncan's chair cast a spin on words that was lost on me. *The only head we won't shave, is a seamhead.* At first, I didn't realize that this was a baseball joke, but this place was a sportsman's haven, and I eventually came to expect that most of what I missed had to do with some sports reference or another. There was always talk of the latest pursuit—Rube Foster's Negro Leagues, boxing great Jack Johnson's conquests, the upcoming 1916 Olympic trials in Berlin, and even a new game called football. It was the language men spoke once a customer climbed into the barber's chair to get his hair trimmed. And as if I needed one more reminder of that I was the only female in the building, the single-stall toilet buried deep in the back of the shop, had a seat that was always getting sprayed by the flush of the urinal, which was right next to the commode.

"I don't have enough cash for a receptionist, but you can surely pitch in. I'm-a have you help direct traffic. The Buffalo Soldiers like a clean cut and shave, nothing fancy. If you are not busy, I want you to direct those war men to me.

"And the new vets is used to getting lice, and the gas mask had to seal real tight, so the hair on their head was short, and no facial hair of any kind was permitted back then. They still thinks they are in the trenches. Those guys want it clean, neat, and no frills. You will get to know the other barbers and who to send the dandies, the kids, and the balding to." Mr. Duncan smiled and ran a hand over his own smooth head. "Each man rents his chair from me, and although I prefer a straight edge with a Royal blade and DeWitt Steri-tool to sanitize my instruments, to each his own. Each barber brings his own tool set."

My eyes drifted to Mr. Duncan's steel tray on his counter, which held numerous straight edges, razors, and what looked like switchblades—the blades could easily double for something in a doctor's bag.

"You, too, Bessie," he continued. "You brings your own files and such. I pays for the water and the lights. So that means don't waste neither. One towel to every twelve shaves, and you get a towel a day, which you can shake out back, Bessie—the towel I mean." Mr. Duncan allowed himself that rare, lewd indulgence, concluding his monologue with a final piece of advice, "Bessie, you real pretty, so smile a lot and don't talk too much." In an effort to show compliance, I flashed a smile and stifled my suddenly meaningless questions.

I met the guys one by one. In a bucket-of-blood joint, a decade ago, Hash, Mr. Duncan's nephew, had burst into a drink-fueled rage over a woman and stabbed his rival to death. Hash was sentenced to a nine-year stretch at Old Joliet Prison. He described the filthy squalor there, hell on earth inside an ornate gothic fortress—a warehouse for Negro and poor whites alike. "Skid Row losers, festering in a giant cesspool," he spat. Hash was chocolaty brown and built real thick. Even with a scar that ran the length of the left side of his face, he was still ruggedly handsome. And although his past frightened me, he himself did not. He was always peaceful towards me, and I thanked heaven for it.

Despite his holy name, Bishop was anything but. "The girls pray to get with me, their fellas pray I don't!" He would say upon meeting both men and women. He was indeed nice to look at. Espresso brown, with a mop of thick, black, curly hair, and all around the sides of his head from temple to temple were sheared, layered shingles of new growth that hugged his neck. The entire affair was perfected in a wavy-sea high-top, aggressively tamed by tonics and pomades, twice a day, every day.

The first time I met Bishop, he shook my hand, but he wouldn't release it. He cupped my hand in his, held my wrist snugly, then wagged his middle finger around and around in my palm. Bishop was obsessed with the pursuit of women, and each of his conquests was more exquisite than the last. All of his girls were glamour dolls, with bodies like Coca-Cola bottles. Hair smooth as glass, skin like porcelain or mahogany, Bishop did not discriminate on the basis of hue. "Man, I like booty, body, beauty, and in that order, too!" Throwing his head back, he would laugh himself silly every time he said it. All jokes aside, Bishop was the best barber in the shop. He was precise and worked hard at his craft.

Then there was Squeeze. The American League White Sox could have sailed into first place in 1915 rather than drifting into third, if only they had had a tall, extra-lean hitter like Squeeze, who instead played ball the only place he could—in the Negro Leagues. His frame didn't reveal the power hiding in his gangly limbs. His beard and mustache were as scraggly as Bishop's was flawless.

Naturally, Mr. Duncan and Squeeze were our resident sports experts, and since the customers talked sports, work, and women—pretty much in that order—every topic had an expert. Most of the time the shop was filled with light-hearted banter, tales of bravado and self-described heroism, but one day the talk turned grim. The film director D.W. Griffith had just released a moving picture entitled, *The Birth of a Nation*, in which President Lincoln's assassination was turned upside down, portrayed not as a tragedy, but rather a reason to celebrate. In Griffith's rearranged history, white actors wear blackface and play defeated Negro soldiers, and a Negro militia of outlaws and rapists who run amuck require the Ku Klux Klan to restore order.

While most moving pictures cost twenty-five cents, *The Birth of a Nation* cost two dollars. For that sum, I could buy a gallon of milk, a loaf of bread, a hunk of cheese, a pound of coffee, sugar, and a dozen apples.

Upon the movie's release in February of 1915, deadly riots in cities from Boston to Los Angeles erupted. The journalistic backlash was intense as well: "Women of Race Fighting Against *Birth of a Nation*," bellowed *The Chicago Defender*'s headline. And "Protest Parade Against *Birth of a Nation*"; "Grotesque, Insolent and Absolutely Barren of Plausibility." My favorite *Defender* headline mocked the cinema title, "*The Dirt of a Nation*." *The Defender*'s founder and publisher, Mr. Robert Abbott, became my hero forever, due to the paper's relentless and fierce attack against the film.

The NAACP monthly journal *The Crisis* protested, too. In its Opinion section of the June 1915 issue, the Hon. Albert E. Pillsbury, a white Attorney General of the state of Massachusetts who had been quoted by the *Boston Herald* said, "The play, like the book *The Clansman* on which it is founded, is a gross perversion of a period of our history about which the people have been persistently lied to for a generation."

In that same article, the real history of what was taking place across the country, and not on movie screens, was also conveyed, as a Memphis clergyman wrote about the lynching of a man. "Hundreds of Kodaks clicked all morning at the scene of the lynching. People ... came from miles around to view the corpse under the bridge, dangling from the end of a rope. Picture-card photographers installed a portable printing press at the bridge and made a fortune in selling picture postcards showing the lynched Negro. Women and children were there by the score."

It would take five years before our own director, Oscar Micheaux would make the film *Within Our Gates* to expose Griffith's lies. The haunting title foreshadowed the plot—a wealthy white landlord, intent on raping a Negro, discovers that she is his own daughter! Micheaux used this anecdote to document what lay in slavery's wake—poverty, illiteracy, orphans. Families were eviscerated either by parents being sold or lynched, and by rape, rape, rape—the ever-present violent threat to Negro women. In the same *Crisis* Opinion column, the author wrote, Griffith "knows but one side of southern life, the sex problem of the 'Aryan and African'."

Insult heaped upon insult, as D.W. Griffith was featured in the *Chicago Tribune*, expressing his dismay at those who, like Chicago's mayor Big Bill Thompson, sought to stop *Birth of a Nation* from being shown in Chicago. Griffith railed on about censorship, calling those who wanted no parts of the downtown destruction that had followed the riots throughout the country after showings of his film, "witch burners." Griffith said that Thompson and others around the country were camouflaging their attempt to censor his film, and that he, like the Salem witches, was the victim. Yet, Griffith did find a bright spot in his dilemma, and he reported that "a great man," had said that *Birth of a Nation* was "like teaching history with lightning."

I think President Wilson was the "great man," to whom Griffith referred. President Woodrow Wilson showed *Birth of a Nation* at the White House! The President did nothing to quell the race wars—riots, murder, rape, lynchings—real ones, and all were visited on real Negroes, in cities from coast to coast. America had become an imitation of the fake vigilantes that Griffith had conjured on screen.

I had been working for the White Sox for nearly eight months when Mr. Duncan called a mandatory meeting for six the next morning. I was worried that he had bad news to announce. Why else would he call us all to meet in such a rush? My worst fear was that if he were closing the barbery it would mean I'd have to find another job—immediately. No way I intended to go back to living with Willie again.

I arrived at five thirty in the morning, and the red-and-white pole just outside the White Sox was already swirling, its peppermint stripes harkening back to the day when barbers used to "bleed" people to heal ailments; the red represented blood, the white, healing. That morning, even Bishop was on time. "What's shakin', Mr. D? Must be bad news if you wants us all together before the cock crows." Bishop smiled nervously. I could see he was worried, too.

"Yep, it is BIG news. First, we ain't closing. I figure I need to get that out the way," Mr. Duncan said, and we all breathed a sigh of relief. "This morning at ten o'clock, we gonna have us a mighty special customer. So I wants everything to be right. The Deluxe Duncan treatment, from a perfect manicure, Bessie, to the best haircut you ever delivered, Bishop. You not too hungover, is you?"

"No, suh, Mr. Duncan!" The rummy fumes from Bishop's breath were hardly hidden by his butterscotch cologne. "I'm-a be better once I gets me a strong cup of joe."

Mr. Duncan rolled his eyes and nodded his head toward the coffee atop the tiny potbelly stove in the back. "Gents and Bessie, Mr. Robert Sengstacke Abbott will be our guest today. Mr. Abbott is the publisher and founder of *The Chicago Defender*," Mr. Duncan explained.

Every Saturday, hot off the press, we always had a tall stack of *The Defender* for our customers. I read the paper faithfully, but I did not know anything about Mr. Abbott, the man. The idea that we would be meeting him made my heart skip a beat. Mr. Abbott was big time!

As if reading my thoughts, Mr. Duncan explained, "Mr. Abbott is a Negro who made a million dollars selling the stories of our people, without ever selling out. He's the son of slaves, and when he arrived here in Chicago, up from the Georgia backwoods, he figured every Negro needed to move north, and he decided that we needed a voice and a guide to make that happen. Mr. Abbott built an empire from the then outrageous notion that our stories deserved to be told." It was clear to all of us that as an entrepreneur himself, Mr. Duncan revered Mr. Abbott's rags-to-riches story.

"Mr. Abbott wants to hold a meeting here, 'cause this is where the everyday man comes to get his hair cut and his nails buffed and to shoot the breeze. He wants to talk about how this movie has affected us. I don't know who yet, but Mr. Abbott is bringing a couple of rich cats with him. I guess they're making their rounds of the barbershops on the Stroll. I want the best from each of you, 'cause if Mr. Abbott becomes a regular here, it will mean a lotta new business, and that's good news for all of us," he smiled like the Cheshire Cat.

Mr. Duncan wanted the best from all of us, and we set out to fulfill his expectations. Sacks of trash were pulled into the back room, piles of papers were straightened, windows washed and dried. I swept the floor clean, while Squeeze followed behind me with the mop. Bishop waxed the barber chairs until they glowed. Mr. Duncan brewed a fresh pot of strong coffee, while Hash poured the day-old cream that we crossed our fingers and drank every day down the drain and went off to fetch a fresh bottle. Squeeze heaped a china bowl, brushed clean of hair clippings, full of Domino sugar cubes. He even polished the silver spoon.

With only minutes to spare, Bishop sharpened his clippers and razors and laid them out like surgical instruments, and by the time the cowbells jingled on the saloon-style doors, we were ready. Six distinguished-looking men strutted into the White Sox, and the air that swirled around our guests was charged with what felt like electricity.

"Good morning, gentlemen," Mr. Abbott said, tipping his rich chocolate homburg. His index finger rested in his hat's gutter, until he clutched the kettle curl of its brim. Flipping it off his head, he bowed regally to me. I didn't know what to do in response to so fine a greeting, so I did the only thing I could think of: I curtsied. It seemed like what one should do in the presence of royalty.

Mr. Abbott was a thickset man of average height, with a barrel chest and sharp eyes. "Milady," Mr. Abbott played along. "I didn't realize that Mr. Duncan had added such a fine accoutrement to his staff. Such beauty is a tactical advantage in business and a fine reason to return to the White Sox." My cheeks flushed.

Mr. Abbott's entourage smiled approvingly as they each cast a look my way. I bowed my head. These men were like nothing I had ever seen before. They were powerful. They were rich. Each exquisitely dressed under a lightweight overcoat, a luxurious accessory in navy, brindle, or camel. Each Chesterfield had expensive bone buttons, was lined with silk, and ringed with a collar of velvet or the swirl of curly lamb. By now Chicago's harsh winter had given way to a cool, rainy spring, and these gentlemen were ready for anything that Mother Nature could dish out. Bishop and I rushed to accept the fine topcoats and then hang them in front so that passersby could gawk.

Beneath the coats, their bodies were encased in fine wool suits, with trousers that broke in a slight crease above perfectly spit-shined leather brogans or wingtips. No one in this crowd wore loud spats. Crisply starched muslin shirts ended in sleeve cuffs that peeked out a perfect half-inch, revealing the tasteful script of their embroidered initials, which floated just below golden cufflinks. Matching gold tie pins made the elegance complete. Clearly, these men had tailors who were many cuts above anything that the Sears Catalog had to offer.

Mr. Abbott broke our star-struck stares by taking a seat in Mr. Duncan's chair, and our small audience of barbers and customers crowded around to see what he would do next. Although I remained at my station, I maneuvered my chair, like a weathervane in the wind, toward Mr. Abbott. We were disciples at the feet of the master. We waited.

His coffee-bean complexion was without blemish. Perfectly coiffed, his mustache was waxed into place. He drew a small, dog-eared pad and finely sharpened pencil from his breast pocket. Prepared, as he was— along with another man, seemingly a reporter—to record our thoughts, he said, "Tell me what people are saying about *Birth of a Nation*."

"Well, I don't know how that guy Griffin can get away with this," Bishop began.

"Nothing but trash," Squeeze complained. "Negroes shouldn't be paying a dime to see that tripe. If we do, we are lining his pockets with Judas silver."

"Yes, yes, boycotting is a given," Mr. Abbott agreed.

"I wanna meet this coward in a dark alley," Hash growled. "I could teach him what I learned in jail about his KKK! When they're in a group, they'll lynch us, but catch 'em alone, and they squeal like little girls. I did my time in a seven-by-seven prison tomb. A single crack in the wall was the only light I had for nine whole years. There was two of us shoved into each cell, Negroes together, whites together. We had a husk mattress on each bunk and a bucket, and the guards would entertain themselves watching us Niggas with glee, while we fought and killed each other over the one straw pillow each cell was allowed.

"We had an hour a day in the yard—murderers and thieves in the sun. One day Percival Turner, a filthy clansman, killed an old Negro friend of mine named Chicken just for fun. He tripped him up, and once Chicken fell, Percival stomped him in the head with his boot, like he was smashing a tomato. The last blow made brains spurt out of his skull. "Anybody want fried Chicken? How's about scrambled eggs?" Percival called out, while he laughed and laughed. The guards, too, was doubled over laughing. So, I snuck up on him and hammered Percival real hard on the top of his head with my fist. I grabbed a fist full of his hair, yanked him back hard by the scalp, and I hacked his throat until he gagged and rolled around in the dust. I was gonna finish him off, but the guards stopped laughing long enough to rescue Percival and restrain me in irons. Percival wasn't punished for killing a Negro, but I got a hummingbird— the guards doused me with a pail of piss then jammed a cattle prod with raw current into my wet back. The shock made my bones rattle and my blood boil. But the worst part was they let Percival watch.

"Percival got out of Joliet long before I did, but I am on the hunt for him. When I find him, I plan to use an ice pick to finish what I started. I'm going to pith his brain and stare into his eyes till I see 'em grow dark."

I had never heard Hash speak of jail before. I don't know if any of us had. We were all still as stone until he stopped talking. I knew that in my case, one more word from him, and I would have thrown up.

"Bloodshed." Mr. Abbott broke the silence. "It's never-ending and we always lose. You ice-pick that man, and you will go back to Old Joliet. No amount of slaughter can restore our loved ones. You go back inside, and they'll use a strapping lad like you to carry on with their slavery. You will be Jim Crow jail-labor, my friend, but this time, because you killed a white man, you will never get out. You are too valuable for that, son! We need strong men like you, Hash, to head and guide our families, not to provide free labor for the state. We must focus on bringing our families north because only through meaningful work can we provide for our families. And only if we are informed can we lift the yoke of oppression. To keep our sons out of Old Joliet's electric chair, we must liberate our people through education."

Hash stewed. But Mr. Abbott had a way with men like Hash. He would not allow the conversation to progress into more fantasies of violent retribution. Hash was real. Jim Crow jail was real. Something had to be done.

"I will make you a promise," Mr. Abbott spoke directly to Hash. "You let this hunt go, and I will personally see to it that we expose this Jim Crow jail for all its horror and bring it to shame. Let me take up the work, let me be the defender. But we do it my way, and that is this: The pen becomes the sword. The word becomes a weapon, for it is righteous and will live forever."

Hash's scowl dissipated as Mr. Abbot lay a finely manicured hand on the younger man's shoulder. We all felt the touch. In it was everything that Mr. Abbott embodied—intellect and action, discipline without impulse.

"You see, this film breathes new life into southern demons. They feel justified in keeping us from living in decent housing, having a fair shot at respectable work, and voting. In many cases, they lock us up for minor offences in Jim Crow jails and throw away the keys. Now, this enrages me because we came up here to escape all that," Mr. Abbott said with dignified fury. "Griffith convinces every racist that we don't deserve better, that we can't be trusted with responsibility. But just as fire knows no bounds, this film has ignited the hearts of our people. *The Defender* has given voice to the noble NAACP, and since this film has been released, its membership has grown by leaps and bounds."

Hash may not have surrendered, but he had been persuaded to retreat. More hate and more violence had not, and would not, cure America's formidable racial divisions. "What you say is the truth, suh," Hash acknowledged, "But you wait and watch, they are gonna fill these jails with us and build new ones now that we flood the North."

True to his word, the May 22 ,1915 *Defender* headline proclaimed,

"JIM CROW JAIL MUST NOT EXIST IN CHICAGO." The article that followed stated, "Investigation shows that discrimination exists in our county jails. Jails and hades should be the last places where men are discriminated against on account of color. Pay Taxes for All Alike … Chicago must and will set a pace to put its heel upon discrimination, not only at theaters and all public places, but in the jails. Let our bar association take the lead in this protest, the citizens will follow."

Mr. Abbott adjusted the tie pin in his collar, signaling he was changing gears. "Has your own behavior changed as a result of this propaganda film?" I could tell that the others were thinking their answers through. No one spoke for what felt like a long time, so I jumped in.

"My name is Bessie Coleman," I cleared my throat and went on, "Your newspaper is a brilliant, powerful gift, sir." All of the men swiveled in my direction.

"Tell me more," Mr. Abbott said. "And speak plainly, child," he encouraged. "I don't get a compliment often, so I want to make this one last." Everyone chuckled politely.

"The jails are deplorable here, and you are right, in the South they use our men for slave labor. But on the outside, sometimes we think all is well here in the North because we ride the streetcar sitting next to whites. But when a white man gets off, he can go anywhere he likes, which we cannot do. What I mean to say is that not all things are as they appear. This film should make every Negro fight for more than a seat on the streetcar. I want better than that. I want to strive for better. I want to go where our people have never been allowed to go."

Mr. Abbott put his head back and slowly began to clap. "My goodness, Mr. Duncan, I saw the beauty, but there appears to be courage and wisdom in the same package. What is your name again, dear?"

I told him.

Mr. Abbott turned his attention to the rest of the group and spent another thirty minutes listening to both barbers and customers. He took copious notes in his notepad and then thanked Mr. Duncan for the excellent coffee and hospitality and declared that he had found himself a new barbershop. From now on, he would be coming to the White Sox. Mr. Duncan was elated at this news.

Following his declaration, Mr. Abbot and the other gents broke up into smaller groups to talk. Making his way to my perch, Mr. Abbott slid into the seat across from me. He drew small gold-rimmed glasses and the nifty notepad from his pocket again. "I want better than that. I want to strive for better. I want to go where our people have never been allowed to go." Tell me more about you, young, brave Bessie. In what way will you be better? What field of endeavor do you intend to pursue?"

"I am not so brave," I said. "It's just that your newspaper inspires us to dream BIG and you make us believe that anything is possible, so I wanted you to know that I found inspiration in your words."

"Well, thank you. So, tell me, what do you aspire to do? What do you dream about?" he pressed.

"I dream of …" I shifted in my seat. "I want to …"

"You weren't so shy a minute ago. Go on, then," he urged.

"I want to know more about the flying machines. It sounds crazy when I say it out loud, but I want to fly those contraptions. Flying is the wave of the future!" I exclaimed.

"Ah, the future. You certainly have a much clearer vision of it than I had at your age," Mr. Abbott said. He slid the notebook back into his breast pocket and removed a cigar.

"What do you mean?"

"I went to law school after college because I wanted to defend the Constitution," he smiled wryly, lit a flame to the cigar, and took a few puffs from it. "But I couldn't find a single person whom I could defend. Whites wouldn't hire me, and Race men and women couldn't afford to pay me. I became a printing apprentice in order to make my way through Hampton Institute, and then a funny thing happened, something I never could have seen coming. I had a lot to say about a lot of things, but I had nowhere to say it. So, I decided to start a newspaper with the seven dollars I had. My landlady became my first promoter. She kept begging me for more and more copies to sell. She called my efforts evangelical. She believed in me, and I believed in our Race. There were stories that needed to be told, businesses that needed a champion, people who needed uplifting, and I could do that by telling our stories. Before I knew it, I was selling advertising and hiring writers, and in less than a decade, I was a millionaire. Mine is an American story, just not one often afforded to those of our race. It was a future I had never envisioned. So, Miss Coleman, if you can already see your future, go get it. Nothing is impossible."

Mr. Abbott handed me his crisp white calling card and stood up from my table. "When you want to talk more about flying, about the future, about your future, call on me," he said. "You remind me of myself when I was young. You have a full head of steam and a heart full of passion. What great fortune it must be to have a gem of a daughter such as you. I am sure your mother is stunning, and I am confident that your father is proud."

"Thank you, sir, for the honor and the compliments," I managed.

One of Mr. Abbott's colleagues had been hovering and closed in just as our conversation ended. This new gent had rakish good looks and was all swagger. He stared at me with an intensity that hinted at playfulness, a complex mix of grown man and adolescent charm. Without taking his eyes off me, he asked for an introduction, and Mr. Abbott obliged.

"I am reluctant to introduce my robber baron friend," Mr. Abbott warned. "But I suppose I must, since he can't stop staring at you. Miss Coleman, meet Jesse Binga, real estate magnate, banker and, as I said before, robber baron extraordinaire."

"Robert, you make me sound so appealing," Jesse said as he flashed a smile, one hundred watts of pure dazzle beneath the most perfectly coiffed cookie-duster mustache I had ever seen. I had no idea what a robber baron was, but the term sounded like a high-class thief. Whatever else he was culpable of, Mr. Jesse Binga instantly stole my heart, which at the moment, I was glad no one else could hear pounding in my own ears.

CHAPTER 8

The next morning, I clutched a cup of steaming black tea and watched the sky transform as the sun rose fully above the horizon. I waited for the predictable charge that I always felt and celebrated as the sun's energy penetrated the earth.

"I am confident that your father is proud," Mr. Abbott had said. But I had no way of knowing whether Daddy was proud or not. I had not seen him in more than a dozen years. I had no idea if he was even alive.

George Coleman was the best of his African and Choctaw heritage. His Indian family had trudged up from the Mississippi Delta and, like his forebears, he was a great hunter and an even better fisherman. When Daddy moved our family to Waxahachie from Atlanta, Texas, he used his bare hands to build our shotgun house near bodies of fresh water so that he could fish. Mustang Creek ran along the border of our property, and steps from our place was a deep pool called the Blue Hole, where giant cantankerous catfish were plentiful. Daddy said Choctaws spoke the Muskogean language and the people were known as Hacha Hatak, or the River People. He told me that Oklahoma is a Choctaw word, that *okla* means people and *humma* means red.

Daddy was a handsome man with high cheekbones and a mop of thick, black, wavy hair. He had smooth, dark reddish-brown skin and narrow, coal-black eyes with thick eyelashes and sculpted eyebrows. His vision was as sharp as the corners of his almond-shaped eyes. He used his keen eyesight to hunt, bragging that he could make out a prairie dog a hundred feet away. "But I s'pose that's useless less'n you can shoot that far and cook 'im up for everybody," he'd laugh.

I inherited my Daddy's superior eyesight, his great health, and his passion for the water, whether for leisure or fishing, swimming or survival. On Sundays while Mama was at church, Daddy and I would steal away to one of the many fishing holes he had found hidden deep within the spring creeks. Surrounded by spikey cattail reeds, I would dig for blood-worms with a long-handled spoon and then plunge my arm deep into the cold, white clay-mud up to my elbow. I'd pull out long squiggling creatures, thread his rod, spear the worms and, like a Tennessee plott hound, point out the flies dancing on the glassy, watery tabletop. Daddy angled and spirited out dozens of sheepshead, crappies, bass, and catfish.

My father remains a puzzle to me. He could kill and skin an animal in no time with the same hunting knife that he unsheathed from his vest in order to bounce a baby on his knee or rock one of his children to sleep in the cradle between his elbow and bicep. His huge, calloused hands could be gentle on a child's brow or savage when he wielded an axe. We all knew how much he loved us and how much he had sacrificed for us, taking on any work, no matter how harsh or dangerous, so that he could feed us. And we came to learn that he carried a rage that lurked below the surface of his calm. While slow to anger, he was fierce when disobeyed, and we grew to understand that he carried a frustration born of the lack of independence he had had felt his entire life. Daddy wanted real freedom. He wanted his own spring on his own land, and he craved the life of a rancher with open space and endless sky. He had worked so hard and for so long, laboring at jobs that made other men rich. And as he aged, I watched him slowly change. During the hottest Texas days, he picked cotton alongside my mother and us children. In the evening, he worked in the cotton mill, struggling to make ends meet.

As a future of adventure and passion slowly slipped away from my proud father's grasp, his whole self seemed to diminish like air from a leaking bellows. The only thing that seemed to spark Daddy were dreams of wandering through Oklahoma, settling on land that we would claim as our own. I was beginning to feel the same wanderlust, the same desire for better, no matter how undefined, no matter where that quest led. But Mama didn't see it that way at all.

One afternoon the overseer, Mr. Louis, eyed my Daddy warily. I wasn't sure what offence Daddy had committed, but Mr. Louis looked hot, bored, and angry, and he loved to pick at us for sport when he was idle. I had a penny in my pocket, so in order to distract him from whatever he was thinking about Daddy, I placed the coin from one side pocket to the other, where a chronic hole in my overalls had worn itself thin again. I spun the penny from inside my pocket so that when it hit the ground, it rolled and stopped right at the scuffed tip of the overseer's boot. In an instant, Mr. Louis went from disgusted to delighted, as the thought of filching a penny from a child in his employ made him as giddy as a child himself.

Mr. Louis bent at the waist, and his considerable girth kept him suspended there for a moment, and in that moment I pounced. I slid into position and placed the toe of my weathered boot onto the pea-scale that measured our family's weekly cotton totals. This weekly accounting was ripe for contrived losses meant to cheat big families like ours who worked every day and depended on an accurate tabulation.

Mr. Louis retrieved and then bit down on the penny with his eye tooth, as if I, a ten-year-old, could possibly engineer a counterfeit coin. As he turned it over again and again between his sweaty fingers, I took advantage of his distraction and increased the pressure of my boot. Mama saw my high jinks and winced, and while I'd never confuse it for a smile, the muscle in Daddy's jaw rippled ever so slightly, and then a trace grin reached his eyes before disappearing in a flash. Mr. Louis never had an inkling of what was going on. As Daddy stared without a hint of emotion straight into Mama's face, Mr. Louis eyed the two of them, but not me. I imagined that he enjoyed what he interpreted as my parents' indignation over their inability to defend their child, as much as he did his own power to control our fortunes.

Mr. Louis kept my penny, but my stunt added fifty cents to our family's total haul, which meant the Colemans were up forty-nine cents! But when we had moved down the road a-piece, Mama boxed my ears real hard. "You could have gotten us in a lot of hot water back there," she whispered through clenched teeth. But Daddy smiled much broader now. Winking at me, he jangled extra coins in his pocket as we shared in a delight of our own. But it was a short-lived happiness and one of the last private jokes that Daddy and I would ever share.

Two weeks before my tenth birthday, Daddy declared that he was going to Oklahoma. He said he would go on ahead and prepare a place for all of us, and although Mama said that she would consider following, we all knew her heart. A third move, this time to some desolate spot in Oklahoma, where I had been told there were more rocks than in a busted-up quarry, was just too much. It represented loneliness, back-breaking labor, and the unpredictable weather of tornados in the plains. I had no way of knowing it but I would never lay eyes on Daddy again.

As the sun kept inching higher, I checked my timepiece, knowing I'd have to abandon my thoughts of Daddy and hurry to work in order to get there before our first customers arrived. I had a great number of appointments that Friday since it was the start of the weekend, so I hurriedly bathed, dressed, and scurried.

Seated at my table, as fine as ever, was my first customer of the day.

"Would you please do me the honor of cleaning up my act?" Jesse Binga said, as he splayed his wide, rugged hands palms-down on my table so that they nearly covered the entire surface of my workspace. As I hung up my coat and hat, I tried to suppress the smile that crept across my lips.

I sat down and slid my hands beneath his fingers, assessing the work. But before I could take a look, he turned my fingers over, engulfed my hands in his, and began gently massaging my hands with his own big thumbs. His nails looked as if they had been buffed an hour ago.

"Your hands are already pretty tidy," I said. "There's little that I can improve upon."

"So, are you trying to tell me that my money is no good here?" he teased.

"I'll happily take your money, sir, but I want to earn it," I heard myself say, and flashed him a flirtatious smile that my facial muscles did not fully recognize as my own. I wasn't engaged in a manicure, yet I still seemed to be holding his hands. Or was he holding mine? Our exchange felt like playing with fire, and it felt so good that I could not pull away.

"Aren't you the cheeky one," he said.

I felt my heart skip when he flexed a muscle in his square jaw. He was much better looking in person than he was in his pictures in *The Defender*. Jesse Binga was a legend, one of the few self-made millionaires who called the Stroll their own. It made sense that Mr. Abbott chronicled Jesse Binga's business affairs in *The Defender*. It made even more sense that these two men were friends and colleagues. According to *The Broad Ax*, another Chicago Negro weekly newspaper, Mr. Abbott was a board member of Jesse's Binga State Bank, so too was Alderman Oscar De Priest, the only Negro serving in Congress. Yes, two tycoons and a politician—these great men were movers and shakers—Chicago's Negro aristocracy, self-made kings of money, influence, politics. And Jesse Binga earned his fortune while single-handedly changing the landscape of Chicago's South Side forever. South Side homes, once owned exclusively by whites, were out of reach for Negro families—that is, until Jesse came along. He was a modern-day Robin Hood, buying houses from white homeowners, sight unseen, and selling them to Negroes or renting them out. When needed, he'd don a pair of overalls and paint a wall or fix a porch.

Often, families would pool their entire life savings for a down payment, but those same families needed to secure a loan for a mortgage, and they needed insurance, too. Stamping the entire enterprise with his own name, Jesse hatched The Binga State Bank, where these same families could safely protect their deposits. He was the only man brazen enough to wash the gangster money that flowed through Chicago's real-estate market, while simultaneously turning hope into picket fences for the everyday Negro family. Feared by many, envied by many more, Jesse Binga was respected by everyone. Now, this same man sat in my chair, fondling my hands, while asking me to take some of his money. I smiled at the irony.

I grabbed a stiff, new emery board I'd been saving from its hiding spot in my drawer and began to reshape his nails. Although his huge hands were well taken care of, it was obvious to me they were no stranger to hard work. No matter how good the manicure, you could never erase a person's past. It was written on the rough palm of the hand and embedded in the pulp of every fingertip.

"Mr. Binga, I would be happy to relieve you of your burden," I said.

I tried to concentrate, but just touching him made that impossible. He smiled at me under his bushy chevron mustache and boldly reached over my table with a free hand to smooth my hair. He neither apologized nor explained, just curled the left side of his mouth into a much smaller, less readable smile. I wondered how many smiles this man had in his arsenal.

Mr. Duncan arrived and was pleased to see our unexpected guest. "Mornin', Mr. Binga. Glad you come back to see us again so soon. Bessie seeing to your needs?"

"Why, yes. Yes, she is," Jesse Binga said softly, and the two shared a suggestive smirk.

As my cheeks flushed, I considered Mr. Duncan's coded query a betrayal, and when he winked at me, I cut my eyes at him to let him know he was not forgiven.

"Say, Mr. Binga, I am so glad to have another opportunity. I wanted to say thank you the other day but didn't have the chance. With what you done here in Chicago, the Negro can hold his head up high and live better. Thank you for that."

Jesse smiled proudly, and tipped an imaginary cap.

"If Mr. Duncan said that, he meant it. He never puts anybody on," I confessed in a whisper.

"Thank you, Miss Coleman. It is Miss Coleman, isn't it?"

"Yes, sir, it is Miss," I responded.

"Miss Coleman, from …?"

"From Waxahachie, Texas, suh." I laid on my thickest Texas drawl.

"Pleased to meet you, Miss Coleman from Waxa-who?, Texas"

"Waxa-what-you-call-it? Waxa-why-you-smack-him, Why-you-wax-it, Texas?" I said, laughing, I could go on with this all day long. Waxahachie, good sir."

"I have traveled all over this country, but I missed this stop. Good place to be from?"

"Like anywhere in the Deep South, it is far better to be from there than to still be there," I said truthfully.

"Listen," he said, "it's time for me to go to work, but I was wondering if you would be free for dinner. Maybe we could continue our conversation outside of the barbershop? Are you available tomorrow evening after closing?"

"I might be."

"Excellent! I'll see you then."

He rose, and I took note of his gray plaid suit and blood-red tie. He moved easily, confidently. It was rude of me to stare, but I needed enough time to memorize his tall athletic build and to summon his vanilla and licorice scent long after he'd walked out.

"I look forward to it," I said.

The flame was blazing hot—too many flames to stamp out now. I looked down at my empty hands and saw that on my table he had left a tip, a crisp, new twenty-dollar bill, the equivalent to two week's wages. I quickly shoved my providence deep down in my brassiere.

The thought of him distracted me for the rest of the day. How did a colored man like Jesse find his way in this world? What in the world did he want with me? How in the world would I wait until tomorrow to see him again? And more importantly, what to wear? Oh, my goodness, what to wear?

For this answer, I needed a seamstress amongst seamstresses. Someone who knew garments, fabrics, and yarns. I also needed a confidant, best friend, and keeper of my every secret. I needed Norma.

CHAPTER 9

P
aired as college roommates in Langston Colored Agricultural and Normal School, Norma and I grew to be as close as sisters. Our friendship had only grown stronger through the years, and now that we were both in Chicago, we spent as much time together as we possibly could. Norma would be able to help me with more than just my wardrobe. If anyone in my small circle knew about grown-up matters, she did. After she had graduated from college, Norma had married, become a mother, and now had another baby on the way. She knew things.

That evening in her kitchen, Norma and I feasted on fried green tomatoes, crusted cornmeal pockets then deep fried in lard. We ate together as we used to do back in school—perched on rickety old ladder-back chairs, sharing one plate and two forks.

With this new baby, Norma liked to eat peculiar things and for some reason did not want to indulge alone. I begged off when she insisted on adding smashed bananas and chopped cheese to our plate and shuddered as she dug into the commingled mash.

"Gurrrrl, you been working so much, I thought you done forgot about me," Norma said, her forearm raised to wipe a bit of banana from the side of her mouth.

"I have been hustling, honey! Have to save my money for flying lessons, that's all," I reassured.

"You really are going to do it, aren't you?" she asked. Her fork, as well as her disbelief, dangled in midair. Perhaps the fact that I was actively saving had finally convinced her.

"Yep, a few more years of squirreling away tips, and I'm going to loop loops!"

"I am frightened for you," she breathed.

We were opposites, Norma and I, in our choice of men, in our approach to life. While Norma avoided risks, I rushed towards adventure. Her husband Moe, who had been our college buddy, was predictable, gentle, loving, and a good provider. I had yet to find a man who could measure up to his qualities.

"Listen," I said, changing the subject, "I need to borrow something pretty for tomorrow night, or maybe you could just whip me up something right quick. I met someone special. He invited me out to paint the town."

"Anything for you, shuga," she said, fanning herself, although it was not hot. "Anyone I know? Who is this mystery man?"

"No mystery. His name is Jesse Binga," I answered.

"Not the Jesse Binga!"

"The one and only."

"Well, I happen to know him, she laughed.

"How in the world do you know him?" There was no way to cloak my surprise. The fact that Norma already knew my bigwig came as a shock.

"He sauntered into my alterations shop one day and ordered half a dozen custom shirts. Wanted the finest linen I could buy. He was so pleased with my work, he gave me a suit order, and I am making him a three-button pinstripe. I designed it for him—has a smart vest, high lapel, and snug-fit trousers, 'cause he is so *foine*, and I want all my other clients to see how a foine body like his can be accentuated. I even added my new label—*Pope Couture*. The pattern and material is resting over there," she motioned toward her worktable. "I was gonna tell you 'bout my new important customer, but you ain't come round to visit Moe, little Pearle, and me in a month of Sundays."

Transfixed, I floated across the room and fondled the sheer chalk stripe that ran down the fine navy wool. Touching the garment that would clothe Jesse felt like spying.

"So, he's who you been keeping company with," she shot me a smile which faded as fast as it had appeared. "Not so shabby, not shabby at all. But listen, and I am in no position to judge, but isn't he a bit … mature?

He gave me license to style him, but I don't know anything about Mr. Binga's personal life. What do you really know about him, anyway?"

"Listen, I came here to get your fashion advice. Slow down on the caution flags, Norma. I haven't even gotten out the gate yet." I could feel my own smile wavering.

"I care about you," she said and crossed the room to hug me. "I just want you to be careful. Jesse Binga is a grown man. You take care of yourself around him, okay?"

Norma disappeared into the bedroom and then returned with a powder-blue two-piece skirt set. The chic hobble skirt that had once clung snugly to her hips and thighs would now cling to my own, and I marveled at the idea that I would be wearing something so sharp. It was one of her original designs, and she knew I had loved it since first seeing her in it the day we met at Langston. What I loved most was that it was bold. This suit refused any notion of demure. The jacket did not attempt to obscure the posterior but hugged it snugly instead.

That evening Norma didn't ask me any more questions. In thirty minutes, she had finished hand-stitching the hem, and when she had sewn the last tiny stitch, she declared, "You'll look better in this than I ever did. I'm not sure if it's a good thing or a bad thing, but you'll be irresistible."

It was I who had found Norma irresistible ever since we'd met. Norma's hair was thick and plaited into two long braids that hung down her back like hunks of midnight. She was the color of Hershey's chocolate and had sharp features and big round eyes fringed by long lashes. Each time she closed her eyes, her upper lashes seemed to do battle with the lower ones just to reopen again, which made for her signature long-lasting blink.

Way back in the fall of 1910, on a bright, sunny morning, each of us had gotten up before the sun and dressed in our Sunday best. Although our clothes were the finest we owned, our cardboard suitcases and hobo totes betrayed our station in life, and we quickly shoved them beneath the benches of the dusty old coach from Langston that met us at the train station. It was pulled by two beastly oxen who seemed as though they had been hitched to that beat-down old rig their whole miserable lives.

"Them brutes look like the sharecroppers I left behind in Sugarland," Norma whispered to me as we pulled away from the dusty curb. Sugarland, Texas was as far from Houston, as Waxahachie was from Dallas. "I worked cane since I was a child. If it wasn't for this chance, I would be working like them beasts still," Norma added.

With very few words, Mr. Timothy, a tall, gaunt, red-brown man in overalls who was Langston's only custodian, drove the wagon on to our new adventure. The sun shone fully and brightly overhead, and after a few hours, as if from a dream, the trio of buildings that made up Langston Colored Agricultural and Normal University rose up out of the flat, red Oklahoma plains—three hallowed structures gleaming like gemstones in a tiara. The rose-gold glow of the ruddy Cimarron River hugged the curvature of land that ringed our school, and although more like a moat than a crown, it encircled us and kept all threats at bay. We would soon learn through hardship and experience that it was Mother Nature and poverty that were the twin threats to fledging students like us.

The lower Cimarron was plagued by flooding, which is likely why the Langston founders were able to acquire the muddy land that slid and shifted above the river's berm. The floods were merciless as the river consumed its own embankment, floating tiny Arkansas shiners to the surface. Giant carp would pursue the minnow lures then snapping turtles and rattlesnakes would pursue the fish. It was as if the creatures of the blood-red water had been waiting to slither amongst us in the muddy earth.

But the greater peril that each of us suffered was the fragile nature of our finances. The meager sums that our families had scraped together had been just enough to get us to college, but they left little margin for disaster—man-made or otherwise. Money was tight, and college was a luxury. I knew I had to claim my education before circumstance snatched my chances away. If I could survive the floods, I could nourish my dream with hard work and would become the first in what I hoped would be a long line of Coleman college graduates.

But there wasn't a single rain cloud in the sky the day we arrived. The oxen stirred up brick-red dust, but I didn't see red haze so much as I saw light glinting off of Page Hall, the largest school building. It shimmered as if caught in some sort of magic, copper powder. Named after our illustrious school President, Mr. Inman Page, the limestone building was solid, massive, impressive. I felt confident that a whole lot of learning went on in there.

The other two buildings were the girls' and the boys' dormitories, separated by an ocean of grass. Our teachers worried deeply about the possibility of pregnancies, but my newfound freedom didn't provoke lust, but rather dread. The girls' building was small and modest, with a flimsy tin roof. It looked as if a strong wind could knock it down. Our dormitory was nothing more than a shack compared to the sturdy limestone boys' dorm, mainly because girls were a recent addition to the student body, numbering only twenty out of the two hundred students.

Although Norma and I had only just met at the train depot, I knew right away that she and I were going to be best friends, and I had always longed for a best friend. It had dawned on me that best friends were an indulgence of time, an extravagance I had been denied while growing up. Caring for my sisters, picking cotton, taking in laundry, being a maid, none of these afforded time for play with friends. But in my new relationship with Norma, I would give and get protection, a generous ear to tell my secrets, and a heart that would not judge. I would also find someone to answer my questions about boys—kissing, sex, and all the stuff I dared not mention to Mama. I was convinced that Norma would tell me her intimate secrets, and I would tell her mine, but even then I had no way of preparing myself for the depth of her confidence.

At five feet six inches, Norma was quite a bit taller than most girls. She had long, slender legs, an ample bust, and the kind of shelf-like buttocks that men looked at twice. You could just see their imaginations running wild as they tarried during a second, lengthy gander as she passed. Norma was exquisite and sensual, and you could see it in her walk. Her slow, long strides contained harnessed energy, and she could, at any moment, stretch those lanky gams and dash like a gazelle. All legs and arms, Norma was the only girl who could beat any boy in a footrace.

She did not realize how beautiful she was. Once I found her wringing her long fingers in her lap, as she cast her broom-like lashes to the floor and spoke so softly I could barely hear her. "When I was growing up, white kids were cruel; but colored kids hurt me even more—'skillet, boot-black, midnight, tar,'—these are the names they hurled at me, then pointed at me and laughed until they couldn't catch their breath. They made me think that all things black were bad and ugly."

I loved her dark cherry color and thought she was the most beautiful woman I had ever seen. We were opposites who attracted—I was short, she was tall. I was light, she was dark. I couldn't wait to charge ahead, while Norma thought about everything before she took a single step. Our differences extended to our visions of the future, too. I told Norma about my fascination with aeroplanes, which she considered very daring, and she told me about her dream of opening a tailoring establishment one day. In the newness of our friendship, dreams of flying and entrepreneurship felt attainable. What we were going to do with our futures, at that moment, seemed as open and as big as the Oklahoma sky, that same blue firmament into which my Daddy had disappeared.

But there was gravity too. For just as hope and optimism made us buoyant, loss and longing clung to many of our southern lives.

"Tell me about yourself, Miss Norma Rae," I said with seriousness.

Norma looked at me sheepishly. "Funny," she said. "I have been waiting my entire life to tell somebody my story."

I joined her on her cot and burrowed my ankles deeply into her soft mattress. "You can trust me," I told her, laying my hand across her warm fingers.

"My father died before I was born and my Mama raised me by herself. I never did have other kin to speak of—t'was just Mama and me." Norma started right at the beginning.

"Mama cut cane in the fields, and she taught me to do the same. When she had extra time, she worked 'cross town in an old cotton mill. She would carry home the scrap-cotton and make skeins of yarn from it. Then, she'd fashion the simple string into all sorts of scarves, sweaters, pretty table linens, and such. Mama learned me to knit and sew," Norma said with great pride.

"Six months ago, Mama died in her sleep. I suspect her heart just gave 'way. She was only thirty-seven." Norma was quiet. Then she said, "I had a decision to make. Either I could stay in Sugarland, Texas, which was anything but sweet, or I could venture out into the world. I chose the world. It has been big and scary, but I promised Mama that I'd get an education. I decided to come to Langston, 'cause it was on the way to Chicago."

"And your Daddy?" I had yet to share the story of my own missing father.

"My Daddy was a Buffalo Soldier and was headed out West to clear the forest and construct roads. He was part of the 10th Calvary and one of the finest horsemen in his unit," Norma paused. "He was murdered."

Slowly, Norma recounted his wasting. Proudly, dressed in his new soldier's uniform, he had been on his way into town to collect provisions for his pregnant wife who was to join him, when he encountered three white men. The story goes that Daddy refused to make way for them and did not budge off the flagstones he was walking on. But the three outnumbered Daddy. They beat him and slit his throat from ear to ear. I was born six months after Daddy was buried. He never laid eyes on me. After his murder, Mama and me stayed in Sugarland, and so did the men who murdered Daddy. They were never brought to justice, of course. All my life, I grew up living next to my Daddy's murderers and their children, too."

Norma talked as though she had stored up her entire life in a bottle and was now turning that bottle over to pour her story out. My invitation uncorked years, and her loss came out like atomized spray.

"After Mama died, I took her place at the mill. Because of Mama's hard work and good reputation, I was promoted to floor boss of all the colored girls—we made yarn, threads, and such. I would work late, often. Most times I was the last to leave. One night, Mr. Dratchet caught hold of me in the dark. He wasn't supposed to be anywhere near the place because he had lost his job there for stealing. White men had the best jobs, and Mr. Clyde Dratchet had been one of the men who ran the machinery and inspected the final skeins. Everybody knew he was also one of the three that murdered Daddy. I hated him for that, and he hated me for having the nerve to have a good job in the place he was fired from.

"Wasn't enough that he had stolen my Daddy's life, now he preyed on me. Mr. Dratchet was a hulk, and he looked like an ogre. But he was older now, slowed a bit. He was drunk, too. He snuck up behind me, and I smelled him before I heard him over the spinning wheel that I was working. He pressed himself against me and then hauled me to my feet and dragged me behind the mill where the cellar door was standing open.

"In those days I used to carry Daddy's Bowie knife concealed in my head wrap, not so much for protection, but 'cause it was one of only two things that Mama left me of Daddy's. I wanted to pull that knife out then and threaten Mr. Dratchet, but I was afraid he would turn things around and use it on me.

"Mr. Dratchet shoved me, and I resisted, so he kicked me and pitched me down the cellar steps. The earthen walls was dank, and the filth from leaking sewage pooled where I landed. I heard the iron clank of him bolting the door behind, locking us both inside. I don't know why, but I played dead. He came down the stairs, real slow like, and I heard him unbuckle his belt.

"He fondled me. I was afraid to look upon him. His ice-blue eyes were a shock of lightning, and they always terrified me. 'You the only decent thing that good-for-nothin' Nigga toy soldier left behind,' he grunted. He unbuttoned his trousers and pulled out his organ. Huffing and puffing foul breath, he took all mine away. I knew I had one chance. So, I took it," Norma breathed.

I felt like I too had been robbed of air. I had been unable to breathe since Norma had begun.

"He hiked up my skirts and tried to penetrate me. He was so absorbed in what he was doing that he allowed his grip to let my hands go free. I reached up to my head wrap, grabbed my knife, and plunged the blade deep into his right flank. He never knew what hit him. I heard a sound, like air rushing out of a balloon. Then I ripped the knife up, gutting him like a shad. Blood was everywhere. The smell of it mixed with the stench of sewage.

"My ankle was busted from the fall, but I scrambled away from him and clambered up them stairs. Somehow, that devil limped up the stairs behind me. He grabbed me, but I kicked him in the face with the boot heel of my good leg and yanked the bolt free. But just as I went to shut the cellar door, he shoved his hand out to grab me one final time. I whacked the door shut. It slammed on the tips of his thick fingers, and they splattered in the door jam. I took that shackle bolt and slid it into place, locking it from the outside. He screamed like a coyote, but wasn't a soul around to hear him.

"It was Saturday night, and nobody worked the next day since it would be the Sabbath. By the time that Monday workers arrived, they would find Dratchet in a pool of his own blood. Divine isn't it?" Norma asked, even though she seemed not to expect an answer. "My Daddy bled to death, and so did Mr. Dratchet."

Neither of us had unpacked a thing and by the time she finished her story, it was dark outside. If we didn't hustle, we would be late for the dinner roundup. We somehow managed to break free from Norma's past, scurried down a quiet, empty hallway, and burst out of the door to the outside, only to find that the other girls were already lined up. They had been waiting for us.

The clock on Page Hall announced the hour—we were four minutes late.

"Good evening ladies, so glad that you decided to join our little party," our matron, Miss Olive Crump, frowned at us. A few of the girls snickered. Even though we were embarrassed, I thought to myself that those girls would be real quiet if they knew what I had just learned about Norma.

Each of our lives harbored secrets. Some were more harrowing and unspeakable than others. Later, Norma told me that on that night, she used the dirt back roads to get home. Before the sun came up, she scoured her privates with lye soap and burned her bloody clothes. "Then I scattered them ashes. They vanished, just like I did." Mr. Dratchet had so many enemies, that when Norma up and left Sugarland, no one ever chased her. Plus, it was assumed that a woman couldn't ever have savaged a giant man like Mr. Dratchet.

"You will brush your teeth," Matron Crump was saying, "wash your face and hands and discard your wastewater into a pail. Do not come to my table without your beds made, fresh breath, and clean face and hands. If these most basic chores are incomplete, you will not eat." Many of us were already skinny from missing meals, and this threat was not taken lightly by any of us.

"Each of you will be assigned a duty," Matron Crump continued.

Just then, a big group of upper-class boys sauntered by our uneven lineup. They were snickering amongst themselves, confident and full of swagger. I was sure that they were sorting through the lot of us, deciding which girl they intended to badger. The one-girl-to-twenty-boy ratio could not go unnoticed, and impending manhood hung in the air we breathed.

Matron Crump would have none of it, and she shooed them away like flies. After threatening to flatten them with her hand, she started in on our chores again. We listened as she ran through a litany of cleaning duties—outhouses, hallways, classrooms. The cooking assignments to feed four hundred students and fifty teachers meant that plenty of work went into breakfast, lunch, and dinner. Then there was a slew of agricultural classes that had a dual purpose—we'd be learning from them, and they would be feeding us, as well. There were chickens to care for, eggs to collect, cows to milk, and vegetables to plant, weed, and harvest. We were young and strong, and the beneficiaries of our own labor, a generation of young men and women who had grown up doing these same chores at home, in places with names as hard to pronounce as they were to find on a map—Autaugaville, Alabama; Escatawapa, Mississippi, and Osceola, Arkansas.

We knew hard work and were not afraid to do it, but at that time, there were two schools of thought about the precious education we were to receive, and it resulted in a philosophical battle being waged by two of the brightest minds of our race. They were like intellectual pugilists, and we spectators were captivated by their national fight. In one corner was the northern scholar and educator W.E.B. Du Bois. He had gone to Fisk University around the same year that I was born, had then studied at the University of Berlin, and by the time I was a toddler, had earned his PhD from Harvard University. He believed that Negroes should seek broad studies in literature, history, language, mathematics, and science with a vengeance, and that in doing so, we could make education the great equalizer of the races.

The University of Pennsylvania commissioned Du Bois to study the state of the Philadelphia Negro, and in 1899 he published the findings of five thousand interviews that he had conducted from a door-to-door survey. Du Bois's research had found that Negroes paid more for miserable housing and suffered poor wages due to a lack of schooling, all of which led to even deeper poverty. He concluded that only by instructing the children of slaves could we be successful in challenging the notions whites had on every issue from land ownership, to jobs, to the vote. Du Bois sought equality without compromise.

Then there was the work, and I mean work, of southerner Booker T. Washington who believed that college should teach each of us a skill or a trade. This post-slavery generation had to make itself invaluable to whites, in his judgment, and to the economy that had previously benefited from the labor of slaves. He had his students at Tuskegee Normal and Industrial Institute build a kiln designed to fabricate bricks so that students could build their own buildings, since he said that there was as much power in knowing how to make bricks and construct the building as there was in lounging inside its reading room.

At first, I embraced Du Bois's philosophy completely and wanted to dismiss Washington's ideas for what I determined was a rebuild-what-the-slaves-had-left-behind approach to education. I wanted progress, not just the same hard work under a different name. But back then our world of colleges was small, and word of what was happening at each one spread like Yellow Fever. We heard that when Washington first arrived at Tuskegee, the buildings were decrepit and leaking and so, borrowing a page straight out of the book of Exodus, he chose to imitate the life of the Pharisees and the Hebrews. But instead of Egyptian clay, Washington had students stomp in an Alabama clay pit. This did not go over well. As the biblical Hebrews had done, the students left in droves. It was dirty, back-breaking labor, and this new generation, the sons and daughters of slaves, saw this as new slavery, whether it was in return for an education or not.

Washington's experiment was a failure. The bricks, as well as a key group of supporters, fell apart. But the effort was not a total loss. In fact, as I was to learn, some of the greatest discoveries come from the biggest failures. He would need a better kiln to make strong bricks so that, unlike with our girls' dorm, a priceless education could not be swept away.

It was said that Washington pawned his gold pocket watch for fifteen dollars, investing the meager and only sum he had left in the world into building a functioning kiln. This time, he had success and made so many bricks that he even sold the extras not needed for school buildings to any townspeople who wanted them. It seemed to me that his power did not just come from his ability to make bricks, it came from his having the opportunity to sell them. He took on the business of supplying a commodity that until then had not existed in his town. As a result, he taught his students about striving, failing, and trying again.

With two such intellectuals hard at work in their respective corners, many were provoking the northern scholar and the southern laborer to spar. But my hope was that these two would line up and fight on the same side, because the way I saw it, together they would be invincible. We desperately needed to read and write, but we also needed to assess the needs of our communities and then to be self-reliant enough to build our own homes and businesses.

During the time that these two men were pursuing their goals, a young coed named Ethel Hedgemen started a sorority named Alpha Kappa Alpha at Howard University in 1908. She saw service and a lifelong affiliation with like-minded women as the key to enhancing a woman's college experience, as well as her own future. My hope was that Alpha Kappa Alpha would land on our campus and would consider letting me join them. It was exciting to dream about sisterhood, and I wanted to join a women's tribe, not so much just to belong, but rather to unite and be stronger together.

I never did get the chance to finish college, not to mention join Alpha Kappa Alpha. By the end of my first semester, boll weevils had struck the cotton crop back home. There was no more money, not even enough for me to complete my freshman year at Langston.

On the day I was set to leave, Norma handed me a package. "Here, I made this for you. It's a going-away present."

I wept as I took the package from her hands. "I am so ashamed. I won't be able to finish college, and worse, I am leaving you all by yourself." My Mama and the girls needed me, but how in the world could I leave Norma? She'd be alone again.

"Don't say anything else," Norma hushed, as tears formed in her eyes, "just go on, open it."

The parcel was wrapped in brown paper and tied with a long piece of twine of the same color. I didn't want to unseal it. I felt too guilty. It felt wrong to be receiving Norma's gift when I was about to betray her by leaving.

"Open it," she insisted. "I made it for you."

I untied the string and folded back the paper. Inside the bundle was the most exquisite gift I have ever received. In our *Housekeeping and Fabrics* course, Norma's final project had been a quilt. The assignment was to make a quiltlet, and just as the slaves had done before us, it had to tell a story. It could be a coded map of the North, with abstract symbols which, when decoded, pointed a slave toward freedom, or through patch-work the piece could tell an ordinary person's life story. Technique was graded, and while applique, backstitching, basting, batting, and bearding counted, it was the story that was paramount.

I hadn't noticed right away, but little by little, a shirt here, and a nightgown there had gone missing from my sad wardrobe. One by one, Norma had spirited away a few items of my clothing that really were too threadbare to miss for long. With just scraps of my garments, Norma had begun to tell my story and had begun to write my future. Her Christmas gift to me was an oracle.

My raggedy blue nightgown was transformed. It became sky. A skirt had been turned into borders around circle-loops and inside each circle was a tattered flower from a shirt I had worn way past its prime, and cloud-white patches from her own sacrificed sheets floated above. My sad, pale pink slip was reborn as the rectrices of a bird's tail.

Without my knowing, Norma had sent away for a piece of deep blue velvet corduroy. That rich midnight sky color became the backing fabric. And from the only other possession she owned from her dead father—his black-and-white bandana—a strip trimmed from its edging created the outline of the fuselage of an aeroplane. I had confided in Norma my secret desire to fly, and this quilt was her way of telling me that I would do so.

This was the treasure that had inspired me to spend so much on the first piece of furniture I would own in Chicago. My big brass bed was more than a place to sleep, it was a place to showcase the story of my future. Beneath that quilt, I dreamt of flying. When I woke each morning, before I did anything else, I'd make my bed, allowing myself an indulgence of time and a prayer of belief. Each morning, I swept my hands across the precious bandana fuselage and absorbed its strength.

CHAPTER 10

When my shift at the barbershop ended, I ran in the back to change into Norma's suit and put on fresh lipstick and rouge. I threw on an intricate shawl that Norma had dyed with beets, its deep Bordeaux color gave my complexion a new complexity, and when I paired it with the powder-blue cloche that matched my suit, the overall look was sophisticated. I said a quick good night over my shoulder to the fellas and hurried out. I did not want them to know about my date.

A little taller than I remembered, Jesse Binga waltzed down the Stroll in a slate-gray suit as if he owned the entire block. And I guessed that in a certain way, he kind of did. I saw him smile as he glided my way. It was a big, easy invitation. I smiled back and quickened my pace toward him so that we would meet before he reached the plate-glass window of the barbershop. Bishop was still inside sweeping up, and I knew he would tell all of my business if he caught a glimpse of us together.

"Hello, Miss Coleman," his smile grew wider still.

"Evenin', Mr. Binga," I said. "Thought I'd save you a step."

"I think you don't want to be seen with me, that's why you met me halfway," he countered.

"Well, suh, you are as wise as you are striking," I heard myself say back. "Men folk in a barbershop gossip worse than women folk any day."

For a moment, I thought that he might have begun to regret asking me out. I tried not to flinch or look away as he seemed to size me up. I sensed that Jesse was not judging me, so much as he was analyzing me, deciding whether I was a place where it would be wise to invest his time. Everything with this man was built on calculation. Time, money, effort, these were all precious resources that I imagined he never squandered. I was like any other investment. He had to determine whether to take a chance or take a pass.

So, I watched him back. With the sunlight fading on our faces, I noticed that he was considerably older than me. But he had aged well. His bronzed skin had a metallic quality, and beneath the gas street-lamp, it shimmered a little like something alive. He had thumbprint-sized dimples that pooled on either side of his smile, and his hair was longish, curly, crowning his large eyes which were a shade lighter than his skin.

"So, are you sure that you are not ashamed to be out with the likes of me?" he asked. I sensed that he was fishing for a compliment.

"I should be asking you that question," I said.

"I am not the one slinking into a shadowy alley. What are you so afraid of?" he asked.

"Once one of the guys gets a little information, he will blab it to the others. They will have more details about my little social life than I have," I lamented.

"I suppose you do know what you are talking about, Miss Coleman." Changing the subject, he asked, "You look hungry, what kind of food do you like?"

"I like seafood," I said.

"I thought you were from the Texas heartland. What do you know about bounty from the sea, my fair maiden?"

My Texas drawl oozed. "You fell for my old-timey joke ... if I sees food, I eats it!"

"I see you have a funny bone. Do I always have to be on my guard with you?" he asked with a chuckle.

"No, suh, not with me." I gave him my best schoolgirl imitation.

"So, it's up to me to show you a good time, then. The pressure is on. I hope I will not disappoint," he said with another smile, more sly this time.

We walked on and talked and laughed, eventually arriving at the Monogram, a fancy nightspot where we were going to have a drink before moving on for dinner. I had wanted to slip inside this place for the longest time, but it wasn't proper for an unaccompanied woman to go alone. Plus, it was expensive, probably a day's wage for an entree.

The Monogram was smaller and more intimate than I had imagined from the outside, and it was glamorous, as well. Everything inside the dining room was either black or white—the chairs, tablecloths, and floors, and even the fancy black letters on the white walls, which suggested where the Monogram got its name. The alphabet was scattered all over the place, the letters spelling nothing in particular.

The ceiling was black, studded with three elaborate crystal chandeliers. They glittered, throwing little diamond-shaped lights over everything. Each chandelier was adorned with hanging crystals, and the arms ended in tiny, modern electric lights that had miniature bulbs in the shape of a flame atop mock candles. I thought about the irony of the restaurant's décor. Like Jesse, like me, like everyone else in the room— our browns, yellows, and reds were in stark contrast to our black-and-white surroundings.

At the front of the room stood an elegant, tall, fair-skinned woman dressed in, of course, black and white who, upon seeing Jesse, came out from behind her podium and was transformed. I had watched her speaking to the guests who had come before us, addressing them with a matter-of-fact, I-am-so-beautiful-but-I-have-to-speak-to-you attitude. Yet, the minute she set eyes on Jesse, she put on the Ritz.

"Mr. Binga, we hoped that you would stop by tonight. I'm-a give you our best table. We have music coming shortly, and if you have any special requests … " She was falling all over herself, and all over him, too.

"Oh, I see you have brought a friend. Very well, then," she said. Abandoning the line of less important customers, she moved into the room, "Please, follow me."

She snapped her fingers high above her head, and from the other side of the room, two men in white dinner jackets scurried toward us. From what looked like thin air, they produced a small round table right in front of the stage, and with waiters and a busboy in tow, a white tablecloth was placed on top of it. Before we had made our way to the front of the room, linen napkins, silverware, a lighted white candle and a tiny bud vase with a white lily had been set upon the table.

"I hope this will do, Mr. Binga." She smiled and then lingered a bit too long for my taste. "I'll be back to check on you. In the meantime, shall I get Bill to send over a fine single malt for you?" Jesse nodded affirmatively, and without ever looking in my direction, she asked, "And for your guest?"

I was angry, but at the same time, I was relieved. This drink business was perplexing.

"Tell you what, Mildred. I'll take the Chivas, and give us a minute. Maybe send Bill over to us in a few. That sound okay?"

"My pleasure, suh. I'll let Bill know that you require him directly. Thank you, suh." I took note: while he seemed to accept special treatment, Jesse was slightly dismissive of the servile.

"So, what would you like to drink?" he asked me.

There was that pesky question again. Should I just be honest and confess that I had no idea what alcohol tasted like? Although I had seen my brothers drink plenty, and watched as it altered their behavior, I had no inkling of how spirits would affect me. Should I ask for a Tom Collins? I had heard of that. Dr. Jones used to suck down a few every evening that I was at the Joneses' helping Mama. On one particularly happy night, he put away five of those concoctions. I remember that he sang merrily after being united with Mr. Tom Collins.

"I don't know what I feel like tonight," was the response I settled on.

"The truth is, you have never had an alcoholic drink in your life. Am I right?"

"I bet there is very little that gets by you," I answered, not wanting to lie.

The older man called Bill appeared, carrying a short glass with ice cubes that left clear streaks through a brown syrupy liquid. Bill set that potion down upon a fancy white napkin with a black M on it.

"Good evening, sir. And good evening, milady." He smiled dutifully at me and then trained his attention back on Jesse.

"Bill, good to see you tonight. The lady will have your best chilled ginger ale with as many cherries as you can spare." Bill and Jesse shared a chortle. I was clearly a lightweight, and Jesse was making fun of that fact.

"Suh, it is always a pleasure to serve you."

Bill disappeared into the thickening crowd as quickly as he had arrived and, in no time, he returned with a delicious-looking tonic. It had a little white paper umbrella supported by a long wooden toothpick, and on the toothpick, someone had crowded a stack of bright red cherries. There were six of them, and at the tippy-top, was a half-moon-shaped orange slice. I smiled so wide that Bill looked away. I knew little about waiters, but I gathered that they were just to deliver food and drink and then leave with minimal intrusion.

"I have never seen anyone get such joy out of a soda pop," Jesse said, pleased with my reaction. "Bessie, you are a delight!"

"This looks so good! But I will try to be a lady," I promised.

He gave me a genuine smile, and at his look of contentment I thought that if our date ended right now, I would be a happy woman. It was going to be hard, but I was determined to be ladylike with this extravagance, which prompted me to ask, "Mr. Binga, would you like to have one of my sweet cherries?"

He threw his head back and laughed deeply. "Young lady, I don't think you realize what you are offering, and I must tell you that I would love to accept, but I don't think that either of us is ready to share that much," he allowed himself just one more indulgence, "at least, not yet."

He was right, I was naïve and hadn't a clue at that moment what my words had suggested. I had been salivating over those little cherries on a stick, and now that I knew I didn't have to share, I couldn't wait any longer. It wasn't until some time later, and with great embarrassment, that I would learn the significance of what I had offered. I used my teeth to grip a cherry, and he watched my face intently as I bit down and it exploded in my mouth.

"I can see you handle the unexpected well," Jesse's low and deep voice dripped with pleasure, and anticipation. He leaned across the table and whispered, "Bessie, I imagine you are a woman of great passion … Taste good?" he asked, gulping down his own drink.

"So, so good," I purred.

We shared a smile that felt good way down deep, and my toes curled inside my shoes.

CHAPTER 11

Norma and Moe had named their first child Pearle, after Norma's beloved mother, and while my best friend and Moe were having a wholesome family life, Jesse and I were carousing, discovering the joys of the Stroll's many haunts. I did not have chick nor child to care for, so I could stay out dancing into the wee hours whenever I pleased.

Experiencing the Stroll's nightlife with Jessie was different from wandering its dozen blocks along State Street during the daytime. These scant square miles made up Bronzeville. It had been so named by the *Half-Century Magazine* founder, Anthony Overton, whose publication took its name from the fifty years that had passed since emancipation. We southerners who had landed here preferred to call it Bronzeville, rather than the name that whites had called the area, which was the Black Belt.

At every turn there was a blend of the ideal and the familiar that we children of slaves had created in our new bronzed neighborhood. Peppered among the glitzy nightclubs you could find an old oil barrel cut in half and converted into a down-home barbeque smoker pitched outside a dry-goods storefront, where one could mail a package to loved ones back home or tear off an ad posted on the bulletin board for a room or flat to rent. Some sort of trade school, a hair tonic, or a job was always up for grabs. Still, labels stuck. The demeaning and confining term Black Belt was used to describe a condition we thought we had escaped. We may have been bound and held in like a cinched waist, but we couldn't let these constraints keep us from dreaming, and so we created the Stroll to feel like the Milky Way, where fine supper clubs and gas street-lamps dotted a galaxy far from the dusty, grim life of cotton picking.

While thousands crowded the Stroll every day, Jesse was among the elite that financed Bronzeville, the star-crusted Stroll, and everything within their orbit. There was a different level of entertainment, casino gambling, and entrée for a kingpin-owner than there was for the average pedestrian. And now that I was no longer an average pedestrian, I got to go where Jesse went. He knew all of the stars of the music and entertainment scene, and they knew him—King Oliver and Louis Armstrong were among the many. They would invite him places, and I got to hang on Jesse's arm and gawk.

"We crept up a back stairwell, and Jesse gave the secret knock," I told Norma. "A little peephole slid open. We saw an eyeball, and when the eyeball saw Jesse, the door creaked open. Turns out, it was the secret upstairs room of the Sunset Café. It was real private up there, and they had made it into one of those black-and-tan affairs. I never even imagined that Negroes and whites danced together, but they did up there! Black-and-tan, but it really should have been called what it was—Black-and-white. Black and white danced and drank, and I saw more than a few couples slip into little private rooms. "The women were all painted up like dolls before they went in, and smeared when they came out," I reported to Norma.

"Oh my God," Norma exclaimed. She gasped and threw the back of her hand over her mouth so that no air could escape.

All in all, there were seventy clubs crowded on or near the main drag of the Stroll. I told Norma how The Pekin Theatre was the only one we never visited. Jesse said that a man called Robert Motts used to own it and that Motts was a Negro who hailed from, of all places, Iowa. I took it that Motts was just as bold in entertainment as Jesse had been in banking, nevertheless we went elsewhere.

"Outta loyalty, on account of rivalries between Jesse's gang and Motts's, we stayed clear of that joint," I told Norma.

I thought that sounded as though we exercised a fair amount of discernment, but the truth was, Motts had enemies. Motts was an entrepreneur with big dreams whose numbers-racket grew to compete against other gangsters. And although he had been to Paris, he named his place after somewhere in the Orient—The Pekin Theatre. We knew he had travelled 'cause he wouldn't let us forget it. Motts was a braggadocious imposter, but he was also a hell of a showman.

His dinner theater boasted four hundred guests, and Motts took out ads to fill every seat. One said—and I read it to Norma—"Enlisting the Cream of the Colored Talent of the World, assisted by Great Singing and Dancing Chorus of 40 Beautiful Colored Maidens. Hear the Big Song Hits. Everything New and Refined."

"We weren't missing much at The Pekin," I shrugged. "We went everywhere else—Lincoln Gardens, the Parkway Ballroom, the Forum. And when we tired of dancing, we'd take in a picture show at the Vendome or the Grand. We went to as many of the happening spots as we could get to, especially The Flats," I reported.

The Stroll rivaled Lennox Avenue in Harlem, and while Harlem may have had Strivers' Row with its soaring brownstones, we had the Mecca Flats. Planned as a ritzy hotel, The Flats hadn't made it as a hotel, and instead had become apartments, mostly for Pullman porters. The upper floor held an atrium, hemmed in only by wrought iron railings that circled the structure like a collar of black lace, and was reserved for private affairs.

"I sure do wish I could get you and Moe out for a night at The Flats," I told Norma, hopeful that I had made an evening out seem irresistible.

"No way, Bess, that party life is not for me and Moe," she smiled and wiped her hands on her apron.

Jesse and I became regulars at private Flats soirées. Jesse would flip the lift operator a coin, and we would soar to the top and waltz out of the elevator that shone like a gilded birdcage. The barmaid must have been sent word the minute we stepped into the marble lobby, because a single malt for Jesse and a chilled champagne flute for me were always poised on a waiter's silver tray when the lift doors parted. Life with Jesse sparkled and was as exhilarating as the bubbles in the wine. I hadn't realized it, but as I got to know the top-floor haunts and basement speakeasy joints, I had become a moll, a gangster's girl. I was living the high life that was far above the seedy affairs where Jesse's enterprises had their roots in the Levee district. The Levee district was a seedy, grimy six-block neighborhood in a red-light district. Custom House Place, that pulsating artery between Harrison and Polk Streets, was home to a dozen prostitution houses that competed for space with pawn shops, opium dens, and gin mills, while Dearborn and Clark Streets corralled the chaos of whores and murderers. A modern Sodom and Gomorrah thrived down by the sands of the Wharf. But all that was far from the dazzle that lit our nights.

We both took a fancy to the women singers—Ida Cox, Alberta Hunter, Ruth Brown, Lil Harden, Bessie Smith, Ma Rainey, and my all-time favorite, Lovie Austin. Lovie was generous with her talents. She either composed for most of the ladies, or had her band, the Blues Serenaders, accompany them. While I never did warm to that willow branch of a hostess, I did love the Monogram. Its duo-chromatic intimacy was home for Lovie, and she played there often. I'd put up with that wet blanket hostess any day because I loved Lovie that much.

Lovie composed, played the piano, and directed the men and women of the Blues Serenaders. She played *Too Sweet for Words, Heebee Jeebies, Galion Stomp, Frog Tongue Stomp, Merry Makers' Twine, Rampart Street Blues,* and *Don't Shake It No More* long before she or anyone else had recorded these numbers. The Monogram was her laboratory, and we were her test-subjects. Depending on how we reacted to the songs, Lovie would record them for herself, change them a bit, or re-orchestrate them for others. My favorite of her tunes was *Travelin' Blues* because the oboe climbed high while the clarinet wiggled low, and Lovie held the whole thing together with the jam from her piano.

Pretty, and a real lady, Lovie would always stop by to say hello to Jesse and me. Then she would blouse outta the joint and hop into her Stutz Bearcat two-seat racer. With its top peeled back, the bucket seats wrapped in leopard skin were revealed, and Lovie would slide right in, her long, black cigarette holder clenched between her teeth and a spiral curl of smoke from her Lucky Strike swirling overhead, Then, just like that, Sheba was gone! To me, Lovie Austin was the cat's meow—talented, gorgeous, funny. There was nothing about her I didn't love.

Then, one evening, we found ourselves at the Sunset Café, where Lonnie Johnson was playing his guitar and then his fiddle. The candle flickered in time with the moaning of his strings, making me feel possessed, as if I had consumed strong spirits that slowed everything down. Even the words I heard warbled in my ears.

"Well, suh, what are we havin' t'night?" asked Mel, yet another waiter who knew Jesse by name.

"Let's keep it simple. We'll have two Porterhouse steaks, mashed spuds—and drown em' in butter—and do you have green beans tonight?" Jesse asked.

"If you would like green beans, I'll go pick 'em myself," replied Mel.

"Don't go through any trouble," Jesse smiled.

Mel wrote nothing down and asked, "How'd you like your steaks, suh?"

"Medium-well, thanks," and before releasing Mel, he turned to me, "That okay by you?"

"That all sounds very okay," I said slowly. The thought of a steak dinner made me deliriously happy. I was from Texas, home of the famed Longhorn, yet I could count on one hand the number of times I had eaten beef. I wasn't sure what a Porterhouse was, but I was confident that if Jesse had ordered it, I was in for yet another treat.

Mel returned in short order with salad, hot biscuits, and a creamy corn chowder with shrimp, none of which we had ordered.

"The chef wanted Mr. Binga and his guest to try these tonight," Mel said.

"Thank you for feeding me," I said to Jesse, as I took my first bite of a flaky biscuit.

"It seems like the right thing to do. Watching you enjoy your pop or a meal is so … " Jesse leaned back in his chair as he searched for a polite word, then settled on, entertaining.

I plunged my spoon into the steaming broth of hot cream and said, "It seems to me that you can see I am an open book, but you are not. To tell the truth, I think I know very little about you, other than what you let me see."

"What do you want to know?" Jesse asked.

"Well, for starters, everyone, everywhere knows your name. But who are you, really? Where were you born? What were you like as a child? What has driven you so hard? You've made a fortune through the work of your own hands, but what do you do when you are not fleecing someone else's pockets?" I smiled to sweeten my last remark.

"Whoa. No one wants to know all that about me. But I'll answer a few of your questions. Which shall I tackle first?"

"Who are you?" I asked again.

"One minute you are sipping pop with a seven-year-old's delight, and the next you are conducting an inquisition. I should be more cautious," he declared. "I thought I was the city slicker, but I believe I am being out-slicked by a country girl. At least, you seem to be a country girl when it's convenient."

"Yes, suh, guilty as charged. But the thing is, you talk for hours, but you say very little about yourself. And that's why this country girl has to pry."

"All right, then, let's see … I love beauty and intellect, most particularly when they come in the same package," he said, holding my gaze. "The way it does in you."

"I thank you, but no compliment, no matter how grand, can distract The Inquisition," I twirled ends of a pretend handlebar mustache, the way the villains in the picture shows did. "What were you like as a boy?" I pushed.

"Well, let's see," he searched. "I can recall that I was a rascal. Or at least, that is what my Mama called me. I was always up to something. Got scraped up every day jumping off of this or climbing onto that. My childhood had plenty of fun in it. There were ten of us, and with so many brothers and sisters, I always had built-in playmates. My Mama was short and fair, and Papa was tall and dark. All of us are a mixture of their opposites—we are mutts. They raised us Catholic, and I continue to be a Catholic."

"Where were you born?"

"I was born up here—well, close by, that is," Jesse said. "In Detroit, Michigan. My mother was born in Buffalo, New York, and my father was born in Ontario, Canada. He became a barber, and like his father before him, Daddy owned his own shop. My parents met when Mama was peddling men's hair tonics. That's why I like Mr. Duncan," Jesse explained. "I know how hard it can be to run your own barbershop."

The fact that Jesse's parents, even his grandparents, had been born free—one in upstate New York, the other in Canada, was so remarkable that my mind, and my tongue, were set still. In the same way that someone might prefer a man who is tall and dark, Jesse's birthright made him immediately more attractive to me. And he was a Catholic. I had never before met a Negro who was anything other than Baptist, or the exotic African Methodist Episcopalian. To my mind, we were all Protestants. We were all protesting. Even our faith led us to protest.

Until that moment, it had never occurred to me that I would someday be sitting at a fancy dinner, holding court with such a Negro man. His cocksureness and complete lack of southern accent was evidence that there was something different about his breeding, and I was finally beginning to learn exactly what that was. If Jesse used slang, it was because he wanted to. Just as a good cook salts a fine stew, Jesse injected the occasional bit of slang, just a pinch here, or a few grains there. He was no mutt to me. The northern soil that nourished Jesse was different from the farm dirt from which I, a cotton picker from the deep Texas flats, had been spawned.

"My mother was really something," he went on. "She bought fish from local fishermen and then packed it in ice and sold it to merchants headed south of the Michigan line."

The violinist took a break, and the pianist struck up Scott Joplin's *The Entertainer*. Jesse raised his glass to the musician who nodded in return. For my part, I wasn't just entertained, I was mesmerized.

"Midwesterners loved fresh fish. It was a delicacy, and so Mama made money hand over fist. She used a combination of her fish money and her inheritance from my grandparents and bought homes in Detroit. People called the street where she owned "Binga Row," and Mama used to take me with her to collect the rents. She was tireless. I don't know how she did it. I don't think she ever slept.

"I mentioned that she was fair-skinned, but that doesn't quite capture it. Mama was light enough to pass, but she would never live a lie. She preferred her life as a Negro woman. My mother was always figuring how to make money and didn't care to be anything other than true to herself."

"And your father? What was he like?"

"Actually, Mr. Duncan reminds me of Papa quite a bit." By now Jesse needed little encouragement and had begun to speak easily. "Like Duncan, Papa had the barbershop and the huge apartment above it, where we lived. "I never want to work for Mr. Charlie," Papa used to declare, and I inherited that point of view from him. Papa's shop was in the heart of colored Detroit, and he employed a half-dozen barbers. I loved going there. It was always bustlin'—some joker always stopping by to sell oddities—socks or sandwiches—and like you said, there was always a lotta gossip. I should have remembered that little detail."

"So, then you know why I wanted to keep things hush-hush," I laughed. "The menfolk in barbershops sure can gossip!"

"My father taught me the art of barbering," he went on with a laugh of his own. "And when I was eighteen, I left home and headed west. I hitched, rode the train, hopped wagons and, eventually, I made my way through Kansas City, Missouri; St. Paul, Minnesota; and Missoula, Montana. In Washington State I lived for a while in Tacoma, and then Seattle. And after that, I made my way to Utah, to both Ogden and Pocatello.

"Each time, in each city, I opened up a new barbershop and stayed for about a year. I had a ton of wild oats at that time and I intended to sow every one of them. By the end of a decade, I made it here to Chicago, and although I only had ten dollars to my name, I had a lifetime of experiences and I had seen a lot of the country."

With this information, I finally learned his age as well as the fact that by the time I was being born, Jesse was already a grown man. For some reason, my Mama's words, "Figures never lie, but liars are always a-figurin'" floated through my mind. Jesse was watching me for a reaction, and although on the inside I was a-twitter, on the outside I never blinked.

"I was tempted to go back to Washington State, maybe even back to Utah," he continued. "But I fell in love with Chicago. It's like Detroit, only better. There's a rhythm—the music, the food, the people, the Stroll. The weather is cold, but the scene is hot! It's alive! I saw that there was too much opportunity to go anywhere else.

"Barbers like Mr. Duncan had that market sewn up, but one thing that was missing here was decent housing. So, I decided to follow in my mother's footsteps and began buying and selling houses with the little bit of money it turned out she had left to each of us. Around this time, I met Robert Abbott. He did a story on my efforts to buy a few buildings, and after that, I advertised every week in his paper—flats with stove heat and flats with steam heat, real estate sales, loans, etc.

"Robert thought that two generations of colored city landowners was noteworthy, and he was right. He said I had cleared a way for our people to own homes. When local banks refused our families mortgages, I began planning bank and insurance companies as logical next steps—housing, mortgages, deposits, insurance—these opportunities both improve peoples' lives and build institutions of our own," he explained.

"Robert and I have different businesses. Publishing may not be like real estate or banking, but we have common goals, and we can help one another. He made me promise to sit on a steering committee that works to help him finance his dream of buying a new printing press. He wants to own his building and take on more photographers and reporters. He wants to grow. In return, he sits on the board of directors of the bank. He keeps me honest. Robert Abbot has never changed his tune, never wavered from the goal we have in common—to bring our people north to opportunity."

"I have accomplished so little," I breathed after he stopped speaking and took a sip of his soup. "Why in the world would you want to spend time with the likes of me?"

"Because, as I told you before, I like smart and beautiful in the same package. Haven't you been listening?" Perhaps to soften his words, he reached across the table, and with the back of his hand he smoothed my cheek. "Beautiful women are a dime a dozen, Bessie. But you are intelligent, and when you're challenged you don't flinch, you continue to think. That is a rare quality, indeed."

His age, his wit, his demeanor, and his achievements were as intriguing as they were overwhelming. I searched Jesse's eyes. They looked like what I imagined a mountain lion's looked like—unpredictable, hungry.

Mel cleared away salad plates and bread dishes. I had tried my best to be ladylike and to leave behind at least a few ladylike green leaves, but I had been unable. The hot biscuits and the melted butter made me want to lose all my manners and lick my fingers clean.

As the dining room filled with well-dressed Negroes, Mel, a white towel draped over his arm, wove his way back to our table, his band of servers trailing behind him. One scrawny man struggled with a huge tray that sagged under the weight of our heavy dinner platters. The other man carried a water jug and steak knives glinting from an ornately carved wooden box lined with velvet.

"Milady," Mel said, placing a thick, white, china dish in front of me. The steak was as large as my thigh and crisscrossed with seared grill marks. Next to it loomed a mountain of mashed potatoes and a heap of string beans, while thick brown gravy glistened on top of the entire affair. I had to restrain myself and use my best manners to wait until Mel presented the other plate to Jesse.

"I have never eaten a meal like this before," I said quietly after the waiters had disappeared. "Thank you."

It was all that I could manage. I did not want Jesse to think that he had gone out to dinner with a wild dog, but inside I felt carnivorous. I couldn't wait to rip into that steak. I could no longer ask or field any questions, I just needed to eat, without speaking or listening or thinking about anything else. My entire life had been spent in pursuit of food, and tonight this steak dinner had been placed in front of me. I had only to lift my fork and chew.

Jesse seemed to understand and did not say a word until only the

T-shaped bone remained on my otherwise clean plate. He had finished less than half of his dinner and then had reclined in his chair to watch me. I could feel the proximity of his long legs. Stretched out, he filled the entire space beneath the table.

"Passionate indeed," Jesse breathed. "I don't think I realized it before now, but I have been hungry for a long time."

"You've left half of your food untouched. What are you hungry for?" I asked quietly.

"I don't think you are ready for my answer," Jesse replied, his voice dropping low again. Then, slowly controlling something deep within himself, he said, "Now it's my turn to ask the questions."

He stared at me, and the sandy color in his eyes smoldered like lava. I didn't know much about the secret world of what happened between grown folk, but I was sure it had something to do with the look I saw in his eyes. It was clear that he no longer cared for the food, for he had pushed his half-eaten dinner out of his way. Shifting in his chair so that his elbows occupied the space where his plate had been, he possessed the entire table now—above it and below it, too.

"Now—tell me about yourself," he demanded quietly.

"No free meals, right? After you feed me, I have to pay up with information?" I smiled and went on more timidly, "I hope you won't be disappointed. There's not much to tell."

"Oh, I doubt that you will disappoint me, Miss Coleman. You have a great deal of courage. I want to know why you made the journey from Texas to Chicago all alone."

I was relieved. With this question, the subject could shift from whatever I had been feeling to my vital statistics—where I was from, my birth order—far less intimate topics. I told him I was born in Atlanta, Texas, and that my parents moved to Waxahachie when I was a toddler. I gave enough clues for him to figure my age, although I was confident that he already knew it. I told him about my Langston adventure and my best friend Norma. He told me how much he appreciated her fine tailoring. I told him that I could just about match him in sibling number, but that unlike his prosperous family, my family owned little, only the tiny house bordering Mustang Creek on a grubby lot where Mama still lived with my three younger sisters.

I told him about my brothers, Walter and John, and how I came to live in Chicago with them. I explained that my vicious sister-in-law was the reason I had moved out and now lived on my own. I added that I hoped my mother and three younger sisters would join me in Chicago soon. Although I missed them, I explained that I had to flee Texas when living there had become oppressive. This seemed like a good place to wrap things up in my narrative, but it was this last detail, which was my ability to live without assistance, without the protection of a husband, which seemed to impress Jesse the most.

"But wait a second, there's more to the story of you leaving home," he said matter-of-factly.

"Nope, that's it, really. I am sorry there's no more drama." I said, intentionally leaving out years of school closings due to cotton picking and washerwoman drudgery, and I surely omitted details of when Mama and I were maids for the Joneses.

Sensing the omissions, Jesse persisted, "A young woman who goes off to college, the first in her family ever to attempt such a feat, then works and saves enough money to get herself to Chicago from—where did you say in Texas, Waxahachit?" Jesse asked, teasing me.

"Waxahachie. You are dreadful when you make fun of me."

"Don't be mad, I'm just having fun." A smile curled his mouth into a crescent.

"Okay, I'm not mad," I lied.

But I was. I felt bruised. His pedigree made me feel less-than. It was nothing that he had said or done, it just made me feel that I was very far from making something of myself.

"Sure do wish I could say that I was from Detroit, or some other important place like you are," I mumbled.

"Okay, I'll ask you what you asked me. Who are you?" Jesse persisted. "I'm just a two-bit hustler with good timing. But you are a different flower in the garden," he said, speaking aloud what he seemed to be thinking. "You're keeping something back, but now that we have filled your belly and you are feeling more comfortable, I hope I can get into your head."

Since it rhymed, I thought he had said, bed, " … get into your bed." But then, I fit the last sentence into context and convinced myself that he had said head.

He smiled slyly, having immediately picked up on my misunderstanding. "You came to Chicago for a reason. You could have stayed in Texas and married, had a mess of beautiful babies, but you came here looking for something. What are you looking for? He paused then added,

"What is your heart's desire?"

"I cannot tell you," I said.

"Why not?"

"Because you will laugh at me."

"No, I won't."

"Oh, yes you will, and if you do, I will be wounded beyond measure."

"What makes you think that I will laugh at you?" he asked.

"Ah … Waxahachit … remember that?"

He laughed again, "Okay, you have reason. But I am serious now. I have learned that where you invest your time and money is where you build your treasure. What will you do with your treasured life, young Bessie?"

The only person I'd met in Chicago who I had dared to breathe my dreams to had been Mr. Abbott, because I believed that meeting in the barbershop had been serendipity, rather than happenstance. I was convinced it was an opportunity not to be squandered, and I reasoned that Mr. Abbott could help me find a school, then publicize my adventures. But Jesse liked me for romantic reasons. I had no idea if a girl with too much ambition might just turn him away. After a moment of hesitation, I decided that if that was the case, then so be it.

"I want to fly an aeroplane. If you really want to know. I want to be a flyer." I said with force.

Although I had prepared myself for the cold shock of rejection or, worse yet, ridicule, I had not prepared myself for his reaction. He did not blink.

"You want to be a flyer. Why, I have never met anyone who wanted such a thing. Why do you want to do this?" I could see the line of questions forming behind his eyes.

"Well, I was just a little girl when I learned of the Wright Brothers' Kitty Hawk adventure back in '03, and in the twelve years since, I have followed every serious advancement in aeroplanes. Not only am I obsessed with flying, I have wanderlust. I want to move at high speeds across huge, open spaces. From your own cross-country excursion, I'm guessing that a wandering spirit is something you and I have in common." Now that my secret was out, I couldn't stop myself. "I used to want to fly far away from the Jim Crow South, to leave all that behind like yesterday's news. But I guess coming to Chicago accomplishes that, at least, in a way it does. But what I want is to be free, and I mean truly free. I want to fly. And I want to be really good at it. I want to be the best."

There was a long pause as he turned the second glass of scotch around in his hand. He did not ridicule me, nor did he tell me that my aspirations were foolish. Above all, he did not mention the most obvious hurdle: that I was a woman.

"I knew that beautiful head of yours had a lot going on in it. You're a prize, Bessie, a rare prize, but you appear to be a prizefighter, too," he said. "So, tell me. How do you intend to turn this dream of yours into a reality?"

And just like that, my feelings of exultation and sophistication at his compliments vanished as quickly as they had arisen. I felt naïve and simple-minded. Yes, my aspiration was extraordinary, but the mechanics of how to—now, that was another matter altogether.

"I thought I would … well, I planned to take lessons now that I am here in Chicago … " Halfway through the lie, I realized it was better not to make things up with Jesse. He would distinguish a well-thought-out plan from a cobbled-together tale any day.

"Listen," I said, "the truth is that I am not really clear on how to do this. The one thing I do know for sure is that I cannot do it alone. I have to figure out where and who will be willing to train me, not to mention how to pay for it."

"I respect your honesty," he swirled his glass again. "So, you decided to hustle the hustler."

"What do you mean?" I bristled.

"Are you really serious about this idea of yours?" Jesse asked.

"You bet your life, I am."

"Then I suppose you accepted my invitations because you needed money," Jesse wore his sense of offense as though it were a coat of porcupine needles.

"Whoa, wait a minute! I accepted your dinner invitations because, well, I was hungry, and because I think that you are interesting and good-looking. Not because I thought I could squeeze money out of you." Now I was the one who was offended. "In actual fact, I had no intention of bringing up my desire to fly. You have to admit, you pried it out of me."

I could tell this last statement had an impact, "You will have to forgive me. I am suspicious by nature," he said.

I was plenty comfortable with the silence that followed and offered no concession, no small talk, nor any excuse. The silence was a fitting response to his implication. In his business he must have dealt with smutty hucksters, cutthroats and bloodsuckers, a circus of two-bit swindlers. But I was no such con.

Finally, he spoke. "I admire both your guile and your ambition. You've got moxie, kid." It was as close to an apology as he would offer. "I do believe that you are serious. So, let's get you an audience with Robert."

"Mr. Abbott already invited me to come and talk to him about my plans," I was happy to reply.

"So, you really don't need me then, do you?"

"Why, sure I do." Now it was I who made light of his wounded feelings. "Mr. Abbott is a luminary, but I'll take help wherever I can get it."

Jesse chuckled at my subtle dig. "And what did Robert say?" he asked.

"He gave me his card, promised to help, and invited me to his office," I answered.

"Why, that sly old dog!" Jesse thumped the table.

I couldn't tell whether Jesse's reaction was because his friend found me attractive, which was entirely off-base, or if Jesse felt he'd suddenly become obsolete.

"Now, hold on a second," I said, "Mr. Abbott was only trying to help. Any progress I make will be advantageous to us both. If I make it, his newspaper will have a new story to prove to our people that we can accomplish anything we try!"

"Well, one thing is for sure, if there is anyone who could help us in our pursuit, it would be my good friend Robert Abbott," Jesse concluded.

"'Our pursuit ... ' I like it," I said. "So, I have become your pet project, have I?"

"I suppose you have. And what a prickly pet you are turning out to be," Jesse said. "Oh, and by the way, during your rant, did you say that you found me 'interesting,' and what else did you say?" Jesse asked, fishing. "Good-looking?" he recalled with delight, plucking out my words that still hung in the charged air above us.

"I just meant to say that I wanted to have dinner with you because ... I do find you interesting, and I only meant to say, I didn't want you to think ... I ... well, I didn't want you to eat alone," I stammered. "You'd probably sit here and talk yourself to death."

"Yes, thank goodness you rescued me! Being inside your head is so much more fun than being all alone in mine."

Seeing my embarrassment for the second time, Jesse smiled wickedly, causing my cheeks to flush with heat. I'm sure I was the same color as the hunk of red velvet cake that we had agreed to share for dessert.

Our forks clinked. Not a crumb remained.

CHAPTER 12

Jelly Roll Morton's *Animule Dance* rumbled from the Victrola. Norma had taken to playing music these days while doing her hand-stitching, and she sang along.

"This baby loves jazz, even old ragtime," she shook her head.

"I still cannot believe that you met Jelly Roll Morton," she purred, taking a break to rub her round belly.

"Jesse took me to the Royal Garden Café to see him, and we had a drink with him between sets." I had already recounted every glamorous detail to Norma but went ahead and did it again for the pure pleasure of it. "They are pals," I boasted. "Jelly Roll banged out *Frog-I-More* and *The Finger Breaker*, and then Jesse had him dedicate *The Crave* to me."

"*The Crave.* Hmm." Norma gave an odd smile unlike any she had ever given me before. "Not so subtle," she said.

"Did I tell you that Jesse promised to help me pay for my flight training?" I needed to turn the conversation, but even though I steered things another way, it was too late. There was no way of avoiding what was on Norma's mind.

"Hmmm. Why, yes, you did. Bess, is he married?"

I shrugged my shoulders and looked away. I had never asked. But if I didn't know before, I knew now. Raised as a strict Southern Baptist, I was taught that adultery was a sin deserving of fire and brimstone, a stoning even. Yet, the temptation of Jesse was too strong. He offered opulence, extravagant evenings, and even the fulfillment of my dreams. How could anyone resist?

"He believes I can be a flyer," I offered, in lieu of a confession.

"Look, you are a grown woman, Bess. Only you and the good Lord God know my cardinal sin. I can't stand in judgment of anyone, especially not you. I just think you should go into this affair with your eyes wide open. Don't fool yourself."

But I was a fool and Jesse and I continued seeing each other. While I secretly wrestled with my moral dilemma, Jesse appeared undisturbed. He was pleased to parade me, trophy-like, in public, as if it were the most natural thing on earth.

Jesse had arranged for Robert and me to speak, not in Mr. Abbott's private office, but rather someplace less formal. The three of us were to meet at the American Giants vs. the Kansas City Monarchs game. I could use this informal occasion, Jesse said, to detail exactly how I needed Mr. Abbott's help.

When I first arrived in Chicago, I knew nothing of sports, but after two years at the White Sox barbershop listening to Mr. Duncan and Squeeze, I'd become a real seamhead and could recite the rankings, stats, and opening lineups about as well as any of the guys. By the time the 1917 season was over, the Giants had a 49-14-2 record and had earned a solid first place in the Western Independent Clubs League. Half of the Giants' starting lineup were southpaws, with Bruce Petway being a switch-hitter. At twenty-seven, Bingo DeMoss was the youngest player, and the grandpa of the starters was thirty-eight-year-old Bill Francis. Whether you were Negro or white, baseball was an American obsession.

The White Sox used to play at Schorling Park, but they had abandoned it once Commiskey Park was built. The Chicago American Giants moved in and made the cast-off field their own. If anyone ever asked my opinion, I planned to weigh in with Squeeze's single-word summary: the Giants in their new home stadium were "UNSTOPPABLE!"

Schorling Park, at 39th and Wentworth Streets, was only a few blocks from my apartment, but since Jesse had just bought a swanky, new silver Rolls-Royce, he came to pick me up. He called this fine automobile "The Silver Bullet," and it glistened in the sunshine, as Jesse's bodyguard,

Deacon, pulled it up to the curb. We drove the short distance to Schorling and parked right in front of the entrance. Deacon hopped out to open his boss's door, then ran around to fetch me. The crowd on the corner near us turned to gawk.

A ticketing clerk abandoned her long line and hurried over to unlock a special gate, and while the audience squeezed single file through a narrow turnstile, Jesse and I waltzed through an open gateway. In dramatic, mafia style, Deacon trailed behind. I shot a last look at that fancy automobile as a boy, with a Giants cap and team shirt, no older than twelve, began shining its gleaming fender. "Thanks, Chief," the boy called out, as he caught an equally shiny dime that Jesse flicked his way.

"Smile, pretty," Jesse commanded. "That crowd is not lookin' at me. They are lookin' at you."

I did as Jesse told me, as complete strangers smiled and waved at us. I hadn't done a thing to earn it, but I felt like royalty.

Just inside the gates we were to meet with a true baseball legend, Rube Foster. Before he had managed the Giants, Foster had pitched perfect games and had single-handedly organized the Negro Leagues. Crowds flocked to see any game that Foster was playing in or coaching because he was a showman, and he always put on a great show. In striking out entire teams, he'd throw screwballs and fadeaways, and then mix it up with curveballs, fastballs, sliders, knuckleballs, and the occasional forkball. That he was standing there before us was almost impossible to believe. I tried not to stare but failed, finally pulling my gaze away to stare at the grout between the tiles along the hallway wall.

We were led into a private alley beneath the grandstand, where the bleachers rose above us, stretching thirty feet into the air. Continuing along, we threaded our way to the dugout, where we found the current kings of baseball, all of whom were actively engaged in getting ready for the game. These men were like prize bullfighters—Bill Francis, Leroy Grant, Bruce Petway, Bingo DeMoss, and John Henry Lloyd. The outfielders sprinted, shortstops paced, and sluggers swung their bats with a force that could have killed a giant beast. I stood and watched, mesmerized, as pitcher Dick "Cannonball" Redding threw balls twice as fast as a Model T Ford could go on an open stretch of road.

In short order Mr. Abbott arrived, followed by a string of people trailing behind him.

"Boss, when you wants the box-receipts count?" another young man in a Giant's cap shouted over the din of the growing crowd.

Without breaking stride, Foster yelled over his shoulder, "I want every red cent of my money collected and tallied by the top of the third." The young man peeled away fast, disappearing into the catacombs beneath the bleachers.

Just then, another page ran up to the group. "Mr. Foster, suh, complaints from the upper tier. Them cheapskates are moaning 'bout pigeons making a mess all over the place." As evidence, he extended his arms to display sleeves that were speckled with the bird excrement that must have splattered guests high above us.

Foster stopped mid-stride. "You're kidding me? I'm trying to patch this stadium together with tacks and chewing gum, and you are harassing my ass about pigeon shit? Come on Dickie! Take care of it. This is a BIG boy job," he shouted. "And you needs to put on your BIG boy drawers!"

But the page looked stricken and did not move. At this, Foster advanced, which made the young man finally begin to retreat. "I can't be losing paying customers to pigeons. If the birds want to pay, they can stay. If they're broke-asses, they got to go! Goddammit, find a scarecrow or be a scarecrow, but clean up that nasty-assed filth up there. And don't let me see you again 'till you cleaned yourself and 'til those damned broke-ass birds is not ruling the roost up there!" He exclaimed. "Now, git!"

The page, his eyebrows rippling in confusion, froze. He either did not or could not move.

Foster curled his right index finger and leaned in close so that the young man's nose was an inch from his own. The page blinked. And then, right into his face, Foster yelled, "BOO!" It was so loud and so fierce, that the young man reeled backward, tripped over a bench, and fell down. Righting himself, he scampered off.

Jesse and Mr. Abbott howled. "Man, I thought my job was tough," Jesse said between guffaws.

"And I thought I had complaints from my readers, but I just didn't know how rough rough could get," said Mr. Abbott. They clasped hands loudly, while laughing from deep down in their bellies. Mr. Abbott laughed so hard, his neatly coiffed frame shook and gently swayed.

As the laughter ebbed, Mr. Foster drew them both in with the same wiggling index finger he had used on the boy. Jesse and Mr. Abbott followed him into a huddle, and with an air of secrecy and solidarity, he wrapped each of his arms around Mr. Abbott's and Jesse's broad shoulders.

"Let me tell you both a little something," said Mr. Foster, and then he paused. "BOO!" he yelled, at the top of his lungs.

The three of them howled all over again. "Y'all some simple mothafu …!" Foster stopped short, as he spotted me. "Oh, shugadee, please pardon us. It's a ballgame and men will act up. So sorry you had to hear about the pigeon shi … I mean mess. My language has gone to the pigs, dealing with the perils of entertaining Jesse's folks and all his cousins." Foster said.

"No apologies to me, sir. I feel a lot sorrier for that young man," I said, sincerely.

"Shoot, I hope those two-cent-paying colored people come back," Foster said. "Add up enough of them skinflints, and I might have me a bloody dolla!"

"Of course, they will, Rube. They have to, man, you're the only game in town! You are now pursuing the Jesse Binga school of economics!" Quoting himself, Jesse continued, "Be good, be the only one, and charge em' what you can, 'cause monopolies won't last forever!"

Jesse spoke the sad truth. With few services, entertainment, and options available to Negroes, we tended to pay more, complain less, and regularly accept the inferior, whether it came to education or grocery stores.

"Sad, but true," I whispered.

"And who are you, my lovely? Why would a girl as pretty as yourself associate with this notorious robber baron?"

"This is Miss Bessie Coleman," Jesse interrupted, introducing us formally. "Don't make her answer that, or she may have to examine us too closely. Say, Robert called me a robber baron, too. What's wrong with you cats?"

Yet another page, with another problem to solve, approached Mr. Foster and caught his eye. "I'll join you folks in a jiffy," he winked at us and made a motion over his shoulder. A stout attendant arrived instantly at Foster's side. "Yes, boss. Whatcha need, suh?"

"Folks," Foster said to us. "This here is Mink. Anything you want, you just ask Mink."

"Mink, these are my good friends. Take them up to my box and make sure they get spoiled rotten," Mr. Foster said.

"Yes, suh, only the best," Mink said dutifully, his accent rich with sounds of Mississippi. From an inside pocket of his jacket, Mink produced cigars for each man and led us up a steep flight of stairs, elbowing a wide path through the crowd to allow us through. Two more turns and we arrived at Foster's box, which to my eyes looked more like a open-air storefront than a place to watch a game.

A massive picture window stretched out before us and looked out onto the diamond on the field. We could see the whole expanse—the bright green grass, the white lines and bases, the banners advertising Camel cigarettes, Wrigley's Juicy Fruit gum, and Cracker Jacks plastering the slats of a wooden fence. Mink brought us hot dogs and popcorn, and there was cold beer for the men and a Coca-Cola for me.

CRACK! The game was off to an electrifying start, as John Henry Lloyd smacked a long drive deep into centerfield, where it hit the Juicy Fruit sign. The ball snaked back into centerfield. The outfielders dived, recovered, collided, and bounced off one another like pinballs. As they were busy chasing Lloyd's ball, he stole second, third, and then home. While Kansas City ended the inning with two injuries, the Giants walked away with an inside-the-park home run.

As if reading my mind, Jesse rested his heavy forearm between our seats and whispered, "Next inning." I had not wanted to badger Mr. Abbott prematurely and, having watched men in the barbershop, had come to learn that there was a rhythm to their relaxation. "Mink, you mind getting us one more round of suds, my friend?" Jesse asked.

"My pleasure, suh." Mink smiled, flashing a gold canine.

I turned to consider Mr. Abbott. Although only five years Jesse's senior, he seemed infinitely older. He struck me as thoughtful, quiet, intense—almost aloof. Exquisitely dressed, his finery was not intended to attract attention, but rather his elegant wardrobe of wools and linens seemed designed to conceal the rags of his past. This man had made a fortune reporting about others, but he himself was a deeply private man. From what I knew, Mr. Abbott was always asking questions but fielded few of them.

When another player was injured during the third inning, Jesse saw an opportunity and plowed ahead. I had worked out my little speech and rehearsed it a dozen times, and I was ready.

"Robert, Bessie's talked to me about her plan to become a flyer. I'm aware that she's confided in you as well, and if anyone knows how to pursue such a thing, you do, my good friend," Jesse opened.

Mr. Abbott's eyes darted from Jesse to me, reassessing my seriousness now that the words were coming from Jesse and not from me.

"Why, yes, I remember quite well," he said. "I must say that I am intrigued."

Here was my opportunity. It was my turn at bat.

"When the Wright brothers dove off that cliff back in '03, I was eleven years old. A few years later, I was working cotton fields with my family on the day that an actual aeroplane flew right over our heads! It was an old sunflower-yellow number and it buzzed us so low I thought I could catch it in my hands." As I grabbed a fistful of air, Mr. Abbott's eyes followed my fingers.

"The pilot dipped and coasted real low, spreading exhaust fifty feet above our heads. My mother was screaming at me to leave it be, as the gray clouds billowed around me, but I didn't see danger, I saw a little piece of heaven. And without even thinking, I spread my arms out and pretended I was flying. The smell of that aeroplane fell down on me like a blanket, but the risk was worth the danger, because to me, there was freedom in those wings.

"A lot has happened in aviation since that day. Just a year ago a man named William Boeing started a company in Seattle, with the plan to deliver mail with aeroplanes between Seattle and Los Angeles. He's also been experimenting with seaplanes—planes that land on water! There's another man, Glenn Curtiss—he's a daredevil for sure. He's been racing his flying machines and even made an aeroplane for an aviatrix named Ruth Law who, as I'm sure you know, has been called a 'Superwoman' in the papers! Curtiss built her plane so sturdy, that they think it can fly all the way across the United States, from the East Coast to the West.

"There's always some new exploit in the papers, and it appears as though the advances that have come as a result of the Great War have catapulted aviation ten times faster towards the future. I have read everything I can about aeroplanes. Everything. I have a passion, sir. And nothing shy of learning how to pilot an aeroplane will satisfy me."

A long pause followed. I had spoken so fast that I had run out of breath, and now sat gulping for air to refill my empty lungs. Jesse finally broke the silence.

"Robert, she's serious. I do believe that if anyone can learn to fly, Bessie can."

Mr. Abbot turned his eyes from Jesse to me. "Young lady, you impress me. The field of aviation is wide open, and a beautiful queen of the sky could inspire legions of our people to literally reach for the heavens. For as long as I've been alive, people have told me, and I know they've told you, Jesse, that we couldn't do what we have done. You, Bessie, also seem like someone who doesn't listen when told what she cannot do." Mr. Abbott's brow remained a wrinkle of reservation. "But this ambition of yours has an added layer of concern. First and foremost, such a pursuit involves grave danger, of which I am sure you are aware. People die, Bessie. Often. It also requires a significant investment in training, time, and money. Isn't that right?" Mr. Abbott questioned.

"Yes, that's right," I said.

Mr. Abbott stared into my eyes for quite a while, as if judging my commitment and my grasp of the enormity of the challenge. When he finally spoke, he addressed both Jesse and me.

"Give me a couple of weeks to mail off some inquiries. I doubt there's anyone in Chicago who will teach you to fly. I will try to find a flight school in the Northeast or maybe in California. Any other female flyers you know of?"

I told him about Harriet Quimby, who in 1912 had become the first woman to fly across the English Channel. Just three months later, papers like *The Dallas Morning News* read, "Woman Aviator Killed at Boston, Miss Harriet Quimby, Together with Passenger, Falls 1,000 Feet."

I pulled the clipping out of my pocketbook to show Mr. Abbott. The article described a test flight in which Quimby had lost control of her Bleriot XI over Boston Harbor. Both she and her airshow organizer had perished, but their demise had been overshadowed by news of another disaster only a day before—the sinking of the great steamship, the *Titanic*. Before she became a flyer, Quimby had spent her career as a journalist, and I had clipped every one of the articles she'd written for the swanky *Leslie's Weekly* that was published in New York. I also told them that I was sorely disappointed to learn that her stories later became plays, produced by none other than the infamous *Birth of a Nation*'s D.W. Griffith.

Mr. Abbott read the entire two-page article silently and the final paragraph out loud.

"'The deaths of Miss Quimby and Willard bring the total of aviation fatalities for the present year to fifty-one, compared with seventy-three during all of 1911.'" His eyes floated to the next article, lower down in the same clipping. "'Aviator Dies of Injuries—Three Other German Birdmen Hurt in Flight but Expected to Recover.'" He lowered his reading glasses with his index finger and peered over them at me. "Are you sure you want to pursue this? The people in these articles are dead, Bessie. They are dead. Do you understand those risks?" Mr. Abbott asked.

"I do."

I began to worry that Mr. Abbott's keen dissection of the facts would lead Jesse to undertake a greater consideration of the risks. His brow wrinkled with what looked like worry, and I changed the topic as fast as I could.

"There are a dozen or so other aviatrixes scattered around the globe, but there is only one Negro flyer and that is Eugene Bullard. He was born in Columbus, Georgia, where his father was nearly lynched. For more than a year Bullard had been a flying ace of the French Foreign Legion and had earned the Croix de Guerre for his kills in the air. But not even he holds the prestigious French civilian license, from the *Fédération Aéronautique Internacionale*. The FAI is the only flying organization that can grant privileges to its civilian holders to fly anywhere in the world. There are no Americans who hold this brevet. And I should add, that when the Americans joined the French in skirmishes with the Germans, Bullard was ripped away from his elite French flying unit and made to fight in the trenches with the American infantry!"

"That is an outrage," Mr. Abbott said, and took a note in the small notebook he pulled from his breast pocket. "You have clearly done your homework, and I admire that Bessie." And although the ballgame had begun again, Mr. Abbott no longer seemed interested in what was taking place on the field. The crowd calls and the sounds from the hollow bowl beneath us no longer claimed his attention. He was keenly focused on what I had to say.

"It may be that you will have to go to another country to train. Bullard's story makes me think you may need to be in France, but you'll have to wait until this bloody war is over. Are you willing to leave American soil to pursue your goal?"

"If I have to," I said, surprising myself with my own rapid answer. "I am willing to go anywhere I have to if it means I get to fly."

"If covered right, this news will play BIG, and not just as a publicity stunt either. Would you be prepared for *The Defender* to follow your progress from entry to completion in flight school? I don't know what the course of study is like, but it has to be rigorous. If you do not pass, that will be news also." He paused. "By the way, what do you intend on doing once you have obtained your brevet, as you call it?" Mr. Abbott asked.

"What is there to do, besides fly in the war or deliver mail?"

"Well, I have a couple of ideas, but I think I need to figure out that part as I go along. I've been learning about barnstormers and wing walkers. Have you heard about them? They do stunts on the wings of the plane at exhibitions. And other pilots are setting records for long-distance flying and highest altitudes. I was also thinking that if it's this hard for me to get training, I could open up a school so other people of our race can learn to fly, both menfolk and women, too." Mr. Abbott drank in every word. His notebook scribbling growing more and more brisk.

"All good ideas. You could become the first and then teach others. Now this would make all of us eyewitnesses to history." Narrowing his eyes, he glanced from Jesse to me, "How do you intend to finance this venture?"

"Gee, Jesse warned me that you would ask all the tough questions," I said.

"It's my job," Mr. Abbott said frankly.

"I have saved every dime that does not go towards food, shelter, and clothing. It's not a huge sum, but it is growing. Jesse has promised also to help me. I wish I could be more specific than that, but I really don't know what it's going to cost overall. All I know is that I take Jesse at his word and know he will help me once I have my plan," I said, looking Jesse squarely in the eyes.

"Robert, I am committed to helping Bessie, and I have no doubt that if she wants this, she can do it. My investment will not go to waste," Jesse said.

"Well, then," said Mr. Abbott, "Count me in." And then, as if working on part of the headline he hoped someday to write: "Tomorrow we start looking for someone who will train our Brave Bess, or maybe it's Queen Bess, or maybe Queen Bee?"

The Chicago American Giants won that night, and so did I. It was the first time that formless vision of mine began to take shape. It was 1917, and my people were spearheading our own transformation. We could manufacturer cars, fly aeroplanes, build houses, open banks, create neighborhoods, and publish newspapers, and I intended to take my place among the most adventurous of us all. That night, I stood at the nexus of two remarkable moments in American history—the dawn of aviation, as more planes rose into the sky—and the dawn of the Great Migration, as more and more Negroes made their way from the South to the North. I was poised to show the world that I could dream big. And just like the migration, I wanted to bring others along with me.

That night Jesse sent Deacon on his way and drove me back to my apartment himself. When we arrived, I asked Jesse to come up for tea. But it wasn't tea he wanted, and with all of the talk of risk, adventure, and vulnerability, our courtship took on a new urgency. Our pull toward each other had been magnetic, hypnotic at times, but now it held a hint of foreboding, a hint that there might be catastrophe at the end of the rainbow.

CHAPTER 13

I put the kettle on, and Jesse dropped onto the sun-bleached, sage davenport that took up most of the space in my tiny living room. I watched him glance around the room, his eyes falling on a small Duncan Phyfe table competing for space with the two white Windsor chairs my brothers had painted for me when I first moved in. Jesse loosened his tie and took off his jacket. Before going to change, I served him a mug of steaming chamomile tea with honey. He winced when he fingered the hot porcelain of the cup. I retreated to the bathroom and opened the tap on the red claw foot tub. I stripped, hung my clothes on the hook on the back of the door, and then plunged myself into the hot water. I thought about this moment. I was twenty-three years old and about to become a woman. For months Jesse had been making me ready. Tonight, he would wait no longer. I thought I was ready.

I emerged from my bath and doused myself in lavender oil. The smell of the field flowers calmed me. I had little choice with regard to night garments, since I had only two gowns. One I had bought since moving to Chicago. It was thick, blue, and frumpy, chosen for its warmth. The other one was very short, with thin straps and small faded daisies. It was clean but old and worn and nearly see-through. It provided just enough covering on sweltering summer nights. My wardrobe reflected Chicago's extremes, one gown fitting the windy, subzero cold, the other for a steamy swelter in summer. The skimpy daisies won.

My wet feet left a trail as I crossed the planks back to the living room, but Jesse wasn't where I had left him. I found him lying on my bed. His shoulders and legs were bare, while a draped sheet hid his midsection. Jesse had lit the taper by my bed. The flame danced around a stiff wick, throwing long shadows along the walls. I had told Jesse about my quilt that Norma made for me and I was grateful that he had folded my price-less gift and laid it on the davenport.

The holster that held Jesse's revolver was first-grade, top-grain leather. Soft and well worn, it was the color of a jackal, and like an animal's skin, he had draped my bedpost with it. The squared butt of his Colt Single Action Army revolver hung low, and the loaded chamber fed a cannon-like barrel. Six inches in front, Colt called this revolver the Peacemaker. Jesse called it that, too. There were plenty of lowlifes ready to snatch the empire that Jesse had built—gangsters, hoodlums, bookies, punks. And he was ready to defend it all with his life. The Peacemaker was all that stood in between.

Once, when my fingers had glanced at his side; he felt me grow stiff at the discovery that he carried a gun. "It's for your protection, too," he had whispered. The sidearm was a part of him. Jesse was never without it. And with his person, money, and mind, Jesse had begun to possess me as well, making me loyal and addicted to him all at once—protection, possession, hunger, danger, yearning.

Jesse watched my eyes float from the revolver hanging on the brass bedpost to his body sprawled on my bed.

"Climb in," he commanded.

His voice rumbled deep inside my brain. Goose pimples peppered my arms as he pulled the sheet back. And just like the long, fine, smooth barrel of the Colt, Jesse was as solid as steel.

As if reading my thoughts, he said, "Go ahead, look."

I had never seen a naked man before. His left foot was planted at the base of his right ankle. With his leg up, the covers formed an open tent as a backdrop. I wanted to look more closely, but I was embarrassed. Curiously enough, the Peacemaker didn't frighten me, but Jesse's naked-ness did. He let the sheet drop and thumped the bed three times hard with the palm of his hand.

"Come," he demanded.

"Will it hurt?"

"I would never hurt you."

He reached his arm out for me, and I gave him my hand. His biceps were well formed, his flanks were lean, and they tapered, V-like, into a trim waist, strong thighs. Then my eyes went back up his legs. There, a giant organ leaped out. Covering large testicles, copious hair curled. I took his outstretched hand and slowly climbed into my bed.

"I've never done this," I admitted.

He did not reply. I searched the darkness for his expression. I couldn't tell whether he didn't believe me or didn't care. We kissed, long and hard, and I could feel him growing bigger and firmer; he pulled me into him, as we lay facing one another. His teeth grabbed the flesh of my throat, and I grew still. I wasn't afraid that he would rip my skin, but I did feel that he might consume me, bite by bite.

Jesse pulled away and reached under the bed near where he had put his shoes. His hand surfaced holding a small object. In the darkness, I could just make out the flowery paper that was wrapped around a small box with a bow. I wanted to open it, but I was having trouble moving my fingers. He seemed to understand. I heard it crackle as he removed the paper, revealing an elegant crystal atomizer. Its attached pink bulb dangled from a flirty tassel. The crystal vessel itself held some sort of liquid.

"I love the way you always smell. I hope I got the fragrance right," he said, and I nodded my head. The crystal held lavender perfume oil.

He tugged at the sides and bottom of my nightgown and lifted it over my head. Now, I too was naked. In an instant, my nipples grew firm and hard. I thought they looked like small bullets. My eyes strayed to his revolver, while Jesse stared only at my body. I grabbed the sheet instinctively to shield myself, but he peeled it slowly back. I sat up, but he drew me down again, so that I lay on my back with my hands at my sides. In a single move, he was on top of me, massaging my breasts and throat.

Slowly, he worked the lavender oil and his lips around my breasts. He kept working the oil down my sides, my belly, and then lower. I felt his hands and fingers pull apart the two lips of my inner self, and then he worked his fingers all around the soft parts of my body. I began to burn deeply, and he breathed harder and kissed me. His mustache tickled, and a giggle escaped my throat. He did it again. This time I laughed.

"Shhh," he hushed. And I did. He smiled, big and round.

He ran his tongue from my bottom lip to my chin, biting me gently, and then he quickly moved down the length of my body.

In a moment he'd parted my legs and worked the oil in feverishly with his fingertips. I only knew that our growing hunger had to be fed. He had maneuvered our bodies so that he lay between my legs. He penetrated me. The lavender oil provided a smooth glide, and he moved his entire pelvis up and down. Then he began to drive himself deeper still inside of me.

At the same instant, I felt a surge of pain that immediately dissolved into pleasure. Slowly at first, in a sort of rising and falling motion, guiding my hips with his fingertips, Jesse placed me in just the right spot. Then, commandingly, he rocked us faster and harder.

"Are you okay?" he panted.

"Yes," I heard myself say, more stiffly than I wanted to sound.

"Oh, baby, you feel so good. You smell so good. I just want to eat you up."

He ran his teeth down the side of my neck and my shoulder. I believed him. I thought that he might just devour me. Biting and licking a spot that I had never even known existed, Jesse moved his mouth down my arm and stopped where my forearm and bicep met. I became so excited that a tiny moan escaped my throat. He switched sides, so that he could do the same to the flesh on the other side as well.

Jesse's big teeth ran along my skin, and I could feel a sort of wetness all around my private parts.

His breathing was hard and driving, and he had moved his hands back to my breasts. I was so sore, so excited, so wanting to please him.

"Can I come inside of you?" he asked.

I wasn't really sure what he meant, so I didn't answer.

"I want to make it last. I want you so much." He pulled his giant organ out of me.

"Turn over," he commanded. I did as I was told.

He straddled my behind and sprayed the lavender oil. All my senses were alive as he dragged his own body back, now straddling the back of my thighs. I could feel that he opened the bottle and poured a tiny pool onto the small of my back. A click escaped his throat as he gently swirled the liquid with a finger inside of the divots above my buttocks.

He slid his body up. I could feel his largeness. He spread my legs to accommodate his size and then, moving his hands up to my shoulders, he moved my hair to the side of the pillow, and I felt him rub then lick the top of my spine. He pulled my hair taut and then ran his teeth down that tiny magic spot on the nape of my neck.

"I can't wait anymore," he breathed.

With that, he flipped me over, and all I saw were his straining biceps, lean belly, and the sheen left from our heat. He parted my legs and tried to enter my body again.

"Ooooo, you are so tight," he said.

"Is that bad?" I asked, hoping that I could somehow loosen up.

"No, baby, that's good."

More oil … this time he rubbed himself. Lubricated, his organ shone in the flickering candlelight. It was enormous.

"Please let me in," he begged.

I lay on my back and felt the oil loosen me open again. He pushed, and the bed springs moaned.

"I want to make love to you," he told me. With his left hand firmly under my buttocks and the right hand massaging that hot spot behind my neck, he mounted me squarely and pushed until he was inside me again.

"Ah," he breathed as the gasps, his and mine, grew louder. "Oh, baby, I am going to come inside of you," he whispered. His hands left my body, and he grabbed the metal frame of my bed's brass headrail. I watched his chest and muscles strain as he spread his arms like wings above me.

"Ohhh, God," he yelled. "Bessie, look me in the eyes!"

The bed knocked against the wall, the gun smacked the bed, he exploded, we both exhaled, and he collapsed on top of me.

Suddenly, I felt a hot, molten, liquid ooze. He continued to glide up and down slowly and I rocked beneath his weight. Although he had released, he was still stiff, and I was glad, because I did not want to stop.

He kissed me and rocked inside me. The Peacemaker banged gently against the brass again, and the sensation that I had felt in my brother's bathtub returned. This time I knew that I would feel the beginning, middle, and end—without interruption. Indeed, I felt a slow, steady climb and then a rush over a jagged summit. A deep need I had never known existed was satisfied. I felt weak and sleepy and sore and good and desired. I was no longer ashamed of my nakedness.

Hours later, I awoke. Jesse had already bathed. He was dressed and lay beside me.

"I didn't want to push myself on you," he spoke as I rubbed the sleep out of my eyes.

"Jesse, I wanted this too."

Then he reached across me, grabbed his holster, and strapped it over his chest. He drew back, and I watched as something caught his eye. He looked past me, and I followed his attention. In the middle of the sheet was a cookie-sized stain of light red blood.

"Oh, God," he whispered. "You really did give me your virginity."

"I told you that I was a virgin. I saved myself for a long time."

I could feel offense mounting like doubt—intimacy, lies, truth, want—they were all tangled together. He must have felt it all in my tone.

"I will be back tonight," he offered. "Maybe we can eat dinner in and—talk some more. It isn't that I didn't believe you, it's just that I have to remember to treat you with kid gloves. Bess, you are so precious to me," Jesse said, as if more to himself than to me.

After making love, my slumber had been anything but peaceful, and now I was overwhelmed with regret. I felt compelled to confront Jesse, yet he had become dominant in my life. I had allowed myself to be swept away. I had lost my virginity to a man whom I knew in my bones I could never have. When the door shut behind Jesse, I was left alone with only the silence of my room and the drumbeat of my pounding thoughts. My tongue remained as silent as the breaking of my hymen had been.

CHAPTER 14

Thus, I embarked upon a life of waiting—waiting for Mr. Abbott to hear back from the training programs on either coast of the country, waiting for Norma's next baby to come, waiting and saving for the day when I could spend the two-thousand-dollar treasure I had amassed, half of which was from my years of labor, the other half from Jesse's generosity. I waited for all these things, but mostly I waited for Jesse.

It was 1917 and the world around me was rapidly changing. The fighting that had begun three years earlier in Belgium and France, and had spread to Britain, Germany, and Russia—the whole of Europe. Both of my brothers had been drafted into the Army to prepare for America's entry into the Great War. Few foot soldiers survived, and many of those who did would return home missing limbs, their sanity, or both.

Yet, time was marked not only by world events, but by events at home, too. Norma's baby girl, who had been named Pearle after Norma's mother, began making her way through the childhood milestones—first smile, first tooth; she sat up, she crawled, she ran. Fortunately, Moe had been exempted from service "due to extreme hardship." Had he been required to serve, Norma and Pearle, and the new baby not-yet born would have become wards of the state without his income. But both of my childless brothers were not so lucky.

Before he left, Walter stopped by to see me and recounted how he had learned that he had been drafted into the Eighth Cavalry. "I come back from New Orleans, and me and Willie quarreled as usual," he said. "I left her in the room to join John for a little bootleg at the kitchen table. Halfway through my drink, John slid two envelopes across the table. One was mine and one was his, both were from Uncle Sam, and we agreed to each open the other's. That damned Wilson campaigned that he would keep us out of the war," Walter said. "Well, now we know that he is a bald-faced liar, 'cause we in the middle of this boiled-up shit-stew now."

John read Walter's assignment: *"Rail operations, carrion removal, London,"* meaning he would be transporting the dead.

Walter read John's assignment: *"Front lines, infantry, Somme,"* meaning he would go to the place where bayonets and grenades worked together as a meat grinder, leaving behind jawbones, limbs, and skulls in the muddy, bloody trenches of France.

My brothers, who had escaped the worst of the South for Negro men, had carved out a life together in a place they had never known, would now have to set out again, only this time they would be separated by war.

"That joker sold us out," Walter said. Negro men who could vote had overwhelmingly voted for President Wilson. "But then what should we expect from that two-faced President? While the world's at war, he's starting one here at home, showing that hateful *Birth of a Nation* right there in the White House! Rule number one," my brother said, thrusting his index finger in the air, "Divide the poor whites and Negroes. Then conquer them all.

"First-class passengers on the Capitol Limited was talking about the headlines, all the way from Chicago to D.C. 'The coloreds was getting uppity after all of white folks' sacrifice and inconvenience.' They mocked us, like they didn't even see me while I was serving them or shining their cheap shoes. This President separated colored and white clerks in D.C., blocked colored clerks from higher-level jobs, and at the same time, convinced big companies up north to hire cheap colored laborers, and even women, to manufacture war supplies—uniforms, weapons, munitions. I read every newspaper the passengers discarded. All across the country, the ads scream JOBS, JOBS, JOBS!"

I remembered my days as the Joneses' maid and how suffocating it was to be a servant who also wanted to use her mind. My brother's work was back breaking, and while the wages were better than for most jobs, the ransom he had to pay for his salary was the extinction of nearly every waking thought. The physical endurance required just to live, day after day, year after year, resulted in an atrophy of the mind in all but the strongest. "Just like the South needed us as slaves, the warmongers need our black backs," Walter had said.

"Marcus Garvey says we should go back to Africa. He's got a whole lot of supporters," I said.

"That group? The Universal Negro Improvement Association? No, I'm not going back to Africa. Chicago belongs to me. And frankly, so does the South. We built this country. Why should we run off?" my brother questioned. "By the way, this city was founded by an African descendant. You didn't see Jean Baptiste du Sable running back to Africa. Hell, nah, he settled Chicago. Why in the world would I call somewhere I never been home?" I watched Walter trying to calm down. He took a deep breath.

"Listen, Bessie, I didn't mean to get off on politics. I came by to talk to you about something else, something a lot closer to home. In case anything happens to me in the war and I can't come back to look after you, there's something I want to say." Walter hesitated, "I try not to stick my nose in where it doesn't belong, but …" I watched Walter's glance as it swept the room and landed on Jesse's crimson tie. It, or one like it, had owned the real estate of the doorknob to my bathroom for months. "Before I ship out, I want to tell you how I feel about this Binga cat."

I stared down into my cup. Until this moment, Walter had steered clear of this territory, but his impending tour of duty had obviously compelled him to finally speak his mind.

"I know Binga and I are in different leagues, but some things are common to all men, rich and poor alike. I don't believe Jesse Binga means you any harm, but he don't mean you no good, neither." Walter slurped another long sip of coffee. "That man is addicted to money and power, Bessie. Don't let him think that he can buy you. You are just as smart as he is and twice as tough, so don't you to settle. Look at me and Willie. I know you wonder what I see in her."

"She is pretty scary." I smiled and my brother nodded in agreement.

"She wasn't always so foul-mouthed. She became more and more bitter after we lost a baby, and then another, seven in all. The doctor says she just can't hold them. Each time we lost a child, I lost a little more of her. Willie was once as beautiful on the inside as she is on the outside. But now she's got those dark circles under her eyes, and she just stays angry all the time. She actually blames God and takes it out on every-body around her. You see, what I am saying to you, Sis, is that life holds so many ups and downs. Some we can see coming, while others are traps that we have no idea are out there waiting for us. What I mean is, when you see danger you can avoid, steer clear of it. I just worry that if you become the other-woman, your flying aeroplanes might turn into a side-show instead of the main event. You need to make your own decisions now, but whatever you choose, I will always be in your corner."

Saying goodbye to my brother that night broke my heart. The thought of him harvesting the dead and the dying was too much to bear. Would his own lungs rot from inhaling human waste and decomposition? Would he have to handle the body of someone he knew? Jesus, what if he had to handle our own brother? These were the thoughts that kept me up long after the sound of Walter's footsteps disappeared down the hallway and out into the night.

Later that night, Jesse came over. I had a simple dinner ready, but I had lit a candle and, family style, had laid out bowls of fresh collards, sweet baked beans, fried chicken with cayenne, and brown-sugar corn-bread dripping with butter and blackberry preserves.

"Mmmm, you really can put it down like a country girl. This is deli-cious," Jesse said. The taper's wick burned to a curl of smoke as we ate and talked, while I danced all around the only subject occupying my mind—our future. When the candle finally flickered out, we stumbled back to my single bed in the dark. His tie was loose and his shirt opened at the neck. He took it off, and I rubbed his back and explored his shoul-ders and muscular arms with my fingertips.

We made love. The penetration made me flinch.

"I can stop," he said.

"No, keep coming to me," I whispered.

If he had shown patience in the past, he was eager tonight. He exploded quickly this time. I stared at him without blinking. When his breathing recovered, he turned to look at me.

"What's going on in that complicated mind of yours?" he asked.

"Are you married?"

"Yes," he answered me flatly.

Jesse inhaled deeply and released the air slowly. "I will never lie to you, Bess. Her brother is a gangster. I agreed to wash his money, moved chunks of cash from his numbers operation through my bank until not one dime could ever be traced back to him," Jesse explained. "In exchange, I got a quarter of a million dollars in deposits. I invested it, quadrupled it, and reinvested the profits in our people. It gave thousands the chance at a better life—to live in decent houses in neighborhoods with good schools and to have work that can make a man proud and a woman want to raise a family. The gangster wanted his sister married and she wanted a husband."

"And you, Robin Hood," I asked, "Did you get what you wanted?"

"I had a grand vision, and that vision needed cash, baby," he said. "It was just business. Until you came along, I didn't know what I was missing."

I hadn't known that marriages could be financial arrangements. All I knew now was that I felt sick. The truth of what I had done, that I had betrayed all I had been taught and believed in, hit me full force.

Jesse fell asleep, and I lay there listening to him breathe. At some point before dawn, I fell asleep and then woke to find him gone. On my pillow there was a note.

You will be the best and most beautiful flyer there ever was. I believe in you.
Here is a little something for your scholarship fund. You are on your way,
my Brave Bess.

Jesse had left me a savings passbook at The Binga State Bank. The outside bore a pen and ink drawing of me. I looked a bit fleshy, but the detail could be forgiven because in this rendition I wore a leather helmet and goggles. I looked noble, daring even. Another hidden Jesse talent— my favorite lefty was quite the artist. Inside the passbook there was a single entry: $3,000.

As I counted the zeros, Walter's words came back to me: Don't let him think he can buy you.

CHAPTER 15

The Great War rumbled on, and America's involvement in its complicated turmoil became all-consuming. On my way home from work one evening, I found a copy of *Aerial Age Weekly* at a newsstand and stayed up all night reading it from cover to cover. The next morning, I mailed in four dollars for a full year's subscription. Then I waited. Each week, like clockwork, a manila envelope from New York City arrived. What was inside was pure gold. I didn't understand every article fully, but what I did understand was that the war had forced rapid progress in aviation, and all over the world aeroplanes were getting faster, more durable, and more dependable. In my quest to understand the technology as much as I could, I memorized the parts of the aeroplane by studying the magazine's advertisements. By September of 1918, I could list them all—barometers, magnetos, die-cast motors, propellers, electrical conductors, cables, cords, strands, batteries, hulls, pontoons, turnbuckles, crankshafts, rivets, ball bearings, gasoline and oil pumps, gauges, nitrate dopes, unshatterable goggles, carburetors, gyroscopes, herringbone gears, and white side wall tires. I marveled with the rest of my fellow aviation buffs when the General Acoustic Company released the Turner Aviaphone. At just over eight pounds of headcaps and receivers, the ad boasted, in flight the contraption "makes conversation possible." I could only wonder what on earth they would think of next.

Wires in Trenton, motors in Milwaukee, propellers in Baltimore, turnbuckles in Chicago, and flying schools were now popping up everywhere—even one in Pittsburg, Kansas. *Thermodynamic Cycles and Internal Combustion Engines* was a study of ways to increase engine power and speed. That, and features like *The King of England Asks for More U.S. Aeroplanes,* or *Making Naval Aviators in a Hurry* made my heart race. The latest in aviation revelations and leapfrog developments had me counting the days each week until the magazine arrived in my mailbox.

Thanks to aeroplanes, the world was growing smaller. The spheres of influence now so much in the news reminded me of a toy I had seen and envied as a child. Dr. Jones had bought his girls Russian nesting dolls, which stood about six inches high and were brightly painted then lacquered until they shone. Each doll unscrewed at the middle and when opened revealed a smaller doll nested inside. Inside that doll was another, and then a third, a fourth, a fifth. Flying was like that. It refined the world into simple systems of geometry, a reliable congruence, coordinates, convergence, and intersections, each of which built upon the last.

Maybe no one else saw a place for me in the future of aviation, but when the writer Benjamin L. Williams asserted that our beloved "industry was at its dawning," I considered myself part of that dawn and saw myself in the middle of those overlapping innovations. Like the smallest of the nesting dolls, I may have been invisible at first, but I was there nonetheless. And I existed in yet another way. While my enslaved ancestors had planted, drip-irrigated, and harvested the crops of their owners, our mothers and fathers had had enough vision to channel a tidal wave of vague but potent ambition into their children. We, the beneficiaries of the generation that dragged itself from slavery and leapt into freedom, grew up to be men like Mr. Abbott, Jesse Binga, Mr. Duncan, Oscar Micheaux—and women like me. And like the scientific progress that was taking place, we were next in line to succeed. Our own institutions—newspapers, banks, entertainment, education, and politics—were all being designed by us and invented from scratch. I was going to be part of this new group of mavericks. To become the first female Negro flyer I would have to conquer not only gravity, but also America's rules about what I could or could not achieve. In order to do that, I had to possess just two things: optimism and fearlessness. I had both.

CHAPTER 16

Although my brothers had been shipped off together for basic training in Georgia, they found themselves separated when they got to Europe. Early on in his deployment, John sent Elizabeth weekly letters in which he detailed his life in the barracks and the day-to-day stories about the people with whom he would be forced to live for the foreseeable future. Elizabeth was kind enough to share her letters with me. But, after a few months, the letters took on an ominous tone and were filled with the grisly accounts of the hand-to-hand combat against the Germans in northern France. Raw, depraved violence surrounded John and poured out of each letter, terrifying Elizabeth and me. There was nothing we could do to help or to reach him, and then one day, his letters stopped. In the year that followed I prayed each day that my brothers would be returned home to us safely. My prayers were answered. They both came back. But they were no longer the men they had been before they left.

Walter was not just plagued by his barren, haranguing wife now, but by ceaseless nightmares and a rattling cough that shook his thin, worn body. We worried that Walter had contracted this strange flu that had killed millions around the globe. I recalled with great clarity *The Defender*'s 1918 headline announcing that all public spaces in the city would be closed due to the "Spanish Plague Raging in Chicago." Had Walter survived the Great War only to fall victim to a killer virus? Had he breathed microscopic death while moving the bodies of the dead and dying? As his eyes grew more and more sunken from exhaustion and his body more ravaged by illness, Walter stopped noticing foul-mouth Willie, or anything else for that matter. Her curses fell on deaf ears, as he became a downtrodden spirit with no fight left in him.

John had changed even more. Before leaving, John had been an easy-going drunk. He would laugh and sing late into the night, pulling all of us into the happy feeling of revelry for no reason at all. Before the war, John would head off to bed with the round Elizabeth in tow, serenading her as he went. But after the war, nothing was funny to him anymore. He found fault with every move Elizabeth made, berating her for the slightest perceived infraction. And when he drank, which he began to do earlier and earlier in the day, he became even meaner.

One late afternoon, John staggered into the White Sox for a shape-up and plopped himself down in Squeeze's chair. While John was getting his hair cut, the place began to fill up, and another customer, Mr. Moore, a good-tipping regular whose little boy always came in with him, arrived. The boy, Thurman, was a precious boy with dimples and a milk-coffee complexion. On the edge of my station, I always had a dish of red-and-white swirl peppermints, the kind I'd discovered on my first night at the Monogram with Jesse. Customers always stopped by to pinch a few from my dish, but I reserved a special stash of sweeties for the kids whose fathers would drag them into the barbershop.

Mr. Moore took his place in Bishop's chair and, as usual, Thurman came to sit by me. I pulled out a little paper sack, my secret reserve. "Go on, pick what you want," I whispered. Inside the bag was a colorful mix of rainbow suckers, Mary Janes, and Tootsie Rolls. Thurman picked a couple of Tootsie Rolls and sat down close to me. After a few minutes, I noticed that he had been struggling to open the wrapper because his fingers were otherwise occupied. In the palm of his right hand was something he refused to put down.

"Here, this is for you," Thurman said, his accent as spicy as the Louisiana gumbo from the parish his daddy must have hailed from. He held his closed fist over my open palm and grinned. His smile revealed a gap where his two missing baby teeth used to be.

"You want me to open this fist? Impossible! You are too strong!" I said, smiling back.

"Open sesame!" Thurman whispered, and his fingers uncurled.

Hidden inside his little hand was a miniature red-and-white porcelain Curtiss Jenny biplane.

My eyes filled with water, and Thurman watched my reaction attentively, pleased that his act of generosity had had such an effect. I hoisted him into my lap, and we hugged each other as if our lives depended upon the strength of the connection this little plane had made between us.

"Do you like it Messes Besssssie?" Thurman fished, whistling through the hole left behind by his missing teeth. "I thought that seein' as you is always cuttin' planes outta picture books and newspapers, I reckon you should own yo' own aeroplane."

"Oh, Thurman," I said, still weeping, "you are too generous. Your gift means the world to me. Thank you from the bottom of my heart." I breathed in the sugary scent of him as he lay his hand in my own. His touch was delightfully sticky from melted taffy.

I wondered sometimes whether running after my dreams would mean I might never have children of my own. The bargain I had struck with Jesse meant that he could never be my husband. Even if I did find a man I loved as much as I loved Jesse, and then went on to have his children, I would have to wait until they were old enough to be on their own before I could fly. By the time that happened, my best years would already be behind me and I would be well past my prime. I was slowly coming to accept that my flying would mean my future would hold only the affection borrowed from other women's children.

Only the day before, Mr. Abbott had invited me to his office to deliver bad news. He had sent off a dozen requests to flight schools on my behalf, and although *Aerial Age Weekly* advertised scores of programs that peppered the country, not one had been willing to train a Negro woman. Thurman's model Jenny now took on even greater significance, and I felt it was a divinely inspired gift. Its message was clear—DO NOT give up! DO NOT take NO for an answer. I had to believe that even though I could not see it clearly, my path would be revealed to me. At the end of our devastating conversation, Mr. Abbot had said that it was time to look elsewhere for flight programs, and upon his recommendation, I set my sights on France.

"No one is doing more in regard to training than the French," Mr. Abbott said. "I can try to find a school there. But you should know, this means that we have to get you into a class to learn how to speak French. Does any of this put you off?"

"Not at all," I assured him. "I can get a primer at the bookstore today and search out night classes in French as soon as I get home."

Mr. Abbott seemed unconvinced and continued to probe, "You sure you can leave your family and Chicago and everything familiar to you? You sure you can pick up and move halfway around the world? You'd be leaving everything, and by that, I mean everything."

His implication was clear. Though he would never outright ask me for more than he already knew about my relationship with Jesse, he had to know that it was strong and that it could easily keep me from wanting to leave my lover. He needed proof that I understood what I would be taking on and what I would have to give up.

"Yes, I will surely miss my family and my new home. I love it here, but Chicago will always be here for me, and I will not always have this chance. As for my … friends, I will miss them the most. But it looks as if I will have to earn a pair of wings the hard way."

"Okay, okay. You've convinced me," Mr. Abbott said, thrusting his hands in the air as though I'd won the battle. "I will let you know when I have found a solution to the flight school problem. And I will find the solution," Mr. Abbott promised. As I turned the little Jenny over and over in my hands, I felt even more sure that he would do just that.

I was aware that John had been sitting in Squeeze's chair the entire time that Thurman snuggled in my lap. John removed a small silver flask from his sock. And in dramatic fashion he shook it upside down, but not a drop came out. Disappointed, he turned his attention to Thurman and me. Something foul fermented in my brother. Thurman eyed John warily.

"Well, suh, would you looky here," John slurred. I had hoped that John would get his hair cut then leave in peace, but he staggered over to my table, bumping into things and knocking bottles from the shelves as he passed. "Got yourself a little aeroplane on a string, a gift, huh?" he said. I had hung the plane from my table lamp, and John bent down and gave it a hard thump. It swung violently on its red satin ribbon.

"I overheard you tellin' Walter that you got some highfalutin' idea you want to learn how to fly an aeroplane. You can't be thinking that you really going to fly, is ya'?" I had never seen my own brother so full of distain. It dripped from each word like poison. Never in our lives had he spoken to me that way. "That's 'bout as close as you gonna get to one," he spat, ready to swat my plane again. I put my hand up and blocked my treasure from further assault.

"John, you're drunk and you're tired, and I bet Elizabeth has a hot meal waiting for you," I said, trying to urge him out the door. "Why don't you go on home now and have a hot shower and a nice cup of coffee?" I pleaded.

The bitterness in his voice oozed like puss. "No, she ain't got nothing hot waiting for me, that's for sure. I think while I was gone, she cooled on me and got hot on some other fella."

"John, no she did not. That's crazy talk. You are drunk and it's time for you to go. I work here. Please, don't embarrass me," I begged.

"Oh, that's right, you work here," he snarled, "filing men's nails. You ain't really so much-in-fuch after all, is you, miss college girl? Didn't finish that either, did ya'? You might as well saddle up on top of your little toy, cause that's as close as you gonna get to a real aeroplane! Shit, colored folk here can't even ride a stupid train south of this sad state. You folks here is just imitatin'. Y'all ain't nothing more than imposters. I never should of come back to this nasty-ass slum. You think the Stroll is so fine. Well, I got news for you, it ain't shit! Paris, now that's high cotton. I been to the Champs Élysées. Had me a bunch of them fine-assed French women, too. They can't get enough of us colored men over there," John spat.

"John!" I whispered and grabbed the arm of his loose jacket. "You are mean and drunk and not the brother I know and love. Go home and sober up before you say another word!"

Mr. Duncan finally intervened, "I'm not one to throw people out, John, but you are being disrespectful and scarin' my customers away. You gotta go. Now."

Ignoring Mr. Duncan, John bellowed, "Bessie, you ain't shit! Neither is this lame-ass barbershop. When you moved out, I thought you was just 'fraid of Willie. I didn't know that you moved out to be with Jesse Binga. You hangin' around with that married man bring shame on all of us. My wife is the same. All you colored women is the same."

The saloon-style doors flapped on their hinges as John finally stumbled into the street, and without a word, I slunk back to my table and gathered my jacket, pocketbook, and hat. Removing my sleeve guards—protectors of my tiny wardrobe of white blouses—I folded them and tucked them in my drawer. I glanced at Thurman's delicate gift and tucked it into the pocket inside my purse. I bent down and extended my fingers to caress Thurman's hair, but he pulled away as if he'd been burned.

Without making eye contact with anyone, I escaped through the same door out of which my brother had just spilled, taking with him every shred of dignity that I had ever owned. I could feel eyeballs pinned to my back. Squeeze's, Bishop's, Hash's, Mr. Duncan's, their customers', my customers', Thurman's. They were all watching as I stole away and out of their lives.

I ran blindly all the way home and somehow managed not to sob until I was crawling up the steps of my apartment building. Inside my apartment, in the tiny vestibule where Jesse and I had kissed for the first time, I fell to my knees.

Jesse reserved Friday nights for us, and he rapped on my door promptly at eight, bearing a jar of maraschino cherries. He smiled irresistibly and pulled me into his arms.

"Thank you," I said, turning my face.

"Thought you might like to indulge," he whispered suggestively and winked.

"I need to speak to you," I said. Everything had changed and I needed him to know.

"How about we talk later?" Jesse replied as he shed the exquisite jacket he had hired Norma to design for him. The *Pope Couture* label inside the collar flashed, as if in warning.

"I am going to France to learn to fly. No one will train me here." I said flatly.

"Paris? When do we leave?" he asked, smiling widely. "We'll paint the town red, baby!"

"No," I told him.

"What do you mean, no?" Jesse asked, genuinely puzzled.

"I can't allow our relationship anymore. No matter how much I love you, I can't continue like this. You parade me in front of men like Mr. Abbott and Rube Foster like a prized trophy, but you will never be mine. Not fully. I don't want a relationship of Fridays. I want Mondays and Tuesdays. I want all the days and years! But I can never have them because the deal you made with the devil means I will only own a piece of you. And I want it all."

How I loved and longed for my gun-toting, self-made millionaire suitor. This handsome, generous man could use those big strong hands of his to fix a squeaky door or find the hottest spot on my body. But his disloyalty to his wife meant that one day he'd betray me too. "How you finds 'em, is how you keeps 'em," Mama used to say. I felt sick to my stomach at the thought. I took Jesse by the hand, slipped his beautiful jacket over his arm and led him to the door.

Humiliated and alone, I did not return to the barbershop for weeks. I did, however, get some good news when a letter arrived from Mr. Abbott saying that he had found three programs in France willing to consider taking on a Negro female student. My brother John had not been so lucky. Jobless and broke, he had turned to Jesse and asked him for work in the bank, without asking me first. It may be that John assumed that being my brother would land him some sort of easy desk job, but Jesse took one look at John, saw him for the sot he was, and turned him down cold. "Drunks and gamblers steal you blind and feed their habit from your plate," Jesse had told me more than once. "They can't help themselves." Some people thought this side of Jesse was cold and hard-hearted. He raised rents and collected on time, and he was never one to give wiggle room when it came to business. But Jesse argued that he had worked hard, remained frugal, and saved all his life. No one was going to steal any part of what his hard work had built, especially if they weren't willing to do the same. This was the gospel according to Jesse. Period.

My brother took out his anger and frustration on me. I didn't know anything about John's interactions with Jesse, yet John raged that I was the reason he had been turned down. The pain of his betrayal and the shame I felt at his accusations made me buckle. My entire private life had been exposed for all those men to see, and John had robbed me of my chance to settle my affairs discretely.

At the White Sox, I had made somewhere between ten and twelve dollars a week. With that income gone, I needed to earn and save a lot more money, and fast. Just around the corner from my apartment there was a thriving chili restaurant that was advertising for a manager, and although I was inexperienced and had never done that kind of work before, I was a hard worker and a twenty-three dollar per week payday felt like a bonanza. I took the job as soon as I found it.

CHAPTER 17

After years of begging from my brothers and me, Mama and my youngest sisters finally decided to come to Chicago. It had taken years and many a prayer to move my family's women up north, and now Mama, Georgia and her new baby Marion; Elois and her children Eula, Vera, Julius, and Dean, and Nilus and her son Arthur were all coming at the same time.

"How will you explain that you and John are not speaking?" Norma asked one afternoon as we sipped tea at her kitchen table.

"Don't really know. I haven't given it much thought," I mumbled.

During this time, Mr. Claude Glenn, an old family friend from Waxahachie who was a regular at the White Sox, called on me at my apartment. After the disaster at the barbershop with John, Mr. Glenn said he wanted to check on me and to see if I was all right. I made him a dinner of meatloaf and mashed potatoes, and then we had glasses of the cheap, sweet wine he'd brought as we chatted on the davenport. In a moment of weakness after my second glass, which Mr. Glenn had poured almost to the top, I had burst into tears and revealed to him how my heart had been broken. He was Mama's age, and although I never gave him much thought as a suitor, he offered me a safe place to land as I fell out of Jesse's arms. The kind Mr. Glenn was neither a gangster nor a married man. We were married three days later at the courthouse. Since there was little to celebrate, there was no fanfare.

But this moment in my life turned out to be as brief as it was painful, and Mr. Glenn was not the answer to what ailed me. Every woman has secrets that she wants to bury, that she not only will not speak of but will not even write. This is one of those, and so I will leave Mr. Glenn in the past where he belongs.

Without Jesse, without the White Sox, and without John, I turned to the one thing left that mattered to me and threw myself headlong in to my studies. My French instructor was a Madame Nancy Montmarie, and she was the first European I had ever met. And although her skin was white, she was different from any white American I had known. A stage actress of some note, with deep auburn hair and eyes that sparkled like emeralds, Madame had come here to marry an American filmmaker she had met in Paris, but upon arriving, she discovered that his films were not the only thing about him that was silent. During their time apart, her filmmaker had become cruel and distant and rarely, if ever, paid her a whit of attention. This was not the man who had romanced her away from the stage with long-stemmed roses and bottles of champagne. This self-absorbed man had become a stranger she did not know. But Madame was an intelligent, vivacious woman who knew how to remake a plan, and that is exactly what she did.

In halting French and at the pace of a novice pecking a Corona typewriter, I painfully forced out each word Madame taught me to say. In the beginning, it was all verbs, regular and irregular, and nouns, masculine and feminine, but over the course of our months together I eventually began sharing everything with her, including my own affair with a married man. We had plenty of man-troubles in common, and with that bond of misery to join us, it seemed natural to tell her of my pain.

"Ah, well, *chérie*," she said, raising her chin a bit and looking above the reading glasses that sat delicately on the bridge of her fine nose. "All women have a married man at one time or another. One must make more sensible choices in the future, that is all."

Her advice extended to more than just my romantic life. Madame developed a genuine interest in my future and considered it her responsibility to play her part in my learning to fly.

"It is ironic, is it not," she asked, "that it is France, with her history of colonialism, that has welcomed America's Negro intelligentsia? It will take some doing, but perhaps one day we can make up for past wrongs. I suppose that while France in many ways has a regrettable history, it appreciates excellence and individual contribution, regardless of its source. Your hard work will bear fruit in *la France, chérie*."

Two weeks later, a letter arrived bearing Mr. Abbott's tightly scrolled handwriting. I stood in the entryway to my building, ripped it from my letter box, and tore the envelope to shreds in my haste.

Dear Bessie:
June 28, 1919

How is your French coming along? I hope it's good because we found a program in France! Do you think that you can be ready by next fall?

Respectfully, Robert Abbott

I ran straight to his office with the letter clutched in my hands. Oh, yes. I would be ready.

o– ◈ –o

I had amassed what to me was a veritable fortune. Stored away at The Binga State Bank, I had squirreled away four thousand, two hundred and seventeen dollars, and even though I had ended our romantic relationship, Jesse had continued to support me and my plans. He had promised that my money would grow with interest, but it appeared that my ex-lover's guilt had led to a significant increase in my grand total, and I came to accept that although I could not trust Jesse with my heart, I could trust him with my bank account. Jesse must have heard about my acceptance into the program because shortly after my letter arrived from Mr. Abbott, I discovered Jesse and Deacon waiting outside the chili joint at the end of my shift.

I felt Jesse before I saw him.

"I didn't want you to walk home alone tonight," he said, slipping his arm through mine.

"What are you doing out here?" I asked.

"The riots have everyone on edge," he said, shuffling me from the side door of the restaurant, through the alley, and into the Rolls.

It was what Mr. Abbott called, "The Red Summer." That August of 1919, all hell broke loose when a young Negro man named Eugene Williams drifted on his raft into the Whites Only bathing section on Lake Michigan's Twenty-ninth Street beach. Sitting next to whites on a streetcar was one thing, but a seventeen-year-old Negro boy bathing that close to half-dressed white women was quite another. It mattered not at all that his actions had been accidental; the boy paid for his trespass with his life. Eugene Williams was stoned to death right there on his raft. So many rocks were hurled from shore that both he and his craft were pinned to the sandy bottom of the lake. Despite hundreds of eyewitnesses, no one was ever arrested for the crime. In the wake of this brutality, the city exploded as it had done after the playing of the D.W. Griffith movie. A wave of riots, arson and, of course, more deaths soon followed.

"Defender Reporter Faces Death in Attempt to Get Facts on Mob Violence; Hospitals Filled with Maimed Men and Women," read *The Defender*. As the chaos swirled around us and dozens lay dead, I prepared for my grand adventure in faraway France. While the city smoldered, my pursuit began to feel like some sort of surreal folly taking place in some other world.

"Well, it was very kind of you to fetch me. I don't take shortcuts up the side streets anymore," I said, sinking back into the plush seat and gazing out the window. As we sped through the streets, we passed a house that had been burned down; the entire block around it was a ruin of charred timber and ash.

"I know. I follow you every night and wanted to make sure you were safe," Jesse said, trying to meet my eyes.

I faced Jesse squarely. "Now, why in the world do you care what happens to me?"

Jesse slammed his right fist against the side of the door and shouted, "I care because I love you, damn it!"

I had never seen him lose his composure, and he had always been guarded in our conversations, especially in front of his men. Yet that night, while a good part of Chicago smoked and burned, and on the eve of my going away for what might be forever, Jesse was suddenly here before me, vulnerable and honest about feelings that until now, he had kept to himself.

"I know you do," I said. "And I love you, too. But you will never leave your wife, and you have made that crystal clear. You've told me that this is a financial arrangement that cannot be undone. I don't want to sneak around with you. I deserve all of you. Anything less and I gut myself."

Jesse held my chin in his fingers. "I would do anything for you. But I cannot walk away from the money."

"No. You won't walk away!" I snapped. "I did some checking, Jesse. Your brother-in-law has been dead for over a decade, and yet you still wash money for riffraff numbers-runners like him. You care more about that numbers game than you care about me, about us. I want you to let go of the strings that come with their filthy money. You have enough. We would be enough." I didn't want to cry. But I couldn't help it.

"See, that's the problem with being young and smart, Bessie. You think you have it all figured out, but you don't even know the half of it." His words came out hoarse and strained. "You don't know anything ..."

I knew enough to know that Jesse had come to support gamblers, dice gamers, bookies, bootleggers, bucket-of-blood saloon owners, scallywags, and crooks, all of whom laundered their dirty money through the first Negro-owned bank in Chicago. Yes, he also nourished the savings of plenty of hard-working porters, barbers, maids, and dreamers, but it was the steady stream of cash from the Levee and from loan sharks that his establishment scrubbed clean that made the dreams of those servants come true. While Jesse's brother-in-law had been the first, since he had died, there had been an endless parade of hoodlums who had slithered through the glass doors of the Binga Bank with a penny to shine.

"One word, Jesse," I breathed. "Neckbone."

"Shit, Bessie, Neckbone's money is my money," Jesse snapped.

Neckbone was the nickname of one of the most terrifying gangsters in Chicago. He got it from his daytime gig, which was butchering pigs on the kill floor in the Stockyards. At night, Neckbone ran a successful numbers parlor in the Levee. He kept order by example, a ruthless, cutthroat example. Two years earlier, a Mississippi man didn't make good on a fifty-dollar gambling debt. The man strolled into Neckbone's place a few days later with new rags and a long story of how he couldn't pay. Next thing you know, Neckbone's barrel chest and square fists came hurtling right at Mississippi. Neckbone beat all of the Mississippi outta that fella and then carved the number 50 into his forehead with his spiked ring. It was the accounting of the debt. People in the Levee talked about that bloody beating for years.

But that wasn't the worst of it. After carefully removing the man's matching corduroy jacket and pants and his newly shined leather shoes, Neckbone's henchmen bound the man with rope then hauled him off to the Stockyards where, under the cover of darkness, they fed the freeloader to the starving pigs. A bucket of lye sat nearby. People said that as the half-eaten man tried to run for it, Neckbone flung lye into the man's eyes. Wounded, blind, his leg missing, the mark hopped then stumbled back into the pen. The pigs, it was said, squealed with delight, even as lye peppered their meal. Within ten minutes, the man from Mississippi was gone. Each time I saw Neckbone coming, I ducked into a shop to avoid him. I thought he was Satan himself.

Jesse called Mickey Finn, another one of his customers, either a "Paddy terrier," or a "mongrel." It was a putdown of the Irishman. But Jesse didn't snub Finn's money. Finn owned a whorehouse and a saloon. Finn would drug a man at the bar, and when the unsuspecting mark woke from being slipped a "Mickey," he'd find he'd been plucked clean of every valuable. Finn was wealthy because Jesse washed his deposits cleaner than any pampered poodle.

"Bessie, my house has been bombed six times! I am building Bronzeville, whether white folks claim I pushed them out or not. They threaten me all the time, but there's no way I'm budging. I know who I'm dealing with. White men hate me because I do what they don't have the balls to do. Negroes need me to help them build a life. And both are jealous. I'm out here trying to build a legacy, and you're busy judging me?

"So many people depend on me, Bess. Sure, there are a few gangsters and hoods, but mostly I bank good, hard-working Negroes. I hold their mortgages. I insure their dreams. Livelihoods float on what I have built. It's complicated," Jesse explained.

"Oh, I understand, all right. I am just one more dependent. I don't want your charity, Jesse. All I have ever wanted was your heart."

I needed to get out. I pulled away and began reaching for the door latch, but he slid across the back seat and enveloped me in a desperate embrace. "You already own it," he whispered into my hair.

We were nearing my apartment, and Deacon was driving so slowly that a pedestrian walking her old dog outpaced us.

"This world isn't about just you. I want to build something, too." I replied more calmly. "I don't want to be anybody's afterthought, not even yours."

"Here," Jesse thrust a heavy envelope into my hands. "I want you to let me come up to say a proper goodbye, but I know you won't." He raised my hand that held the envelope to his lips and held it there for a moment before letting it go.

Jesse liked cash. After a lifetime of making it and moving it around, he used it to express admiration and respect. And love, too.

"You should have a little scratch for when you get to Paris. Go knock 'em dead, baby," he said and turned his face away.

As Deacon pulled away from the curb, I let myself into the building and opened the package as I slowly walked up the stairs. The inky smell of cash floated up from around the wrapping. Inside was $1,000.00. The second I saw it, the scent made me gag, and what made me sick was that my brother had been right. I could be bought. There was no way I was giving back that money.

I would set sail on November 21, 1920.

CHAPTER 18

Thanks to Walter's connections, Norma, Mama, Georgia, and I traveled to New York City from Chicago on one of the Pullman lines. My family would also ride the ferry with me across the Hudson River to Hoboken, New Jersey, where my ship, the *U.S.S. Imperator* awaited her passengers.

"Bess," Norma whispered, "Jesse came by to pick up some more shirts. I think he puts in his custom orders just so we can talk about you. I was prepared to hate him because you were young and naïve, but now I think he is the one who can't live without you."

"Oh, no, you don't," I snapped at her. "You told me to keep my eyes wide open. Remember that? And you know what I saw? I saw a future of waiting around for a married man. Don't you dare get soft on me now!"

"It's just that it's hard to find real love, and I never thought I would say this, but I believe he truly loves you. But you're right, if he orders one more shirt, I think I am going to refuse his business," Norma said.

"Oh, take his money. Please," I said cruelly, "He feels no guilt."

"Now, Bess. That doesn't sound like you," she said. "Don't turn bitter."

Mama and Georgia came to stand alongside us, so Norma dropped the subject. With so much love around me, I suddenly felt homesick, even though we had not left the dock.

The activity on the Manhattan pier had become frenetic as the U.S.S. *Imperator* crew set about busily loading passengers and cargo onto a huge ferry to cross the Hudson River so that we could get to the deep-water dock and the *Imperator* in New Jersey. And although the ferry looked huge, it felt puny alongside the mammoth barges that swarmed the New York Bay.

We set sail across the river, and our little ferry was like a bottle cork bobbing up and down in the wake of the hulking cargo ships crossing the horseshoe bay. The sun rose over Manhattan, and the city glimmered like a case of shimmering gemstones. Mama tapped me on the arm. Her color faded as the same dread that was slowly leaving my body had invaded hers. She pointed her worn index finger at the enormous sea monster of a ship straight ahead of us, its massive hulk growing exponentially before us as we drew closer. Above the Plimsoll line, or water line, the ship's midsection was drenched in pitch. The black keel plunged beneath blacker water, its wide decks spanning one hundred feet across the middle of the vessel. Ten stories above, there was a luxurious upper deck that spread itself out over the water as though suspended. But that's not where I would travel. I would be in steerage, where the engines pumped and roared.

"How in the world could they ever conceive of building such a thing?" Mama asked. "It makes me think of Noah's Ark, only bigger."

"And blacker, too," Georgia said. "That ship's as big as Texas!"

Georgia was right. I felt awe at the size of the ship, fear of the ocean I still had to cross, and thrilled that the adventure I had worked so hard for was beginning. We passed beneath the vast overhang, the shadow of which pitched our pocket-sized ferry into darkness. An eagle was affixed to the bow of the ship, its wings spread out across fifteen feet of steel. Stiff, gold-leaf feathers kept the statue aloft, as the creature's wings swept back, frozen forever in place. Iron chains, each link the size of a truck's tire, grew out of the massive hull and were attached to submerged anchors. Three giant smokestacks climbed into midair, belching thick curtains of smoke. The *Imperator* was longer than three football fields and a hundred feet longer than the *Titanic*. The ship was a leviathan.

The ramp leading up to the ship's mouth was so huge that my entire family stood on the gangplank, and still a dozen people were able to pass shoulder-to-shoulder. Forty-five hundred passengers and crew would traverse the three thousand miles of the North Atlantic at one time. Up ahead, waiting on the giant gangplank, was Mr. Abbott's reporter from *The Defender*, who had brought along a skinny young blond kid from the white press. Mr. Abbott had wanted the white press to make a big deal out of my flight school story, so he made an anonymous tip. The white press took the bait.

"Say, Bessie," the white reporter shouted at me, "Bessie Coleman! How do you feel about going to France to learn how to fly? Where'd you get the notion to do such a thing?"

I found his familiar tone disrespectful. Until you knew a man or woman, Mr., Mrs., or Miss was appropriate. And besides, this was more than a "notion." The word alone devalued the time, money, and effort I had invested into my venture. But I decided to ignore the slight, since saying nothing would allow the reporter the last word, and in print no less.

"I reckon I've wanted to fly ever since I was a girl. And as a woman, I felt I had to protect that child's dream. I always want that girl to be proud of who this woman becomes, and I am duty-bound to make room for little girl dreamers and women who are prepared to fight for what they hope to accomplish," I explained.

"You think they gonna treat you right in Paris?" he sassed.

"The French admire winged pursuit. I am sure I will find fair, like-minded men and women of the sky over there," I beamed.

I had known that Mr. Abbott's reporter would be there to see me off, so I had been plotting how to position myself. I also knew that while The Times was here today, I would need *Aerial Age Weekly* to follow me in the future in order to make a name for myself. If that was to happen, there was no way I would reveal that I once picked cotton and took in laundry, so I planned to talk about my latest pursuits as a manicurist and restaurant manager. I made this calculation, not out of shame, but for the same reason I had taken Jesse's money—it brought me closer to my goal.

The Defender reporter finally got in a question. "What do you think your efforts will do for our race?" This question required more thought and not a fabricated answer and, happy to answer, I flashed him a genuine smile.

"I think that aviators are the future. Race men and women will need to know how to design, fly, and fix an aeroplane and then to train others. I am just playing my part in that process," I said confidently.

A few more photos were snapped and a few final questions asked. But my moment of fame soon dissolved. I was glad, since I felt as though my sudden celebrity status was undeserved, as it was still unearned. The whole group of Colemans, Norma included, had stood during the questioning, looking very noble and prominent, but it was clear that they, too, were shocked at the sudden attention. Although I tried to look brave, I felt anxious. It was finally time to say our goodbyes, and I would have to leave all of them and everything I had known. I hugged each one in turn and climbed the final tier of the gangplank alone.

When I reached the top, I began waving madly at my family. I focused on Mama, who was wiping her eyes with a small white handkerchief she had pulled from her purse. Georgia leaned over and comforted Mama, pulling her into an embrace and smoothing her hair back with a calming hand. I tried to imagine what Mama must be feeling. What must it be like to see the child you had nursed and taught to speak and walk, and for whom you have sacrificed your own youth risk everything that you have invested. And on what? A gamble? My flying was just that—a long shot, a mountain-sized hurdle that I had convinced myself I could clear in a single leap.

Making an arc in the air with my own handkerchief, I waved back to the people I loved. I was uneasy and already lonely, but the hope that had brought me to this moment was with me still, and as the hulking ship began to pull slowly away from the shore, I made peace with my good-byes and turned my face towards the Atlantic.

PART TWO

LEARNING TO FLY

FRANCE

CHAPTER 19

On the final day of our ten days at sea, we approached what I had been told was the most treacherous part of our trip. The Sea of Iroise was the lonely gateway to the harbor of Brest, a medieval seaport at the westernmost tip of France's Brittany peninsula. Turbulent waves crashed against jagged cliffs that lined hundreds of miles of coastline. Shoals and rocky islands peppered this coast in what made for a demanding navigational gauntlet even in the mildest weather. The crew had warned us at the muster drill that the Iroise suffered ill-temper because of differences in the depths and temperatures of its surrounding bodies of water—the English Channel bordered the extreme north, the Celtic Sea hugged the west, then the half-moon Bay of Biscay flanked the south. Stories of the dozens of shipwrecks in those waters were proof of what happened when conditions turned foul. I had chosen to travel at the end of November as the steerage tickets were least expensive during the storm season when hurricanes typically raged all the way into the fall. Up until now, we'd had the gift of fair weather, but as we neared the sea monster Iroise, an endless wall of black clouds grew in the distance, and the weather turned foul.

A wicked storm began brewing before dusk on November 30, 1920. The curdled dark-gray sky turned rapidly into a premature night. Pregnant clouds, heavy with water, hung low over the ocean and began to grumble with thunder. Within minutes, the ship's steeple-high smoke-stacks were lit with blue spears of light as they became a lure to electric bolts. The wind whipped up the surf, and the ocean no longer restrained its fury but loosed twenty-five-foot waves against the ship's hull. The Iroise had us in thrall, tossing the *Imperator* about like a toy boat in a bathtub.

Storm-gawkers braved the black water and pea-soup sky, but soon they were forced to crawl about the deck on all fours to catch even the briefest glance at the seething ocean. They were ordered to enter or be sealed out, and like coins in a slot machine, they slid down the flights of wet metal stairs and tumbled onto the floors below. The ceiling's circular metal door was lowered above them, and a massive wheel, like the one on Jesse's bank vault, was turned clockwise while eight-foot-long pins on grinding gears sealed the hatch with a clank. Remanded by the crew to our tiny cell-like cabins, our bedside portholes were the eight-inch-wide seasick-producing lenses from which we watched the sea and sky fuse as the ship rolled and heeled. We clung to our bed frames as untethered items flew about our cabins. Punishing waves deluged the ship, leaving behind a coating of water so thick that the portholes looked like they were coated by a roux of smoke and haze.

As the ship faced the gigantic swells, its stern snagged, pivoted, and turned, lifting the enormous ship out of the water and slamming it down again on what felt like concrete. Waves as wide as a freight train threw themselves against our side, and metallic moans began to escape the ship's hull. We were completely at the sea's mercy, and passengers sang hymns, their faint voices floating through the air-shaft vents. Sheer terror robbed most of us of the ability to sing, and as I prayed silently to myself, I knew that others were joining me.

I thought of the countless times that I had read Mama the parable from Luke 8:22-25 about Jesus taming the storm,

Now it came to pass on a certain day, that he went into a ship with his disciples: and he said unto them, Let us go over unto the other side of the lake. And they launched forth.

But as they sailed, he fell asleep: and there came down a storm of wind on the lake; and they were filled with water, and were in jeopardy.

And they came to him, and awoke him, saying, Master, master, we perish.

Then he arose, and rebuked the wind and the raging of the water: and they ceased, and there was a calm.

And he said unto them, Where is your faith?

My own faith that we might survive the storm sagged as low as the menacing clouds just above us, as we swayed nauseatingly into the Passage of Fromveur at the end of the Iroise. Notorious for its rapids, the channel writhed with swirling currents, which slithered like serpents in its own deep-water trench that carved a narrow gully through miles of saw-toothed islands. Having made it to this place, we would have to wait, for it would be another six hours until the tide would swell high enough to allow us safe passage. The minutes ticked by as we rocked and fell, holding on to hope that eventually the channel would grow deep enough to make way for the keel of the *Imperator*.

Rising out of the sea and set on rocky mounds, were dozens of defiant lighthouses, called *les phares* by the French. Our captain was expected to follow these red-and-white guiding lights directly into the harbor while remaining within the markers that identified the deepest part of the channel into Brest. As if in a misty dream, we trekked through the wild and watery forest, and as if in Grimm's fairy tale, our only chance for survival was to follow the breadcrumbs of those flickering lighthouses, connecting the dots without touching them. I had read about the *phares* in a pamphlet I had pinched from the upper deck, but I could not remember the name of each. The pictures of these ancient lighthouses on their giant bases thrashed with swirling waves had left me spellbound.

Still holding the metal bunk with one hand, I steadied my fingers and slipped them beneath my pillow. Next to my Bible was the pamphlet about the lighthouses, and I prayed that looking at it again would keep at bay the sour liquid that kept pooling at the back of my throat. Swallowing hard as the words danced across the pages, I read, "*Le Phare de la Jument* was completed in 1911. It took seven years to build. Its coal-fired light can be seen twenty miles out to sea." I could see why, as our ship heaved and rolled, nearly glancing the crumbling ancient pillar, which I could see from my rain-streaked porthole. "In 1896, a ship wrecked itself against rocks at this spot, claiming two hundred and fifty lives and motivating French engineers to construct this string of rock lights. For the next fifty years, dozens more *phares* would be erected. Perched on granite, their bases gouged out of bedrock in the middle of the sea, these stubborn colossi defy the power of the tides."

The Sea of Iroise reluctantly filled her vein with the gray, foaming tide. The boxcar-sized anchors crept slowly up from the seabed and were recoiled into the ship's belly. The engines were fired. Slowly steaming forward, we headed towards the medieval fort in Brest Harbor, and when we pulled in at last, the shipmen pulled down their sheets, and the dock workers lashed the ship to capstans as high as my shoulders, binding the *Imperator*—at last—to rock.

All around us were the castle-like towers of a long-abandoned fort, the Château de Brest. Last touched generations ago, the garrison's cannons lay cold, leaving behind nothing but an ancient, toothless memory of sentries who were now only ghosts staring out at the sea. Still shaken, it took me quite some time to trust that we had truly arrived. But as the ship pulled into the port, I took in the colorful awnings of the restaurants and quaint shops, the people slowly meandering from café to market, their parcels dangling from their hands. As the last beads of rain outside the porthole ledge burned off in the sun, I whispered softly to myself, I made it.

"Bonjour," I managed. *"S'il vous plaît, Monsieur, où est la gare?"* I asked an older man who was busy untangling his fishing net. He looked at me blankly and then returned to his task as if he hadn't even seen me standing before him. The three-hundred-fifty-mile trip from Brest to Paris was a ten-hour affair, and I needed directions to the station if I was to make my train. I asked a second man and then a third, managing to overcome the paralysis of the tongue that had set in at my fear of mispronouncing the words.

Mercifully, the third sailor, who had just cast his rod from the pier, seemed to understand and explained in perfect English, "You must cross this street, make a right at the next corner, and there you will find the train station."

With a rush of *merci*s, I dragged my heavy suitcase across the cobblestones and down the quay, humiliated but relieved.

"Puis-je acheter un billet pour Paris?" I asked politely, once I had made my way to the front of one of the wrought-iron kiosks at the station.

The seconds ticked by as the clerk stared directly into my face without speaking. "*Paris, s'il vous plaît!*" I finally barked in exasperation.

"*Oui, oui,*" the clerk snapped back.

Cautiously, I ventured onto the waiting train. There were no signs for a Colored car, so I chose a premium seat, right by the window. Soon, a man about my age sat down next to me, pulled a novel from his bag, glanced my way and said in French, "Are you on your way to a holiday?"

"Not quite," I managed to stammer back.

"And where are you from?" he asked.

"I'm from Chicago," I answered.

"Ah, I've never been."

We chatted on and off for the duration of the trip and shared a lunch as we talked. I had bought bread and chocolate at the station during my wait, and he offered creamy cheese and cold water from a flask. With some relief, I discovered that he was as eager to practice his English, as I was desperate to shed my fear of making mistakes in French pronunciation, so we stumbled through our conversations in a mix of French and English, hand gestures, and some hilarity.

"We will call this "Frenglish," he proclaimed in his easy way, and I was struck at once by how immediately alien the world around me had become. Had we been in Dallas, I might easily have been kicked off the train for sitting there, chatting and sharing a meal with a white man. But this Frenchman treated me as an equal, and not a single soul around us batted an eye.

When our train pulled into the station, he gave me directions, and we said our goodbyes. Following the rudimentary map he had drawn for me, I made my way to my hostel in the neighborhood called La Rive Gauche, which was the left bank of the Seine River. I had rented a tiny room, where I would have to share a bathroom with several people. The skinny bed and bolster pillows came right up against the door, but a place to sleep had rarely looked so welcoming, and I crawled under the stiff wool blanket and fell immediately into a deep sleep of exhaustion and relief. I awoke with a growling, hungry belly at mid-morning and headed out to the Boulevard Saint-Michel. It was alive with meandering pedestrians, the honks of automobiles and the smells of fishmongers' wares, pastries, and roses. Bicycles whizzed by like birds, and pigeons pecked their way across gray sidewalks where little dogs were walked on tight leather leashes and shopkeepers swept invisible litter with brooms made of twigs.

This neighborhood, where the Seine River flows west, separating the city into halves, was home to artists, writers, actors, and singers, and in this beehive of activity, creativity was currency and beauty was wealth. This district was many times larger than the Stroll and could not have been more different in look and tone. The French ladies and gentlemen leaned themselves against light posts with their notepads, or lounged at *Les Deux Magots*, sipping a coffee and pecking thoughtfully on their Corona typewriters. My brother John had been right when he had thundered that the citizens here reveled in their nonconformity. You could see it everywhere.

The smells of roasting chicken coaxed me inside a restaurant with a yellow awning bearing the name, in a delicate scroll—*Café L'Artisan, Paris*. Inside, the white Carrara marble floors were veined in blue-gray swirls, and a delicate chandelier hung from an ornate plaster ceiling medallion. While the customers lined up behind me, I stood spellbound in the midst of such opulence and was only startled out of my reverie when I felt a gentle tap on the shoulder.

"Here, sit down," said an apron-clad woman bearing the name of the café. "Drink this," she said in French, handing me a tiny cup of *café au lait*. It had a crown of milky cream on top.

In moments she returned with a delicate quiche. It was round and about the size of my hand. I thanked her and she smiled knowingly. The warmth of the pastry struck me first. The outside shell was crumbly and filled with a custard of perfectly baked egg, spinach, ham, and gooey cheese. The entire affair melted in my mouth. It was so good that I had to force myself to slow down.

I had pulled out money, which she returned to my hand. "You look like you are in a hurry. I hope you are now ready for your journey," she smiled. "You had better go."

I was confident that God had placed an angel in my path. This woman was only a little older than my mother. She had a large bosom and a smile to match. But more than that, she had seen both my hunger and my urgency. How could all this be communicated without me explaining who I was, or why I'd come so far?

"Try this," she said. The lemon-yellow macaroon she handed me tasted just like sunshine.

o— ◈ —o

Only days before I had arrived in Paris, two women were killed during an accident while on a training flight, and the school I was set to attend would no longer accept women students. Mr. Abbott's other option, the *École d'Aviation des Frères Caudron* in Le Crotoy—the Caudron Brothers' School of Aviation—which was in the Somme Valley, would be where I would go instead. The *école* was the most famous flight school in all of France and vastly more intimidating because of its reputation.

From Paris, the *Haine Saint Pierre*, an aqua-colored steam locomotive that drew half a dozen bright red passenger cars through the French countryside, brought me the city of Rue. Because I couldn't afford to live in the seaside town of Le Crotoy, where wealthy Parisians took their holidays in mansions that lined the coast, I arranged to stay nine miles away, where I could afford a place.

In order to get there from the station, I hitched a ride with a fisherman and his wife in a buggy drawn by two big old draft horses. As we pulled away from town, the smells of the sea and fine French cooking swirled in the air about us—garlic simmering in butter in a giant saucepan somewhere, just waiting for a trawler with its haul of fresh mussels to arrive. The old couple dropped me off a mile from my destination. Before they were out of earshot, the fisherman yelled directions over the clip-clop of the horse's hooves, "Just keep walking until you see the wings on the sand ..."

The flight school was perched on the banks of the Somme Bay and was part of an enormous aeroplane factory. Its airstrip was the beach that defined the town's western border. The entire complex grew in size as I made my way slowly towards it, making each step more intimidating than the last. The front door of the office was ajar, and when I knocked, it swung farther open to reveal a dark, wood-paneled room.

"*Bonjour*," I said to the man standing behind a glass display case. "May I speak with either René or Gaston Caudron?" I asked.

"Sadly, Mademoiselle, you are too late to meet Monsieur Gaston. That was my eldest brother, he died five years ago in a crash. Perhaps I can assist you? I am René Gaston."

"Please forgive me. I meant no harm. I am so very sorry," I stammered.

I was mortified. I had read all about Monsieur Gaston's death in the flying magazines I devoured, but standing there in that hallowed hall of aviation, I had been completely star-struck and had said the first thing that came to mind. These brothers' names were synonymous with pilot training and the best aeroplane designs in the world, and that I was standing there in their holy hanger stretched the bounds of reality to the point that I could hardly make sense of the miracle of it all.

"Of course, I take no offense. Time softens, but my loss is without measure," he replied.

"Although both came home, two of my brothers fought in the Great War," I said. "I can only imagine how painful it must be to lose a brother. It is impossible to separate the halves of a coin," I hoped I had adequately conveyed the remorse that I had felt at my gaffe.

"You are as wise as you are beautiful, Mademoiselle. Your accent is American, but I have never seen one such as you. Your skin is bronze, yet you speak French. Where are you from, and what is it that brings you to our marshy little outpost?" Monsieur Caudron asked.

"Well, sir, I am from Chicago, by way of Waxahachie, Texas."

"Chicago I have heard of, but this Waxa-*vieu*? What is this? A place? A food? Fish of some sort?"

"Wax-a-ha-chie, sir." I sounded out the name of my hometown, with the emphasis on the third long A. When dropped into a romance language, even to my ears the name sounded awkward. "It is difficult to say in English, not to mention in French," I laughed. "My friend Robert Abbott is the founder of a very famous Negro newspaper in Chicago, and even with his connections throughout the United States, we could not find an establishment that would take me on as a student and teach me to fly."

I dug into my satchel and handed him a letter that was his own affirmative response to Mr. Abbott as to whether I would be admitted to his school. Monsieur Caudron looked at me searchingly. Pulling up a stool next to the display case full of goggles and books, he asked, "So how did you find our school?"

"Mr. Abbott helped me," I began.

"And do you know much about Le Crotoy?"

"No, sir," I said. "I mean, *non, Monsieur*," I corrected myself.

"Well, perhaps you should know a bit of history, *non*?" He asked. "It would be beneficial to know who proceeded you in this quest to fly?"

"Yes, I would appreciate that. Thank you, Monsieur Caudron," I responded.

He told me first that before she was burned at the stake, Joan of Arc was imprisoned there in Le Crotoy. And that in 1910, the first woman licensed by the *Fédération Aéronautique Internationale*, the FAI, was the Baroness de Laroche. Before most men were even driving motor cars, the Baroness was setting distance and altitude records, flying all around the world, and racing in Budapest, Russia, and Africa. She had one son, called André, with Léon Delagrange, who himself was famous as a leader of the FAI, but who died tragically in a crash in Bordeaux. He was flying in heavy winds, when a wing snapped, and he fell; his skull was crushed under the engine. Monsieur Caudron glanced at me, as if to assess my stomach for such a story.

"The Baroness, herself," he continued, "survived a plane crash shortly after her husband's, then an automobile wreck after that. But, her perseverance brought her back to good health, and she went on to set a new world altitude record of four thousand, seven hundred and fifty meters. Months later, she and her co-pilot met their deaths in a crash on this very field. Imagine poor André, orphaned, both of his parents lost." Monsieur Caudron seemed to drift off for a moment while imagining the devastation of that loss. "There have been so many dead and I have talked too much. Please, tell me your name."

"My name is Bessie, sir."

"And after all that I have told you, you still want to learn to fly? Even with the stories you have just heard? This is the passion of fools, of course. What does that say about you?"

"I suppose it means that I am either passionate or a fool, but my passion has gotten me here. I have learned French, I have invested everything I own, and I have crossed an ocean to come here. I could never live with the regret of stopping now. If that makes me a fool, then so be it," I answered.

"Ah, *oui*, regret is waste—wasted time and wasted effort. I hope I do not regret my own decision to accept you," his chestnut eyes sparkled. "Besides, you may be too hard to get rid of. Tomorrow we start a new class of recruits. Have you a place to stay?"

"Yes, sir, I have found a room on the outskirts of Rue. I must watch how much I spend," I said.

"How in the world do you expect to get to and from there?" he asked with surprise.

"I will walk." I replied.

"You will walk!" he bellowed. "It is nine miles—each way. You had better run along, then. It will take you all night to walk there and back in time for class tomorrow." Shaking his head as if he might, indeed, have made a mistake in accepting me, he rose from the stool and walked through the door to where the aeroplanes were awaiting his attention.

I kept my face perfectly calm until I could no longer see him through the doorway and then ran out the front door, jumped the four steps to the cobbled sidewalk and took off down the sandy lane. The idea of walking didn't scare me, and I went back to the counting I had done as a child when I had walked a mile each way to grammar school. With my books and gear, I could easily walk a mile in fifteen minutes. Nine miles would take two hours and fifteen minutes, each way. I would just get up earlier. Or maybe I would splurge on a bicycle. I would skip or dance the whole way because no matter how I got back and forth, the trip meant that some day, and not some fantastical day of my dreams, but some actual day in the near future, I was going to fly.

CHAPTER 20

The next morning, when Monsieur Caudron arrived, he shook his head again.

"You are here before all of the others, and they live nearby!"

"Good morning, sir," I said. "I bought these last night." I handed him a paper sack full of sweet pears. Their perfume floated out of the bag and reminded me of the pear tree back home that Mama had grown in her garden. "Juicy," I grinned.

He did not take the bag from me, but rather used an index finger to pull open the paper and then peek inside. He looked me over suspiciously before drawing in a flared nostril full of the sweet fragrance. At last, his large mustache twitched, then turned up with the corners of his lips.

"Juicy, indeed."

"Come inside and bring your little bribe with you," he said, fitting a skeleton key inside the lock of the door to the whitewashed hangar.

"Thank you. But I was hoping we might first talk about tuition," I said carefully.

"I think I underestimated you. Don't worry, we will work this out. You will not have to bring bribes every morning, or give me any other sort of … gift," he said meaningfully. "I want to see if you can string together a couple of days, maybe even a few weeks, before I take your francs. The course is rigorous, and many do not accomplish even the initial training. Let's talk after this first week, *d'accord?*"

I sincerely hoped Monsieur Caudron's integrity was genuine. He was about Jesse's age, fit and ruggedly handsome, with hair and mustache that matched his dark brown eyes and a dark olive complexion from years spent in the sun. He had a tiny scar in the shape of a miniature boomerang that hovered below his left eyebrow and sharp cheekbones that dove into an angular jaw.

He was in a perfect position to take advantage of my lack of funds and lust to fly. I wanted my flight training badly and hoped that he would not force me to make a choice, to compromise my morality or my dignity. I wanted to leave all that in the past.

We were fifteen students from all over the world, but we had one goal in common—to learn to fly. Behind an old whitewashed hangar at the back of the school, we lined up and faced Monsieur Caudron and the four flight instructors, as they assessed us from some meters away. Each one of the instructors was smartly dressed in neatly pressed identical shirts, black ties, black trousers, and brown leather skull caps that had protective earflaps and goggles pushed above their foreheads. Their boots were spit shined. With their hands clasped behind their backs, they stood like a neat row of chess pieces.

"Please toe the line," Monsieur Caudron commanded, at which a ripple of confusion and rapid, uncertain glances spread through our small student body. "When I say 'toe the line', I mean put your toes up to, but not on, the line," Monsieur Caudron demonstrated as he spoke. "Look at the line. Your attention to detail may one day save your life," he barked. He pointed to the four-inch-thick chalk line used to straighten the aeroplanes, and we quickly organized ourselves with the tips of our shoes just touching its edge.

"You will be as orderly as the aeroplanes. Discipline, precision, attention, these are the first and most basic requirements of any pilot, or mechanic for that matter, wouldn't you agree, Luc?" Monsieur Caudron bellowed above the crashing of the waves just beyond the hangar walls.

"Yes, sir, I do agree. Order first, sir," Luc, the head mechanic, yelled in response.

By this time, we had finally assembled at the line. "I am expecting one more student to arrive," he said. "But we will begin, because the one thing that you can never be in aviation is late." He said this with considerable disgust, as if the student's tardiness was a disagreeable characteristic of which he intended to rid us all. I began to sense that we were a motley, ragtag group of misfits in desperate need of Monsieur Caudron's discipline.

"You are about to embark upon a serious pursuit. The skills that you learn here will lengthen your time on earth. What you do not learn will hasten your demise. You will learn from the mistakes of others so that you do not have to repeat their dangerous or deadly errors." He paused and regarded each one of us from beneath his dark brows.

"I want you to look to your left and to your right." Each of us took furtive glances. "*Allez-y*, look at your neighbor," he paused for a long moment. "By the time we complete this course, neither of your neighbors will be here. Out of the fifteen of you, we will lose ten during the course of our training." He fell silent and allowed this to sink in.

I looked to my left and then to my right. As I did so, I noticed that most of my fellow students were now looking at me. It sure did feel like a lot of the boys' eyes had skipped over their neighbors and were now resting on my flushed face. Not only was I the only woman in the group, I was pretty sure that for many of my classmates, I was the first Negro they had ever encountered in the flesh.

"Are there any questions before we make assignments?" Monsieur Caudron asked.

A scrawny redhead with a heavy cockney accent raised his hand. "Does that mean that ten of us are going to die, sir?"

"We have already predicted our first casualty, I see," Monsieur Caudron mumbled. "What I mean is that only one-third of you will make it through training. The rest of you will not. Either the academics or the stick work itself will help you to select some other field of endeavor.

"You will suppress your ego. You will rely on one another, and you will use each other to review lessons or to prepare for your next flight. How you interact with your fellow classmates will be part of your grade for the simple reason that nothing in this life is achieved by you, and you alone. If you are to survive, you must figure out how to help one another."

Clipboard in hand, he called off the students' last names and assigned three of us to each instructor. I was paired with a blond boy named Tristan and a dark-haired boy named Pierre. The three of us were to be taught by Monsieur Caudron himself. Each student received two books—one, a heavy red volume entitled *Manoeuvres*, and the other, a blue book entitled *Aerodynamics: Sourcebook for Aviators*. Each of these texts had been well used before they came into our possession, but the wrinkled edges and worn covers did nothing to diminish their value in my eyes. I took them from Monsieur Caudron's hands and placed them carefully into my rucksack like the treasures they were.

"Each flight lesson will have the same structure," he continued. "We will have a *Brief*, which will outline what we are going to do and the principle that we are demonstrating, followed by the *Flight*, in which we will do the thing that we have talked about, followed by the *Debrief*, in which we discuss what we have just accomplished. If this sounds simple, then you have already learned your first lesson. Flying is about repetition. It is repetition that will allow you to execute a sequence of events dependably.

"As you know, you will not touch an aeroplane until you complete ground school. Now, off you go. Come back tomorrow when you have completed the first exercise in your blue book."

I ran almost every one of the nine miles back to my hostel and tore into my room. On the edge of my bed was what was left from the *Café L'Artisan* that I had found in Paris. The baguette, although now a bit harder than before, and a hunk of goat cheese made for a suitable supper, and the one pear I had saved for myself was the perfect dessert. I read the assignment and then read it again. I had gone through nearly half the text for a third time, before I fell asleep with the books as my pillow.

For many weeks throughout that winter, I hunched over my spartan desk of oak planks set upon brick pillars, meticulously recording into my logbook the weather, cloud types, and atmospheric conditions including temperature, wind direction and speed, sunrise, sunset, and quantities of rainfall. The tides, and the moons that controlled them, were of critical interest, as was the beach itself. The beach was our landing strip, and so knowing the moons and how they controlled the tides was essential to landing on sand and not in sea water or muddy, shifting ground. The eight phases of the moon—New, Waxing Crescent, First Quarter, Waxing Gibbous, Full, Waning Gibbous, Third Quarter, and Waning Crescent—were all part of a new world of knowledge that we would need to commit to memory and understanding long before we ever took our first flight. These logbooks would become a permanent record of our individual training experiences.

At the same time, the concepts—and for me, the French translation of the terms involved—were fired at us fast as the bullets from a Vickers machine gun. And there were many. Lift, center of lift, center of gravity, center of pressure, dihedral angle, dihedral effect on stability, anhedral, interplane strut, undercarriage, cowl, flying wires, landing wires, incidence wires, angle of incidence, angle of attack, fairing, fuselage, landing gear, leading edge, trailing edge, tail skid, fin, drag wire, ribs, spars. Then there were the three primary control surfaces: *elevator, ailerons, rudder*; the three different ways to rotate in three-dimensions: *pitch*, or nose up or down; *roll*, turning about a line running from nose to tail; *yaw*, or moving side to side, with nose pointing left or right. There was lateral control, along the plane's longitudinal axis, tipping the plane side to side, with one wingtip up, one down, and longitudinal control, or pitch stability about its lateral axis with rudder and rudder control cables. There was also *attitude*. It was not how one felt, nor was this condition related to temperament at all but rather, it was the angle of the aeroplane's nose relative to the horizon.

Half of our fleet was new and had carburetors, a recent advance in technology. Carburetors allowed fuel and air to be mixed, which controlled power and thus, airspeed. Before carburetors, it was all or nothing, which meant either fast or off. You'd hear the whir of the engine and then you'd hear the engine chop. It was either land the plane or drop out of the sky.

And then there was the rotary engine itself, which we had to know as if we had fashioned it with our own hands. These were either two- or four-stroke, gas-powered, internal combustion engines, with their four stages—intake, compression, power, and exhaust—that converted thermal energy and chemical energy into mechanical energy, which made the plane go. We learned that the cylinders were arranged around a crankshaft and that the propeller was bolted to the engine; that the propeller and engine assembly spun around the crankshaft. We learned that the engine was lightweight and air-cooled, and that its parts were magnetos, crankshaft, camshaft, connecting rods, spark plugs, pistons, valves, and the engine block. There was so much to learn in such a short amount of time, and doing it all in French made my head spin 'round and 'round like the rotary engine itself. There were British aeroplanes, named

after animals—the Camel, the Rhino, the Pup. They were sturdy and reliable. Then there were the German aeroplanes—the Albatros, the Fokker,
and the Roland, and they were heavy, fast, and lethal. And finally, there
were the French, which were my favorite—the Caudron, the Farman,
and the Nieuport. They were fast and nimble and squirrely. During the
war, new models were being conceived, designed, and produced in rapid
succession, and mistakes in war became lessons earned in bloodshed.
Often fighter pilots got the test before they learned the lesson.

The first student was cut less than a month into training. The skinny
British redhead who had asked about casualties was dismissed one afternoon and was not in line the following morning. A week later, the young
man who had arrived late on the first day and had continued to over-
sleep, was sent back to his native Poland. The schoolwork grew harder
and the length of the days at the school grew longer, and when two other
students couldn't keep up with the academic demands, they too were told
to go home.

Over the course of these weeks, I had shaved fifteen minutes off my
nine-mile trek back and forth to school and had cut the time down to two
hours flat. But as the season changed from fall to winter, no matter how
fast my trot, the way back to my hostel had to be made in darkness. This
was not Chicago where street-lamps dotted the way along a paved lane.
This was the northern French countryside, where the rugged beauty of
gray sea and sky flowed into one another, and the sandy soil led away
from the shore into a forest so dark green that it was black.

The terrain I passed had deep valleys and breathtaking lookouts that
one could only see from a steep climb to the most dangerous outcrops. In
the mornings, I enjoyed the view, but on crystalline nights, the moon cast
eerie shadows, turning trees and branches into what looked like living
things. Even the vines seemed as if they grew arms and knuckles in the
dark. Each night, I would make my way along the road as quickly as I
could, trying to suppress my fear by concentrating instead on whatever I
had learned that day—going over take offs and landings in my mind and
analyzing the areas where I would improve them if I could.

On one drizzly night, my reflections were cut short when, not far
ahead, I saw what looked like a puff of smoke in a wedge of moonlight
shining on a patch of trees. It turned out to be a cloud of vapor, and
within it, three wolves stood silently on the rocky dirt path. In unison,
they turned their heads to look in my direction, giving me the impression

that, although the sight of them was a surprise to me, they had been aware of my presence for some time. The wolf in the lead was light gray with a black mask pattern tattooed into his fur that made him look like a harlequin, and when he dipped his head to stare straight at me, I felt a surge of fear rush through me like an electric current. The harlequin's tail went from limp to standing up straight, the tiny bones at the end bending into a hook.

I knew instinctively not to run. Each wolf stood as high as my elbow and only fifteen meters spanned the distance between us. The lead wolf took a step forward, and his movement caused his pack to sidestep closer to him. A low growl rumbled from his chest. At the sound, I reconsidered the idea of making a run for it, even though I had always been good at climbing trees and had spotted an old oak nearby with an outstretched limb low enough for me to grab. While I could never outpace all three wolves, I might be able to make it up that tree.

Just as I was getting ready to scramble for my life, I saw what had drawn the wolves out onto the road in the first place. A farrow of boars wandered directly across the strip of path that separated me from the wolves. Without a sound, the wolf pack shot after the baby animals, leaving behind nothing but moonlight where they had just been standing. A few seconds later, I heard loud scrambling and scratching coming from the woods, and then high-pitched squeals as the piglets were devoured. As I bolted down the road, I could hear their animal screams, which were so gruesome that I had to suppress the instinct to cover my ears, but the death cries stopped abruptly, and silence fell once again around me.

Over the course of the run home, the story of Booker T. Washington, which had so intrigued me as a child, came back to me. How fitting, I thought, that it should come to me then, as if by way of direction, as if to say exactly what I needed to do. Just as he had pawned his pocket watch in order to buy a kiln, I would have to sell the one thing of value I owned if I wanted to get through the winter. I would have to sell the small gold cross of my Mama's that I had worn around my neck on a thin leather strap every day since I had first left home. The following day at a pawn shop in town, I handed it across the counter in return for a bicycle that would get me to and from school. As I rolled the rickety old bike out into the rain, my tears and the raindrops slid down my cheeks at the heartbreak of letting go of my mother's cross.

On many a morning, I would have to jerry rig the seat to keep it from slipping or push a broken spoke back into place. There was always some sort of last-minute repair to be made in order to make the bicycle go. And then, one morning two months later, it was gone. Outside my hostel, against the tree where I had left my bike night after night, there was nothing but an empty chain. That morning, as I rushed to school, once again on foot, I cursed the thief whom I would surely never find and tearfully mourned the loss of Mama's treasure. I was so upset that I did not adjust my pace for the unevenness of the cobbles in town, and within a few feet of dashing across their uneven surfaces I rolled my ankle and collapsed into the street. The gutter smelled of urine and stale ale, and I dragged myself up onto all fours. I plopped down on the curb to take a look and saw that the outside ball of my ankle had already begun to swell. For the second time in as many months, I allowed myself to weep in exasperation and exhaustion.

No matter how well deserved, I could not give in to self-pity. If I sat on the curb crying, I was sure to arrive late to class. In my bag I had the ruler I used to plot my course on charts. I also had an exquisite flyer's scarf that Norma had fashioned and given to me as a going away present on my last night in Chicago. I retrieved both and wrapped my ankle tightly in the splint I made from the ruler's long, flat edge. I drew my pant leg down around the bandage, gathered myself up and onto my feet, and hopped and hobbled to class, arriving just as Monsieur Caudron was shutting the door.

"*Bonjour!*" he cheerily began that Monday morning's class, "Today, let us begin with Mademoiselle Coleman, shall we?" I must have registered surprise and alarm, because he added, "Yes, you, Mademoiselle. There is only one mademoiselle here, *non?*"

He did not wait for a reply. "How does an aeroplane fly? How exactly does something heavier than air pull itself from the clutches of gravity?"

On that day, I had been expecting quite another question, since we had spent the previous week studying checklists—an all-important list of every task and its sequence which had to be done before, during, and after each flight. We had also memorized the parts of the plane, and I was ready to explain each part's function.

"Mademoiselle Coleman, did you hear me?

Breathe I reminded myself as my ankle throbbed painfully. You can only think when you are breathing and oxygen is able to get to your brain.

Monsieur Caudron's expression gave no indication of what he was thinking, but I imagined he would make no further investment until I could demonstrate a return.

"Well," I said, gathering my thoughts, "what you are asking is to describe the definition of lift. It is an aerodynamic principle. I could talk about Bernoulli's Theorem and this answer would be correct—technically, that is. All energy, despite disturbances, according to Bernoulli, must be conserved. So, in the case of an aeroplane wing, which is curved on top and flat on the bottom, air travels more rapidly over the curved top, and relatively slower under the wing. This creates a relative difference in how the fluid air is disturbed, as it causes a greater positive, or upward, pressure beneath the wing and, relative to it, a lesser negative, or downward, pressure on top of the wing. It is this relative difference in pressure that literally pushes the wing up, creating what the physicist called lift."

To emphasize the point, I extended my arm and curled my hand, with my knuckles pointed toward the ceiling. I elevated my hand, simulating an upward lifting motion, dragging the curve, and my curved hand, toward the sky.

"Sir Isaac Newton's third law of motion explains that every action has a paired reaction that is equal in force and opposite in direction. In the case of a hunter, a pull on the bowstring draws the arrow back with a force that is equal in strength, but opposite in direction to the arrow once it is released and propelled toward the deer. Similarly, the air pushes an aeroplane up, forcing the wings to push down, or ride on top of a cushion of air."

I used my two index fingers to make antlers that now sprouted out of my hair. Even after I took my fingers away, the tiny antler buds stood at attention in twin peaks in my hair. My hair was soft, but not at all silky, and so it remained tented, like meringue on pie, its tiny stiff spikes persisting. Monsieur Caudron laughed at this, and the others laughed too, as they dutifully followed the direction of their leader.

"The angle of attack, or the angle at which the air flows over the wings, has everything to do with how fast, or how high, the aeroplane is lifted into air." I concluded.

I got up, and having forgotten my sore ankle, nearly tumbled from my seat. With a stifled wince I steadied myself and walked stiffly to the head of the classroom where I picked up a shard of chalk from the blackboard's ledge. My classmates sat in complete silence, now. On the slate, I sketched a stick-figure aeroplane surrounded by four directional arrows. One pointed in an up-direction, toward the sky. Next to it, I wrote the word lift. The second arrow was its opposite force and pointed downward toward the floor; here I wrote the word weight. One arrow sprang away from the nose, I wrote the word thrust, followed by the last arrow shooting out of the tail, where I wrote drag.

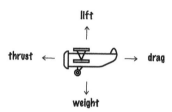

"These are the four forces on an aeroplane in flight. If an aeroplane is flying straight and level, all four of these forces are equal. The only factor that is a constant is gravity, or weight. The other three forces, when the craft is in flight, are variables."

Before hobbling back to my seat, I recited a quote from the Manoeuvers book, "A sixth sense for the art, as well as the science of lift, is the difference between competent and expert."

Monsieur Caudron had, until that time, remained stonily silent in a seat to the right of the blackboard. After a moment more of silence, in which I could think of nothing to do other than straighten and re-straightened the books on my small desk, he finally stood. All eyes were on him as he carefully placed his pen on the seat where he had been sitting and slowly, deliberately brought his hands together in a series of claps.

"*Bravo, ma belle*," he said. And then gesturing to me with one hand, said to my fellow classmates, "This is how you answer."

At break, the ten remaining students puffed on their Gitanes and chatted nervously about the day ahead. Pierre, who came from a privileged background and whom Monsieur Caudron considered haughty, had been dismissed that morning for laziness after showing up late, and so Tristan and I agreed to study together at a nearby café after class. I was glad for his invitation, because I thought that as study partners, we might make twice the progress together as each might make alone.

"You are the teacher's pet," he said sullenly, pouring the last of his coffee down his throat and setting the tiny white cup onto its saucer with a clink. "It's a mystery how you managed to become his favorite.

Perhaps our work together will mean that some of that good luck will rub off on me."

The off-putting remark made me feel as sore as my busted ankle, but I said nothing, preferring to ignore the slight and concentrate on our studies instead. After a few hours, we agreed to meet again another time, and when Tristan asked me where I was going and whether I needed a ride, I jumped at the invitation. Any resentment Tristan may have harbored at Monsieur Caudron's partiality toward me disintegrated when he saw me favor my ankle as I stepped onto the running board of his automobile. He glanced down at my foot and saw the scarf still wound, if more loosely now, around the wooden ruler.

"But, what have you done?" he asked, looking back up at me. "Has it been like this all day?"

Before I could answer, he knelt down and began to gently unwind my makeshift splint. This time, it was he who winced as he uncovered what had been hidden beneath the soft silk of Norma's gift.

"Sit down," he commanded. "Wait right here." I nodded, trying not to let his kindness overwhelm me, as he ran back into the pub. He returned a few moments later with a bar cloth and a champagne cooler filled with ice. By now my ankle was turning black and blue, and with confident hands, he expertly packed the ice into the cloth and wound it around my ankle. When he was finished, he dragged his rucksack over and carefully placed my foot on top of it while I waited for him to return the cooler to the café.

When we pulled up to the dilapidated inn that I called home, Tristan put the car in neutral, and surveyed the chickens that pecked about the front and at the overgrown flower box, now filled with weeds and a few dandelions that survived only because the chickens could not reach them.

"How do you get to school each day?" Tristan asked as the motor rumbled in idle. His fine Renault Touring machine was raring to go. I had admired that car for months, its mustard-gold paint and the walnut panel inserts on the doors. Now that I was inside it, I was able to experience it for myself. The black leather seats, with their neck-high tufted backs, made for a luxurious ride. It may not have been a Rolls, but it had its own kind of class.

"I walk," I said.

"You walk? To school? And back?"

"Yes, Tristan. I walk," I said quietly.

I may have been poor, but I still had my pride, and at that moment, I wished that I had asked Tristan to drop me off at the top of the road so that he had never had to see this dismal place.

"From here to school must be fourteen kilometers," Tristan nearly shouted.

"Fourteen and a half." I corrected.

"How long does that take you?"

"Two hours and fifteen minutes. If I run for a bit, I can cut off fifteen minutes, more or less."

"Each way?" Tristan shrieked.

"Well, yes. The bike I bought was stolen, and I can't afford to replace it. The thing is, I may not have a lot, but I have a strong will, and until this morning, I had two strong legs."

"Good God," he breathed and looked back at the chickens. He turned off the engine, yanked up the parking-break and got out of the car.

"Look, Tristan," I said. He had run around to help me out, but I had already done it for myself. I slammed the door before he could get to it. "In spite of what it might look like around here, I don't need your pity. But I sure could use a friend, as long as that friendship comes with your respect."

"Of course, Bessie. I am sorry. I did not mean any disrespect. It was only that I was shocked to learn that this is how you live," he said. "Perhaps, by way of explanation, I should tell you something about myself, eh?" Tristan took my arm and began to lead me carefully toward the hostel. "If you sense my competitiveness, you are right. I am competitive. But with good reason. My father was a legend in the French Flying Corps and was famous for one thing. He earned the coveted Croix de Guerre. That is the equivalent to your Purple Heart, is it not?" I nodded. "My father had six confirmed kills in the Great War and flew a G.3. You understand the significance of a Gaston 3, *oui*? He was a close friend of Monsieur Gaston, Rene Caudron's deceased brother."

I actually did not understand the significance, as he seemed to sense.

"That connection is likely the only reason that I was admitted to *l'école*. If I do not succeed, I will be a failure in my family's eyes." His watery blue eyes filled, and he turned his face away.

I studied Tristan as he struggled to contain his emotions, taking in for the first time how very slight and fair he was, how soft his hands were compared to my own, which had known the hard work of picking cotton and scrubbing laundry. Perhaps he had never worked at all, I considered, and this cutthroat education he now had to take on was more than he had been taught to bear.

"Tristan, you will succeed if you honestly love flying. Is this even what you love or are you doing this because you are expected to?"

"I do love it," he said with emotion. "I really do. I just don't feel as though I belong. You are all far more accomplished than I am. But my father's legacy looms above me."

"Then there is only one thing to do," I said.

"What is that?"

"Tomorrow is Saturday. The senior cadets do not train until late morning. Can you come back and pick me up?"

"*Mais, oui*," he said without hesitation. "It sounds like you are doing me the favor. It is the least that I can do."

"Now there's something that we agree upon!" I laughed. "I will see you then. *Bonne nuit.*"

"*Bonne nuit*, Bessie," he said in return, smiling genuinely for the first time.

Before stepping through the inn's sagging doorway, I stopped and pulled a couple of sunflower seeds from my pocket and tossed them onto the ground. As the chickens pecked and squabbled loudly, I called over my shoulder in English, "Here you go, girls."

"What did you say?" Tristan called after me.

"Never mind. See you tomorrow morning at zero six hundred hours!" I replied in French.

"So early! Yes, okay, six o'clock." Tristan called back as he jumped back into the shiny Renault.

"Early bird catches the worm, isn't that right?" I directed this last question to my chicken-headed companions. There was a great deal of squawking and I smiled.

"Bessie come inside," beckoned the kindly old woman at the inn. Seeing me limping, she met me halfway as I hobbled up the slates. I threw my arm around her hunched shoulder and she became my human crutch. "We cannot have you all broken up. I made soup and baked bread for you, daughter," she smiled kindly. "It's vegetable soup again tonight! As you requested, I have spared your chicken friends."

PART TWO

CHAPTER 21

Tristan's Renault took fewer than thirty minutes to travel the length of my walk to school. When we arrived, I checked the giant schedule board hanging on a slate outside the hangar. There were no flights scheduled until zero nine thirty.

This gave us three hours. I looked in every direction to make sure that we would not be spotted, praying at the same time that our tire tracks in the sandy soil would not betray us. We ran a zigzag pattern to the building, laughing at ourselves as we went. "We would make terrible spies," Tristan said, and we shared a quiet chuckle.

Inside the unlocked hangar, rows of planes were perfectly aligned; their wingtips only inches apart, the rudders angled up like a row of shark fins. The twin-engine bombers were all muscle and grace, boasting two Le Rhône engines mounted on struts that were sandwiched between the two wing layers. The fighters were sleek and agile, like serpents with wings. I chose a Caudron G.4.

"Go on," I whispered, shoving Tristan forward.

"You are going to get us in a lot of trouble," he whispered back.

"Only if we get caught," I countered. "Come on, hurry it up. Make sure you step on the black roofing tile. There is plywood underneath. If you step anywhere else on the wing, your foot will go straight through the cloth."

I had listened to Monsieur Caudron tell the senior cadets in the class ahead of us that the wings were made of muslin in order to be flexible as well as lightweight. Like skin, this fabric was draped taught over a wooden skeleton of short ribs and long horizontal spars and, although fragile, the entire apparatus was as sturdy as it was agile. But the delicate wings suffered a vulnerability other than their fragility. In order to make the fabric weatherproof and stiff, the muslin was lacquered with layers of nitrate dope that was highly flammable.

"There are so many dials and gauges," Tristan lamented. "And look at the ends of these wings, just wing warping on this one; there are no ailerons."

"Do you know what the ailerons do?" I questioned Tristan.

"They allow an aeroplane to turn left or right."

"To roll left or right. They control movement about the longitudinal axis," I corrected. "But no ailerons here, this design is a throwback," I mused, more to myself than to Tristan. Instead of ailerons, lateral control was achieved by wing warping through cables and pulleys within the wing. The trailing edge mimicked the serrated edge of a bat's wing.

"First, you must get this thing started and then you have to land this sucker." I gave all but the last word of these instructions in French, not being able to think of a French equivalent.

He laughed. "What is this word, 'sucker'?"

"Never mind, don't get distracted," I said. "The reason for all the practice is that every aspect of flight is made up of only four fundamental maneuvers—climbs, turns, descents, and straight and level flight. If you can climb, turn, descend, and keep straight and level, you can make the plane do anything. All of the complex work we are about to do is made up of simple, fundamental elements.

"Pretend that you are on your way to fetch Greta Garbo, Clara Bow, or maybe Mary Pickford. You have to swoop down, pick up Mary, then skedaddle before Douglas Fairbanks realizes that Mary is missing. You want to return to your love nest with her. Get it?" I gave him an exaggerated wink.

"Ahh, now you are talking," he chuckled. The pale, unsure Tristan had become a bit manlier. Perhaps he had just needed the proper … motivation.

In the space of thirty minutes, we had flown all over Paris in our minds. We climbed, we descended, we flew straight and level, and we turned around a whole bunch.

"Time to practice our landing," I said. "I understand Douglas Fairbanks is pretty sweet on Mary. No telling what he might do if he caught up with you." I teased.

"We Frenchmen are great lovers. I am quite sure she would leave him for me!" he smiled suggestively.

"Right," I said, rolling my eyes.

Eventually, we switched seats, which meant it was my turn to pretend. I made my choice and we hopped into the G.3, a single-engine fighter from the Great War, the same kind that Tristan's father had flown. Long before the senior recruits arrived for Saturday practice, we had played around in all kinds of prototypes that were being tested, and before the first student walked through the front gates, we were back in the Renault and headed for the outskirts of Rue, our secret safe and our getaway secured.

"Tristan, you will be a good stick," I told him honestly.

"Ah, the stick, it moves the elevator, the horizontal tailfin, pitch, or movement about the lateral axis, up or down controlling climb or descent," he said. "This is correct, yes?"

"Sure is!" I smiled at him, genuinely this time. It was December, and in a month I would turn twenty-nine years old. I hadn't noticed until now, but Tristan must be at least eight years my junior.

"How do you know so much about all this, Bessie? You and I have not had our turn flying, yet you are so very good at making complex things easy to understand. Have you flown in the United States?" Tristan asked.

"I've never flown in the sky, but I have logged miles and miles of chair-flying. Every day last week, I arrived an hour or two early and climbed into those cockpits. When we finally go up next week, I will already have been, in my mind, where we are going to go." It was harder to manage the conjugations in this string of verb tenses than it was to chair-fly maneuvers, and I was relieved when I came to the end of my explanation.

"Say, may I pick you up on Monday morning?" Tristan said.

"That's very kind, Tristan, but no. I do my best thinking during my morning walk. And I like the exercise," I replied. "I should be healed up by then."

While our friendship was making progress, I still didn't trust Tristan entirely. Had he neglected to fetch me and if I had waited for him before walking to school, I would have arrived hours late. Better to save his charity for when my future did not depend upon his following through on his better nature.

"One more question, Bessie. Where did you get the notion to chair-fly, as you call it?" Tristan asked.

"Have you ever heard of the magician The Great Harry Houdini?" I asked.

"Oui, of course," Tristan said.

"Houdini is a master of manipulation of ordinary elements. With the snap of his fingers," I said, snapping my own, "he makes objects—rabbits, even people—appear and disappear. He creates optical illusions, and since we cannot explain what we see, we call it magic. But what we really see in his slight of his hand is what our imagination directs us to see, which is what he wants us to see."

Tristan seemed confused.

"I wanted you to imagine yourself flying the Caudron G.3. Once you have pictured yourself flying in your father's shoes, perhaps they will not seem too large to fill," I said, as the Renault rumbled to a stop in front of the inn. "You are never going to do it until you see yourself doing it. Your active imagination is more powerful than your passive fears."

"Who said that? Did Houdini say that?" he asked.

"Nope," I called to him over my shoulder, as I navigated the chickens that rushed out to greet me, "I said it!"

That afternoon, while reviewing my work for the following week, a notion that had been inching its way into my mind finally broke free and moved front and center. If I could inspire confidence in someone like Tristan, surely, after learning as much as I could here, I could teach others what I knew. The only optical illusion I'd have to create was to convince my people that they could fly.

That Monday morning, each student was issued goggles and a leather helmet. It was one of the proudest moments of my life. I refused to let a soul see me cry when tears pooled in my eyes. Thankfully, Tristan was picked to fly first, which gave me the chance to organize my thoughts. He had clearly made good use of his secret lessons and stepped on the black roofing tile at the base of the wing and clambered inside the cockpit as if he had done so a million times. Luc, the mechanic, was summoned and came sauntering out of the dark hangar carrying a battered oilcan to which he had welded a long tin straw-like spout. Luc went over to the engine, hoisted the can, and squirted gasoline into small primer cups that sat atop the cylinders.

"Ready!" Monsieur Caudron called out.

Sticking a rag in the back pocket of his overalls, Luc yelled, "Contact!"

"Hot!" Monsieur Caudron responded.

With a crouch and a hard turn of the propeller, Luc threw the giant prop into motion and ducked out of the way. The engine sputtered, then grumbled, and I felt the sand beneath my feet shift as the machine sprang to life.

Tristan and Monsieur Caudron maneuvered the plane into the wind. The idle engine was revved for testing before the flight. As the ailerons were checked, I could see the right aileron deflected up, while the left one faced down. Then, Tristan and Monsieur Caudron were off, racing down the straightaway along the length of the beach. The skid, a little pad at the rear of the aeroplane, went a little right then a little left. "Steady, steady," I heard myself saying. Seconds later, the tail rose then the wings magically lifted the aeroplane, suspending it in the air. My eyes followed the plane across the sky until it became a speck and then disappeared into the pale blue.

An hour passed.

I heard them before I saw them. They set up and landed on the beach, and I watched Tristan climb out of the front bucket seat first. I couldn't make out his expression fully, since his face was pointed downward. Had he done that poorly? I couldn't tell. I pretended to adjust my goggles and walked off toward the water fountain, hoping the space would allow him to slink off without having to face me.

Before I reached the door, I felt his slight arms wrap around my waist. Tristan snatched me up, lifting me off the ground, spinning me in a circle as he yelled, "Bessie, that was *génial*! Your turn!"

Monsieur Caudron nodded in my direction, confirming that it really was my turn. I wanted to run towards the plane, but I gathered myself and walked as sedately and seriously as I could. Although Tristan had completed a thorough pre-flight inspection only an hour before, Monsieur Caudron shut down the engine and had me do my own examination before taking off. I used my checklist, an inspection of parts and systems, just as we had been taught. Luc added fuel, the cork and float bobbed up and down, and I checked the new fuel level and secured the cap when he was finished. I sumped a couple ounces of fuel, checking to make sure there was no water, sediment, or contaminants. Finding none, I moved on down the list before Monsieur Caudron double-checked my work.

I poked about the engine, examining it for any obvious signs of defect. Finding none, I searched the wings for any tear in the skin. Then I crawled beneath the plane to check its underbelly, as well as the delicate skid pad that resembled a thick spade. Its job was to scratch itself into the ground, creating friction to stop the plane after landing. Although the beach worked fine for landing, there were necessary adjustments. Our tires needed to be reduced to about three quarters of the pressure per square inch of what it would be if we were landing on hard pavement. The tires appeared soggy, and they landed like pillows on granular sand.

Finding everything to my amateur satisfaction, I chirped, "Checklist complete."

"Well, then, climb in," Monsieur Caudron replied. I climbed into the front bucket seat, and he climbed into the rear, which would allow him to observe me as I flew.

Luc ambled out of the hangar, and Monsieur Caudron began, "Okay, Bessie, here are the rules. I will do the takeoff, but as soon as we are airborne, you will take over. Our controls are linked so that you can follow me and, later, I can feel you at the controls. If you want to speak to me, pick up the Gosport. This tube has a funnel at both ends, one for speaking, one for hearing. Okay?"

"Okay!" I barked.

"When we return, I will land, but throughout the takeoff and the landing, I want you to follow along with me. Place your hand on that big stick. It will be right there between your legs. Go on, do it, let me watch you," he said, flashing a row of small square teeth at me.

For the first time I noticed the tiny brown lines that separated each of his teeth, no doubt the deposits of the tar left behind from the hand-rolled cigarettes he enjoyed. The brown scars served to punctuate his odd smile. I felt intimidated, yet I did as I was instructed. I grabbed hold of the thick wooden stick. Greased with petroleum at its base, it rotated smoothly in its socket.

"You follow me just as if I put you on top of me. I will guide you and pull myself into you. I will place you exactly where I want you. When I am inside of you, don't fight me, just allow me," he said.

This was the first time that Monsieur Caudron had ever spoken to me in such an overtly suggestive way. Sexual innuendo dripped from each word, and I shuddered at the thought that he was sitting just behind me, and that at this moment he held absolute power over whether I lived or died. He had become a completely different man in the cockpit, and it caught me off guard. Sidetracked by the unexpected, I froze.

"Bessie, focus! You allowed me to distract you! Don't allow me, or anything, to divert your attention from what you are about to do. Ever. Do you hear me? This is a life-or-death lesson you are learning," he practically screamed.

Never having been put in such a position before, I hadn't realized how easily my emotions could be manipulated. I had admired him and trusted him with my life. The thought of his betraying that trust was still a shock. Yes, he had thrown me off. Yes, I had been distracted. I shook my head to rid myself of the whole moment, and I remembered the gratitude I had felt before now for his instruction. Whatever he felt for me, I was clear about one thing—he was committed to seeing me accomplish my goal.

"Now, place your feet on the rudders so you can steer," he demanded. "Each rudder pedal is connected by a cable and pulley to the tailfin of the rudder. Remember, on the ground your hands are useless for locomotion. It is the same in the air. Those pretty feet of yours are going to do all the work, so steer the aeroplane with your feet, not with your hands. Okay?" he repeated himself so that this instruction would sink in as deeply as possible. "You will hold the stick back tightly into your body, and as the plane gathers speed, the stick will come forward. Let it. The tail will fly itself off the ground, as naturally as a baby crawls, then walks, then runs."

While I had logged hundreds of hours of chair-flying, and even hangar-flying with Tristan, I had never experienced this foot-steering before, or the feeling of the tail simply lifting itself into the air.

"While we are flying, I want you to listen to the engine. You will get used to how it should sound. What does the strain of a climb sound like? How about the rush of a descent, the buzz of cruise flight? You listen to it purr or growl, and your ears will tell you all you need to know about the engine's performance."

I didn't know this either, but I nodded.

"I want you to listen to the aeroplane's frame too. The frame is like the plane's skeleton. If we are coming in too fast for a landing, the wires will whistle. If they are whistling a tune, we gently pull that stick back, pull our nose up slightly to bleed off a little speed, and she will settle into a nice hum again. Hum is good; whistle, too fast."

From below his seat, he produced a long metal rod that looked like a lance. "If the Gosport doesn't work, and I need urgently to get your attention, I will poke you three times in your back with this. At this signal, I want you to release both stick and rudder, and I will take over. Barring an impending catastrophe, you will be flying us. Any questions?"

"No, sir."

The threat of being speared through was quite enough, thank you very much. One jab, and he could have whatever he wanted.

"Seat belt?" he prompted.

"Check," I snapped it, as we had been trained to respond. I heard the big steel pin click into place as he secured his own. I pulled out my checklist.

"Bessie, this is why you have walked so far and worked so hard."

Luc had come back out again and was leaning against a fence post, watching as we got ready. Monsieur Caudron glanced his way, "Luc!" he commanded. "We are going flying!"

I eased my goggles down over my eyes and straightened my leather helmet. In the short seconds that it took Luc to execute Monsieur Caudron's directions, the weight of the moment settled in on me. I felt a surge of energy in my spirit unlike any I had imagined possible.

As he had done for Tristan just an hour before, Luc gave the propeller a forceful turn, and Monsieur Caudron kicked the warm engine to life. At the sound of the engine, I felt a rush of blood flow through my chest and then my brain, as though whatever had turned on in the machine had turned on in me. I became acutely aware of my surroundings, as if the world had suddenly turned from black-and-white to color.

Takeoff!

The eighty-horsepower Le Rhône engine grumbled and then roared as my heart beat wildly and my feet tingled as they felt the pedals beneath them. I had prepared for the cold of an open cockpit at altitude, where oxygen is sparse and the air holds a razor-sharp chill, so I had decked myself out in every piece of clothing I owned—a cotton undershirt, woolen pullover, thick overalls, thicker sweater, and stiff canvas flight suit. What I had not factored in were my smoldering nerves, and now the lower layer of clothing clung to my skin with the damp of perspiration.

Monsieur Caudron taxied us forward. We sat so low in the fuselage that we could not see a straight line in front of us and so we snaked our way along. Swerving left to look right and swerving right to look left, he moved us to where we could take advantage of the wind. During takeoff we were going to drive arrow-straight, directly into the wind, giving us more lift to grab our wings.

We were in position. Ahead of us was the straightaway of the beach. Monsieur Caudron pushed the throttle forward, and I got a snout-full of foul-smelling exhaust from the huge exhaust pipe that stuck up above the engine and ended in midair like an upside-down oboe. The fumes wafted away as we moved faster and faster.

The rickety axle between the twin front tires bumped and knocked as we sped ahead down the beach. Sand sprayed against us and the tiny grains pelted my face. With a third of the distance necessary for take off now behind us, the stick gently urged itself forward and the tail nodded up ever so slightly as we gained speed. At twenty-five miles per hour, the rudder was effective. Our feet danced on the pedals to maintain direction.

Just when it seemed like my brain was being rattled to bits inside my skull from speeding over bumpy sand clumps, we increased speed and, at fifty miles an hour, the pulsating wings came alive. I felt the engine surge as Monsieur Caudron tugged the tandem stick back, and with the nose pointed to heaven, the machine lifted and the ground fell away beneath us. No more beach, no more pulverized clamshells, no more rattle. Just smooth air.

Beyond the salt marsh, beyond the acres and acres of opal expanse of sand lay the mighty Atlantic. As we climbed, I could see past the Somme Bay and into the English Channel. At this height, the water, which was a cold steel-gray from the shore, became a deep, dark indigo and seemed to flow on forever in gentle, undulating waves.

My feet had been resting on the rudders since the beginning, and now my eager fingers grasped the stick. Monsieur Caudron had been maneuvering both stick and rudder, and just as if we were dancing, or making love, I followed his every lead. At first, we were doing the foxtrot down the beach, dancing fast—left foot, then right foot, right foot, right foot, then a little left foot on the rudders. But as we climbed through tranquil air, our dancing slowed to a waltz.

My palms were moist with sweat, my knuckles were white, but the resistance of the stick was gentle and there was no need to grab hard. Just the lightest touch made the aeroplane respond. Handling the stick felt more like caressing a baby than massaging a man. Same with the rudder. Kick it either way, and the aeroplane heeled off in the direction of your boot. "The pedal leads the stick," Monsieur Caudron had repeated over and over. These two, stick and rudder, were meant to work in concert.

Being aloft felt like nothing I could ever possibly have described. No sensual pleasure could top the feeling of leaving the earth behind. It was as close as I could imagine to what it must be like to actually go to heaven. I began to cry into my goggles and they immediately steamed up. It hurt to break the suction seal around my eyes, but I stuck a finger under the rim and wiped each eye and lens as best I could. Worried now that Monsieur Caudron would notice my loosened grip both on the rudder and my emotions, I glanced over my shoulder to catch a look at his face. His face, which had been so serious only minutes before, burst into a wide grin. I looked down and saw that he had let go of both stick and rudder.

"Whooooo-hoooooo," I yelled into the wind at the top of my lungs. No matter that I was in France, I let loose a whoop and a holla Texas-style—big enough to erase years of silence and full of the pure joy of doing what my brother Walter said he knew to be true. I was doing what I had been born to do. I was flying.

My joy was contagious. Monsieur Caudron's laughter soared above the engine, and it poured into my ears through the Gosport. It was as if he himself were experiencing flying for the first time all over again, just by witnessing my joy.

An hour passed in a blink. Soon enough, the stick was aimed at the center of the beachy air strip where the windsock showed that we flew straight into the wind. My boots followed as Monsieur Caudron thrust a heel-full of right rudder to counteract the aeroplane's left-turning tendencies. I cast an eye out to sea, where the tide was coming in and the bay was slowly creeping over the sand. Soon our air strip would disappear beneath the waves.

We descended slowly, and trees, rocks, and figures grew in size as we neared the earth. Finally, Monsieur Caudron set the two front wheels down on the ground, and the skid pad in the rear fished gently back and forth. We rumbled and bumped until friction on the skid's tail pad forced us to a stop.

Although others appeared unfazed upon our landing, I could not stop grinning. The muscles in my face were frozen into a smile, but who cared what I looked like? I felt joy. I felt contentment. There was no way now that I would ever be able to get enough of the rush I had just experienced. It was like a drug that brought on euphoria, and I would spend the rest of my life seeking it.

"Another cherry plucked," Monsieur Caudron chuckled as he sent me on my way.

That night in my dreams, I relived everything that had happened during the day. Monsieur Caudron's crude ruse—complete with its lesson—the takeoff, the floating on air, the landing on mother-of-pearl sand, the warm, genuine hugs from my fellow students at the end. It all happened again, just as vividly and with just as much joy. And the conversations in my dreams were, for the first time, in French.

CHAPTER 22

Dear Bess:
January 3, 1921

I received your last letter about your upcoming solo flight. I gathered your
Mama, Eloisa, Nilus, Georgia, and Walter together at my place. John said
that he would come next time. We have taken to meeting every Sunday after
church. We each bring a dish and your latest letter. Then we share your
adventures while we break bread! Keep telling your story Bess!

Love, Norma

Norma had once told me that my greatest gift to her was the gift of my family, and now that I was gone, the rest of my kin clung to her as if she were another sister. She had spent the months comforting my mother while trying to make amends on my behalf with John. "Instead of a lonely only, I have an entire tribe of Colemans," Norma had said, and her warm descriptions of life back at home made that clear.

I had intentionally left out of my letters some of the grimmer, Machiavellian details from flight school. By this time, only eight of us remained, the others having fallen away through some lack of motivation or act of disobedience. One young man, a slender Italian who spoke perfect French and did exceptionally well in class, suffered from such acute motion sickness that he had to withdraw. By the time he finally packed up and left, he was nothing but skin and bones, and the planes reeked something awful. And while I tried hard not to allow the young men who washed out of the program to unnerve me, the thought of me washing out made me shiver. I thought it just as well to keep these stories to myself so that my family didn't have to shudder along with me. A calm heart was required. If I could stay the course, soon I would be ready to solo.

"The weather is perfect," Monsieur Caudron said, appearing from a shadow that overhung the hangar. I had not heard him approach.

"Yes," I answered, looking towards the sky. He was right. Winter flying was spectacular. The cold, dense air of a December morning made the engine perform well. It was the perfect day for my first solo flight.

Luc and I dragged the Nieuport single-seater out of the hangar. Its fuselage was painted bright white, and the empennage and rudder were striped in the French tricolor of royal blue, pure white, and blood red. In the middle was an exquisitely painted red fighting cock. The Nieuports were chosen for solos, according to Monsieur Caudron, because, "in case you wreck them, it won't hurt me quite so much." The joke may have been funny to him, but I could barely manage a smile. It seemed like the wrong time to be bringing up a wreck.

As I walked around the aeroplane to inspect it, I began to tremble. I had walked thousands of miles in my nearly twenty-nine years, yet my knees had never before come in contact with one another out of fear. What was this? I was shaking and, at the same time, propelled forward.

"Are you ready?" Monsieur Caudron asked.

"Yes, sir," I said with a confidence that suddenly I no longer felt.

"You are going to make this a very simple affair, Mademoiselle," he said. "You will depart from the beach and fly in a giant rectangle. Once you give me the thumbs up that you are fine, you may go back and repeat this exercise two more times. After that, we call it a day. C'est bon?"

"C'est bon," I said, repeating his directions silently to myself.

You can do this. I told myself.

"When you are ready, just let me know," Luc said and took a deep drag on his rolled cigarette. He seemed a trifle more sympathetic than he had been before, perhaps it was all the talk of a wreck. He gave a little wave in my direction.

Take one giant step, I told myself. Do what you have been trained to do. And breathe.

I went through the steps of the preflight examination. While I checked the plane, I was breathing as deeply as I could, exhaling slowly, taking the time to put myself at ease. All the while, my anxious stomach grumbled in protest.

A bit ungracefully, I clambered into the cockpit. Settle, I told myself. Settle. The final review went through my head. On the inside left wall, the throttle and fuel mixture knobs were where they were supposed to be. Throttle meant fuel; the mixture knob controlled the ratio of air-to-fuel blended. A small box for maps and charts was mounted on the right.

"Shall I summon Luc?" Monsieur Caudron asked. He took an extra moment to look at me closely, and then stepped up onto the wheel so that he could lean in. He tucked a stray tuft of my hair beneath my leather helmet, and his hand was cool against my skin. I knew he felt my perspiration. He searched my face, making sure that he saw no signs that made him reluctant to turn me loose.

"Yes," I said. "Get him."

Luc came forward from where he had been waiting in the sun, and the other students moved forward as well. Each of them grabbed one of the metal wire hangers that were bolted to the frame and hung beneath the wing's tip. Taking care not to grip the fragile skin of the wings or the delicate flying wires which made up the network of thin steel cables suspended between the top wing and the bottom one, the boys dragged the craft into position. My plane's nose was now pointed directly into the wind.

I threw up my right thumb, as I had seen others do before me. And this time, I was the one who made the calls to Luc.

"Ready!"

"Contact!" Luc yelled in response.

"Hot!"

Using all of his weight, Luc clutched the top of the prop and heaved down on it to give the engine a start. The giant eighty-horsepower Le Rhône coughed, choked, then backfired in a series of pops as loud as a shotgun blast.

Three violent shots: Pow! Pow! Pow!

I had not been prepared for the sound and nearly jumped out of my seat. Luc wore a frown as he approached and instructed me to turn off the switch to the aeroplane's single magneto. Although he had already told me to do so, he hopped up and checked that I had turned the mag switch's little silver toggle to the off-position. If the aeroplane had been "hot" rather than off, what he was about to do could have cost him his head. The magneto provided the electrical spark to fire the pistons and drive the shaft that turned that blade of the eight-foot long propeller.

Assured, Luc knelt down beneath the prop. From where I sat, I couldn't see what he was doing, but I smelled fuel and heard a noise that sounded like a racehorse peeing.

"You didn't sump the fuel at its lowest point in the engine," Luc scolded me. "It had water in it. Cold last night, warmer this morning," he muttered, his voice trailed off in disappointment.

Luc held up a glass jar for me to see the offending evidence: giant dirty water globules sunk to the bottom of the jar, with fuel pooled on top. Water is heavier than fuel, and so big water droplets sank and lay there skulking at the bottom of the jar. While fuel burns, water boils. As soon as the water entered the carburetor, it made the engine backfire, hiss, and cut off. I slumped along with the droplets, feeling useless.

"I must have missed it on my checklist," I admitted.

"It was a mistake, yes, but one that you will never forget," Luc said.

It was the most I had ever heard him say. And he was right. I would never forget my mistake or my humiliation. I had followed my checklist, I checked the fuel quantity, but in my anxious state I must have missed the fuel sump at the bottom of the engine, the lowest point of the fuel system.

As I regained my composure, a thought popped into my mind. Yes, it was embarrassing, and it was painful to see my colleagues standing about, whispering to one another as they too learned at my expense. But so what? I was glad this was discovered on the ground and not in flight. Had I been taking off, water globules would have made the engine cut off in midair. As if carried on the wind, my father's voice whispered in my ear, "Don't stay inside your mistake. Take from it. It is already in the past, only carry its lesson into your future."

We sumped the tank till all the water was gone. This time Luc spun the prop, dove out of the way, and just like that, the engine throbbed, hissed, and then hummed.

I pulled out my next checklist, *After Start*:

Rudders clear—push left, push right, I looked over my shoulder to follow each movement. The giant tail fin swung left, then right.

Controls free and correct—the stick moved about in its socket. The ailerons dipped left and right as I commanded.

Mixture full/rich—the device that allowed a blend of fuel and air was set to allow the maximum amount of fuel to flow for takeoff.

All checks were good.

I gazed down the long strip of beach that lay before me, stretched out like a magic carpet that would lift me into the air. I thought about this moment, and a surge of emotion swelled in my chest, knotting up into a lump that plugged my throat at the thought of how far I had come in years and miles to get to exactly this spot—from Waxahachie to Chicago to the shores of the Somme Bay, and from washing laundry and filing nails to this.

I was about to solo.

I held myself completely still, waiting until the lump eased itself back down my throat. I swallowed hard. My mouth was dry and my mind raced. I grasped the stick with my right hand and used my left to slide my goggles in place.

Let's go, baby, I whispered to the Nieuport.

I accelerated. The speed kept building and the grains of sand pelted my face, but this time in a way that felt familiar. Soon the swinging silver airspeed indicator on the wing read twenty-five miles an hour.

The stick eased itself forward.

The tail lifted up.

The nose lowered a bit.

My speed was building.

At fifty miles an hour, I made a gentle sweeping motion and pulled the stick back tightly into my body, and the plane lifted itself off the ground.

I was flying.

I turned inland, afraid to defy Monsieur Caudron's orders not to fly out over the open water. Just as I had pulled the stick to turn, I pulled back too far, and I heard a sputter. Shit! Not now. Don't die on me now!

Just ahead I saw a hedge, or some sort of row of shrubs. At three hundred feet above the ground, they were not shrubs at all, but rather a row of pine trees. I gave my frozen hand directions: just release the stick a bit and aim for the trees. This way speed will build. Then just pop up right in front of these raggedy old trees. I knew this strategy was right, but my fingers were unwilling to follow my mind's directions.

"Wake up! Release your grip on that stick!" I screamed out loud at my disconnected hand. I held my breath, said another prayer, and lowered the nose, while shoving the throttle to the firewall. Full fuel flowed and the wind poured smoothly over the wings. I could hear the engine roar and feel the speed begin to build. I was headed for the trees.

In no time I had reached eighty miles an hour. I was trading speed for altitude. When I pulled the stick back, the Nieuport groaned, but responded. A second before I would have smacked directly into the top of the upper branches, my plane complied and hauled itself up and over the trees.

I looked down and saw my clenched white knuckles. I unfurled my fingers one at a time, only to reveal the imprint of my fingernails in the palm of my hand. The light crescents left by my grip were enough to remind me of Monsieur Caudron's command, which he had issued to me over and over. Light touch, Bessie. Light touch.

I sailed out past the trees, and the village of Le Crotoy sprawled out before me. In minutes I had reached an indicated altitude on the altimeter of three hundred meters, which was about one thousand feet. Maintaining my altitude, I made a left turn. This first leg is called cross-wind, and when I judged my distance sufficient, about a half-mile or so, I made another left to enter the downwind leg of my rectangle, followed by a third left turn to base. One more left turn put me on final approach. The finish line was dead ahead.

Learning to land had been a painful affair. Monsieur Caudron sat in the rear seat, while I fished, spun, and bumped us to smithereens over and over again. But the rule was that there would be no solo until he was thoroughly convinced that a student could land competently. If he had confidence in my ability, I would have to as well.

"Steady now, steady," I said aloud to myself. A flag of orange fabric on a pole shoved into the sand showed wind direction. The material was limp, which meant that there was a gentle wind of about five knots or so and conditions were favorable for an easy landing.

I had to remind myself to be calm and not to rush, but the excitement of my first solo landing and the anxiety of following my own orders made it almost impossible to breathe. I checked my descent. I was losing about six hundred feet per minute. With the airspeed bleeding off nicely,

I was just a few knots above stall speed, at which air would cease to flow smoothly over the wing.

Closing in on the distance, I let my instincts take over. I knew exactly what to do. I would push the stick gently forward in order to set the main front landing gear onto the ground, and then once the two mains were firmly in place, I would give it a gentle tug back in order to lower the tail skid onto the beach.

Then, out of the corner of my eye, I saw one of the boys inspecting his parachute. What looked like yards and yards of silk was unfurled in a long sloppy heap on the beach. Just as I began to lower the main wheels, a gust of wind caught the material and it floated up into the air like a giant mushroom. And that overgrown fungus was headed in my direction. Monsieur Caudron had seen it, too, and had taken off screaming and waving his stick in the direction of the boy and his parachute.

What I knew was that, in an instant, I had gone from being poised to have a perfect textbook landing to having a full-on disaster, and that the transition from air to earth had been interrupted. If that cloth so much as touched my propeller, it would get caught and pull me straight out of the air. If it were to float in front or on top of me, I would lose my ability to see and would have no idea where the ground was in relation to my plane. Monsieur Caudron began swinging his arms in wide circles, signaling to me that I should go around the rectangle pattern again.

In order to build up speed, I let the aeroplane's nose sink toward the ground. I was in a tight spot, and that spot was getting tighter by each fraction of a second. With only fifteen meters of air between the sand and the plane's belly, the fabric cloud was billowing and floating right toward me. On my right was a pier full of fishermen. Surely, I would sheer off the mast of one of their schooners if I could not raise myself faster. I tried not to think about the sunbathers scattered across the beach below.

I sliced left and prayed a solitary word, Jesus.

Looming in front of me, rising triumphantly into the sky, were the two spiny, carrot-colored turrets of the Castle Guerlain. The Paris perfume magnate had built the fiery-orange castle as a monument to his love-ly-smelling self, and now his massive Rapunzel towers stood perfectly in line to impale me.

My engine growled, black exhaust poured from the pipes. I clenched my teeth hard, aimed at the spires and, with meters to spare, I pulled the stick back, hard. I skimmed the top of the castle and thought for sure that I had snagged my belly on the spires, but I had missed the towers by centimeters. Everything had happened in less than the time it took to sneeze. There had been no time to panic.

At the end of the beach, I saw Monsieur Caudron on one side and Luc on the other with huge sticks in their hands. Either they had chased the boy away or had beaten him senseless, but either way it didn't matter. The floating chute was gone.

My breathing began to slow again, and my heart rate leveled out. I checked the triangle airspeed indicator and saw that it was at fifty-five miles an hour.

Check!

Stick slightly forward, the wind telltale showed that I was flying into the wind.

Check!

Within moments, the main front wheels were bouncing along the sand. I felt the rough bump and crumbles of a thousand clumps of seaweed and clam shells being ground into pieces, mashed down by my tires. My legs and bottom shook along with the rough ride. The stick was exhausted. When it could be pulled back no further, I returned the tail skid to the beach and the skid dug itself down into the sand like a garden spade, insisting upon a complete stop. The airspeed was zero, the transition from air to earth complete.

Monsieur Caudron hopped onto his motorbike and raced to where I had landed.

"*Mais, c'était supér ça! C'était incroyable!*"

"Well, thank you" I panted, pulling my goggles up and onto my helmet.

"*Ça va?* You okay?" he asked.

"*Formidable!* I am ready to go again!" I said at once.

"Again?"

"*Encore!*" I confirmed and pulled my goggles back down.

He acquiesced.

I went on to complete two more takeoffs and landings without incident—no pines, parachutes, nor castle spires. One landing was terrible—I bounced all over the beach and then fishtailed wickedly. Another involved much less fishtailing, but a lot more bounce. Each of them was ugly, but together, they got the job done.

Hopping out of the Nieuport after my last flight, I couldn't help

myself and reached back and patted the aeroplane on the side of its fuselage. There was no other way I could think of to express my gratitude to
this marvelous machine that had taken me into the air and back safely to
earth again. The taut skin shuddered in response.

I had learned many lessons from my first solo in that plane. Transitions
matter. Never ignore them. Don't overthink a problem. Let your mind
take in a situation. Decide on a course of action and commit to it. Trust
your instincts.

On my walk back to the hangar I turned and looked over my shoulder
one more time. I had flown that marvelous contraption up into the sky
and over the sea, and then landed it all by myself. I did that.

"Mademoiselle Coleman, please come here," Monsieur Caudron
called from his dimly lit office inside the entrance to the hangar. He
walked out just as Luc and my fellow students had finished gathering in
a wide circle opposite where I stood.

"It is your turn," Monsieur Caudron said, handing me a finely
sculpted wooden baton shining with lacquer. His voice was solemn, full
of the emotion that every person in the room shared. This was tradition.
I was to ring the bell and I was also to have my shirttail cut to commem-
orate the milestone I had just passed. It was the way of the flyers. It was
our rite of passage.

We stood in front of a giant brass dinner bell like the one that had
been used to summon us to dinner on the *USS Imperator*. I held the stick
firmly in my grip and then whacked that bell so hard that it wiggled on
its hinge. Then I hit it again and again.

"Once for each time I landed," I yelled, and then I hit it one more
time. "And that one's for the damn parachute!"

"Bess," Monsieur Caudron said softly when I had finally passed the
baton. "Once you have rung the bell, no one can ever un-ring it. What
you have done, no one can ever take from you."

His eyes smiled gently, and my own had begun to fill. When a tear
too big to stay put finally splashed against my cheek, Monsieur Caudron
reached up and brushed it away with the back of his hand.

"Okay, you know what comes next. Turn your back to me,"
he commanded.

Yes, one more ritual. The cutting of the shirttail, symbolizing that
the instructor, who sat behind you, no longer had to yank on it to tell
you what to do. I turned my back towards him and heard the sound

of his giant fishing knife as it was pulled from its leather sheath. As the tiny circle of my male colleagues tightened in order to better witness the momentous event, I realized that by lifting my overshirts I was about to be exposed. I had worked so hard to keep my gender from being emphasized, but now all that would finally fall away.

So be it. I took off my heavy Sidcot flight suit. It was a hand-me-down that a senior cadet had given me after he bought himself a brand-new leather one. The oil-coated Burberry protected against extreme cold, but the oil coating stank something fierce and held the inherent danger of being highly flammable. I unbuckled the neck and ankle straps, then unbuttoned the trousers and vest sections. The military-issue gear slid to the ground and piled up in a crumpled heap around my ankles. I stepped out of it, happy to shed it. A paper-thin, man-tailored shirt with faded blue doves that flew in every direction came next.

The front buttons pulled and splayed where the boy's shirt fit me too snugly around the bust, and the tail resisted coming loose from my denim trousers. I jerked hard to free the tail from my sweaty back. With all the excitement, I was wet with perspiration, and that made the thin cotton cling. I wished that I had put on a chemise. Even with my back to them, I could feel the eyes of my fellow male students inspecting every inch of me as it was revealed.

Monsieur Caudron held up the knife. He made a ceremonial plunge, slicing through material. I felt the cool shank of the blade glance the small of my back before he re-sheathed the knife and tossed it onto a nearby worktable with a loud clunk. With two ends of the material now flapping from his sagittal cut, Monsieur Caudron took an end in each hand and ripped hard. He hoisted the torn piece of material high in the air, and the scalp of victory flapped from his hand for all to see.

The men cheered loudly. "Well done!"

"Welcome!"

"You are one of us!"

Warm embraces and the kissing of cheeks all around followed the applause. Champagne flowed. For this fleeting moment, I felt entirely accepted, part of an elite group of humans who had taken flight. I belonged with the Wright Brothers and with Tristan's father. I belonged. But even so, this boisterous togetherness was not what I wanted. More than anything, I wanted to be alone to celebrate this milestone and so, when I could, I slipped away and walked out to where I could see the ocean from the fence along the airfield. What I needed was to pray a humble prayer of thanksgiving. I pulled open the fence gate, let it creak closed on its rusty hinges behind me, and walked down to the water.

The sea crawled towards me and then away. These beaches were home to merlin, nightingales, peregrine falcons, and swallow-tailed kites, but at this moment, a lone osprey screeched overhead and then hurtled itself into the shallows for an easy meal. Low tide was feeding time for harriers and prey alike. Another osprey shot down from the line of trees and joined in. Together the birds sounded like competing teakettle whistles, hushed only when they plunged.

I inched out to where the water lapped my boots and stopped to watch a tiny greenish-yellow seahorse bob along in the shallows, its little fins fluttering to keep it upright in a foot of sea swirl. I marveled at the tiny creature's will, the way it curled its tail tightly onto a stem of glasswort, swaying but not allowing the rush of swell to push it out to sea. This unlikely creature—delicate, thorny, with a dragon's armor, was small in stature but big in presence. And, like the seahorse, I too was an implausible assemblage—Texan, Negro, woman, flyer. But we shared more than our unlikely characteristics. What I had most in common with this ancient animal was resolve.

It had been a month and one week since I had begun flight school and at the end of each week, I had asked Monsieur Caudron how much my tuition would cost. Each time, he had put me off or would change the subject. It was becoming clear that I had become his charity case and, although I was grateful, I did not ever want him to think that I was taking advantage of his generosity. Determined to have the conversation, I cornered him in his office where he was working behind the desk. Closing the door behind me, I came to stand in front of him.

"Oui?" he said, without looking up.

"Monsieur Caudron, you have been very kind to me. You have taken me under your wing," I began. "But I do not want to take advantage. Please allow me to pay for my lessons. I don't have much, but I have saved for my own schooling."

He screwed the silver cap onto the pen he had been holding and placed it on the stack of papers before him. He leaned back against his chair and looked up at me.

"Bessie, *chérie*. I have never had a student like you before," he said, as though he, too, had been prepared for this conversation.

"It is clear to everyone that you want to be a flyer and that you are willing to do whatever it takes to succeed. You have studied and travelled and given up everything you have known. That is something few people are willing to do. I want you to do me the honor of accepting my patronage."

For the first time in my life, a man with power wanted nothing in return for his gift. "Monsieur Caudron, I am grateful. I don't know how I could ever possibly thank you, but I do know that I will never forget you or this gift. I am truly humbled."

"Let me tell you something, Bessie. Something I have not said to you before. Every pilot gets two bags when they start flying," he said. "One bag is filled with luck and the other is filled with experience. The bag of luck for the brand-new pilot is large, and the bag of experience is nearly empty. As you learn, you will fill up the experience bag, and at the same time your bag of luck will grow smaller. Are you understanding so far?" he asked.

I nodded.

"Okay. *Bon*. I want to be sure that you also understand that I am not suggesting you avoid all risks, because as I have said, you only learn by doing. But every risk you take should be carefully calculated. Never allow your ego to talk you into something that your skill cannot buy you out of. This is a lesson that I had to learn in the most painful of ways. It was because of my own arrogance that my brother was killed. He flew a plane that I had designed, a prototype that was not yet ready. I should have flown it myself, but my brother insisted on taking it on the test flight. The plane was not ready ... " His voice trailed off.

The thought of losing a brother while also feeling responsible for his death was more heartbreak than I could fathom. What if I had lost Walter? What if it had been my fault?

"Right now, you are in a period of what I call adolescent discovery. You are eager and you are dangerous. You will be presented with a situation, and a voice in your head will say, 'It can't happen to me.' That voice is lying to you. Crush it. And if you ignore my advice, it will happen to you."

When he finished, there were tears in both our eyes.

"Enough. That is enough for today. When I feel you are ready, I will tell you more. But for now, enough *ça suffit*."

I walked back to the hangar in silence, ignoring the calls from my fellow students who were ready to go in search of dinner. When I reached my wooden cubby, I gathered my gear and looped my satchel up and over my shoulders, hoping desperately that my bag of luck was chock full.

CHAPTER 23

What helped us neophytes survive to live another day of flight school was that our work was clearly defined—and limited—each day by Monsieur Caudron. We had a specific set of skills arranged in a specific order that we had to master. Each of these was described in a preflight brief, and while we had no choice as to which assignment was dictated, there were options as to how a task could be accomplished.

One day, the task was to find *Le Château de Rambures*. That posed a challenge, as there were dozens of spectacular castles in northern France. We were to identify this fifteenth-century *grande dame* first by pilotage and then by dead reckoning, and afterwards return to home base. "The fortress can be found west of Amiens and south of Abbeville, and the two cities are approximately fifty kilometers apart. Triangulate your position and the castle will jump right out at you," Monsieur Caudron had instructed.

The village of Abbeville still had charming cottages and its churches still had their ringing bells. In bleak contrast, the spires of the churches in Amiens had been blown to bits by German bombs. I could practically see the smoke and hear the screams of ten thousand Frenchmen, as well as the final caterwaul of Manfred von Richthofen's own disbelief. For it was here, not long after his seventieth kill, that von Richthofen, the Red

Baron, had met his fiery end.

Anton Fokker designed the lethal D.VII biplane, as well as the squirrely Dreidecker triplane, but von Richthofen gave life to the latter. Just as he painted his plane red, von Richthofen made the Somme run red with blood. Born the same year as I had been, von Richthofen was twenty-four when he made Squadron leader of the *Jasta 11, Jagdstaffel*— the allied squad of hunters.

It was heresy to fantasize about Fokker masterpieces. For Herr Fokker and Monsieur Caudron were locked in a ruinous, bloody battle during the Great War—Fokker's precision vs. Caudron's agility. Monsieur Caudron had said that the real battle was a duel of minds. Their fight did not begin in midair; it ended there.

Each student would be required to compare our hand-made charts and see what we had missed that others had observed. We needed to be aware of mountain ranges and their leeward winds, to be able to spot farms that could double as landing strips, and to follow ponds and streams that threaded their way to the marsh near the banks of our school. Straight ahead loomed *Le Château de Rambures*. The medieval fortress, which was the first in France to be entirely made of brick, sprouted out of a field of emerald grass. Its red walls climbed to a wide band of white halfway up, and then another layer of red. From there, eight towers and half-towers with roofs of black slate laid in a perfect Herringbone pattern, rose into the sky. Far below, a drawbridge crossed a dry moat.

Stretching my arm out as far as it would go, I reached over the side of the open cockpit and pitched out a rock I had wrapped in a magenta cloth. It landed right in front of the giant castle doors, and a puff of dust billowed up around it.

I still had plenty of fuel and the cold January sky beckoned. My impending birthday made me feel like celebrating, and so I allowed myself to do something that I had never done before. I wanted to fly, not as part of an exercise or trial, but rather for the sheer pleasure of it.

"At some point, you will have had enough experience and will feel secure enough in your abilities to enjoy the ride without thinking about the mechanical. When that happens, you can really notice everything around you. Not only that, you will feel tremendous peace," Monsieur Caudron had said.

In the open cockpit, the air flowed over the wings and over my head.

It was clear and cold, dry and smooth. At that atmosphere, the air was thin, causing me to breathe deeply and exhale fully. Without the swerving and turning, the wind was docile, like a breeze blowing over a baby carriage—quiet, soft; smooth and gentle.

Clouds, exquisite cotton-like puffballs cleaner than any that I had ever picked, surrounded me. We were told not to fly through clouds. The aeroplane had no instrumentation to determine the horizon once inside them, no way of telling up from down, down from up. A flyer could become perilously disoriented without that knowledge. This cloud formation dredged up a memory that I had not thought about for years

The day I turned eleven, Mama came home from work carrying a package. It was larger than a bread box, wrapped in brown paper and dark green string. She set it on the kitchen table, where I watched it hour by hour until dinner was over and I could look inside.

Even now I can hear the paper crinkle as I ripped it off to reveal the most exquisite doll castle. It was a hand-me-down that had come to me by way of Mrs. Joneses' girls who had either outgrown the toy or moved on to others that covered the floors of their pink playroom. The origin mattered little to me. All that mattered was that it was new to me, and that it was mine.

Painted marble white with a series of tattered purple flags that projected out of towers, it was the most beautiful toy I had ever owned. I played with it for hours at a time, peering through the tiny curved windows, raising and lowering the drawbridge that hung from tiny strings. There was no end to the adventures that I, as queen, and my sisters, as maidens, could create. For years, we lived mostly in the miniature world of our own kingdom, the citizens of which required daily rescue from one threat or another. With wisdom and the assistance of my faithful flying dragon, whom I had named Scales, I ruled with magnanimity and pride.

And now, far from the castle daydreams of my childhood, I was gliding through the land of real castles, all alone in a plane that I could fly myself.

But you can't glide along in fairyland forever. In the real world I found that I had been sucked up about three hundred meters by the updraft of a cloud. I slowed to a maneuvering speed of about seventy miles an hour so that any further abrupt changes in wind speed or direction would have less of a chance of causing damage to my fragile cloth wings. It was similar to driving on cobblestones. You'd slow down across a rough patch, then speed up as the dirt road smoothed out.

Climbing three hundred meters higher, I saw what seemed like a mirage in the clouds. From a mile above, the stratus swirls of circular towers and cumulous turrets grew into a massive palace, ten times taller than Rambures. The clouds slowly fortified one another, growing taller as I watched until they formed into the shape of my childhood castle. Where the purple banners had flown from my childhood castle, giant blue ribbons of sky now unfurled.

"Just what is a cloud, anyway?" I had asked Monsieur Caudron.

"A cloud is nothing more than visible moisture," he had answered.

And so it was, for the skin on my face and hands was dewy. The smell of the air reminded me of earthy wet rocks that one might find in a soggy riverbed and was nothing like what I would have predicted of the breath of heaven.

I had plenty of fuel but darkness would be falling soon and, although we had begun to study celestial navigation and I understood it in principle, finding the shore by the guidance of stars with only a wobbly compass for aid was not something I felt ready to take on. The tide was already coming in, claiming the shore as her own, and soon there'd be no place to land. Eventually, a black sky and a blacker sea would become a blur, leaving me no horizon whatsoever to connect my vision to the shore.

I pointed my nose toward the beach and opened the throttle wide, and as the sun plunged with gathering speed and the moon began its stealthy climb upward, I flew forward. But like Lot's wife I could not resist one last look back at my palace of clouds. In the distance, the clouds, my clouds, burned from the raging fires of the setting sun. My castle was being consumed as the purple-and-orange rays of light splintered into pieces its towers, turrets, and gables, plunging my enchanted dream beneath the horizon and consigning all that I had seen to memory.

CHAPTER 24

Dear Bess:

We greatly enjoyed your last letter and your story about your landings. How exciting! A bit of news from here: I reckon your three youngest sisters seem to be faring well, as your nephews and nieces are finding their way in their new Chicago schools. But I promised to always tell you the truth and the rest of your brethren is not quite as well. While I do not want to burden you, you deserve to know what's going on. Walter and Willie have lost another baby, which as you know, sours her even further and makes poor Walter's life a living hell. To make matters worse, John and Elizabeth have separated, and the news was very hard on Mama. Sometimes I think that she is quite lost here in such a big city and surrounded by so much noise and commotion. These are surely trying times. I am doing my best to keep everyone together. Please take care of yourself and come back to us in one piece. Until then …

With much love,
Norma

By the sixth month of my training, I had only spent money on food and my room at the inn. I didn't want to rush this experience, but I remembered the lesson of Langston and how not having enough money had thwarted me once before. Our course was a scheduled ten-month program, but in an effort to get as much experience as I could, I took all of the extra flying that I could get. If someone cancelled a flight because they were ill or ill prepared, I eagerly took their spot.

I had practiced all our maneuvers until I had them down cold, and as I did, Monsieur Caudron added more to our repertoire. From dead-stick landings—touching down with no engine—to simulated short-field landings, turns around a point, and figure eights, as soon as I mastered one task, there was another right behind it. My logbook pages were becoming softer and more wrinkled from use. In the end, I was able to cut three months off of my training schedule. Yet, as my program was drawing to a close, I grew more and more melancholy.

I began to think about what I would be able to do with all of this flight training when I got home. Would I truly be able to open a school and do for the Negro what Monsieur Caudron had done for me? Where in the world would I get the aeroplanes, the use of an aerodrome, and hell, even the students with money to pay for their own flight time? Now that I had wings, I was deeply worried that I would not be able to use them or take anyone under them.

My fantasy began to feel far-fetched. Either that, or reality had begun to settle in. There I was, within striking distance of everything I had ever wanted, with no way of knowing if the work would be valuable to anyone but me. It could easily be that my coveted certificate would amount to nothing more than a piece of paper with an official stamp on it. What good would it do me if I could never use my flight training to teach others? Often during the long walks to and from school, I began to sink into uncertainty, and rather than reciting checklists, reviewing maneuvers, or practicing French grammar, I pictured all the ways in which I might possibly spend the rest of my life. And none of them held a moment spent in an aeroplane. My dream had taken me halfway around the globe to a place I would soon leave with more questions than answers. I had begun to doubt myself and my purpose and, once again, I had come to a point where I couldn't discern my way. Not only that, but how could I return to an America that espoused racial discrimination after the freedom and generosity I had experienced in France? Although I myself had grown, the America I had escaped—the America that suffocated my dream—remained unchanged.

On some mornings, Tristan would pick me up. We traded moods. I was somber, he was cheerful. At times, he was painfully chipper. As we sped along in the Renault, he'd hum some dreadful French ditty while I tried to drown out my doubts and focus on preparing for my looming examinations. My final test would be given by an examiner from the prestigious Fédération Aéronautique Internationale and would take place in a two-seat trainer like the ones I had flown at first. To get ready, we returned to the Nieuport, with Monsieur Caudron riding in the rear once again. In the weeks leading up to the test, he had grown significantly harder on me than he was on Tristan, or any of the other students, for that matter. Before our very last flight, he had drawn all sorts of paint marks along the sand, making a series of targets on which I would need to land.

"No, no, no, Bessie. When I tell you to land on the white line in the sand, I mean it. If you must, you may land before it, but never after it. By now you should know this," he barked into the Gosport.

If one of my landings was more bumpy than usual, he would bellow, "Bessie, you could shake the pee out of, and the devil into your examiner by bouncing him along like that. So, don't!"

If I pointed out too many checkpoints along the way of a navigation flight, he would scold me. "Dear God, woman, you are going to drown the man in details!"

These days, it seemed as though nothing I did pleased him.

"What have I done to make you so dissatisfied with everything I do?" I blurted out after another of his tongue lashings. I had grown accustomed to being the teacher's pet, and his new disappointment was unsettling, to say the least.

Placing both his hands on my shoulders and putting his face within inches of mine, he said, "You are going to be tested by one of a dozen examiners, and to my knowledge, you are the first Negro woman that any of these men have ever laid eyes upon. They do not know you as I do, nor will they get to know you. They will not learn why you have come so far, nor hear of the admirable purpose you plan to pursue with your training. Not only that, they will not care. My hope is that the man who tests you will be fair and will want to test your skill. I pray that he can see beyond any of your physical characteristics, whether they are color or sex, and that he will not use you to make an example of why women should stay at home with their apron strings tied to a cook stove."

If he had meant to make me realize the gravity of the examination, he had succeeded. I understood for the first time what I was up against and why his attitude had suddenly changed. He was afraid for me and wanted me to be on my guard. I had felt confident enough to accelerate my training, but now I wondered whether this had been a good idea and whether my decision might make the examiners more inclined to fail me. I had already faced the anxiety that I might fail, but it had never occurred to me that I might be failed.

"Thank you for speaking so directly," was all I could muster.

Tristan and I went to work with renewed vigor. He declared that since we had begun together, we must finish together as well and that he was prepared to graduate with me—a surprisingly noble and unexpected gesture of loyalty in my eyes. We began our preparations for the three-part examination, which included a written test, an oral inquisition, and a flight test in the aeroplane.

"What do you do if you are flying and the weather turns dark and stormy?" Tristan rattled off.

"Land!" I said, and he laughed.

"Best answer, yet," he said. "Okay, I have a tricky one for you. What happens if lightning strikes your Caudron biplane?"

"You become a French fry in a basket?" I responded innocently.

"Humor from the gallows then, Bessie?"

Tristan had taken to driving his Renault to the inn and parking it next to the hens. From there, we would walk the nine miles to the beach together. This gave us plenty of time to prepare for oral exams.

"This distance is extreme," Tristan complained one morning. "But I can see what you like about the walk. We know how you like to talk to yourself. And there is no one out here to correct you," he teased. I elbowed him playfully.

On the morning of our dress rehearsal, Monsieur Caudron was waiting when we arrived. Already headed for the flight line, he called over his shoulder, "Bessie, you first, then Tristan."

Our instructions were succinct and precise. Take off, fly north at a steady airspeed, climb to fifteen hundred meters, and perform two stalls—a power on, and a power off—which were nothing more than mock take off and landing maneuvers completed with the great safety net of altitude. While a stall in the air sounds terrifying, it is a momentary condition, not a mechanical failing. A stall takes place as the critical angle of attack is exceeded, meaning the angle at which the relative wind strikes the wing no longer produces lift. Our task was to correct that condition, alter the angle of attack, and make the wing literally fly again.

Next, two steep turns—one to the right, followed by one to the left at a forty-five-degree bank angle, without vertical loss or gain of more than thirty meters of altitude. Completed, the two circles would resemble a figure eight in the sky.

Next, complete a chandelle—a one-hundred-eighty-degree slow, climbing turn while gaining one hundred and fifty meters of altitude.

After a few more maneuvers we were to return to the beach and make three landings, two routine and one simulated short-field landing as if landing on a shortened airstrip. Often, we would land in a farmer's field, and an ox, or its cart, could make the patch of grass beyond it useless. For that reason, we practiced landing "short."

We had practiced each of these maneuvers as a separate effort and would obsess over the smallest detail, whether in altitude, entering the wind correctly, or recovery procedures, but now we would have to combine all of these maneuvers with their various intricacies, condensing the entire lot into one thirty-minute, graded performance.

The test would be brisk, and like a musician during a recital, there would be no time to go back and correct wrong notes, or wrong turns. This was, of course, the opposite of what we had been doing. During my practice flights, when I wasn't crazy about my steep turns, I'd execute the turns again, and again, and again.

"Bessie, your turns were weak. Tristan, your landings shook my brain! We will take a break and do it again!" *Monsieur* Caudron demanded.

"Oh, good grief, maybe I should just go back home right now," I muttered to myself. "What good will a break do?"

Gloomily and without interest, I unwrapped my bread and cheese from their waxed paper, wondering all the while why the good Lord would allow food to be wasted on the likes of me. I hated feeling this way. It wasn't in my nature to wallow, but my anxiety was hard to shake. And it was getting increasingly hard to hide my dread from others. Pretending that everything was just fine when it was anything but was also not a skill I had mastered.

Feeling sorry for myself I glanced up when Henri, whose skills I envied, took off and headed west to begin his routine. Henri, a sculpted blond who was a native of the Brittany coast, was a natural pilot—effortlessly graceful, he also knew the territory cold. He could likely draw a perfect map while blindfolded. Henri had been flying Caudrons, Spads, Sopwith Camels, and Nieuports around these banks and shores since he had been a teen, learning at the knee of his father, who had been another one of the Great War heroes whose stories we had come to know. I looked down at my textbook as Henri climbed into smooth air, but within moments, I heard a loud crack.

The right wing of Henri's plane had snapped off at its root.

Immediately, the aeroplane began to spin violently in a column of its own air. And as it came hurtling toward the water, it twisted like an oak seedling in the wind. The propeller sheared off and spun like a saber, the blade striking Henri and severing his head. Broken wing first, the plane plummeted into the waves, disappearing beneath the surf.

We ran then swam the half-mile to the wreckage, which floated everywhere. Soon, the wail of sirens competed with our splashing and screams for help. Instructors, students, and medics all tried in vain to extricate his headless body. But what was the use anyway? Red water swirled around us, and the smell of fuel burned the back of my throat, leaving an oily film in my mouth. The taste of petrol and the gruesome sight of his mangled body, pinned inside the vice of twisted metal, made me retch like a dog.

Henri's death was the most horrific thing I had ever witnessed. Not only was the trauma the kind I knew would haunt me forever, but I had to face the realization that his fate could be my own. With only two weeks to go before my scheduled flight exam, I was now beset with the two most dangerous and debilitating foes a flyer could face—self-doubt and unshakeable fear.

After the ambulance and the priest had long since driven away, *Monsieur* Caudron gathered us together.

"Henri was an excellent student. We believe that a structural failure was the cause of his accident. However, if anyone chooses to walk away right now, you are of course free to do so, and I will understand. I lost my brother to this passion of ours." No one moved. *Monsieur* Caudron remained silent for a long while, as if unsure how to go on.

"I am not practiced at inspirational speeches. Producing flyers, truly talented ones, who love what they do is my life's work, and I do it well. I am quite confident that if you have made it thus far, you are well placed to succeed. In honor of Henri, we will fly no more today, but for those of you who return tomorrow, we will continue on."

I had no way of knowing who would be coming back tomorrow or even whether I would be one of them. With Henri's death we were now five.

Tristan gave me a ride back to the inn. We did not speak the entire way.

He broke the silence as we pulled up to the inn. "Shall I pick you up tomorrow morning?"

"Yes, thank you. I would like that," I said, although I was not at all certain I would.

"I will be here at zero seven hundred," Tristan replied softly.

I nodded my head in acknowledgement and climbed out of the Renault.

I crawled inside and put all of my books and checklists away in the bookshelf I had built over my wooden desk. I lay down on my sagging cot and prayed for sleep to come quickly, not wanting to see any more gruesome images from the day. I squeezed my eyes tightly shut and hoped that I would not dream of the propeller's cruel path as it hurtled towards Henri's elegant neck and golden curls. He had been the best among us and now he was dead.

CHAPTER 25

The next week was a blur. The five of us had all returned, and we rotated mechanically through our drills like sleepwalkers. Compacting all the moves into a routine that became more familiar in a certain way gave us a respite from reality. But the tragedy of Henri's death hung over us like a dusk that would never lead to dawn.

My flight test was scheduled for nine o'clock, June 15, 1921. I arrived at seven wearing my best khaki slacks, a wide brown belt and a snug white blouse. It was a little risqué but I chose a short-sleeved blouse anyway. I didn't want to invite distractions, but this was my tidiest outfit. At home in front of my smoky mirror, I had sprinkled on lavender and practiced making my cheeriest smile.

"*Bonjour, mademoiselle. Vous êtes Mademoiselle Coleman?*"

Seven minutes past eight. The man was early.

"*Oui, oui! Bonjour, Monsieur,*" I replied.

He was not at all as I had expected. I had pictured a crusty old man, maybe with a mustache and eyeglass, but this man was nothing like that. He was in his thirties, slight of build, with thick russet hair that was a little longer than was the custom. His most notable characteristic was a deep L-shaped scar on his neck, which ran along the length of his white starched collar. I wondered what had happened to the soldier who carved his mark upon my examiner's throat.

"May I get you a coffee? I've just made some," I asked him.

Kicking myself for sounding more like a waitress than a flyer, I immediately regretted putting myself in a subservient position. But it was old instinct hammered home by years of lessons in good manners from working in many a kitchen and laundry room. The question somehow oozed from my nervous tongue.

"No, thank you. I would like to get to work," he said curtly, and reached out his hand for me to shake. "I am Georges Morel."

"Enchantée," I replied and returned his handshake. I admired, and at the same time found his all-business approach intimidating.

He asked to see my logbook so that he could examine the record of all my flights, ground school lessons, and work that had led up to this day. He asked me several dozen questions and then, using the slate in the front of the classroom, he wrote another dozen in thin, precise cursive. I was to record my answers on a smaller slate of my own, and I had a moment of panic because my spoken French had become stronger than my written work. I read each of my answers over several times looking for any grammatical errors or misspellings, and there were plenty. I went about fixing each of them methodically.

Monsieur Morel had left me alone in the classroom, but every now and then I became aware of his eyes on the back of my head as he peered through the ten-inch-square glass window at the top of the door. After an hour, I heard *Monsieur* Caudron's footsteps and then the rapid-fire French of their conversation just outside the door. I couldn't hear every word and had to continually remind myself that I didn't want to. Managing the answers was more than enough. When I had finished, I put down my slate, folded my hands on the desk in front of me and stared straight ahead.

Monsieur Morel must have been watching, for he returned a moment later and pulled a chair up next to mine. While I tried desperately not to fidget, he silently read over each of my answers and then wiped the slate clean with a cloth.

"I understand that you learned French in order to come here to fly," he began.

"Oui, *Monsieur*," I said. "No one would teach a Negro woman to fly an aeroplane in my country, so I learned French and I came here for my training."

"This must have been quite difficult for you, *non?*"

"Being away from my family has been difficult, but the training itself and learning French has been well worthwhile since it's what was necessary in order to achieve my goal." I paused. "I suppose the hardest part was Henri's death. I think it made all of us take a close look at the path we have chosen."

I felt his entire mood shift. His shoulders sagged as if the confidence had faded from them; his voice grew softer. "I too lost many friends in the war. You never get used to losing your own. I still hear their screams."

For what felt like ages neither one of us spoke and, while the silence may have been soothing for him, it was painfully awkward for me. Henri's death was still fresh and raw. Dwelling on death, grief, and fear threatened to rob me of every bit of what little confidence I had left. *Monsieur* Morel eventually tore himself away from his memories, "I fought in Spads and Nieuports. But the Caudron G.3 became my personal favorite, and this is what you will fly today. So, if you are ready, let's see what you can do."

The momentary confession was over. My examiner, and all of his swagger, was back.

We left the classroom and walked over to the flight line. *Monsieur* Morel was silent while I completed a preflight examination, but he observed my every movement. "Are you ready to go flying?" I asked. He nodded in the affirmative.

I hopped into the front seat, and he climbed in behind me where *Monsieur* Caudron had spent hour upon hour looking over my shoulder and poking me with his stick. The takeoff was routine and in short order we were flying south toward our practice area, where I had memorized the hundred-mile expanse of flat onion fields and meandering farms that awaited us. I was still as nervous as a cat, and although the breeze was flowing around the open cockpit, I was sweating as if it were a summer day back home in the Texas heat.

I performed my program robotically until I felt a poke in my back. He gestured to the Gosport and I picked up the funnel tube. Over the sound of the wind, he yelled, "I will demonstrate to you a chandelle," which was the maneuver I had just completed, or perhaps botched. I relinquished my grasp on the tandem controls and, without adding any excess pressure from my touch, I let my fingers graze the stick and snuck my feet gently onto the tandem rudder so that I could feel the subtleties of his control inputs.

Monsieur Morel looked left and led the plane that way. As if by telepathy, the plane slavishly followed his lead. He added power with the throttle, raised the nose and then, facing a flagpole as a target, he smoothly climbed one hundred fifty meters in a steady one-hundred-eighty-degree, climbing, left-hand turn. Just above the speed of a nearly stalled wing, he finished the maneuver, and we were once again facing the flag, albeit from the opposite direction.

His turn was smooth, positive, aggressive, and determined. The entire maneuver was executed as the masterful exchange that it was intended to be. While consuming a minimum of fuel, the chandelle was designed to reposition a fighter above a target, without ever losing sight of the enemy. This man was a master fighter pilot and it showed.

Either to show off a bit or for the sheer joy of it, he initiated a gradual pitch increase, nose up, and began the slow but steady climb of a second chandelle in the opposite direction, while simultaneously changing the bank of the aeroplane about forty degrees. Steadily, he altered the tilt throughout the one-hundred-eighty-degree turn, adding power during the maneuver, and at the very end, he straightened out the wings, reduced the power, and achieved another perfect horseshoe turn that delivered us to yet another plateau one hundred fifty meters higher than the last one. Throughout the two giant turns, he had formed a three-hundred-meter vertical S in the sky.

He poked my back again and his voice roared through the Gosport, "Now you do it!"

I said nothing, fearful of ruining my concentration and breaking the spell. I tried to imitate his smooth, positive control in a chandelle. My flying lacked his purpose, but nevertheless, I tried to make my fingers and toes reproduce through muscle memory what I had just felt him do, and I sought out the sounds of the engine as it strained to its maximum performance.

I finished my chandelle and swung my head around to see if I should proceed with the flight. The words all students feared hearing from an examiner were, "The ride is now over. Return for a try later."

"Better. Not good ... but better," he yelled through the funnel tube. He flagged me on with a couple of flicks of the back of his hand.

I finished my program and was returning us to the beach when I felt his weight shifting from side to side in the rear of the plane. I turned just in time to catch *Monsieur* Morel, one eye closed, pointing his index finger as if firing machine guns at the cows below. POW-POW-POW-POW-POW-POW, he gestured. I knew that if he felt comfortable enough to hang off the side of the plane and mow down a few dozen cows with his finger guns, that I had probably passed my examination thus far.

One more test remained—landings that had to be completed to his specificity. The four huge Caudron hangars that looked like big white hat boxes littering the marshlands of Le Crotoy were getting closer as we descended. I waited for his direction as we approached. *Monsieur* Morel pinched his thumb and index finger, which was the sign for short. I would have preferred that my first landing be something else. Anything else.

With thousands of feet of beach to play with, he had chosen the most difficult task first. He wanted a short-field landing. I came in high then shut off the power. In a fit of anxiety, I put the two front main wheels down hard which meant that we skidded with the back of the aeroplane fishtailing all about the sand. We stopped with only inches to spare before the line that *Monsieur* Morel had previously gouged into the sand. He immediately began scribbling on his tattered pad of paper.

"So, you were trying to make me vomit on that one, eh," he said, in what seemed to be all seriousness. We were at a complete standstill, and the Le Rhône engine spit and coughed in response to my harsh landing. What I wanted to say was, "Well, sir, you asked for short and I gave you short." But that seemed unwise, so I said nothing at all. I gave my him my best placid look—blank eyes and a hint of smile. There. Take that!

"Give me two more landings that don't make me sick, and we can be done with this test," he grumbled.

It was hard to recover from his disapproval, but since I was pointed into the wind, I didn't bother taxiing back, but just took off and said another fervent prayer. Lord do not leave me now, I begged. I have come too far. I pushed the throttle forward, advancing it slowly—no more fast fingers, no sudden moves. The wind had picked up, and I whispered another silent prayer that these next two landings could be greasers. I just wanted to slide this plane right on down the beach, as if the path had been oiled smooth in anticipation of my arrival.

I flew a rectangular box pattern around the beach, and the next landing was smooth as glass. I turned to him and he flagged me again. "Go on," he said, "let's see if we can do that twice in a row." The third landing made up for a lot. It was smooth, if not smoother than the second.

Taxiing slowly, I returned us to the flight line outside the hangar. We bobbed along, crunching tiny mounds of shells and clumps of seaweed.

I cut the engine, and *Monsieur* Morel unfastened his seat belt, hopped out and, without a word, sprinted back to the classroom. I tied the plane down with the ropes that were attached to two giant tires, anchored by deep stakes that ended far below in the sand.

I hurried to catch up with my suddenly mute examiner. I had no idea what to think. My chandelle was not so expert as his, and the first landing was indeed a short-field and not meant to be smooth, but after that, I had set him down gently, hadn't I? But he hopped out of the plane so fast and just scooted off, as if I had offended him or as if he really were going to throw up.

He had gone immediately to speak to *Monsieur* Caudron. I could hear their voices coming from behind the closed door of the classroom. I put my ear to the solid oak door and strained to eavesdrop, but I could not hear a single word clearly. Their voices fell silent as if sensing that I was there, and I heard the sound of a chair scraping the wooden floor.

"Enter," said *Monsieur* Caudron.

I tried to gauge from their faces what was going on. I turned directly to *Monsieur* Caudron, but he looked straight down at the desk in front of him. I began to panic. Had I actually failed? Why on earth were these men not looking me in the eye?

With great ceremony, *Monsieur* Morel undid the buckles of a brown leather briefcase, reached inside and removed a stiff card from a stack of papers inside, along with a small bottle of glue, a smaller capped jar of ink, and an old-fashioned quill. He shut the case and buckled it again. He lay the first paper on the table and began to write with the quill. I inched closer as he began filling in the blanks.

He asked me my birthplace and date of birth. I told the truth about the former, and lied about the latter, making myself four years younger. Why not? The day of my birth, he recorded incorrectly as the 20th rather than the 26th. He then wrote the French word for January, *Janvier*. And the year he had been told, 1896. I started to correct him, but then changed my mind when I saw the two words printed below the date:

Pilote—Aviateur.

CHAPTER 26

I repeated these words to myself, first in French and then in English. I tried them on just as one would try on a suit of fine linen. Norma herself could fashion no finer wardrobe for me, and I draped myself in the title I had dreamt of since I was a child. My path had been uncertain and often harsh, but today, on this fine spring day, in the middle of the year, I had done something miraculous, I had earned a pair of wings, and my place amongst those who had received the prestigious FAI was forever to be brevet #18310.

Once all the blank lines on the license were filled, *Monsieur* Morel took the bottle of glue and ran a thin bead of sticky paste from corner to corner of my photograph, placing one more dot right in the middle, he then flipped the picture over and mashed my image firmly down with the heel of his hand.

I stared down at the face of the woman in the photo. We had had our pictures taken in anticipation of examination day, and although I had only just sat for the photograph, I was taken aback on seeing it again now. Just as in Jesse's drawing, the woman in that picture was a pilot. She was serene. She did not sweat profusely, nor did she suffer from a roiling stomach as I so often did. She was confidence itself in the sky—helmet on, goggles up, looking sideways toward something only she could see.

"Congratulations, Mademoiselle Coleman. You are now a member of an elite club. On this day, by the power vested in me, you have been granted a certificate of completion by the *Fédération Aéronautique Internationale*. We hope that you will exercise your privileges with great pride and even greater caution." Shaking my hand, *Monsieur* Morel smiled thinly. "Civilian FAI Brevet number 18310, will forever belong to you. You are the first American to achieve this civilian distinction."

"The first," I parroted, not out of disbelief, but rather because the fact seemed to need an echo. "I am the first," I said again.

"Congratulations, Bessie!" *Monsieur* Caudron beamed and shook my hand heartily before drawing me to him for a full embrace. He smelled of the sea and sky, and I breathed his sent in deeply, hoping to remember forever how he smelled. I knew that the overwhelming gratitude I had for him at that moment would stay with me for the rest of my life.

That night, Tristan and I celebrated in high style. He had passed his own examination and his suggestion was a night out at the *Pilote—Aviateur.* at 18 rue Victor Petit in the center of Le Crotoy. Part shrine, part local watering hole, this restaurant was all legend amongst flyers. I had wanted to go inside this place the entire time that I had been in flight school, but I had been too busy flying, walking mile after mile, and keeping a close eye on my dwindling savings to indulge. Now that I had my tuition money to live on, I decided to treat myself to a proper celebration. And it was well worth the wait. Inside the wood-paneled, candle-lit establishment, the lives and heroics of every flying ace who had ever graced the town were memorialized along the walls.

Tristan and I were directed to a table in front, where we could welcome other classmates and watch the people as they ambled by. Vacationers from Paris packed this tiny seaside resort. Children licked their ice cream, women in fancy hats pushed prams and chatted, and men sat in groups at the café across the street, smoking cigarettes and sharing an evening wine. They all looked as though they had not a care in the world. And for the first time in my life, I felt the same.

Tristan ordered us beer and the traditional mussels and fried pota-toes. The shiny black shells floated in a broth of garlic and wine and smelled deliciously of the sea. I ate and drank until I was stuffed. My emotions were full too, and I kept feeling as if I were going to cry. Not wanting Tristan to see how moved I was, I got up to study the pictures, posters, and memorabilia that covered every inch of the walls. Propeller models dangled from the beams that spanned the ceiling, and rudders hung along doorways. A faded photo of *Monsieur* Caudron and his brother Gaston, their arms around one another and smiles shining out, allowed their winged pursuits to remain immortal, a living monument to the brothers and their work.

Monsieur Caudron was an elegant pilot—smooth and artful. Each turn of the wing was fluid and had a graceful sweep. That day I had learned that *Monsieur* Morel was a different kind of stick. He embodied mechanical precision, as he had learned the ways of the dogfighter—kill or be killed. In the hands of *Monsieur* Morel, the plane was a warship. In the hands of *Monsieur* Caudron it was a schooner. How each man lived was reflected in how he flew. One brings everything to the stick and the rudder—love, passion, aggression, respect, anxiety, fear.

Among the many images of planes and the heroes who flew them was a photograph that took me by surprise. Upon closer inspection, it seemed to show a Negro helping to dig a propeller out of a field.

"That's *Monsieur* Eugene Bullard," said a waiter as he slid by, balancing a full tray of wine glasses with practiced fingertips. He winked knowingly. "He is quite famous here, you know. He was awarded the highest medal of honor for his bravery, the Croix de Guerre." I looked back at the picture. It seemed to cry out: Tell them that you saw me! Tell them that I was here! Or maybe that was just how I felt upon seeing his image—the world needed to know that he was real. That I was real.

Hours later, Tristan and my classmates were still singing. I bid my goodbyes and stepped out into the cool night air, the full moon lighting the way like a beacon. I started walking, following the wedge of light cut by the moon. When I arrived back at the inn, I staggered into the thatched-roof building, crossed the creaking, worn planks, opened and then bolted my lopsided door, and fell onto my straw cot. Dragging my rucksack close to me, I pulled out my certificate and stared at it in the moonlight.

The photograph of my face was a reflecting pool. In it, I saw my mother, my lost father. Walter was there. So too was John, his humiliation, as well as his dare. Norma's love shone through my eyes. Jesse was there, too. A thread of generosity went from one beloved friend and family member to the next, each of whom had played a part in what I now held in my hands—Mr. Abbott, Tristan, *Monsieur* Caudron, even the angel in the restaurant who had fed me on my first day in France. I saw an unmistakable pattern that led me to believe that my life had not been a series of random coincidences, but rather deliberate convergences directed by a merciful, loving God. As Mama used to tell us, "Every one of your steps has been ordered."

Two days later, Tristan picked me up in the Renault and drove me to the train station in Calais for the three-hour trip to Paris. My passage on a ship from Cherbourg to New York was not scheduled to depart until mid-September, which meant I had three months—and the tuition money *Monsieur* Caudron had refused—in which to do whatever I pleased. A summer in Paris sounded grand, and I intended to enjoy every second of it.

As the Simplon Orient Express pulled into the station, Tristan and I said our goodbyes. He pulled me to him and we shared a long embrace. I said a prayer for his protection, and I could tell by how tightly he clutched me that he feared for my life as I did for his. Finally, I pulled away from him and tearfully boarded the train, looking back only once. Alone on the platform, he looked small and forlorn. Steam wafted in front of the window as we waved through the thick glass that separated us. As the train pulled away from the station, I felt great sadness at the thought that I would not likely ever see my friend again.

During the next three months I ate, slept, and shopped under the Eiffel Tower's shadow. The *Moulin Rouge* had burned to the ground, but in its stead, copycats had sprung up, and I went to each one of the cabarets as they opened. I saw Mistinguett, who was glamorous and raucous, and I searched all over town to find a pink peignoir like hers, complete with trailing silk tassels and satin ribbons. This rosy extravagance was to be one of my gifts for Norma. It was almost beyond my means, but I could happily sacrifice a dinner or two to bring it home.

I flopped at a rooming house whose glassy black doors and giant brass knocker resembled every other ancient doorway along the stretch of aging houses in the Latin Quarter. The street was alive with bookstores, cafes, churches, restaurants, cinemas, and open-air markets. There were specialty shops for every conceivable need here, as well—cobblers to heel, jewelers to bedazzle, ateliers for the creative—all housed in glamorous boutiques and matchbox storefronts—and alongside them there were tiny places offering confections or tobacco.

There were even shops for things that I didn't know were a need. One elegant establishment sold nothing other than ostrich feathers. "Quills for pens, fans, or elaborate centerpieces for weddings. We will gladly decorate a room or a body," the shopkeeper grinned through unusually sharp teeth. He held up two plush plumes and in one dramatic motion crisscrossed them against my chest. One was the purest white I had ever seen. The other, blush pink.

Above the fitting-room door, a gold-leaf frame held a sepia photograph of Josephine Baker. Smiling from beneath a cockatiel headdress that pitched a two-foot spray of feathers, her private parts were hidden by a patch of spangled gems and her sculpted arms were bare, but her bottom was draped with so many ostrich feathers that an entire flock must have been plucked just to make her fantail skirt. The manager saw my eyes float up to the picture, and his did the same.

"I'd like to see less of your clothing, would you like to see more of my feathers?" he said revealing his jagged teeth for the second time. "You look like her," he leered, his beady hazel eyes travelling up and down my body.

This gaunt man with greasy, slicked-back hair was as slimy as his plumes were elegant. I did not turn my back on him for a moment, but gradually made my way towards the front of the store and told him regretfully that all the feathers were making me sneeze. I did so twice, with great exaggeration, and then ducked out the door and scooted down the alley to the safety of the busy street.

Undeterred, I still wandered into every shop that caught my fancy. I would leave my room after a breakfast of coffee and a freshly baked croissant, and I would return long after dark, having strolled through as many Arrondissements as I could, stopping every so often to rest in a rattan chair of one of the cafés that lined the sidewalks. I visited the Louvre and charged my way up the steps of the Sacre-Coeur. I stormed the magnificent Arc de Triomphe just to see what John had boasted about. The boulevards radiating from this monument dedicated to the French military under Napoleon made the seventeen-story-high structure spectacular, but what truly drew me to it was a stunt I had read about by one of the great French dogfighters. Charles Godefroy had flown his Nieuport Bébé right through the middle of the arch. With nearly forty-six meters between the inside walls, there was plenty of room to accommodate the Nieuport's eight-meter wingspan, but even with the extra room, what a thrill it must have been to duck down, gun the engine, and go whipping through. Even now I can imagine the sound of the flying wires winnowing through the arch, with the high-pitched whistle of a piccolo audible above the percussive roar of the crowd. BRAVO to the French flying machines.

CHAPTER 27

New York City
26 September 1921

I t was finally time to go home. The voyage home seemed shorter than the voyage out. Too eager to sleep on the last night at sea, I lay awake for hours, looking out at the starless sky. The first sliver of light began as a white vein along the horizon before bursting into a river of orange. Fire burned through navy. In the newness of first light, the Statue of Liberty's torch shimmered like a bundle of pavé diamonds.

I had not had my foot on land for more than a moment before Mama made her way to me and held me like a child. Mama's hug was fierce as she wrapped me up in her arms and then held my face in her hands. All around her and gathering like a storm, were reporters from *The Chicago Defender*, the *New York Amsterdam News*, and even the *New York Times*. The growing mob and their attendant photographers penned me in a circle and peppered me with questions.

"What made you go to France, Miss Coleman?"

"What kind of aeroplanes did you fly, Miss Coleman?"

"How does it feel to be a real pilot?"

"What's it like to be the first?"

"What will you do now that you're back?"

I created a past. I didn't specifically mean to deceive, but when the *New York Times* reporter asked for my story, I quickly stated that I had been a Foreign Legion nurse and had learned to fly in the Corps. Neither of which was true, of course. But I figured these aspirations carried with them a greater nobility than simply wishing to fly. Somehow, my actual story didn't seem as though it would be enough to satisfy this throng. So, according to my imagined past, I had joined a growing number of Negro expatriates who had sought refuge from racial oppression at home and had gone in search of a better life in France. And despite its colonial history, France had welcomed us. Now, while this was true for many Negro expatriates—scientists, artists, writers, musicians—I had a feeling that we were treated well over there because we were comparatively few in number and had brought expertise from America.

I wasn't ashamed of my background, but over the course of the weeks at sea, I had determined that my past might not inspire the support of investors, and I needed backers if I wanted to buy aeroplanes. There was just no charm in the truth—in picking cotton and taking in laundry. Besides, I had returned to a new world on that September day in 1921. The 19th Amendment—women's Suffrage—had been ratified just a few months before I had left for France, which meant that many women could now vote, but the price had been that white men had turned on their sisters, wives, and even their own mothers, causing scars that would take long years to repair. And the year before Suffrage, Congress had also passed the Volstead Act, to add teeth to the 18th Amendment— Prohibition—banning the manufacture and sale of alcohol. It seemed to me that compared with what I had just experienced in France, everyone here was on edge. Maybe they all just needed a good stiff drink.

Mama held onto my hand as reporters yelled and scribbled and photographers snapped away. The thin puff of vapor wafting above exploding flash bulbs faded as quickly as the fanfare that had surrounded my arrival. Eventually the reporters wandered off and Mama let go of my hand. In their wake I found myself alone with my mother, my pile of suitcases standing between us.

"I am proud of you. You shouldn't be ashamed of your past, nor of me," Mama said softly.

"Mama, I don't think anyone really wants to know about a cotton picker turned flyer. It sounds ridiculous even to me when I say it aloud," I whispered hoarsely. "And I need my story to inspire people to pay for a fleet of aeroplanes. Every flyer I know adds a little fringe to his story. It isn't real, Mama, it's just what we have to do to survive."

"But, Bessie, 'To thine own self be true'," Mama said, and the line from *Hamlet* stung.

Twice a year, the book cart had rumbled through town and, having saved her pennies, Mama had let me pick anything I wanted. Since the Grecian Nicholas P. Sims Library did not allow a colored girl like me past its august marble colonnade, this was my one chance to read a book. Sitting on the dirt floor in front of our tiny potbelly stove, I would read *Hamlet* aloud to Mama hour upon hour.

I resented not being able to stroll into the grand Sims, especially since it always seemed to be empty. I rarely saw anyone going in or coming out other than Dr. Jones, whom I had overhead talking with a neighbor about a lecture that he gave in the *lyceum*, a word which became a constant source of fascination to me. He boasted that the lyceum had a pressed-tin ceiling, rows and rows of amphitheater-like seating covered in plush red velvet, and a grand marble arch over the stage where he gave his lecture from a podium carved out of cherry wood.

I daydreamed endlessly about luxuriating in the lyceum seats while reading about Mary Shelley's Frankenstein, or *Othello*'s Moor, or even Kipling's feral boy who had been raised by wolves. I pictured myself at the cherry podium, my voice echoing as I read from the pages from Du Bois's *The Souls of Black Folk*, which I had had to read five times just to understand it, and I had wept each time I encountered the passage in which his infant son is refused medical assistance and dies. The story was as painful on the fifth reading as it was on the first. I had read *Uncle Tom's Cabin*, too, but I had rented it only once. The story made me furious, and I determined that none of that Tom stuff would ever be for me. After reading Fredrick Douglass's story of starvation and enslavement in *My Bondage and My Freedom*, I vowed that although I was not permitted to set foot in the Sims Library, I would allow my mind go anywhere it pleased.

In Paris I had gone each week to an eclectic bookstore called Shakespeare and Company that sat in the shadow of Notre-Dame and was a second home to expat writers and books lovers of all sorts. If the sky was my heaven here on earth, I had discovered that Eden had an address—7 rue de l'Odéon. And while the Sims's lyceum had been an apple that I was not allowed to eat, this bookstore was everything else in the Master's garden. Starting or ending my days here, I reveled in the vanilla scent of old paper and the weighty feel of the antique leather-bound volumes. I skimmed some and indulged in others, both of which deeply satisfied the bookworm in me. The store was packed to bursting, with not an inch of shelf space to spare, so duplicate books were packed onto carts outside, manuals were jammed in sideways around door jams, plays were stuffed in bins. Everywhere, shelves sagged beneath the weight of knowledge and pleasure by the pound. There were BOOKS, BOOKS, BOOKS!

Reaching into my largest bag, I rooted about for a book of photographs of Paris that I had gotten for Mama at Shakespeare and Company, hoping to distract her from the conversation about my newly invented past.

"Good evening. Miss Coleman?" A handsome pecan-colored man interrupted my search. "The crowd of reporters gave you away. I am Bill Whitaker and I am very pleased to meet you."

Mr. Whitaker and his wife were our New York City hosts and had been kind enough to offer to put us up in their Harlem brownstone. In a letter that arrived from Mr. Abbott on my last days in Paris, I had learned that he had arranged not only for these accommodations but for us to attend a special performance of the hit musical *Shuffle Along* where, on the following evening, I was to be the honoree.

We took a taxi from the midtown pier to our hosts' home, and while I was as polite as I could be, I was deeply disturbed throughout the ride. I hated that Mama felt that by denying my past I had also denied her existence. She had toiled for years to clothe and feed us, while loving us unconditionally all the while. In the blink of an eye, I had erased that reality by inventing a past that didn't include her. But there was no way to explain to her that it simply was not fashionable to celebrate poverty. If I wanted to reach my goals, I would have to leave my humble roots where roots belonged—buried deep.

I begged an early leave from our hosts and their two pampered toy dogs, who had taken a liking to me and followed me from room to room. Mama came too, and we changed into our bed clothes and tidied our things. Before falling asleep in our shared room, I gave Mama her other present. Never wasteful, Mama removed the brown string and wrap and folded both, saving them to be used again. Inside the smooth white box beneath the paper was a crystal bottle of Chanel No. 5 *parfum*, created by the haute couture French designer Coco Chanel. Mama refused to cry, but her top lip quivered as she reverently placed the bottle on the table by her bedside. "Thank you, Bessie. I've never smelled anything so delicious," she whispered. At sixty-six years old, and after a lifetime of doing without, this was the first perfume Mama had ever owned.

The next evening, Mama dabbed Chanel No. 5 sparingly against her wrists and behind her ears and we headed out to join two thousand Negro and white patrons who crowded the Cort's 63rd Street Theater to see *Shuffle Along*. "The *Shuffle Along* Premier," declared the *New York Times* review, "had the distinction of being written, composed, and played entirely by Negroes … and a swinging and infectious score by one Eubie Blake."

On that night, Ethel Waters, Paul Robeson, Josephine Baker, Eubie Blake, and Noble Sissle would earn cheers for their performances, but the final round of applause would belong to me. At the end of the sold-out performance, I would be invited on stage to receive an achievement award for being the first American, Negro or white, male or female, to earn civilian flying credentials from the most recognized aviation organization in the world.

I slipped the ruby-red dress, with its V-neck front and draped back that I had bought in Paris, over my head and let it slide down. Its low-cut front was modern and required no brassiere, and only an inch of fabric held the dress on my shoulders. The back fell away and pooled at the top of my buttocks; the rest of the rich and heavy fabric poured down around my ankles, trailing like a mermaid's fantail. A thousand sparkling sequins were sprinkled across the bottom of the skirt, sending confetti of light in all directions.

Racy?

Maybe. But then, this was New York City. I wanted to be as bright as the Broadway lights. I glanced at myself in the mirror above the dresser, and the gravity of the moment began to loom. My garter-belt grabbed slinky stockings at the tops of my thighs, and neutral colored T-strapped heels clicked beneath my train. I spun a blood-red bayadère scarf around my throat so that both ends cascaded behind me, popped on dangling red crystal earrings the size of holly berries, and then doused myself in French lavender cologne. I couldn't wait to show off to Norma, who would approve of the sumptuous fabric and the fine stitching.

Finally, I put on the headdress. It was the shape of a gentleman's bow tie, but many times larger, and constructed of sheer white lawn. At the center, a jeweled knot of rhinestones tied the whole blazing affair together. I swept the left side of my hair with the lower end and the right side of the headdress rose into midair. I sank the comb deep into my hair. Finally a bit of rouge, real French red lipstick, and Maybelline mascara, which at seventy-five cents had been a worthwhile splurge. I felt confident and was ready to greet the stars.

Our velvet seats in the balcony overlooked the stage, and we had a perfect view of performers and audience alike. Every number was met with thunderous applause, and when *I'm Just Wild about Harry* started up, the audience joined in to sing along.

During the closing number, one of the dancers appeared by my seat. She escorted me to the back of the theater, down some stairs, and through a labyrinth to the wings of the stage. Thick navy velvet curtains hung like midnight, and while the musicians began a song medley, the singers lined up to take one final bow. At the end of the number and to massive applause, Eubie Blake tried to quell a minute-long standing ovation that rang out in appreciation for his songwriting and composition. Reluctantly the crowd finally hushed, and speaking into the microphone before him, he said, "Will the illustrious Ethel Waters please to make her way to the stage."

Cloaked in a brilliant emerald gown and sparkling like new money, it was hard to believe that Ethel Waters had endured a life of poverty and abandonment. She made her way to the stage with the grace of an angel and nodded like a queen to Mr. Blake.

"I am thrilled and humbled," Mrs. Waters began, "to be in the presence tonight of a sylph, a spirit of the air. And it is with the greatest of respect and admiration that I present this lustrous silver cup to Miss Bessie Coleman, who has flown over the skies of Paris, yet on this evening is kind enough to do us all the honor of gracing us with her presence."

Blinded by white floodlights, I eased my way onto the stage. A year before, no one had known my name, but on that night, I sashayed out among the brightest stars that shone. Glowing in their acceptance, I received a silver cup and kisses from the great Ethel Waters. I embraced Eubie Blake and greeted the breathtaking Josephine Baker who stood behind him. The picture in the ostrich feather shop had not done her justice. Whether dripping in a sea of ruffles and feathers or mocking the casino gents when she donned a tuxedo and top hat, or even on the stage that night in a modest cloche, Josephine would be hands down the prettiest woman in any room. She was exquisite, with skin the color of honey glistening under pearly powder, eyebrows drawn into crescent moons, and a smile that flashed far brighter than the stage bulbs, which illuminated her from below.

My ruby dress slinked around my ankles. I slowed my walk to a strut, praying all the while that I wouldn't trip and make a fool of myself. I was so taken with these faces and the magnetic pull of their glamour, that it dulled my sense of everything else going on around me. And then, I heard it. The thunderous applause this time was for me! The love emanating from the crowd was so pure, so intense, that for a moment I could not breathe and just stared out into the sound and the light.

"Thank you for your generosity," I finally managed, trying to project my voice out into the audience as far as I could. I'd always had a deep voice for a woman, and in my mind I sounded as loud as thunder, but stage fright caused a squeaky mouse-like sound to leave my throat.

A ripple of nervous laughter spread throughout the theater. I felt it and my cheeks grew as scarlet as my gown. Mr. Blake came back on stage to my rescue, handed me a megaphone, and took the silver cup from my shaking hands. Holding down the trigger to amplify my voice, I tried again, "Thank you for your gen—" I took it away from my mouth, this time startled by the power of my own voice.

I extended my arm fully and examined the bullhorn head-on. "This thing is loud!" I shouted in my deepest Texas drawl, feigning surprise. "I could use this contraption in my aeroplane!" The crowd roared back with laughter, and the feeling of solidarity I had in that one moment made me feel forever connected to the throbbing mass of humanity that pulsed out there in the dark. I felt as if every one of us shared the same heartbeat.

"But truly, thank you for your generosity. It is an honor to be recognized by such a fine group of professional performers. Learning to fly has been a joy, and I want to share this training with members of my race. You see, flying doesn't depend on your gender or your color because the aeroplane doesn't know, nor does it care, about either. Your abilities are what count, and just as fear and hatred can be taught, so too can confidence and skill."

The crowd erupted in applause again. I wanted to continue but I divined that on stage, brevity was best, especially for a non-performer. Adulation was always short lived and being a bore was criminal.

"Before I go, I must thank my Mama, Mrs. Susan Coleman," I said, extending my left hand to the balcony. "She encouraged me to believe that anything is possible and to strive for more than was expected of me. A female Negro flyer might have seemed out of the realm of possibilities for a girl like me, but Mama didn't think so." The crowd got to its feet, and Mama was pulled gently to her own feet in the balcony. I waited for the applause to subside.

"This kind of thinking might not come naturally to a woman born of modest means in the Texas heartland, where I'm from, but it was the only way she knew how to raise us. So, this award is a tribute to my Mama, who also taught me that before I study the compass to find out where I am going, I should first seek deep within myself in order to be sure that to my own self, I stay true. Thank you, Mama, for teaching me to believe in myself and for making me the woman I am."

The crowd went wild again, but this time for Mama. All eyes were on her where she stood, lit by a single klieg light shining on her in the balcony. I passed the megaphone to a stagehand and used both hands to take my trophy back from Mr. Blake. I thrust the heavy silver cup high above my head and tipped it in the direction of where Mama stood.

Mr. Blake took the Whitakers, Mama, and me to the upper floor of a haunt on the corner of 142nd and Lenox Avenue in Harlem. We crept up the dark stairwell and then were led through a maze of tables of diners and bustling waiters buzzing every which way. We followed the length of a long oak and brass bar until it ended at a reserved table in front of a stage so narrow that it could have doubled as a church alter. It may not have been a church, but there were many of the faithful here at Club DeLuxe, where Mr. Blake was clergy and prohibition was a joke.

Jack Johnson, the World Heavyweight Champion owned the joint, and he hurried over to greet us. Thirteen years before, Johnson had gone to Sydney, Australia where he had pounded away on Tommy Burns, beating him in the Heavyweight Championship bout. Back then, Jack London wrote in the *New York Herald* that, "The fight, if fight it could be called, was like that between a pygmy and a colossus … Jim Jeffries must emerge from his alfalfa farm and remove the golden smile from Jack Johnson's face. Jeff, it's up to you! The White Man must be rescued." Johnson's blackness threatened and petrified his white opponents, white audiences, and white sports writers like London. Just two years later, Johnson and Jeffries met again in the Nevada desert, where Johnson beat Jeffries once more. I was nineteen at the time, and I remembered the headlines. Jeffries had been the Great White Hope, and the fight was dubbed, the Fight of the Century. But that hope was dashed with a one-two punch that knocked Jeffries out cold in the 15th round.

"My word," Mama whispered to me, "That Black Jack aged well!" I smiled in the dark in agreement. Johnson was just my cup of tea. If Michelangelo had seen him, the Italian master would have had to re-do David—out of onyx! But Johnson was also loud and arrogant, and that bravado was what kept him ferocious. It took more than talent, it took guts to beat a white man within an inch of his life with twenty thousand spectators watching, whether abroad or here on American soil. That he avoided being lynched was testimony to why coming north was the single wisest thing a Negro could do. Another attribute may have been more dangerous than any of that. I knew, as did everyone in the world, that Jack Johnson preferred the company of white women. Nevertheless, I felt that we had plenty in common. Both from Texas, both the first generation to be born free from slavery. He and I had burst out of the same slave shacks that had caged our parents.

Our styles may have been different, but we were both unapologetic and bodacious in our own ways. To be the first at anything meant being different, and Johnson was even more complex than he appeared. He was a pugilist, a stevedore, an entrepreneur, and a fine fiddle player to boot. After a few rounds of drinks, Johnson did not have to work hard to coax Mr. Blake to the grand piano waiting on the stage. The two began playing as if they had been rehearsing together for years.

By extension, we too became royalty, gorging ourselves on feast and drink, trying everything on the menu that appealed, and slurping champagne that rained down on us like water. When we were full to bursting, Mr. Blake took Mama by the hand and led her onto the dance floor, where he taught her the Charleston, and then the two stomped their way through the foxtrot.

"Oh, my word!" an exhausted Mama exclaimed as she plopped down like Jell-O on her cabaret chair. "I could never imagine!" She was winded and happy, and I had never before seen my Mama this carefree. Feeling her spirit soar, seeing her boundless delight made me as giddy as a five-year-old. Both of our childhoods, Mama's and mine, had been robbed of this kind of joy, and this was the first time we had shared a moment of unfettered happiness together.

The evening ended all too soon and we reluctantly said our good-byes. It seemed that just as quickly as our comet had streaked across the sky, it dissolved into dust. On the following morning, the Whitakers accompanied us to Penn Station where, like Cinderellas, we boarded the westbound train that would speed us back to Chicago and an uncertain future.

CHAPTER 28

I had settled into a smallish one-room flat of my own, two blocks from Norma's new shop. Its greatest features were its nearness to my best friend and that it had a giant southeast-facing bay window—the sunrises from that spot were glorious. I knew I was getting somewhere when *Aerial Age Weekly* did a story about me, and when the current issue arrived, I ran from my mailbox to my cozy window seat to read the words. "Chicago Colored Girl Learns to Fly Abroad."

They said I was twenty-four years old. I was twenty-nine! And evidently, was, "having a Nieuport Scout built ..." and "intended to make flights in this country as an inspiration for people of her race to take up aviation." Although there was nothing at that time that might have pleased me more, this tidbit was also invented.

"Chicago Girl Is a Full-fledged Aviatrix Now," read *The Defender*. The headline floated above the photograph from my license. "With the exception of Miss Coleman and a Chinese woman, all aviatrixes are white. A special Nieuport Scout plane is being built for her by French airplane builders. It will be sent here shortly. Miss Coleman ... will give aero-exhibitions in the hope of inspiring others with the desire to fly." While the latter was true, and I wanted to inspire legions, no matter how many newspapers reported that I was having an aeroplane specially built for me, it was a straight up LIE! There was no special construction and certainly no such plane was being shipped.

Nevertheless, the press persisted. Just a week later, another headline, taken from an interview I had given, read, "Aviatrix Must Sign Away Life to Learn Trade ... Walked Nine Miles Each Day While Studying Aviation." I had talked about how our Race men and women were behind in the field of aviation. I talked about how Japan and China were buying planes from the French and that fighter planes were outfitted differently from passenger planes. I also said that flying was safer than being in an automobile.

The many stories in the press, whether true or not, were responsible for one of the most precious correspondences I had ever received. I returned home one evening after a full day of interviews and discovered a handwritten letter of congratulations. The return address bore the name, Mrs. Ida B. Wells. I studied the return address. Only blocks away, I decided to thank Mrs. Wells in person for her kindness and after carefully re-folding the letter and putting it with my most cherished papers on my desk, I set out in the direction of her home.

Mrs. Wells, who had been born a slave in Holly Springs, Mississippi, had become an anti-lynching crusader. She was also a journalist and author, and I had decided to bring my treasured copy of her book, *The Red Record*, in case she would do me the honor of autographing it for me. *The Red Record* was a meticulous account of the gruesome lynchings she had either seen or covered in her journalistic work. It told in harrowing detail of the agony brought to countless human beings and their families at the hands of white men. And her writing not only shone a bright light on these brutal injustices, it simultaneously made her the target of the Ku Klux Klan and a hero among our people. I thought often of Frederick Douglass's letter to her, which she had included in her book:

Dear Miss Wells:

Let me give you thanks for your faithful paper on the lynch abomination now generally practiced against colored people in the South. There has been no word equal to it in convincing power. I have spoken, but my word is feeble in comparison. You give us what you know and testify from actual knowledge. You have dealt with the facts with cool, painstaking fidelity and left those naked and uncontradicted facts to speak for themselves.

Very truly and gratefully yours,

Frederick Douglass

As I approached her building, I began to feel overcome by the fact that I might soon be in the presence of a crusader, a woman who had made some of the most historic contributions both to our people and to the country. Mrs. Wells's courage and righteousness must have transformed her from a slave into a queen, for she lived in what appeared to be a real castle. I stood looking up for quite some time at the giant three-stories of granite that cast a literal shadow over the entire city block. The arched windows, columns, and friezes, along with the towering, window-lined turret made it clear that the person who commanded this home was as powerful as the stone cornices that loomed above the street. I carefully peeled open the shoulder-high, wrought iron gate and walked up the eight steps to the door. Then I turned and walked right back down again. I sat down on the bottom step. And then I got up and headed up the stairs again. How would this liberator, this journalist, this larger-than-life matriarch receive me?

I knocked on one of the muntin-paneled doors. A minute passed and I turned to leave. Just then, one of the twin grand doors swung open, and I spun around. The aroma of fried fish wafted past the doorway, swirled around me, and floated off into the street. There, standing before me, was Ida B. Wells. She was not, however, the Ida B. Wells I had imagined coming face to face with when I had set out that afternoon. Her hair was piled up in a high chignon, and she had a dusting of flour on one cheek. As she dried her wet hands on her blue cotton apron and looked me up and down, I grew embarrassed, for I had interrupted her dinner preparations.

"Oh, my goodness, how lovely!" she said, as though she'd been expecting me. She reached her warm hand out to shake my own. "I know just who you are! All four of my children are home for a visit and we are fixin' to have supper. Please do join us. You'll be another daughter and they will be thrilled to meet you."

Mrs. Wells was thirty years my senior, and Mama had raised me never to arrive at someone's home without a gift. I had brought along a small box of French confections I had saved from Paris, and now handed it to her. She smiled broadly, opened the door further to allow me in, and I followed her inside like a puppy. There was something in her motherly nature that made me feel as if I were her own.

The entire family embraced me in the same way at dinner. Their boisterous, loving conversation put me right at ease and made me feel as if I had been eating at their table since I was a little girl. The flaky fish tasted as good as it had smelled when it washed over me at the front door, and Mrs. Wells seemed to notice my appetite, for she served me a second helping that was even larger than the first.

Over dessert, Mrs. Wells caught me eyeing a framed photo of a hulking wood-burning locomotive that hung near the dining table. "That was the train I was riding when the conductor ordered me to leave the women's car. You know that story … "

"Yes, you refused outright," I answered without hesitation, still looking at the photograph.

"That's exactly right," she said, looking with me. "The trainman was embarrassed that I wouldn't budge. He commenced to harangue me," her thick Mississippi drawl lingered over the word *harangue*. "But when that bigot laid his hands on me, I did the only thing that I could think of—I bit him!" she exclaimed. "Nearly yanked a sour chunk right out of his arm!" She chuckled and we all did the same.

"After that, he had to get three other white men to help him throw me off that train! No way he was coming back by himself! People said I had courage when I sued the railroad and won a five-hundred-dollar judgment," Mrs. Wells went on. "But three years later, the Tennessee State Supreme Court reversed the lower court's decision. I didn't mind because I had already won. Fighting back meant I had won." She smiled at me gently. "You understand that, don't you, Bessie."

"Oh, yes, ma'am. I most certainly do."

Here I was, in the house and at the table of this great luminary, a woman who fearlessly stood her ground on a moving train as well as having stared down her own mortality at the hands of the KKK. Yet at the same time that she was a fierce revolutionary, she could cook the meanest piece of flakey golden-brown catfish that I had ever eaten. Mrs. Wells was a series of contrasts—complex yet simple; beautiful yet practical; funny one moment, then deadly serious the next. Not only a fearless crusader, she was also a tender mother to a brood of children and strangers alike.

Before my thoughts had a chance to settle, she asked me pointedly, "And what about you, Brave Bessie? What are your plans now? My good friend Mr. Abbott tells me you live up to that name and I assume he does not lie." She smiled and adjusted her topknot so that she could more easily lean her head back against her dining chair. Her sons and daughters stood up and cleared the table, as if to give us a moment alone together. Her grandchildren sat silently, concerned with nothing other than the big wedges of homemade pecan pie and sweet whipped cream they had been served.

"Well, I certainly don't feel at all brave compared to the kinds of things you have done," I said truthfully. "While I can pilot an aeroplane, I sure can't make a living out of it, which means it's unlikely that I'll be able to convince others to follow in my footsteps. So far as I can see, the only way to reach our people will be to spread my flying gospel as a barnstormer. It's the only way I'll be able to reach as many with my flying as you do with your writing." I explained that most newly minted flyers during peacetime were barnstormers, pilots who performed tricks with their planes to large audiences. The problem was that I had no idea how to do these tricks.

"Maybe not yet, you don't." Mrs. Wells corrected. "It seems to me that the solution to your problem is to go back to Europe, for you have a great deal more to learn."

Right then and there, we began to plot my next trip to Europe, including excursions to Paris, Berlin, and Amsterdam, which were home to the best aviators in the world. Mrs. Wells had been to Europe and traveled extensively on her own lecture tours. "War heroes honed their abilities as dogfighters during the Great War. They became masters in the art of aerial combat. You will need to find them and learn from them," Mrs. Wells said. "You will have to return to Europe."

Mrs. Wells offered logic and a plan just as I was starting to flounder again. I had begun praying that I wouldn't have to return to obscurity, that all my hard work and travel would not end in another barbershop or chili parlor. She felt confident that if I could explain my expanded plan to Mr. Abbott, he would be amenable to helping me once again. By the end of the evening, my belly, heart, and mind were full. As she walked me to the front door, I bashfully pulled *The Red Record* from my satchel and flipped to the opening page. Mrs. Wells smiled and took it from my hands.

"You brought this all the way over here for me to sign, honey?" She pulled a fountain pen from a vase on the secretary in the marble entryway and began to write in the book. I did not dare look at her inscription until

I was many blocks from her house, but I eventually stopped and under the glow of a streetlight read her swirling script:

"Bessie," she wrote, "I am so proud of you, daughter. We crawl about down here in the muck, while you have a pair of wings. GO FLY!"

CHAPTER 29

I began my second training tour in Europe with an advanced aerodynamics course at Le Bourget Field, seven miles northeast of Paris. *Monsieur* Caudron had introduced me by way of a letter to a friend, a war hero named Jacques Dumas. Dumas, *Monsieur* Caudron promised, was a first-class instructor from whom I could learn a lot. "Jacques is a good man, an exceptional stick, but he LOVES a good, thigh-slapping practical joke. Do not be surprised when he finds a way to make every one of his students the butt of his tomfoolery. Be prepared!"

Monsieur Dumas was slight of build and pleasant looking, with eyes the color of forest fronds and skin that had seen its fair share of sun, wind, and smoky spaces. I watched him carefully over the first few days, keeping my eyes wide open for some sort of booby trap, but as the weeks passed and nothing at all happened, I thought that perhaps *Monsieur* Caudron had been mistaken. *Monsieur* Dumas was a straight-laced professional and an exceptional teacher. As far as I could see, there was nothing much to him other than that.

"How do you like our loops and twists so far?" *Monsieur* Dumas asked one morning over a coffee.

"I love them!" I exclaimed immediately. I knew I needed a lot of practice to become good at them, but just going through the maneuvers at his direction had been a thrill.

"I think you are a natural," *Monsieur* Dumas replied. "About talent,

I never joke … Today we are going to learn about barrel rolls. Let us, begin," he went on.

With slate and chalk he illustrated how our job was to combine both a roll and a loop, forcing us to rotate about the lateral and longitudinal axes of the aeroplane. It was like an end-to-end cartwheel that finished in a loop, almost like a ball of yarn unraveling. It looked convoluted and it looked exhilarating.

"Let me explain further," he said, "We used to do this to force our enemy in front of us. Once you were on top, you'd shoot down the guy below like a fish in a barrel!"

At the recollection, his green eyes flashed. Every maneuver he taught was rooted in hunt, locate, annihilate. Even maneuvers with frilly sounding names, like whifferdills, were deadly. Dogfighters used this half-S turn to reverse course without losing airspeed before the kill.

He picked up his chalk again. He was a Leonardo da Vinci of chalk illustration, for every one he drew was a work of art. He used his artistic ability, as well as his skill at breaking down a complex task into simple parts, to demonstrate perfect loops, parachute jumping, and wing walking, all of which I eventually was able to add to my repertoire. It did not take long for me to realize that to call what he did stunt flying was an insult. He was a dogfighter, a master strategist in the art of evasive maneuvers, and his gift was in making those maneuvers look elegant and effortless.

"Now, let's try a barrel roll on the ground first," *Monsieur* Dumas declared. He led me over to an enormous oaken wine cask. "Hop inside so that we can demonstrate," he said. The wood inside smelled of a thousand hangovers. I felt drunk just inhaling. And that was before he began to spin me around with gleeful vigor.

The spinning went on for only a few minutes, but it felt like an hour. *Monsieur* Dumas had likely exhausted himself with the wicked rotation of the barrel, made heavier by my weight, but when he finally stopped, I had the distinct impression that he would have continued for longer had I been a bit lighter.

Dizzy and nauseated, I spilled out of the cask and onto the dirt, where I collapsed in a heap. At the sight of my crumpled body, *Monsieur* Dumas began to laugh, "Ah, Bessie, you are too funny!"

The sound of his laughter, which seemed somehow to push my nausea past the point of no return, was enough to make me vomit. And

I did—right onto his shoes. He just laughed even harder.

Nothing seemed to rile him, not even when I tried the actual maneuver and dipped the aeroplane perilously close to the Somme River, maybe even close enough to dampen the tires. "Okay, Beastie," he mocked my name, letting it echo through the Gosport, "You already puked on my shoes. Are you trying to clean them off in the river?"

We flew every day of the eight weeks that I was at Le Bourget, and by the time I left in May of 1922, I was a different pilot. "Learning to fly is all about how to stay out of aerodynamic trouble, but aerobatic training is about how to get into hot water and escape without getting burned," *Monsieur* Dumas had said. As my first aerobatic instructor, his artistry and flawless execution created a model of excellence for which I would always strive. I loved his generous spirit and the way in which he shared his knowledge without reservation. Yet, I feared his nature, for deep inside him was the instinct to lure, trap, and slaughter, and these instincts could exist simultaneously with his boisterous laughter. His smiles made the sharp corners of his mouth leap up and grab the edges of his eyes, which, regardless of their mirth, glowed green at the thought of the hunt.

CHAPTER 30

From France I went on to Holland. South of Amsterdam was the Universiteit Leiden, in the town of Leiden, the Netherlands. There, lecturers were propounding the work of Nobel Prize winners Madame Curie and Professor Albert Einstein, but while I would have loved to have listened to the latest developments in radioactive medicine, or the theory of relativity, the great mind I wanted to learn from was a certain Anton Fokker.

I slipped into a dimly lit lecture hall, claimed a seat near the front, and along with two hundred and fifty others, I waited eagerly for the guest speaker to arrive. Anton Fokker was to present a morning address on "Aeroplanes of the Future." Scientists, politicians, engineers, and professors had gathered here to listen to the talk. And so had I.

He was tall, well dressed in a vested herringbone suit, and carrying his papers in a leather attaché case. A spotlight followed him dramatically as he made his way from offstage to the podium.

"Aeroplanes will one day take us further than our wildest imaginations," Folker began. "One day, aeroplanes will fly five miles high, cross oceans at their widest spans, and use instrumentation in the cockpit that will allow them to circumnavigate the globe."

I was not only convinced, I was smitten—not by the man, but by his vision. Yes, he was charismatic and passionate, but it was the future he described that I could not get enough of. And those of us listening had good reason to believe him. Not only was he one of the most famous living pilots, but the synchronization gear he had invented and engineered had quite simply changed the course of the Great War. It allowed a bullet to shoot through the arc of a moving propeller, which meant that the gunner had the highest likelihood of striking the target rather than his own moving propeller. This invention revolutionized the way the Germans flew during the war. Fokker had sold his talents to the German Luftstreitkräfte to outfit its squadrons. Rumor had it that he had first approached the Americans, but without revealing how this mechanical device operated. Declaring his price too high, the Americans turned Fokker away. The Germans paid, and during the Great War, Fokker designed and built aeroplanes for Max Immelmann and Manfred von Richthofen, the Red Baron.

Thanks to his ingenuity and to the foresight of the German military, over the course of 1915 the Germans shot Allied planes out of the sky like skeet. All the other fighter planes were unsophisticated by comparison with the German. With machine guns mounted on top of the dash, the shots ricocheted off of tin, crudely smelted on the back of the propeller. It took a year, but when one of Fokker's planes was downed due to fuel starvation, the Allies pounced. They recovered and dissected the machine to learn its synchronization mechanism. This was a turning point in the air war because now the Allies, too, had access to Fokker's technology.

Fokker had shaped aerial combat in the past, and now I sat listening to him forecast the future. At the end of the lecture, I waited my turn in the line of admirers. I came forward, and Herr Fokker smiled at me, his eyes sparkling with good humor. We talked about his legendary D.VII and his plans to build a trimotor. Soon the hall emptied, but we continued to talk.

"Enough of my stories," Fokker said seriously. "Tell me about you. Why have you traveled so far? Certainly not to hear me prattle on."

I told him of my desire to be an aerobatic pilot. I told him of my humble beginnings in Texas and how I had learned French in order to complete my primary training at Caudron's. I told him of my desire to learn from him in particular. He listened intently all the while.

"Being an aerobat requires a great heart. You chase the elusive—you pursue demons or angels, and you demand that the aeroplane follow. You are the will, which means that the aeroplane becomes a prisoner of your desire, your passion, your temperament. If you are afraid, it will reveal your anguish. If your spirit is open, rapture awaits."

I grew still. I hadn't expected such poetry from an engineer whose aeroplanes dealt death. Once again, I was faced with the complexity of war. How could something involving such pain also carry within it so much beauty?

"Now," he continued, "you give me a life-changing, inspirational story, and what shall I give you? A thrill-ride that lasts for a moment? It doesn't seem equal, but it is all that I have to give."

A thrill-ride? I was sure I had not heard him correctly.

"It looks as if we are quite alone," he continued, glancing around the empty auditorium. "Perhaps you would like to see where I work. I would be honored for you to accompany me. Should you be interested, I could show you a D.VII … "

His shiny Mercedes was egg white on the outside, blood red on the inside, and it housed a souped-up aeroplane engine under the bonnet. A noisy, straight-eight-cylinder engine he had designed himself with a chain drive, the car was a speed demon riding on a sturdy chassis. At idle it growled; at cruising speed, it purred and, let loose on the open road, it would take me to see a real D.VII.

Like the endless emerald fields and dykes we traveled through, Fokker spread out his life before me. Although only two years my senior, Anton Fokker had been building and designing aeroplanes since he was an adolescent. He built his first plane in 1910, when he was twenty years old, seven years after the Wright Brothers' historic flight. The M.1 Spinne, the German word for spider, was modern in its day and years ahead in its sleek design, for it was a monoplane when everyone else was still designing biplanes. Young Fokker built his arachnid from scratch using bamboo rods and a cobweb of wires.

"Every famous flyer has a nickname, you know," Fokker announced with boyish delight. "We must think up a good nickname for you. I am the Flying Dutchman," he proclaimed, "named after Wagner's opera which is an ode to a phantom ship that never docks." I knew his nickname and how he had earned it. As far as I was concerned, everyone knew the tale. Fokker had been flying high his entire life.

"Well, if these aren't the pearly gates," I said, as we rolled up to a pair of fifteen-foot-high iron gates that guarded Fokker's sprawling factory. Maybe this wasn't heaven, but I heard the rapture of Wagner, violins cresting, horns blaring, as we skidded to a stop, dust flying just shy of a row of gleaming brand-new D.VIIs.

"I thought the Versailles Treaty made these illegal," I said, eyeing the plane's long fuselage and stubbed nose. It had a beautiful tail that fanned out like a hawk's.

"In Germany, yes, but not in the Netherlands. Want to give her a go?"

Out came one of his helpers. He handed me a flight suit to borrow and then quickly sketched a map of the local area for me, which mainly consisted of the roof of the factory and a bunch of fields. I took off and flew loops and barrel rolls. I was so taken with the ride that I lost track of the time as it slipped by, and that was a serious mistake. The heavier engine consumed more fuel than I had expected. A glance at the fuel gauge showed nothing more than a cork and a float, but I had to assume it was accurate. It was nearly empty.

I slowed down and, without stalling, I headed back towards the gold crown that was emblazoned on the factory's red roof. No more loops. Dear God, what if I run out of fuel and have to put this thing down in a field? I screamed at myself as I limped along. As luck would have it, I aimed for the airstrip just as the engine starved. Deadsticking the landing, I came down a little hard, but gratefully rolled to a stop. The fuel was completely gone and so were my nerves. The plane and I had both landed on fumes.

It was a mile walk to the hanger to get more fuel. I got it, walked back and filled up the plane, then drove it back to the flight line, still cursing myself all the while.

"I ran out of fuel! I've NEVER been out of fuel before!" I whispered to Fokker as he greeted me at the line.

He laughed a hearty laugh, "Listen," he said, clapping me on the back, "now you have a good Fokker story to tell!"

"Sure, but I could have wrecked your beautiful aeroplane!" I said, still mortified at the thought that I could have done exactly that.

"Well, you didn't! And the good news is that you will never run out of fuel again!" he said. "Listen, you are far too pretty ever to be a man, but if you insist on living amongst us, you must learn to think like a man. Learn from your mistake and move on. It makes a superb pub story!"

For the rest of the day, we stayed on the ground and talked about our plans for the future. Folker was planning on taking a trip to the States in order to meet Henry Ford. He admired Ford who, like himself, was both businessman and inventor, and Fokker wanted to see Ford's factories for himself. Folker intended to mint a second fortune by promising his future creations to adventurous Americans.

As we said goodbye, Fokker gave me a letter of recommendation addressed to Herr Robert Thelen, the famed German aircraft designer, who had been one of his colleagues.

"When you get to him, make sure to tell him your nickname," Folker said. "I will give it to you as a parting gift. You are from this point forward, the exquisite Daredevil!"

What made it painful to leave him was not so much the end of the grand adventure I had had at his factory, it was rather that I knew for certain that the freedom we had enjoyed during our time together, the ease with which a Negro woman and a European man could come together could not, and likely would not, be repeated in my own country. Although he had promised to meet me in the States, I was confident that our paths would never cross again.

CHAPTER 31

The Great War had left its stain on northern Germany, and in the wake of Allied bombing, castle ruins and skeletal hulks dotted the landscape. Like jagged spines, brick fireplace stacks jutted up from the fields and clung to the edges of farms. It had been four years since the Great War's end, but Germany continued to endure devastating inflation and hardship, and the great German trains, which had once run like clockwork, now struggled to leave or arrive on time. The train I took to get to Aldershof Airfield, where I had planned to meet the legendary aircraft designer of the Albatros Flugzeugwerke, Herr Robert Thelen, stopped some eight miles shy of the airfield.

So, I walked.

Fokker had explained that a dozen years had passed since Thelen had taken on and then summarily dumped Germany's first female licensed pilot. Amelie "Melli" Beese had suffered a mechanical failure on her second lesson, which had caused a crash. She recovered and returned to flying, but Thelen refused to participate in her training and said he would no longer instruct her. He had sworn off taking female students ever since, which meant that my acceptance would be a long shot.

An eager cadet ushered me to the hangar. Thelen, I was informed, was out flying and I would have to wait. Twenty minutes later, I heard the distinctive whir of an Albatross engine approaching—loud, grumbling, straining to stay attached to the fuselage of the aeroplane it overpowered. I watched as Thelen touched down smoothly and handlers scurried out to guide his wingtips. One of them looked at me, and Thelen began a slow, determined walk in my direction. He glanced once at an engine as it started. The rotating blade became a whirling machete just centimeters from his face, but he didn't even flinch. This man had no fear. I had seen this look before. The war-weary were not disturbed by life-threatening provocations.

I, on the other hand, had plenty of fear. I heard them before I saw them—what seemed like a full pack of snarling Rottweilers suddenly charging me from behind. The term "dogfight" flashed briefly through my mind. As they got closer, I could count them. Five. Their paws ate up the distance to where I stood. A Texas-deep survival warning rumbled in my ear. It had accompanied the warning Mama had given me since I was a girl. "Gal, don't never get caught out there on that dirt road by yourself."

Yet, here I was, out here alone with no protection. Around me were nothing but attack dogs, German soldiers, and loaded Spandau machine guns still attached to military fighters. I was alone, all right. I had finally strayed too far. As my hands began to tremble, I fought every impulse in my body not to turn and run like hell. Thelen was less than fifty feet and closing, his thick, round goggles glinted in the sun as he walked.

Thelen bellowed a command in German, and the dogs immediately stopped where they were, sat down, and fell silent. As he passed them, he said something else I could not understand and then came to stand directly next to where I stood. Looming inches above me, he stared me down with such intensity that I took a step back.

"What can I do for you?" he demanded, or at least that was what I thought he said.

I turned my eyes away from his dogs to face him and exhaled the air I had been holding in my lungs. The war might have been over for some, but Thelen had not surrendered yet, and his demeanor showed it. He ran Aldershof Aerodrome like the military installation it had once been, and it seemed evident that he would not have the patience to hear me blunder through an introductory explanation with the dozen words I knew in German. By way of escape, I decided to just hand over Anton's letter and to let it speak for us both. His steel gray eyes never blinked as he opened the letter. His massive, dirty hands tore open the envelope, staining the linen lining with oil.

It occurred to me as he read, that I didn't even know what Fokker had written about me. I had so thoroughly trusted our quick, intimate exchange that I hadn't thought to ask him to reveal his letter's contents. Looking up finally, Thelen said, "My old rival, Anton Fokker says that I should speak to you in English. It figures that he would ask me to put myself out for him ... again. Always the opportunist. I suppose he has conveniently forgotten our past. Now, what do you want from me?"

"I understand that you take good pilots and make them exceptional." I paused, debating as to how to continue. "I'm good. Or at least I have been told so, and I want to learn as much as I can from the best instructors in the world. They say you focus on the finest details. I want that." By the time I finished, I was shaking again. This man was more intimidating than his dogs.

Thelen snorted with what sounded like disgust and said nothing. Without a word, he turned and began walking back toward the aeroplane he had just parked. I remained where he left me, until he yelled over his shoulder in English, "Well, are you coming, or would you rather be my dogs' dinner?"

I hurried to keep up with his long strides. His men had emerged from the hangar to watch the odd couple—unlikely newcomer and grizzled fighter. He dismissed them with a glare and they went back to their jobs, fixing, polishing, preparing to fly.

"Have you ever seen one of these?" he asked, gesturing toward a plane.

"Not up close, but I think it's a Roland."

"Yes. Most Americans do not know this plane. It is an LFG-Roland CII, 160-horsepower, with a Mercedes III engine. A stupid, slow, heavy pig that would sink in a dogfight. But the engine is better than good," he said. "If you can maneuver this pig, then you can handle anything."

Thelen eyed me curiously. "Fokker likes checks issued by governments. But then he is also a leg man. Perhaps that was it." He put a quid of chew in his mouth, then spat, missing my shoulder by a hair.

The suggestion that Fokker's letter of recommendation had been given in return for a sexual favor was beyond galling, but as the fury rose up in my throat, I worked hard to suppress it. It was not the first time I had been accused of such a thing. But I certainly was not going to launch into a long-winded defense of what I had or had not done. If anything, this would make my story even less believable. As usual, I let the man concoct whatever story he needed. My outrage was nothing compared to my desire to learn what he knew. I swallowed hard, turned the heel of my boot into the dirt, pretending that his face was underneath it, and gave him my best expressionless gaze. I only hoped that his skill was greater than his contempt for women, his mistrust of Fokker, and his disdain for the German surrender.

He agreed to an assessment flight. And fly we did. Thelen had me execute every maneuver I knew and then execute them all again. The Roland had a five-hour range, and I had never before flown for that length of time. Nieuports and Caudrons were agile and lightweight, carrying only enough fuel for a couple of hours. I was mentally exhausted and chilled to the bone by the time we landed.

"I'll take you on," was all he said.

He handed something to one of his assistants who seemed to be in charge of managing me for the time being. After setting up a training schedule and payments, which included staying in the barracks connected to the aerodrome, I stumbled to the spartan dormitory and let myself into the tiny, windowless room. Despite my weariness, I couldn't fall asleep until I had wedged the top of the only chair in my room under the doorknob.

This German base, with its tyrant Thelen, his unquestioning devotees, and his menacing Rottweilers made me homesick for my predictably racist America. At least there I knew what to expect, and my fear was based on solid, concrete experience that had taught me what to avoid. The dread brought on by what I had encountered here was different. I wondered whether it was going to be worth it to be trained by a man who was so full of fury. He didn't seem to want students at all, let alone female ones, so I assumed he needed the money. Could I even trust him at all?

"He is nearly deaf," a young soldier confided to me as I walked to the barracks the next morning. "His years spent in and around these war birds robbed him of his hearing. He stares so intently because he is reading your lips."

Well, now finally something was making sense. Eager for more, I asked, "How old is he?"

"He's thirty-eight," the soldier said, backing away. Had he been caught having a private conversation with me, it might have been misconstrued as a betrayal.

As I suspected, Herr Thelen was younger than he appeared. After a war that he was still fighting, thousands of hand-rolled cigarettes, and a lifetime in the elements, he had aged at least one hard decade beyond his actual years.

Early one morning, I found Thelen fixing an old radiator. I had seen him doing the same on a number of occasions and knowing that he had made the transition from air-cooled rotary to heavier, beefier radial engines, it made sense that he would then have to do the unglamorous work of keeping them up and running. The bright side was that he was never more pleasant then when he was tinkering, and all the workers, from the lowliest cleaner to his assistants, seemed to collectively exhale when he was consumed by these tasks.

Thelen had an appreciation that was akin to reverence for mechanical precision. He finely tuned every aeroplane part by hand himself and rarely needed a second set of hands to assist. But on this particular occasion when he did, I was commanded to hold a radiator firmly so that he could work on it from an awkward angle. Not knowing exactly what to do with the silence between us, I cleared my throat so that he would be sure to hear me, "Herr Thelen, your English is perfect. Where did you learn to speak it so well?"

He flashed me a blazing look. Gripping in one hand the long screwdriver that I feared might become a weapon, he snatched the radiator carcass from my fingers with the other.

"You should always learn your enemy's tongue. And you should be sure to mind your own," he growled.

His searing rebuke followed. "Your barrel rolls are uninspired. Your figure eights are more like a giant letter B. You must enter the wind precisely, not haphazardly. Do not rush. Try counting to eight—you know, the way you Americans do it, one Mississippi, two Mississippi—go all the way to eight, before you roll out. Then fly decisively away from your maneuver."

He paused then added, "You Americans are lousy at geography. How in the world did you people ever find the war to win it? You probably don't even know where Mississippi is."

It had been more than a few weeks of this kind of assault, and I felt myself growing as irritable as he was.

"Yeah, I know where it is, Jack. It's Jim Crow east of where I'm from," I snapped. I may have needed what he had to offer, but I couldn't contain my anger any longer. His genius was exacting a steep price and I was running out of emotional funds.

That spring of 1922 in Berlin was raw and rainy, with a cloud cover that rarely seemed to give way to sun. Nevertheless, I managed to log seventy-six flights during the ninety days that I was at Aldershof which, looking back now, seems almost impossible to imagine. As my time and money began to dwindle, I made plans to leave, and although I had learned an enormous amount, I was more than happy to put this part of my education firmly in the past. I was not going to miss the daily humiliations and tongue lashings doled out by my cranky instructor.

"I did not expect much from you," he said out of nowhere one afternoon as we were working on another engine. "I figured you were part of a publicity stunt, or a practical joke designed by Fokker. But you are obviously truly committed to flying."

"It hasn't been easy," I responded.

"I know," he said, and for the first time he did something I had not known he was capable of. He smiled.

"You have teeth! I had no idea!" I shouted.

"Shhh!" he whispered. "Keep your voice down or the others will discover this, too."

At the sound of my raised voice, his dogs appeared. They trotted towards Thelen, then turned abruptly and sat at my feet. Whimpering and whining, and with their tails wagging, they trained their soulful brown eyes on me.

"What is this betrayal?" Thelen asked, his brow now a squiggle line of confusion.

I indulged in a self-satisfied smile.

"When I first got here," I explained, "I was terrified to go anywhere since I never knew when your bloodthirsty metzgerhunds would appear. And since the potted meat from the mess hall was unidentifiable as mutton or beef, and because it made me retch, I decided it might be worth more to me as a way to befriend your dogs. I carry a spoon of it with me wherever I go." I tapped the pocket on my haversack and the ping made the dogs whimper, they wagged their tails and were transformed into drooling, guileless goofs.

"It only took once or twice, but I'd pull out this spoon and sling a couple of dollops along my path. Once the dogs accepted the fact that I was carrying the food rather than being the food, I knew I would be fine." I batted my eyes playfully to soften what I said next. "In the beginning you snarled at me, too."

"Yes, I suppose I did. I was skeptical. And maybe I should have been. After all, you've turned my dogs into traitors!" He smiled for a second time. "I still don't understand why you sought me out in particular. Perhaps I never will understand," he said.

I rewarded each dog with a spoonful of meat and a head rub.

"I love everything about aeroplanes—how they sound and smell, how they handle and respond to anything I command. I love looking down on the earth and seeing a bank of clouds hug the fat thighs of a winding river. I love the feeling of control that comes from landing on a stretch of grass that looks like a strip of bacon from thousands of feet up in the air. I love that this machine doesn't know, or care, that I am Negro or that I am a woman. But in my country that was precisely and only what mattered, and I was barred from learning how to fly."

He nodded. Then, for what would be the third time in my life, a white man of foreign origin allowed his name and reputation to be used as an endorsement of my skill and ability. Thelen handed me a letter of reference that proclaimed without equivocation to the broader world, that I was who I claimed to be.

"I hope this will help you in your efforts in America," he said. "It is a record of our training." Thelen's record keeping was, of course, as meticulous as he was. Every single maneuver we had completed had been precisely documented, along with the dates and the weather for each flight time. His penmanship was impeccable; it looked as if a machine had typed each word.

"Thank you. I am humbled," I said sincerely.

"Your time with me is almost over, but there is one more task you may enjoy. A film crew from Pathé News is coming tomorrow to document the flight training taking place now that the war is over. A rather touchy subject for me, since your friend Anton Fokker stole my best pilot from me, but none the less … " Thelen grumbled. "Perhaps you can use such a film to your advantage. You are quite a novelty and they may be interested in filming you."

Though the term novelty stung, I was not about to let the slight keep me from such an opportunity.

"Yes, I would like that very much," I tried my best to sound casual, but the self-promoter in me was electrified at the thought of how I could use this film back home to spread the gospel of flying. I also couldn't let the comment about Fokker go by without at least trying to understand the rift. "So, he stole your pilot? Is that why you hate Anton Fokker so much?" I braved.

"I don't hate Anton," he answered. "The Red Baron, as you lot call him, started flying in my Albatros, which was a bomber, and it meant that he made most of his kills in my plane. But he became famous flying a Fokker. The truth is that my aeroplanes were good, but Fokker's were great. As you well know, the synchronization gear allowed bullets to fly through the propeller's arc. It was simple. It was genius. It was Fokker."

"Your machines had a different purpose," I reasoned. "No Dreidecker, even with three squirrely levels of wings could carry a two-hundred and fifty pound bomb. But your aeroplanes could. And they did." I felt the need to offer a consolation, but we both knew that while dogfighting maneuvers were becoming my expertise, war strategy was not.

"Oswald Boelcke, Max Immelmann, and Manfred von Richthofen became friends. They called their Jasta of the Luftstreitkräfte, the Flying Circus. Jagdstaffel, translated, means hunting squadron. But, Flying Circus? How did such a child's pursuit become a nickname for a hunt-and-kill squadron?" Thelen asked, then answered his own question. "It was because during the year that Fokker aeroplanes were outfitted with the synchronization gear, the German planes won every dogfight. A dog, as you have seen, Bessie, fights to win. He will fight to kill." He was right. I had seen that.

Thelen went on to explain that Boelcke, Immelmann, and von Richthofen chose bold colors to paint their Fokkers. Manfred chose red. "It symbolized the blood he spilt. He had probably eighty kills, seventy confirmed. That's how he earned the name, the *Red* Baron. Their choice of primary colors suggested a circus, and thus the name. But make no mistake the Jagstaffel meant deadly business. Boelcke was the innovator of some of the most lethal fighting tactics. Immelmann was known for his wicked turns to gain a surveillance advantage, but without Fokker's fighters to protect them, my machines would have been blown to bits," Thelen brooded.

"Caudrons, Nieuports, and the French Spads were all agile, but with his synchronization mechanism, Fokker created a German fighter that was both nimble and lethal. Although it may be painful, the truth is without dispute. German pilots who flew them were invincible and so, too, was their creator. History will memorialize Anton, while I am already a footnote," Thelen concluded.

"You are wrong, Robert,"—I dared call him by his first name, as well as contradict him—and before I bid him goodnight, I offered my humble, if not sophomoric, opinion. "I think history will remember you far more than you believe. You men are not happy without your war medals celebrating your kills. But history takes into account much more than that. Your engineering and designs will count for more than a foot-note in a bloody legacy. They will allow those not engaged in killing to travel great distances, perhaps even across whole continents. And it will be your contributions that made the way for that."

We were both lost in thought as we walked in silence to my dormitory. The dogs trailed a few paces behind and stopped when we arrived at my door. With a curt nod and a command, he and his pack turned and headed back in the direction of the hangar. I took note for the first time of his broad shoulders as I watched him walk away.

Early the next morning, I was fully dressed in the French tailored uniform that I had had made for myself during my first trip to Paris. Thelen watched me approach, lifted his goggles, revealing briefly the permanent grooves etched deep from the heavy eyewear.

"You look stunning," he said and walked in the opposite direction before I had a chance to say thank you.

The film crew arrived in two shiny automobiles, packed with men and equipment. Each ragtop was peeled back to accommodate the cameras, tripods, and other odd contraptions that poked out in every direction. Thelen met the entourage at the gate, exchanged a few words with a man who appeared to be the director, and then disappeared again. Apparently, whatever came next was not something he wished to play a part in, and so he had left the crew and me to figure out the details.

"You are the flyer?" the director tried in German. My three months in Berlin had allowed for a slight improvement in my understanding, but I still could not respond without stumbles.

"I am so sorry, I understand German, but I speak English and French much better," I managed in halting German.

"Ah, then, I am Niko Roth," he replied in English. Although good, his English was not flawless, but what I did understand was that he was interested in my story and thought that the best way to tell it was to show it—to show me flying. "People will believe what they see long before they believe what they are told," Roth said. "Let's get you into formation and then get it on this film," he gestured back towards the stuffed automobiles. "That will really do the trick!"

I had never flown in formation.

I glanced in all directions, hoping to find Thelen. Just as I was coming to terms with the idea that I would have to ask one of the other pilots to fly beside me, he emerged from the dusty shadows of the hangar. Gone were his formless baggy trousers covered in grease stains and snags. They had been replaced with sharply pressed gray wool jodhpurs and a brown leather bomber jacket lined with fur. His blonde hair had been tamed into a lake of waves. And one other thing had vanished with his old soiled wardrobe—I no longer felt his rage.

"Since you have never flown in formation, I figured I would teach you shadow maneuvers while they set up. I will show you a series of hand signs and wing signals and I will fly alongside you."

While the director unraveled cords and set up his camera and tripods, we retreated behind the hangar. We used a wide patch of dirt for our slate, and after each explanation in which I sketched the lines that Thelen had described, we acted out the maneuvers. He went ahead, arms extended, and I followed behind like a shadow, glued as tightly as possible to his every movement.

Without warning, he stopped abruptly in the middle of his demonstration, dropped to the ground and did an awkward somersault. Because I was literally riding on his heels, so did I. Dust went flying as we tumbled over top of each other, making me wonder whether we looked to onlookers as if we were doubles in a Charlie Chaplin movie. Laughing, he apologized for the mishap and helped me to my feet. While I brushed dirt off of my bottom, arms, and legs, he brushed a smudge off my cheek, below my eye, and then the dust out of my hair. In return, I swept his sideburns with the palm of my hand then tugged at a stubborn smudge on his earlobe with my thumb.

Somehow the act of grooming one another passed for affection. While I had felt no attraction before, there had been energy. Something in the way I'd had to win this war-wounded dogfighter had made me warm to him and feel protective of his injured spirit. And although he had taken me on reluctantly, and let it show, he had worked harder than he probably ever intended to shape me as an aerobat—a gymnast of the air.

We stared at one another for a long moment and then we each turned away, embarrassed by our newfound intimacy.

"So, where were we?" I said, brushing the last bit of dirt from my hands.

"Ah, we were discussing the entering, middle, and end of each step, fuel output for each part of the maneuver, where exactly the throttle should be—full forward, balls to the wall." He stopped himself at the crude reference. His voice was different. He was different, trying to fill the awkward space between us with directions and, uncharacteristically for him, far too many words.

"Why did you take me on?" I finally asked the one question I felt as if I really needed to know.

"I liked you," he smiled. "Wasn't that obvious from the start?"

"Well, not exactly ... " I whispered, and he laughed softly before he reached out and took the collar of my jacket in his hand. Pulling on it gently, he drew me into his arms for an embrace that I never imagined happening, and that I never wanted to end.

"Boss, they are ready for you," a voice called from inside the hangar.

That morning, Thelen and I flew in perfect unison. Was I his wingman, or was he mine? He was precision personified. While Anton Fokker ribbed me for my pursuit of perfection, flawlessness mattered to Thelen. In a dogfight, when you're trying to elude the enemy, being precise meant staying alive, scoring a kill. I was a long way from Thelen's skill level, but on that day, we flew together as gracefully as if we were making love. And in the end, I would have a brilliant piece of film to show for my efforts. Yes, a picture really was worth a thousand words, for while people may not have believed my adventures when they heard about them, they could never again deny what they had seen for themselves on film. At nearly a foot across, these heavy film canisters would forever be proof that I had once soared and looped over the ousted monarch, Kaiser Wilhelm II's Palace in Potsdam, Germany.

As Thelen banked hard and headed back to the patch, I followed his magnetic pull back to base. After our final landing, one of Thelen's men snapped a photo of the two of us. A cadet developed it and slid it beneath my door the next day. In the picture, I am staring straight into the camera, while Thelen is leaning in, lavishing a rare smile in my direction. It is this image that I carried with me from that day forward.

As my time in Berlin drew to a close, I began to think about ways in which I could thank Thelen for all he had done to teach me and mold me as an aviator. I had witnessed his frugal and resourceful nature and assumed that whatever he was saving for went towards maintaining his beloved aeroplanes. What small thing could I give him that would not be too much or too little, but would remain a simple reminder to him of our time together?

I rustled through my cardboard suitcase and found my long, white flyer's scarf. Norma had embroidered my initials into the layers of sturdy silk that for years had protected the nape of my neck against wind and sun, and from the chafing of the rough leather collar of the flight suit. Long before I had ever flown a plane, I had used the strength found in Norma's gift to splint my twisted ankle, allowing me to hobble back and forth to Caudron's. I wrote Robert a note and slid it inside the folded rich fabric:

Dearest Robert:

Your instruction has been one of my life's great gifts. Because of you, I have learned the difference between precision and perfection. Perfection is a vague notion to be chased and chased, while precision is an active pursuit. I promise that I will always seek precision.

You once told me that your "respect had to be earned," and I hope that I have earned it, for you surely have mine. Please accept this scarf as a gift of thanks. It was made for me by my dearest friend, and I pray that it will always protect you in the same way that her friendship has long protected me.

Yours, in eternal gratitude and from my heart,
Your Student, Your Friend Always,
Bessie Coleman

I wrapped the scarf and placed it, and the note, on the seat of Thelen's favorite aeroplane. He had nicknamed the grass green Albatross D.V with a black Maltese cross painted on the rudder, "*Claudine, die Ehefrau,*" which meant, Claudine, the wife. I had no idea whether Thelen had ever married, but since he guarded his privacy so fiercely, I never thought to pry. Had Claudine been his wife? Had she died in the war? The Maltese cross with its ancient roots in symbolizing the four cardinal virtues of prudence, temperance, justice, and fortitude seemed somehow to represent eternity. As I ran my hand along the side of the plane, I began to imagine a life other than the one I had planned. It was not unreasonable to imagine returning to France and making my new home there. In France, I would have access to aeroplanes as well as a public that adored aviators, no matter their color. And perhaps just as importantly, from Paris I could see Thelen whenever I wanted. Giving the aeroplane a last glance, I walked slowly back to the hangar. If Negroes were ever to gain exposure to the sight of other Negroes flying planes, I would have to be the one to do it. Even a future as appealing as one with Thelen in it could not tempt me from my path. I could not stay.

I prepared my belongings, making a hobo-style rucksack for the film canisters. I slung them low and tight across my back, but as the strap fell along the edge of my jacket, I felt something pressing into my side. I unzipped the lining and discovered I had been outdone. Thelen had left me a present, too.

I recognized his trench watch immediately. He was never without it. A Breitling design, protected by a heavy-gauge shrapnel guard on the front and back, the double-lug strap made it a thing of beauty yet, typical of Thelen, functional as well. On the steel back, a single-word inscription was engraved—*Flieger*. Flyer.

The leather smelled of Robert. I strapped it on my wrist.

The worlds we belonged to were entirely different and separated by an ocean, yet, for a brief moment, we shared an intimacy so great that those differences and distances were rendered irrelevant. As I straightened my bag over my shoulder, I had the realization that of all my singular encounters, Robert's was the one that had left me with the greatest and most varied of gifts. And as I pulled my coat sleeve down over the watch, I had the further realization that I would miss Robert Thelen for the rest of my life.

PART THREE

BARNSTORMER

CHAPTER 32

When the ship docked on August 13, 1922, a throng of reporters met me once again. Mr. Abbott had written to alert me that reporters from the *New York Times*, the *New York Amsterdam News*, as well as *The Chicago Defender* would be there, and that he would be there, too.

I felt more confident than I had after my first trip to France. While I had learned to fly at Caudron's, that training had been all about staying out of trouble. This time, I was returning from Europe after six months of advanced training. This time, I had learned the most aerodynamically compromising parts of the art. But more than that, I now had something to say, and I wasn't afraid to say it. I squared my shoulders and walked straight in the reporters' direction.

With the backdrop of a busy New York City pier—ships docking and departing, passengers scurrying, baggage being loaded and unloaded, seagulls screaming above our heads—the reporters rushed towards me. Without a moment's hesitation, I told them all that I was thrilled to be back home, and that after flying with Anton Fokker and training with Robert Thelen, I had come home with two goals: I wanted to be a barnstormer and I also wanted to open a school where Negroes could learn to fly.

And then, because I couldn't help myself, I added, "I plan on purchasing a dozen Fokker aeroplanes for my new school."

No one ever did challenge the particulars of how that purchase might be made. They merely reported it the way I had said it. Most of the barn-stormers I met had some sort of gimmick or had added a little extra to their own stories. They were part demigod, part showman, part hustler, and all of us did whatever we had to in order to keep flying. One flyer had a routine where he stumbled along, a drunken farmer with his pitch-fork, but when he tumbled into the cockpit, he flew entirely sober loops. Others stuck to their roots as military flyers, dogfighting an imaginary enemy, mounting Max Immelmann's turns, dive-bombing phantoms, reliving old battles for crowds who only wanted to be entertained in return for their quarters. Another flyer, named Roscoe Turner, flew with a live lion cub named Gilmore in the cockpit.

While I would never be a demi-goddess in the minds of the white American public, I had captured their curiosity, which was enough to get me some coverage. I was determined to take whatever fame I earned, or was given, and to use it to raise up my own community. And even though I laced my story with a few frills, my commitment to advancing my people in aviation was never a fabrication, and it never wavered.

The *New York Times* did write a story about me—"Negro Aviatrix Arrives." The article wasn't long, only three paragraphs, but it was strong and informative and bolstered my confidence. They reported, "Termed by leading French and Dutch aviators one of the best flyers they had seen, Miss Bessie Coleman, said to be the only Negro aviatrix in the world, returned from Europe to give a series of exhibitions in this country, particularly among her own people ... without instruction, flew a 220-horsepower Benz motored L.F.G. plane, winning for herself ... the distinction of having piloted the largest aeroplane ever flown by a woman." I smiled and slid my fingers across the face of my watch. I had Robert's Roland to thank for that accolade.

I watched Mr. Abbott beam like a proud father as he held the *New York Times* in his hands. We were in the lobby of my hotel, huddled over several newspaper articles.

"You planted this seed with the *Times*." I said to him. "I know it was you."

"You give me too much credit," he said, smiling proudly.

"Without you, there would have been no French lessons, no trips to France, no training on fancy machines. If anyone has been like a father to me in my life, it's been you." I said honestly.

"Well then, come now, daughter, you look skinny," Mr. Abbott was back to himself, in command of the plan.

The Defender's Harlem office had grown considerably since I had last seen it, and in the time that it took me to finish training, Mr. Abbott had built an entire editorial team. They greeted us heartily in the presence of Mr. Abbott, who had become the boss's boss. His affluence and prominence had attracted layers of editorial staff and ad salesmen.

We ordered sandwiches and, over lunch and coffee, Mr. Abbott challenged us to create "an event" the likes of which our people had never seen. The airshow and my barnstorming would be the obvious centerpiece, but we needed "bookends," Mr. Abbott explained. "An act that introduces Bessie, heralds her achievement, and then puts an exclamation point on her American Race story."

Although he was as complimentary as ever, some almost imperceptible change had taken place over the course of the conversation. It was as if Mr. Abbott was now only focused on addressing the reporters, and with this change, it occurred to me that while the show still revolved around me, I was no longer included in their planning.

"We want to show her beauty, charm, and talent, not just talk about it. This could be a grand opportunity for *The Defender* to be the first to proclaim this defining moment in history!" Mr. Abbott boomed.

And while I knew I had been important to Mr. Abbott, and that there had been real altruism in his generosity to me, I wondered whether it was mostly in an effort to add value to yet another one of his assets. I did not speak falsely when I said Mr. Abbott had been my champion. Yet, I stuffed down the ugly thought that I was becoming nothing more than a useful commodity to him.

Nevertheless, *The Defender* was much more expansive in its reportage than the *New York Times* had been. There were dozens of copies in the office. The headline read: "Bessie to Fly Over Gotham: QUEEN BESS TO RIDE AIR NEXT SUNDAY." The paper had me owning a Fokker, ordering several others, and even turning down an offer to fly in Moscow, "owing to Soviet Disturbances." I hadn't the slightest idea where this detail had come from.

Nevertheless, while we conjured up more ideas, a young copy assistant was busily tidying up the room around us, stacking newspapers and filing folders into steel drawers. When he had finished, he asked me for my autograph. I was thrilled. Someone had noticed that I was still in the room!

I preened.

"My uncle fought in France, close to where you took your flight training," the assistant said. I was new to celebrity, so I was busy thinking of something profound to write before scribbling my name.

"Where was he?" I stalled.

"Somme, France. He was a Harlem Hell Fighter. He was a New Negro."

"New Negro," he had said. While I was gone, almost every colored person, or Negro, had begun calling himself a "New Negro." While Mr. Abbott continued to urge us north and renamed us Race women and Race men, Marcus Garvey, the radical Jamaican wanted all of us, Caribbean and Southerners alike, to leave the U.S. and go to Africa. My brothers called Garvey, who fancied parades and a brigadier's hat, a "Crazy Nigga." But I thought that Garvey's description of "New Negro" had a rebellious sound to it. The term felt laced with anticipation—perhaps Old Negroes would be left behind while something big and better awaited the New Negroes? Although I did not want to be disloyal to Mr. Abbott's neutral term, "Race men and women," I too, was eager to make the switch. After all, I was a modern woman—New Negro, yes, modern indeed! Maybe Garvey wasn't so crazy after all.

"Young man, that's it!" Mr. Abbott proclaimed. I knew that look— Mr. Abbott had just hatched a plan. "There were four million Americans soldiers, of whom three hundred fifty thousand were Negro who served our country proudly. Their sacrifices have never been acknowledged."

Mr. Abbott added, "We will feature Bessie along with the local Harlem veterans of the 369th Infantry Regiment, the Harlem Hell Fighters, in a coming-home airshow. They have a drum corps, a marching band, and vets who would love to appear in full military regalia in order to get the approbation and gratitude they have never yet received. These men have had to stave off poverty and joblessness for the last three years. It's up to us to celebrate them for the heroes they are."

"Boss, this all sounds grand," one reporter braved. "But where on earth are we going to get an airfield? Who will lend us an aeroplane?" Jeeze, even the reporters appeared to suspect that published accounts of my aeroplane ownership was mere fantasy.

"Good questions, keep 'em coming," Mr. Abbott encouraged. "Money is green. We can rent Glenn Curtiss field in East Elmhurst, Queens, on Long Island, and an aeroplane too. At the end of the performance, we could sell rides. People of our race, up there flying around! Why, I can just see it! We will give the veterans of the Harlem Hell Fighters their due, while at the same time, we will lift up our very own angel—that would be you, Bessie!"

Once he made up his mind, the show took on a life of its own. With only three weeks to plan and promote, the arrangements had to be made quickly.

Mr. Abbott made most of the arrangements himself by telegraph. The reality of my fictional aeroplane ownership was simply a wee, teeny, tiny detail that no one had yet addressed, and so Mr. Abbott negotiated a price to rent an aeroplane, as well as all of Curtis Field in Garden City, Long Island. By now, news articles had been transformed into advertisements in *The Defender*. In big, bold, block lettering the headline read: "WORLD'S GREATEST EVENT! HEART-THRILLING AEROPLANE STUNTS BY THE ONLY RACE AVIATRIX. Her First Flight in America in Honor of 15th New York Infantry." Admission was $1, the ad stated, "with tickets on sale in the NY Office, UNDER THE AUSPICES OF THE CHICAGO DEFENDER—THE WORLD'S GREATEST WEEKLY."

According to this article, I had just returned from France, Germany, Holland and, now, Switzerland. And on top of that, I would be flying my own plane which was "made in Holland" and "doing tail spins, banking, and looping the loop." Then, according to the splashy ad, there would be "eight other sensational flights by American Aces."

This was the greatest exaggeration of all. There were not eight Negro flyers in the whole world, new ones or old ones!

When I told Mr. Abbott that my performance would be substantive, but would likely last all of fifteen minutes, he was clearly disappointed. He didn't say much, but before I knew it, he had taken the liberty of lining up one other flying act.

"I promise that you will be the star, but I have to give the people their money's worth," Mr. Abbott said. By the others, he meant the entire real world of New Negro flyers: me and three others—Captain Edison C. McVey, Hubert Fauntleroy Julian, and Eugene Bullard.

Bullard had war experience, McVey was a mechanic as well as a pilot, and Fauntleroy was a parachutist who flew occasionally, but I remained the only American—Negro or white, male or female, who had earned international civilian FAI flying credentials.

Part of me secretly pouted like a spoiled child. After all, this was supposed to be my introduction to the public, my grand debutante coming-out party. But later, I came to be truly glad for the introduction to McVey. He had been a mechanic for field troops in the U.S. Army's 95th Aero Squadron, attached to the Air Services First Pursuit where he had learned everything there was to know about finicky rotary engines. I was hoping that he would pass some of that knowledge on to me.

Anticipating thousands, Mr. Abbott had the aerodrome carpenter erect a split-rail fence between the bleachers and the airstrip. "A little crowd control can't hurt," he said, throwing in his own resources, both money and staff, into organizing buses from the Bronx, Brooklyn, and Harlem out to Curtiss Field. This caravan would take the 369th soldiers to Long Island, so that they could set up before the show, and then those same buses would return to Manhattan to pick up spectators for a fare of ten cents per passenger.

"'Sides that," Mr. Abbott said, rubbing his chin, "I will get sponsors to advertise on the buses and at the air strip. We'll plaster the inside and outside of the buses."

These expensive advertisements brought him more cash, as he convinced sponsors to sell their pomades and tonics to captive riders. According to the copy in *The Defender*, readers were to take the "Long Island Railroad from Pennsylvania Station, or Flatbush Avenue, Brooklyn, to Garden City or Mineola, [where there would be] Sightseeing Buses to the Field." Or, spectators could take *Defender* buses that left from its Harlem offices every fifteen minutes between noon and 2:30 p.m.

And so, the show was booked. It was scheduled for Sunday, August 27, 1922. And that was that!

Meanwhile, Mr. Abbott secured a commitment from the 369th Infantry Regiment, called the Men of Bronze, or the Black Rattlers, who were earlier known as the 15th Infantry Regiment, or the Harlem Hell Fighters. He rounded up scores of war heroes, or "Doughboys clad in overseas togs," as Mr. Abbott called them. As part of a grand ceremony these warriors would be honored with *The Defender* Medal of Honor, a special bronze memento, to celebrate each man's dignity, valor, and contribution to the Nation.

At the end of one of our longest days of planning, Mr. Abbott suggested that we get dinner—just the two of us. A steady rain had begun, so we sprinted to the closest lunch car we could find. Just as we slid into our booth, thunder boomed, and the clouds released sheets of rain, casting dark shadows against the walls around us. The early-bird special of chicken and waffles should have cheered me, but the thought of the two drowning in brown gravy, made my insides churn. My nerves had returned to plague my weakest link—my stomach.

My first show loomed. I was exhilarated and sick with anxiety all at the same time. I didn't want Mr. Abbott to doubt me, so I had to pretend that everything was normal. The waitress came by, and I ordered what I hoped would be a safe choice—chicken soup and coffee, but my mood grew more somber as the rain beat against the windows, and we waited out the storm. As we hashed out details of who would come first and do what, my sense of calm slowly returned. For a time, active planning seemed to take away some of the queasiness, but when the waitress brought our food to the table, I tried not to look down at the mushy carrots and chunks of chicken swirling around in a greasy broth. I left my soup untouched.

I was thankful for the strong distracting smell of coffee, for it brought me back to the present and to the feeling that I had some control over what was to come. Mr. Abbott's secretary had found me a room in a small hotel, and I planned to chair-fly the minute I got there—close my eyes and visualize every part of my routine: a normal takeoff, a climb, a barrel roll, a figure eight, and a couple of loop the loops, followed by a circuit of the airfield, with a landing directly in front of the grandstands. I knew Mr. Abbott liked pizzazz, and I hoped I could do enough to make him proud of me.

CHAPTER 33

The morning of my show, I eased back the covers and walked to my hotel window. I lifted the shade and was greeted by blinding shards of lightning. Mr. Abbott sent word that the rain date would be advertised, and that my show would now be a week later on September 3.

On September 2nd, I tossed and turned all night and rose hours before the sun. I had had another Henri nightmare in which I had been trailed in shallow, bloody seawater by a sinister shark fin in place of Henri's battered rudder. But when I looked below the waves, it was not a shark at all, but rather Henri's headless body that pursued me. I woke up just in time to see a paper-thin tear in the sky through which ripples of pink and orange ribbon waved.

The magnitude of my first show felt like a crushing weight, and that weight represented the thousands of my people who were counting on me to perform. The anxiety seeped through my pores, and even though I had scrubbed and scrubbed, a sour smell still clung to my skin. I was used to perspiration that comes from walking many miles, but distress produces something else—an oil, a musky stink. I had smelled it on others. It is unmistakable, memorable, and now this odor clung to me.

I sought calm through order, and I found it in the preparation of my armor. On the bed in my hotel room, I laid out my uniform, the same one I'd worn for the British Pathé news film. I had emulated the uniform of the officers whom I had seen wear theirs with unwavering authority. Their rich dark wool suits, with padded shoulders and cinched jackets, were girded by a stiff leather belt and anchored by thick leather boots. Each outfit had a smart cap with lots of gold braid like scrambled eggs plastered on the visor, and they all sported medals over their brave hearts.

I wouldn't copy the medals, but I had found the finest army green wool in a Paris shop, as well as a tailor of whom Norma would approve. When I returned, Norma copied the double-breasted jacket, and made me two more that were identical. On my brass belt buckle were my initials, BC, and on my visor, the same letters rested on the breast of an eagle with outstretched wings.

So as not to sprinkle any loose strands on the immaculate white cotton, I combed my hair before putting on my shirt and then styled it into a severe bob that fell above my shoulders. I kept working and slid my jacket over my shoulders and, with a fit like a glove, I snapped it into place. My belt buckle clicked; my cap sat low over my eyes. My boots were shined to a fare-thee-well; I pulled them up and laced each eyelet. In the looking glass, my father's face flashed back at me.

Holding onto the wrought iron handrail to steady myself, I descended the hotel's marble staircase. At the foot of the stairs, I collected myself and crossed the lobby. A large black Ford touring car was waiting directly out front, and the driver already knew who I was. His greeting was formal, "Morning, Miss Coleman. Are you ready?"

From Harlem, it was an hour's ride to the air strip on Long Island. The field was already abuzz with preparations when we arrived. Vendors were setting up carts of lemonade and popcorn. Buses were arriving, and members of the Hell Fighters' drum corps and marching band had started to assemble and practice. The grandstand was being adorned with red, white, and blue streamers.

I made my way over to Long Island Aviation Academy, the flight school from which we were renting the Curtiss JN-4. It was a two-toned aeroplane, cream colored and red. On the side, it had once boasted the letters and numbers: SC3034. But today, the letters peeped through mud spots splattering its sides. This plane had definitely been a workhorse to someone in our military, and it had clearly seen its better days. I walked a full circle around it and prayed that the engine had been maintained better than the skin.

I greeted the eager flight student at the scheduling desk. When he reviewed my FAI credentials, he said nothing, turned, and ran like he had seen a ghost. After a few moments in which I stood alone in stunned silence, a rail-thin middle-aged man, who introduced himself as Chief Pilot Becker, returned and demanded to meet the "real Bessie Coleman," as the aeroplane had been reserved in her name, and not for a Negro woman.

I don't know why I was shocked. Two years before, I hadn't been able to find anyone to train me. Apparently, not everyone kept up with the *New York Times*!

As he always did, Mr. Abbott showed up at the pivotal moment. He had heard that I had arrived and was swinging by to make sure that everything was in order. I had never been so glad to see him.

"Yes, the school did lease a plane to *The Chicago Defender*," Becker admitted, but he had no idea that a Negro woman would be flying it, he now explained to Mr. Abbott.

"Well, I assure you, young man, you don't want me flying that plane," Mr. Abbott wore a smile that was as thin as veneer. "Miss Coleman is qualified. We merely rented it for her."

It was clear that Mr. Abbott intended to be the defender of Chicago, this show, and me. During the tense stare-down, a muscle above Becker's right eyebrow twitched and then, finally, he blinked.

"Fine, then!" he snapped, trying to regain control when he was clearly unaccustomed to having it taken from him. "There are two conditions that she has to submit to before she can take the aeroplane out on her own." He didn't even give me the courtesy of speaking to me directly, and in this case my gender appeared to be a greater hazard than my being a Negro. "She will have to fly a test flight with me, and because this is a former military field, there can be no trick flying, no aerobatics, and no barnstorming!"

I couldn't believe my ears. "What am I supposed to do? Zoom around the traffic pattern and land? That's not what the people want to see. They paid to see a show!" I snapped.

"Those are the field rules, take 'em or leave 'em!" said Becker, snatching his power back. "Oh, and I almost forgot," he added slyly, "here's a written flight test that she'll need to complete."

I snatched a pencil that lay on the desk and shot Becker a menacing look. He returned my glare with a condescending smirk. I read the questions quickly. Within five minutes, I had scribbled the answers and thrust the paper and pencil back at Becker across the counter. I refrained from asking whether he would like me to complete a second set of questions in French.

Whatever Mr. Abbott's previous calculation of my value, at the moment, he and I were in lock step. Our indignation toward Becker united us. He glanced at me with a mixture of pride and proprietorship, popped his cigar into his mouth, and glared at Becker from under his black bowler hat and through a haze of blue smoke.

Becker read each answer and then looked up at me in complete amazement. I suppose he thought that I would be stumped, or maybe even that I was illiterate.

"Your answers are all correct," he said grudgingly. And then, still looking somewhat angry and mystified, he added, "let's see how you do on the flight test."

Without excusing himself, Mr. Abbott took me by the elbow and escorted me out the door of the flight school. "A brevet from France is the best in the world," he strained to keep his composure, he had apparently planned to give me an entire speech, but for the first time ever, I cut him off.

"I would be willing to bet that this guy doesn't have a third of the training that I have. And he is going to road test me?" I could feel my anger mounting. "I had an entire show planned, and now he tells me no tricks!"

"Bessie, I don't like this stick figure or his foolish rules any more than you do. But we have a job to do." Mr. Abbott placed an index finger over his pursed lips. "Listen, do you hear that? There are thousands of people out there. They are here to see you. I can't allow some scrawny Yankee to spoil our hard work. You must never allow someone else to determine your path," he breathed heavily.

Despite the message, Mr. Abbott was wounded; his own dignity was shaken and the patience that he was trying to exemplify to me was being sorely tested.

"Besides, this may be a blessing in disguise," he huffed as he changed tack.

"Oh, yeah, how so?" I snapped.

"Bessie, this is your first public showing. I don't want anything to go wrong. Go out there, stretch your wings, show that a Race woman can fly an aeroplane, and we will have already won the war of assumptions.

You don't need to show off for me. I already know what you can do. You always say," he reminded me, "that I believed in you and what you are capable of long before you did." For a moment, the calculating tycoon was gone, and he and I were in cahoots against the world.

"We have a lot to do this morning. Get up there, fly this skinny little pecker around. I have a program set up, and the men of the 369th are waiting. I've got interviews lined up for you, too. After the show you are going to take our people up for flights. You get to keep one dollar of the two dollars per ride that we collect," he said, cheery now at the thought of profits to be made.

"I keep half of everything?" I asked, delighted.

"Half!" he reassured me.

We walked over to the aeroplane where Becker, his helmet and goggles already in place, had climbed into the rear bucket seat. While I completed my preflight, he impatiently drummed the side of the plane with his index finger, as if he had a million better things to do with his time. Still, I did not rush. Nor did I speak. Rather, I followed every procedure as I had always done and took off, flying the closed-circuit pattern that he demanded. The aeroplane was a baby carriage, with handling far easier than a Caudron. I landed smoothly, taxied back to the flight line, then shut down the engine.

We both hopped out. I began to fold the seat belt and neaten the cockpit. Becker cleared his throat, but I didn't turn to face him. Since this test had not been on the schedule, I felt even greater pressure, as my start time now loomed.

"You did a good job up there. I didn't know what to expect, but you know what you're doing," Becker said and abruptly marched away. At least I had the satisfaction of his admission that he had underestimated me, but it did not make up for the fact that I was now running two hours behind schedule.

When I returned to the grandstand to tell Mr. Abbott everything was a green light, I couldn't even get to him, as he was surrounded by a ring of fans and acquaintances. The field was teaming with thousands of people, both Negro and white. It was at that moment, that the full weight of the crowd's presence struck me dumb. I took a moment to gaze at the crowd. I was sure that many just wanted to see if I were real. It was, after all, 1922. Many Americans didn't even own motor cars yet, and women had just earned the right to vote two years before.

Many ladies were there that day, still dressed in their Sunday church hats and dresses. People were patient, occupying themselves with the business of waiting—the crowds were festive, but not rowdy, indulging their children with lemonade and treats to while away the time. There was an air of celebration without a descent into carnival.

I walked along the outskirts of the crowd, enjoying the festivities and the anticipation in the air. At the end of my walk, I discovered a stairwell in the back of the hangar next to where I had parked the Jenny. To my delight, it led to a hatch that opened onto the roof that I had seen from above while flying with Becker. I climbed out and perched myself on the edge. From my roost, I could see for miles. A neat row of buses snaked in a long line entering the parking lot. The bright colored hats of the ladies and the black bowlers and caps on the men were like thousands of multicolored sails, moving in what looked like tides. Having my own private bird's-eye view was both exhilarating and terrifying—there were so many people, and so many expectations!

From somewhere inside the building, I heard my name being shouted, and I scrambled down. McVey had arrived, and even though I didn't know him, I could tell he was profoundly agitated. There was a crisis, he explained. He needed to borrow the Curtiss Jenny that we had just rented because, he confessed, the aeroplane he had planned on borrowing wasn't airworthy. His agreement with his plane's owner had been that if McVey was able to fix it, he could borrow it, but that plane was in such bad shape that it could not be mended in time. It needed expensive parts and was in no way ready for that day's show. I acquiesced. Yes, he could borrow my rented plane. What else was I to do?

The show began. The brave men of the 369th marched, the bands played, and the medal ceremony moved many, including me, to tears. Next, Captain McVey and Hubert Julian were to perform.

McVey pulled the aeroplane around to the front of the hangar and parked it in front of the grandstands, where the men from the 369th were seated. When McVey chopped the engine Julian, who had been doubled over, popped up from the front bucket seat like a jack in the box. Julian, known as the Black Eagle of Harlem, was a tall, lanky mahogany-colored man. His handsome face looked as though it had been chiseled out of a solid hunk of wood. On that day he was wearing his bright red jumpsuit, and while McVey was dignified in a military uniform, Julian's good looks were wasted. He looked like a giant tomato—a red, preening orb. Julian's costume billowed as he sprang out of the plane to walk across the wing—his limbs delivered structure, but he looked like a starfish, demonstrating on the ground what he planned to do at altitude. A huge cheer went up and Julian took an exaggerated bow.

"Oh, for heaven's sake," I mused aloud. He hadn't even left the ground yet, and in my rented aeroplane no less. Then, as if he'd heard me grumble from hundreds of yards away, Julian donned his rucksack parachute and belted himself into the Jenny behind McVey.

With a hand prop from an aerodrome worker, McVey's engine was started, and then he maneuvered the Jenny into position at the takeoff line. In no time, he was airborne and climbed easily, flying upward over the field in a spiraled cylinder. In circling up like this, the crowd never lost sight of the two. It would take McVey twenty minutes to climb to ten thousand feet, a distance of two miles above the crowd. During that time, the drum corps would perform for the expectant crowds.

At the top of their climb, Julian somersaulted out of the plane. Like a rock dropped from a window, he plummeted a couple thousand feet, hurtling toward the earth at breakneck speed. A collective gasp went up and shrieks hovered above the crowd. Hands covered mouths, fingers shielded eyes, children were pulled against their mothers' skirts.

Then, just as it appeared that he would splat like the tomato he resembled, Julian ripped a cord and released the rainbow-colored parachute. Sections of red, white, blue, green, and yellow fabric all stitched together provided a balloon of silk that stopped his fall and righted his long frame. The drag from the chute allowed Julian to float to the ground, where he came to rest at the feet of the cheering, adoring crowd.

With a bow, a wave, and kisses thrown from hands still attached to ropes and thirty yards of trailing rainbow-colored fabric, Julian gathered up his silken cloud, shoved it into his rucksack, and poof! he was gone—vanishing behind the grandstands into a waiting automobile. In less time than it had taken him to descend, Herbert Julian, The Black Eagle, had flown the coop!

My flight was next.

The crowd's excitement had been mounting. From a high wooden pedestal that looked like a lifeguard's tower, the announcer proclaimed my upcoming flight: "And now, without further ado, ado, ado … " his voice echoed, vibrating through air, "it is my pleasure to introduce to you the world's first and only licensed Negro female flyer, flyer, flyer …

She is the only American to hold French flying credentials granting her the privilege to fly anywhere in the world, world, world ... but she chose to share her talents with you, loyal New York readers of *The Defender, Defender, Defender ...*"

The applause sounded as if it might lift the heavy grandstands into the air.

"Just back from Paris, Amsterdam, and Berlin, I present to you, Miss Bessie Coleman, Coleman, Coleman!!!"

As if in a trance, I clambered down from my lifeguard's tower and floated over to where McVey had parked the Jenny. When they caught sight of me, the crowd roared. I felt the vibration of their cheers reverberating through my body and braced myself by planting a hand on the SC3034. The plane's skin under my fingers palpated, too. I climbed into the cockpit and then stood on top of the seat so that I could be seen above the frame of the aeroplane. That didn't feel tall enough, so I balanced my weight and climbed onto the top wing's spar, being careful not to step on the fabric in between the ribs.

Finally, I could see the entire crowd. And they could see me. I pushed my goggles up and thrust a gloved hand into the air, waving like a queen—wrist, wrist then elbow, elbow.

Then as if on cue, a bugle player played the first few notes of *My Country 'Tis of Thee*. Its melody forced thousands of people to rise to their feet at an ode to a country that used us and then spurned us. And then, after the crowd fell silent, a hundred veterans from the 369th advanced with military precision across the field. The bugle player was joined by the entire marching band of the Hell Fighters. They added flesh to the bugle player's solitary notes, and they all encircled me as I stood atop my muddy rented plane.

I turned to my right then swung left. Balancing my weight upon the spar, I saluted the uniformed soldiers. I hadn't planned a salute, but it surely seemed like the right thing to do. Only after they returned the salute did I slowly and respectfully lower my hand. The men returned the greeting by saluting almost in unison, yelling, "HOOAH!" The giant blue pennant of the 369th waved. Embroidered with French inscriptions of bravery and fearlessness, it felt in some way like a fitting sign.

The energy of three thousand was united in rooting for the success of one of their own. My purpose was the purpose of a people. And I, too, was overcome with emotion. The bugler then played taps, as McVey emerged from the sea of military uniforms with a boy of about ten years old, wearing round, gold-rimmed glasses that were too big for his tiny face. The owl boy climbed fearlessly onto my plane to pass me a bouquet of flowers.

Poof, poof … I heard the cameras flash, saw the glints of light, and smelled the magnesium from the flares of fifty flashbulbs as they burned instantly and curled into thin spirals of smoky vapor; the moment before my first air show had been captured forever.

"Thank you, my friend." I cupped my hands around my mouth and yelled so that McVey could hear me over the roar of the crowd. "Never thought I'd ask so many foine men to disperse, but could you please move all of these warriors far, far away from the prop? I am ready to go."

With McVey's command, the uniformed troops peeled back and marched in lock step to the solemn beat from the drum corps. They reassembled in reserved front-row seats, where they formed a line of black, uniformed masculinity. I felt great pride well up in my chest as I looked back at the strength emanating from these mighty men.

I inspected the aeroplane. With the preflight complete, I dropped to one knee to say a prayer. The entire audience was silent. When I stood up again, the crowd cheered. McVey returned to hand prop my start, and I yelled that I was ready. Unsure as to whether he could hear me over the din of the crowd, I gave him the thumbs-up sign. He cranked the engine and dove out of the way.

A light but steady breeze ran straight up the grass strip. Everything was in my favor. I was as ready as I would ever be, so I gave one more long wave to the crowd, said one more simple prayer, and latched my seatbelt, "God, thank you for this day. Please help me to always stay true to myself and your purpose." It was a magnificent fall day. The air was warm, but not hot, and the clear blue sky was full of promise.

So that I wouldn't send prop wash over the folks who had just cheered me, I began gently advancing the throttle. Once past the grandstands, I pushed the throttle to its limit—full speed. With my feet dancing on the rudder pedals, grass clumps bounced me, mud splattered over me, and then, a third of the way down the strip, the tail lifted up. After another few hundred feet forward, the aeroplane just lifted off the ground.

I was mindful of all the restrictions placed upon me—no trick flying—and although I thought the rules were silly and wanted to do what I had trained for, Mr. Abbott's name, as well as a hefty deposit, was on the line. And while I honored my promise, I felt that my audience deserved a thrill.

So, I flew away from the field. Unlike McVey, who spiraled upward, higher and higher so that the crowd never lost sight of him, I flew directly forward until I could no longer see the grandstands. I was confident that people had their hands cupped high across their brows, shielding their eyes from the sun, trying to see the red and white tail of the Jenny against blue sky.

When I was sure that I was nearly out of sight, I turned back and flew like a bat out of hell, aiming straight for the field, losing altitude as I plowed forward. As my descent increased, so did my speed: 60 ... 70 ... 80 ... 90 ... 100 ... 110 miles an hour. When I was in close range of the grandstands, I dove through the air, gunning the engine, and skimmed the crowd at a thousand feet.

I roared right over their heads.

The screams and cheers made the aeroplane's skin pulse, and it beat along with my own. I did a hairpin turn, reversed direction, and flew back over the grandstands again. This time I sliced the air at five hundred feet above the crowd. I saw dozens ducking and covering their heads as exhaust wafted out, descending like thin fog. This was getting good! I was laughing out loud and having a ball! So, I went out for a third pass.

I fished around next to me on my seat where I had secured a sturdy haversack. Inside were a hundred silk scarves that Norma had given to Mr. Abbott to bring with him from Chicago. I had told her of my gift to Robert, and she had diligently sewn a less luxurious commemorative version for my first show. They were cream colored with a delicate fringe, and instead of my initials, each one had a tiny sky-blue biplane embroidered on one corner.

On my last run, I flew at one hundred feet above the crowd and, as I did, I shook out the rucksack to sprinkle out the scarves as I shot overhead. The crowd went wild. They screamed and went diving for the scarves. Or maybe they were ducking for cover? All I knew was that their sense of wonder, pride, and joy was fuel enough for me to keep doing this until I breathed my very last breath.

The low flyover was packed with all of the exhilaration of a barrel roll for me, and it thrilled and chilled the people I had come there to entertain. I gunned the engine and, as it growled, I whooped with delight. After another tight hairpin turn, I shut down the engine and dead sticked a smooth landing. A dozen uniformed men flanked the JN-4 on each side, parking me right in front of the crowd.

That was it. In fewer than fifteen minutes, the thrills were over. The audience was on its feet with a standing ovation. I decided then and there that, like a signature, I would make the low flyover a staple in my routine.

Mr. Abbott reached my side first. As I climbed out of the cockpit, he practically lifted me over the air frame. He twirled me around, and I was surprised to find that Robert Abbott, the intellectual, could also be so demonstrative. He planted a big juicy kiss on my forehead and squeezed me in a big hug.

Within seconds, others descended upon us. Every camera froze that moment forever. Together, Mr. Abbott and I had accomplished the impossible.

"You really do stretch the rules, don't you?" Mr. Abbott whispered.

"I learned from the best," I whispered back, as we smiled big for the cameras.

I removed my bronze tie pin, a gift from *Monsieur* Caudron—a gilded pair of wings—and pinned it to Mr. Abbott's lapel. A tear welled in his eye. Before it could splash, he wiped it away and gave me a smile instead. We hugged once more and turned to accept the congratulations of the long line of admirers waiting to be acknowledged.

Late that afternoon and into the evening, I gave rides to people who paid two dollars to buzz around the airfield. I thought this was a huge sum, but then Mr. Abbott reminded me, "This is New York City. We can't be giving away anything up here!" I knew he was right. And even at this price there was no shortage of customers.

"I never in my life thought I would climb into one of these contraptions," one old man said.

"So, this is what a bird sees," said another, younger man.

"I never imagined I'd ride in the sky!" a woman exclaimed with tears in her eyes.

And then there was my favorite, plain and simple, from an eight-year-old boy upon landing, "Wow, thanks Daddy. I love you!"

"BESSIE GETS AWAY; DOES HER STUFF," *The Defender* headline read. They said two thousand people had attended the show, and the reporter called my landing "perfect." Now that was good news.

CHAPTER 34

When I returned to Chicago, Norma was the only one waiting to welcome me at the train station, and while I was thrilled to see her, I asked her why only she had come to greet me.

"How come Mama and Walter at least didn't come to the train station?" I grumbled my own answer, "Guess everyone is just too busy."

"My, you sure are becoming mighty important. Aren't I, the best friend you ever had, good enough?" Norma teased.

"Sorry, Norma," I muttered.

I was quiet while Norma chatted merrily about all of the new happenings on the Stroll. The streetcar lurched to a stop in front of her building, and Norma practically ran me down to get to the door in front of me. I struggled with packages and dragged my steamer trunk as far as I could, happy to let her lead the way to the top of her third-story walk-up above the alterations shop. When she threw the door open, she ducked inside. I was busy fussing with packages when a dozen voices called out, "Welcome Home!"

They were all there—the entire Coleman tribe, shoehorned into the front room of Norma's apartment. Even Mr. Abbott was there. Norma batted her long eyelashes. "There," she said, proud at having pulled off the surprise, "is this enough of a welcome party for you?"

Walter went downstairs to retrieve my heavy steamer trunk. In addition to my books, it stored a treasure trove of gifts, for I had something for everyone. Elizabeth shrieked as she unwrapped her fine clutch coat from Paris, an overdue replacement for the one she had lent me. It had huge black velvet cuffs and a luxurious matching collar, white silk lining, and a giant pearl button to shut out the Chicago wind that had chased us inside her apartment so long ago. Elizabeth was speechless.

My nieces went wild over a bone-handled looking glass, French paper-dolls, pinwheels, and Chiclets. I had beaded lace and a bolt of royal blue silk for Norma. I bought dangling pearl earbobs for my sisters and for Mama. For Mr. Abbott I had bought a fine, French, leather-bound notebook to replace the dog-eared notepad he always carried. The doeskin glove leather was a buff color that enveloped small linen pages.

Finally, it was Walter's turn. Walter loved trains, but he loved automobiles, too, and I knew he lusted after his own. "I brought you a fine French model," I said, giggling as he opened a six-inch rectangular box. Inside was a miniature 1920 Peugeot Landaulet. So detailed was the burgundy and black model that the little steering wheel turned, and the soft top folded down. Walter declared he would take all of us out for a Sunday drive in his new automobile. "We are all so proud of you, Bessie," he beamed.

But it was John who broke my heart. "Bessie, I am sorry for many things," he whispered and gave me a long hug. He looked as though he had aged a decade during the six months I had been away. I could not stand to see my brother, a grown man, wounded by war, cry on my account. I set my index finger on his lips and handed him a cast iron replica of the Arc de Triumphe.

"I love you, brother," I said. "Paris was everything you said it would be. From now on, we fight on the same side."

Elizabeth smiled bravely. John put a hand on her arm and then drifted away from us. He said he would be back, but we did not see him again that evening. My triumphant return must have been both healing and painful for him, not because he was envious, but because he struggled so.

"I am also proud of you, Bess," Norma whispered. "But I worry about you in those rattletraps. I sure wish we could buy you your own aeroplane. One we know is safe."

Yes, buy my own plane. Teach at my own academy. That was the plan. But the day when that might happen felt far away once again. At least I had pocketed three hundred and fifty dollars from the New York show. This was a king's ransom for a day's work! My next stop would be at The Binga State Bank, where I would deposit my earnings. I knew that before long I would be seeing Jesse again, but right then I only wanted to slip into the bank and slide out again unnoticed.

Mr. Abbott was planning our second airshow, to be held in Chicago this time, and if there was one thing I did not want, it was to get distracted by my former lover. Sooner or later, though, I would have to deal with Jesse because, if the New York show was big, my hometown celebration was going to be even bigger—anything big and Negro in Chicago would necessarily involve Jesse Binga.

As he'd done in New York, Mr. Abbott was making the arrangements. This time, my sisters, brothers, and their wives; my mother and a gaggle of my nieces and nephews; Norma and Moe, and even my former White Sox customers would be at this show. While there had been no trick flying in New York, people in Chicago were expecting to see some fancy stunts. My hometown folks had read all about my aerobatic training, and the more death defying, they likely thought, the better.

"Everyone loves a winner," Mr. Abbott explained. "You have proven that our race is strong and, not only that, you have succeeded in spite of overwhelming obstacles. And besides all that, these shows make a pretty penny for the promoters. And money always talks."

We found a taker at Checkerboard Field, an aerodrome northwest of the city. The show was scheduled for October 15, 1922. Nearly three months had passed since I had been able to practice my routine of barrel roll, figure eight, loop the loop, Max Immelmann turns, low flyover—the works. I was going to need to get out to the airfield to bone up.

During the next week, I traveled to Checkerboard and flew the checkered red-and-white aeroplanes as often as the weather would allow. While I was flying, the future felt promising, as if I could raise our entire race upon a feather. By mid-week, though, we had unexpected rain, and my heart sank. The idea of a rained-out show put me in a blue mood all over again. With less than four days to go before my show, practices were going well, and postponing the show due to weather would break the momentum that was propelling me and raising *The Defender*'s readership across Chicago.

The day was soggy, and I sulked on my window seat, watching the rain drum in endless streams across the glass. Below me, a long silver

Rolls Royce pulled up in front of my building, and my heart skipped a beat and then thundered in my throat. The driver got out, unfurled a tent-sized black umbrella and held it over the rear passenger door. Two shrouded figures hurried to the stairs through the pelting rain. Big, black, shiny, leather wingtips solidly mounted the flagstones. Taking the stairs leading to my front door, the two figures were in lock step. The doorbell rang. I couldn't see the passenger, but I knew who it was.

I had already bathed and gotten ready for bed in the thin cotton pants and long-sleeved top I wore beneath my flyer's uniform. I wore no brassiere or underpants, and when the doorbell rang, I didn't have time to change, so I hurried down the steps in my sheer underclothes and looked out through the small glass window in the front door. My visitor's face was hidden behind a dozen sumptuous red roses, but I didn't need to see his face. I had spent enough time with Jesse to know his long limbs, wide shoulders, and bowed legs. I exhaled deeply and opened the two locks that kept strangers at bay.

"These are for you."

His voice, deep and gravely, resonated inside my body. His fist was somehow gentle as it grasped tender stems, thrusting the open blooms forward. I tried to ignore the parts of me that warmed and softened in his presence. Jesse made me feel vulnerable and needy—all of the things that I could ill afford to be anymore. It was selfish of him to have come.

"Are you going to let me in?" he asked, this time peering over the flowers. "I just wanted to wish you well and see you before the show," he smiled, and it was the smile that he knew I liked—the big, confident one, the one that had opened more important doors than my own. It was a smile full of self-assurance, poise, and control.

"Come in," I said, convinced that I was making a poor decision even as I spoke.

I took the bribe of flowers.

Jesse's driver returned to the car, and then I heard the tumblers of the two locks clicking into place as Jesse bolted the door to the building behind him. I felt his eyes on my buttocks as my weight shifted from hip to hip mounting the staircase and so I went up as quickly as I could without running. He quickened his own pace and stayed right on my heels. When we reached my door, he extended a long, gentlemanly arm to push it open for me, and I placed the flowers between us to shield myself from rubbing against his body as I walked through.

The attempt backfired. Tense, I grabbed the stems tighter than I'd handle the aeroplane's stick, and one of the thorns pierced the palm of my hand. I dropped the roses as if they were on fire. In one swift movement Jesse closed the door with his foot, bolted the latch, and swept me up into his arms the way a bridegroom would lift his bride. He carried me to the sofa, where he took my bleeding hand in his own.

Jesse looked into my eyes and tucked me into his waiting lap. He sucked the droplets of blood from my palm, rubbing my wrist with the fleshy part of his thumb. He lifted my arm to his mouth and began working his tongue and teeth up my forearm. He sucked and stroked me, and his tongue traveled up to my neck and then, somehow, he was devouring the nape of my neck.

Beneath my buttocks his manhood had risen fully, and he gripped my hips and slid my bottom ruggedly across his lap.

"No!" I protested.

As it always had, the sweet smell of his breath on my neck had caused the desired response, but I had to force my mind to take control.

"I can't. We can't ... I don't want this." Fighting the desire inside myself, I said, "I told you I would never kiss you again."

He was breathless, and I couldn't see his face because his mouth was on my ear. "We don't have to kiss," he laughed at his own joke, and I was glad he did. It was just what I needed to make me pull away.

"Please don't. It's too hard for me to resist you. I still want you, but ... " I said, breathing a little harder than I wanted to.

He slid to the front of the couch with a self-satisfied smile, "I can see that."

I needed to be both firm and clear because Jesse was persuasive, and I was lonely. This man was an opportunist in business and in love—he knew me well and had calculated my vulnerability.

"Jesse, you know I have always been stirred by your body. You have a way with me. But you and I have one big problem. You are married to another woman. I don't want to be your gal on the side. A relationship like that would be my undoing, and I would never be taken seriously again. I am my own person now, and not only that, but I have people who look up to me, who count on me. But I could be so much stronger with you fully in my corner ... as my husband."

There! I had said it. I had finally worked up the nerve to say what I really wanted.

"Bessie, I have built an empire with my brother-in-law's money. If I divorce my wife, I give it back. If I let go of the string now ... "

He didn't need to finish. I knew he loved me. But Jesse's fortune rested upon a gangster's early investments, and his rough and tumble brother-in-law made sure that the transaction was ironclad in the eyes of the law. If Jesse left the marriage, he would forfeit both the principle and any profits earned from the seed money. Jesse's first love was money and the second was like unto it—power. That put me in third place and I could never settle for that.

Jesse sat on the sofa and pulled me down next to him. He wedged his body along the length of mine and draped his big black coat across the two of us. We fell asleep listening to the rain pelting the windows.

When I awoke, he had gone. His heavy overcoat was still wrapped around me.

In my bare feet, I went to the window. The rain still fell, washing the empty parking space where the Rolls Royce had been. I had thought a lot about that Silver Ghost Rolls over the last few years. I had been fascinated by the hood ornament—a figure of a woman, Valkyrie-like braving the wind with her face, as her arms swept back into wings. Called the Spirit of Ecstasy, she was poised to take flight. But even though it was she who stood atop the assembly, it was not she who held the power. The might of six cylinders was what caused the engine to rumble just beneath her feet. She was merely a figurehead—a demonstration that things were not always what they appeared to be. Yet, in the rain of last night and on every occasion, it appeared as though she never faltered.

In the Daru Staircase of the Louvre, I had set eyes upon the statue of Nike, the goddess of victory. I had rounded a corner and there she was. Headless, armless, but winged, she towered—an eighteen-foot goddess, a massive, ancient expression of power. Her triumphant war-like stance was as haunting to me as the battlefields over which I had flown. She had also conjured up the image of the hood ornament on Jesse's elegant Rolls, and as I stood looking up at her, I had recalled Jesse's excitement at the notion of coming with me to Paris to "paint the town."

But no matter how powerful Nike was, she soared by herself. Likewise, the hood ornament was poised straight into the wind, braving every element with only her body. I felt an undeniable kinship to them both. Whether sculpted out of stone or metal, or of flesh and bone, we each flew alone.

On the table, I saw that Jesse had placed his flowers in a vase, next to a note.

You are the woman I have always wanted.
And while I will not push myself on you, I will always want you.
I will be at Checkerboard to watch you fly unless you tell me otherwise.

Love, Jesse.

I opened Jesse's envelope on the kitchen table, and the familiar whiff greeted me. Tender. Legal tender. Money that had been handled by ten thousand sweaty fingers carried a smell like no other. Human stain and tallow made the inky cotton that I had once picked for a white man's profit smell fetid to me now. Inside Jesse's envelope was two thousand dollars. I counted the bills, all of them hundreds—cold, hard cash, Jesse-style—and I wept as the money fell from my fingers and floated onto the floor. The smell was the same but the stain was deeper. Dropping back onto the couch, I buried my face in the collar of his overcoat, where I could drown in another scent—his. I stayed there for a long time, listening to the rain that threatened to wash away everything that I had worked so hard to cobble together.

CHAPTER 35

Just as he had in the New York show, Mr. Abbott intended to celebrate Negro soldiers in our hometown. This time he invited the Eighth Infantry Regiment, which meant that this show was personal, for my two brothers would guard each of my wingtips. The men of the Fighting Eighth, as they were known, were also joined that day by older men, in their forties and fifties, who had fought in the Spanish-American War in 1898. What they shared in common was that they had all fought for a country that was ungrateful upon their return. Mr. Abbott planned to seat these veterans front and center, and I planned to salute them with all the gratitude that they had never received.

And so, it was on another warm fall morning that I rose at dawn to fulfill the headline Mr. Abbott had chosen: "Queen Bess to Try Air. October 15" Although the day held the first scents of autumn, the air was toasty, and I headed out to Checkerboard Field with my head buried in the newspaper. Just as he had in New York City, Mr. Abbott sent a car for me, arranging my world, getting me from here to there. He had told me to expect a wave of publicity, and he did not disappoint.

The article I held in my hands stated, "Miss Coleman will straighten up her plane in the manner of Eddie Rickenbacker and will execute her glides after the style of the German Richthofen. In the second flight the daring aviatrix will cut a figure "8" in honor of the men of the Eighth Illinois Infantry, afterwards presenting to the Regiment a flag made by herself and named Inspiration in honor of the record of the Illinois soldier boys."

These Greats, mentioned in the same sentence as my name? Now, this was more than hoopla. In a matter of a few sentences, Mr. Abbott had turned me into the Queen of Aces.

I took off in front of the grandstands in an aeroplane we borrowed from the Checkerboard's owner. As I climbed, the words of Jacques Dumas came to me: "When you are upside down, everything is opposite. But you can't think about it. You must only allow the plane in this condition for a fraction of a second. Any longer, and fuel ceases to flow through the carburetor and oil pressure decreases to zero. When this happens, the engine shuts off. There is no second chance to restart the engine in the air in this model, so your plane will fly like a manhole cover. You feel the loop, let it happen, then recover swiftly."

My loop was followed by a spin. To create it, I simply stalled one wing. Once air ceased to flow smoothly over the wing, I would kick the rudder pedal and throw the stick in the same direction. The aeroplane heeled over, looking like a corkscrew, winding itself farther and farther toward the ground, pirouetting on the tip of its propeller. I would pull out at a thousand feet above the grass. Like a contortionist, the aeroplane coiled the air around itself in a corkscrew spiral as I pointed my nose toward the ground. *Monsieur* Dumas had told me that three turns were enough. They happened as quickly as a sneeze.

I pulled the stick over hard to the right then stomped harder on the rudder in the same direction, and the aeroplane responded. This time, I had forced a lateral tumble. A barrel roll, a loop, and a roll followed. Then, I looped the aeroplane. A loop by itself is a graceful maneuver. It is less thrill and more majesty, but these barrel rolls were spiky, athletic somersaults.

I climbed back up to five thousand feet. A mile above the surface of the earth, I pointed the aeroplane's nose down and sped through 80, 90, 100 miles per hour. When I reached 110, I hauled back on the stick, pulling it between my legs, hugging the wand close into my body and keeping my feet even and steady. With the rudders neutral, I pointed my head to the sky and climbed straight up toward heaven. I watched a puffy cloud tumble over my head. I knew I had completed a rotation as I passed through the horizon. This time, with less thinking and more feeling, I had caused the aeroplane to flip over itself. Like a child, with knees buckled in a mid-air cannonball, I flipped the aeroplane around in a tighter loop. I did it again, but this time I lost nearly a thousand feet of altitude in what felt like an instant.

I was soaring above my friends and relatives. I was entertaining everyone I knew and loved. I was content. The stick was easy. I felt at home in the air.

I punctuated my show with the low flyover, sprinkling a batch of Norma's scarves, then dead sticked a landing, coasting to a stop right in front of the grandstands. People jumped to their feet, showering me with a standing ovation.

"We honor brave Bess and the brave men of the Fighting Eighth," the announcer's voice boomed over the loudspeaker.

I had plenty of fuel left, and seeing all the waving of hats and clapping of hands gave me an idea. I climbed back into the red-and-white checkered plane, thinking I must have looked like a tablecloth flapping in the wind. "And what can we expect this time from our own Bess ... Bess ... Bess?" the announcer went on. I grabbed my haversack. Inside I had several quarts of Castrol Motor Oil. I realized that if I drizzled the thick oil into the manifold exhaust pipe that ran along the side of the plane's engine, the wind would reveal my flight path.

Half a mile in front of soldier row, I began an infinity figure eight to celebrate the fine gentlemen of the Eighth Regiment. Vaporizing into thick, heavy smoke, the sign for forever was etched upon a resolute cyan sky. And although this second flight lasted only minutes, the crowd went wild. Mr. Abbott had promised something that I had not been sure I could deliver. He had stoked the crowd, and I wanted to live up to both what he had advertised, as well as his expectations of me. The warm wind was light and didn't disturb the symbol of infinity—I hoped it would last in people's minds forever.

CHAPTER 36

I went home that night and I slept like the dead. When I awoke, I was starving and went in search of breakfast at my favorite café down the street. Every stranger hailed me as they passed and seemed to know exactly who I was. It was as if I had woken up into a whole new world. Once, it had been I who had admired the fine and famous men and women who owned the Stroll, yet today, it was I who held court, waving in greeting and thanks to all who passed by in the street, and then later, ensconced in a corner booth, autographing napkins, patting the heads of children, and greeting elders with adoring smiles.

Thankfully, my siblings kept me grounded a-plenty. At a family gathering that night to celebrate my successful show, my sister Nilus teased me from the kitchen.

"Bessie, I mean Queen Bee, or shall I just call you Queenie?" Nilus ribbed. "Think you can put yer hands in this here dish warta?" She handed me her dirty plate.

I knew that my siblings weren't jealous or mean-spirited about my success and cheered me on more than anyone at all, but Mama sat as still as a stone, saying not a word. I took a seat beside her and put my head on her shoulder.

"What's bothering you, Mama?" I asked.

"Bessie, before the rest of the world discovered you, you belonged to me, and I felt as if I could keep you safe in it," Mama said, as she stroked my hair. "But I'm troubled, honey. One minute this fickle world loves you, the next, they turns on you. You flyin' round in these flimsy contraptions. That biplane is like a kite strapped onto your back! Who's gonna fix these rusty old things for you?"

"Mama, I'm going to be fine. You always taught me to let go and let God. And that's what I'm going to do. That is what I do."

"Humph!" Mama snorted. "God wants you to use your common sense, girl. Some of these planes are beat-up old tin cans. And not just that, who's gonna keep track of the money that flows all round you, but don't make it into your pocket? There are gonna be people who sees you as their meal ticket. I'm just afraid 'cause I can't protect you in the world you are fixing to fly into."

"Oh, Mama. You're just being a worrywart."

"A worrywart, huh?" she pulled away from me and held my shoulders in her hands. "I was just ten when I came to freedom, but I still remember one of the last things my master said to my own mama, your grandmother. He had seen me from his winda when I was kickin' up some dirt on the sheets that hung on the line, and he came runnin' out to whip me. My mama put her body between me and the lash and promised to clean every one of his bedclothes good as new. He said, 'You better had, gal. You and your daughter, your son, all your children, y'all are just money in my pocket. I'd be glad to sell that little pickaninny if I see her pissin' away any more of your time'." Mama's eyes blazed at me, "I don't care if these managers are colored or white, when one of these men tells you you're money in his pocket, believe him. For you flying is freedom, but for them your flying is their payday. All they wants to do is to own you and every bit of your labor."

While I didn't want to admit it, Mama was right. Many of the aeroplanes that I could borrow were junkers, and many of the men who wanted to "manage" my affairs turned out to be con artists. I had to acknowledge that her trepidation was not unfounded. But for right now, I couldn't afford to give in to that kind of paralyzing fear and worry. Not only that, I needed to resist being swept away by the tidal wave that followed my successful Chicago show, and just as Mama's warnings foreshadowed, I started receiving all sorts of offers from "managers" who tried to sell me on their services. What was true was that I did need help keeping track of the places I had to be, the travel required to get there, the amount of money that would be promised, and the ability to collect every red cent I was owed.

I needed his guidance, and so I went to see Mr. Abbott at his office and brought along a list of the people who had contacted me over the past week. He did not know of half of the characters I named, and so I dismissed those people outright. But Mr. Abbott did know one man. His name was J. A. Jackson.

"What's the J. A. stand for?" I asked Mr. Abbott. I was suspicious for some indefinable reason, as if the initials indicated that he might not want his name to be known.

"I don't know, Bessie," Mr. Abbott said. "You will have to ask him that for yourself. I don't know what kind of agent he'd make, but I do know that he has a lot of experience in publicity. He's created hugely popular fairs that entertain a ton of our people down south. Says he wants to bring these fairs up north. Wherever he is, he makes a big production, advertises in my newspaper regularly and, supposedly, he makes a whole lot of money."

"No doubt for himself," I muttered under my breath.

"If you pursue this, Bessie, you will be on your own. I am not so sure that I can stay in the show-producing business," he went on. "Pulitzer and Hearst are printing twenty-five thousand newspapers an hour with their modern presses. I need a broader reach if I'm going to minister to all the folks I've convinced to come up north."

"But you produced the New York show and then the one right here in Chicago! And look how well they did! I think by every measure those shows minister to our people. They teach the message of big risk and an even bigger payoff. And not just that, they show our ability to achieve in the sciences. Plus, they were profitable, too, right?" I pleaded. No matter what our relationship was, the idea of not having Mr. Abbott help me was a new and terrifying prospect.

"Bessie, you are one of the best investments that I have ever made, and I will always have your back. You can count on that. But you're ready to go on without me. Truth is, you have been flying solo all along."

He smiled. I cried.

I had such mixed feelings. "One of the best investments," he had said. Once again, the familiar confusion of emotions came with that phrase—both the pride I felt from it, as well as the disturbing thought that I was only that—an investment to him, gold bullion to trade. But I couldn't dwell on that because all I felt at that moment was fearful and alone.

"How will I manage without you?" I begged.

"Something tells me that you will always find your way," he reassured, lifting my chin between his thick index finger and thumb. "You're very pushy, you know."

In the end, I accepted Mr. Jackson's proposal. And although I did so, some of Mama's doubt and distrust ran right through me. I could not bring myself to call him J. A., so I just called him Jackson.

Jackson was a short, light-skinned man who was prone to large lunches and therefore a heavy abdomen and hips. He was always dressed in a matching ensemble, done up with gaudy spats and a bright feather in his bowler. He carried a briefcase that spilled over with papers, and it had a way of making him look busier than he needed to be on every occasion. But none of that was the problem. What troubled me was that so much of him felt contrived. He was trying to sell his acts to the Negro fairs, but he felt like all packaging and no substance. I told myself that this was how it was with the promotion business and that he really was the best of the lot. But from the beginning, there was just something about him that I did not trust.

It was greed, pride, and inexperience that led me into trouble with Jackson. He promised me that he could book me on a lucrative tour throughout the South, where I would be the main event in a series of barnstorming carnivals. Our first stop would be Memphis. In addition to the Negro state fairs, he offered to make me a movie star in a cinema feature production. This represented a level of publicity that would lead to the kind of financial windfall I never could have imagined. But I made the mistake of not telling myself often enough what Mama had told me, "if it sounds too good to be true, you better reckon it is."

Although I accepted him as my new manager, I told Jackson that before we agreed to any of these deals, whether air shows or moving pictures, that he and I should have a written contract spelling out exactly what he was going to do and what I was going to do, and how much money would change hands, or more precisely, how much of my effort would remain as grease in his sweaty, plump palms.

Yet, exactly what words should be put into such a contract remained only a vague notion to me. I had sketched out a few terms that came to my mind—like who would pay for travel, how much of the gate I would keep, who would schedule hotels in the North, or when traveling down south, in people's homes. Negroes, New or Old, couldn't stay in hotels south of the Mason-Dixon line, the way I had in New York City, and even if it may have seemed an indulgence to Jackson, I really did require a room all to myself while a guest in someone's home. Sleep was critical to performing. Without it, I'd never be able to enter a loop or pull out of a spin. Rest kept me calm and kept the anxiety at bay.

Remembering that Mr. Abbott had been trained in the law, I took my single page of notes to him, and he told me I was on the right track and that I should return in a day to retrieve his recommendations. "See, I told you that you don't need me," he said.

But, surely, I did need him, for when I returned, he had expanded my scribbles to a three-page agreement. It was typed, professional looking, and outlined everything I was concerned about, as well as other things I had not even thought to put into writing. He had added a rain clause, a guaranteed amount I was to receive, regardless of how many spectators showed up, or didn't show up, and there was even language in there about renting aeroplanes. If I deemed the craft unsafe for any reason, I did not have to perform in it. I knew that particular one would make Mama rest easier, and I didn't mind it so much myself.

"One day, when I buy my aeroplane, we can change this clause," I said wistfully.

"Yes, dear, one day soon," Mr. Abbott reassured me.

Mr. Abbott's secretary had made carbon copies and when I met with Jackson, I gave him one. He read it and we both signed the purple-tinged documents that outlined the rules of our game. He proclaimed that he really had the ability to fill up my schedule, and he promised to make me wealthy enough that I could buy an entire fleet of my own aeroplanes. Jackson was a fast talker, and I knew to be wary of people who talk too fast.

Our agreement was that my travel expenses, as well as big items—the plane rental, gas, air strip rental—all had to be covered by the take from the gate. Any additional profit would be split fifty-fifty.

But Memphis was our first show together, and since we were just starting out, I gladly paid the up-front costs for my trip. Just in case, I meticulously saved receipts and train ticket stubs and dutifully filed them in an envelope in the pocket of my rucksack. Likewise, I paid a local family eight dollars up front for a room and five meals over the course of a week's stay.

The family's home was humble, but that didn't bother me. The meals were like those I had eaten as a child: loose, runny oatmeal for breakfast, and fatback, collards, and corn pone for dinner. The husband was hard-working and the wife soft-spoken. They were kind, and their children were well-mannered. The only part of the arrangement that gave me pause was that all four children had to sleep along with their parents in the common front room, while I luxuriated in the only bedroom in the rear of the shack. I felt guilty that my demands for privacy had cost them their own, but I also knew how far that money would go in a household such as theirs, and I would be sure to leave a little extra cash on my way out the door.

The Memphis show was stacking up to be a success. I now had a solid program and I delivered it with growing confidence. But the atmosphere at the Memphis show was altogether different from that of *The Defender* shows in New York and Chicago, both of which had been dignified, meaningful affairs. Mr. Abbott had seen to it that Negro soldiers came decked out in their uniforms, medals, and pride. There was no such effort at the Memphis show. It was pure carnival. The people loved my loops and figure eights, and they squealed with delight when I flew low over their heads, but the thrill was just that—an amusement. In the Bible, Egypt's Memphis was the New Kingdom; this was anything but. The crowd just wanted to be distracted. They wanted, for one day, to forget about sharecropping and slaughtering hogs.

Many in the South barely subsisted, as I had myself a decade before, living job to job, hand to mouth. But once or twice a year, for a nickel or a dime, as many people as possible would pile atop of the Strongest-Man-Alive's wagon. Sometimes there would be two of these he-men, and they would compete to see who could pull the massive groups of people the farthest. Poor folks would wager a penny and throw their coins behind the man in the snug blue tights or the hulk in the red stocking feet.

There was cockfighting, too, and contests for the fattest cow, the best blueberry pie, or the prettiest hog. A pair of local baseball teams challenged each other, as did the prettiest girls in town. Maybe, I told myself, as I watched a line drive sink into the outfield, there is nothing wrong with just plain old amusement. I could still encourage and uplift our people at these events, too. Over the course of three days and my three shows, more than three thousand people attended the Memphis Fair.

The plane I had rented was another beat-up Curtiss Jenny from the War. On the third and final show, and less than a mile above the field, the engine sputtered and then died. Thank God, I was really just over the field, or I would never have made it down in one piece. I felt like spitting on that hunk of junk and on the people who rented it to us, as well. They had charged us a lot of money for that old wreck and had not taken the time to care for it properly. By this time in my fledgling career, I had dealt with plenty of engine outs. I wasn't afraid. I was just angry.

When I landed, a little boy ran over to me. "Hey, lady, did that thing quit on you up there for a little while?" he asked, out of breath from his gallop.

"It sure did," I said, shaking his small hand. "You sound as if you'll make a great flyer one day," I added. "You have a super keen eye and ear for what just happened."

"Jeez, thanks, missus," he drawled. "Would you please sign my program?"

"I would be honored. What's your name?" I asked.

"Gage," he replied.

"Gage," I repeated. "Always keep your eyes and ears open, and you will make a fine flyer. Love, Bessie Coleman." I scrawled.

"Gee, thanks, missus!" he called as he skipped off with his prize.

"Hey, Mama, look what I got me!" Gage yelled as he flagged his mother down. Her belly was heavy with another baby, and she had to lean over it to see what her little boy held in his hands. A handsome man in overalls joined them, and the boy handed the program to his father, then he pointed to me. I nodded to the parents and they smiled back.

While the waves of people swirled all around me, I kept my eyes on the round belly and then on Gage's little hand as it slipped into his mama's. What if that had been my life? What if, instead of scud-running clouds and doing loops for those below, I had left my feet planted on the ground and had others I loved planting theirs alongside mine? I threw the family one long last look before I moved on. It was in moments like these that I drowned in regret. They came upon me when I was least expecting them and when I felt least prepared to sort through them, and they left me longing for the children I did not bear and the husband I did not have. As a local reporter flagged me down and beckoned others to us, I pushed away the familiar anguish and set my face back into its practiced, easy smile. It was time to promote the next event. I reminded myself that regret was an indulgence for which I simply did not have time.

Expenses from the Memphis show, including the aeroplane, fuel, my train fare, and room and board, amounted to one hundred and seven dollars. I expected to recoup all this, plus one hundred and fifty dollars from the split of the gate profit when Jackson and I reconvened. But before I could collect on my payday, Jackson informed me that I would first have to hurry to a studio in Manhattan for the filming of *Shadows and Sunshine*, the film that I had agreed to star in.

Making a movie sounded so glamorous, and I still had trouble believing that Jackson had gotten me a gig as an actress in a moving picture show. He said the film would boost my popularity and recognition and that making me a starlet would command bigger payouts at my air shows for sure, so, as always, I kept my eyes on the future. I still needed money for my own plane, and this seemed to be a novel and glitzy way to get there.

My travel expenses grew another seventy-five dollars, as now I took the train from Memphis to Manhattan and had to stay in a hotel. Jackson had asked the hotel manager to give me a copy of the article that Jackson himself had written. The headline in *The Baltimore Afro-American* read, "Bessie Coleman to Star in a Seminole Super Film." In my first starring role, I was to be cast as a young mother named Malinda Suggs. Her character was that of a dignified mother of a handicapped girl called Eliza who, despite grave birth defects, grew into a remarkable woman and author. My character, born into slavery, was like many of my mother's generation who burst out of bondage and poured determination and hope into their children.

I knew this history, because I had read Eliza Suggs's memoir during the fifteen-hour train ride from Memphis to Manhattan. *Shadows and Sunshine* was a well-written testament to Eliza's love for her family, their will to survive, and their determination to achieve a dignified life for them all. They had bought their way out of servitude and were moving into a new world in which they would have at least some control over their own destinies.

But when I arrived for the first meeting, I found that the director had a very different vision, both from mine and from reality. He had cast Malinda Suggs as a hunched-over, rag-wearing, cane-dragging old hag. I was to dress in tatters. I was to stoop. I was to hobble like a broken bird across the stage. And worse than all that, the script I was handed was peppered with such slang that there was no way my character would even be understood. They wanted Malinda Suggs the slave, not Malinda Suggs the proud lioness.

I told myself that there had to be some mistake. I had my copy of *Shadows and Sunshine* in my hand, and figured I would simply introduce myself and show the director the picture of Malinda Suggs on page sixteen. She was a proud, exquisitely dressed and well-coiffed woman. He just needed to see that he had made an incorrect assumption. Making my way through the hundreds of extras who were on hand to show the toil of working under the hot sun in the fields of our constructed set, I went in search of the director.

I found Nip Preston wrestling a clipboard of yellow papers. He was a tall man, with beady eyes that peered out from behind horn-rimmed spectacles. Walnut colored, he had a pencil-line mustache and wore a scarlet beret on his small cone-shaped head. I wondered what French picture show he had seen that had made him do such a ridiculous thing, because his beret was a terrible imitation of what real Frenchmen wore.

We exchanged pleasantries. But Nip, like his name, was short on small talk.

"Good to meet you. Wish we had more time. These rented studios are at a premium, of course. So … " his voice trailed off. "If you wouldn't mind getting into costume, we will walk you through what to do during the opening sequence. This first scene has no dialogue for your character, but you'll have the rest of the week to memorize your lines, and we'll bring you back at week's end to finish shooting your part. Sound good?" He asked, already looking back to his dog-eared papers.

"Oh … well, that's just it," I began. "I think there has been a mistake. In the first scene, Malinda is dressed in rags, and I think I am supposed to hunch my back and limp across the stage with a walking stick? In the book, Malinda didn't need a cane, she was perfectly robust."

If he had been annoyed at my presence before, now he was angry.

"You know, Betsy …" he began.

"Bessie," I corrected.

"Yes, right. Bessie, is it? They tell me that you fly aeroplanes. And I guess you think that since you fly planes, you can direct cinema too. Well, this is my job, and we are going to do things my way. Is that clear?" People had begun to gather around us. There was about to be a showdown and everyone was ready to watch a real drama unfold.

"The script is going to reflect the general condition of slavery," he went on. "Maybe Malinda was the luckiest little slave girl ever, but her life story is unique. I don't want the charm of unique, I want to capture the routine."

"Why, that's just the point!" I said, louder now. "Malinda was not some 'little slave girl'. She literally worked her way out of bondage. She was a devoted mother and wife who saw to her daughter's needs. She had dignity! To dress her up in rags and parade her about doesn't honor any of the real-life heroes in her story. If you want to portray the life of a poor southern slave, then you should do that, but don't call it the life of Malinda or Eliza Suggs."

As I spoke, Nip's cheeks began to turn as red as his lid.

"That's right! No Uncle Tom stuff for her!" A man dressed as if he'd been working in the fields cried out from the gathering crowd. It dawned on me that I should have insisted on a private conversation, maybe taken a softer approach. But Nip was in such a hurry and so rude to me that my sense of self-restraint had failed me.

With his back against the wall, it would be tough to retreat in front of all of these people. He was, after all, the director, and he was being challenged by what he saw as an arrogant, just-arrived upstart who wasn't even an actress.

"Get back to work, all of you." Nip flung his hand at the throng of extras.

But they wouldn't budge. Without having met a single one of them, I knew that each of us had lived through the same ordeal, suffering through the post-emancipation world. The struggle bound us together. The deprivation was with us every day.

"I said, get back to work!" he tried to bellow, but his voice cracked.

"Listen ... " sensing the inevitable, I tried to turn down the heat. "I didn't handle this in the best way. You have already forgotten more than I will ever learn about making moving pictures. I just think this character deserves respect. I think she earned it."

"Yeah, well, I am pretty sure my good friend J. A. was wrong when he thought you had earned a part in this picture. If I had known how difficult you were going to be, I would not have let you within ten feet of this set," Nip hissed at me. "I have actresses, real ones, not ones I have to teach to act, and they are lined up to star in this film."

Now I was the one who was angry. I had given him an out and he had refused to take it.

"That's it!" I said, throwing my hands up in disgust. He flinched, as if afraid I was going to hit him.

"I am not going to harm you, mister, but I agree with my friend over here, no Uncle Tom stuff for me! Keep your movie and keep your Raggedy Ann costume, too!"

On my way out, a young woman grabbed my arm. "I can't believe you stood up to Nip Preston! He is the biggest director in all of Negro cinema!" she whispered, "it's about time somebody did. That man is always Tomming his own people. There is another up-and-coming director. His name is Oscar Micheaux. One day," she breathed, "I hope to work with him."

"I saw *The Homesteader*," I replied. "It played twice a day at the New Center Theater in Chicago. It was excellent. Go! Get away from here and go find Oscar Micheaux. Time is the only resource you can never buy more of. Don't waste another minute of your life with this fool!"

I followed my own advice and ran out of that place.

Eager to catch Jackson before Nip had a chance to do the same, I hurried to *The Defender*'s New York office, where Jackson rented space. I was too late. Word had already reached him, and for the second time in one day, I was face to face with an angry man, and Jackson was even angrier than Nip.

"So, this is how you treat opportunity?" was the first thing he spat at me when I walked into the office.

"Hi, how do you do?" I asked. "Now that our pleasantries are out of the way, would you like to hear my side of the story?"

"I don't need to hear any of your lies. All I know is that you seem to think that you are better than everyone else. Yet, you yourself are a nothing but a cotton-picking, gold-digging social climber. That tattered dress was too poor for the likes of you, you choice piece of Calico!" Jackson shouted.

"Malinda Suggs was born a slave," I shouted back, "and come to think of it, she had more prosperity before emancipation than I do as a free woman. Not only that, from the little I've read about her I can say for a fact that she had more dignity and decency in her pinkie finger than you have in your entire fat body!"

"Here, take this and then get out," he said, tossing me an envelope.

I caught it in midair, opened it and counted swiftly—ninety-seven dollars.

"This doesn't even cover my expenses!" I snapped. "Plus, you still owe me for my cut of the Memphis gate!"

He didn't answer.

"You fat cheat. Where. Is. The. Rest?" I growled.

"That's all you're worth to me," he said, without looking up.

"So, that's how it is, is it? I expected the overseer to steal from me, but my own people, my own manager?" I hissed, "J. A. must stand for Jack Ass because you are a lousy, filthy thief! If I were a man, I'd whip your ass!"

But it was Jackson who had the last word. Two months later, J.A. penned another article for *The Baltimore Afro-American*. This time the headline was ugly, and the worst press I had ever gotten. "BESSIE COLEMAN BREAKS CONTRACT. Quits Seminole Picture Co. After Agreement to Feature in Film Drama. NEW STAR SUBSTITUTED ..." He called my replacement "a pretty little girl" and condescendingly referred to me as "eccentric." But the worst lie Jackson told was, "the lady seems to want to capitalize [on] her publicity without being willing to work." Nothing could be further from the truth; my track record showed that. But I had another lesson still to learn—I could never control what the writers would write or what the readers would believe.

CHAPTER 37

I complained to Mr. Abbott, and the next day the money was waiting for me at the Western Union on State Street. But my break with Jackson had cost me a lot more than my grand total of three-hundred and thirty-two dollars. While Mr. Abbott had been my most loyal supporter, and I had come to know him well, he steadfastly avoided friction in his personal and business relationships. Jackson rented space in *The Defender*'s Harlem office and he advertised weekly in the paper. Mr. Abbott would not relish disharmony between himself and a business associate, and he did not want to be drawn into the middle of my fight.

I left New York and returned to Chicago, where I confided in Norma, "when I first came home, I was on top of the world. Now I feel like the world is on top of me."

"Well, Bess, the air is sure not smooth right now, but you know how you are. As soon as you are flying, everything will make sense again," she consoled.

"Thanks, Norma. I know you're right. But this time it might not be that easy." I smiled. "Jackson's partner, another of these Negro Fair promoters, disappeared on me, too. He controlled the chittlin' circuit— fairs throughout the Carolinas, and now he wants nothing to do with me, either. These men have knocked me on my ass."

The sad fact was that I was fighting on two fronts. I was a Negro in a profession where our numbers could be counted on one hand, and I was a woman trying to make my mark in outlets controlled, owned, and managed by men. The fact that the latter fight involved men of my own race wounded me profoundly.

A few weeks later, I ran into Stanley Jacobs, an old customer of mine from my days at the White Sox. An enterprising man in his fifties, Mr. Jacobs owned a half-dozen storefronts along the Stroll, which is how he came to be one of my clients. He said he had read of my earlier adventures in *The Defender* and he was proud of me. I thanked him and then, perhaps because I was worried about my future and respected his business sense, I poured out my troubles to this man I barely knew. He already knew most of it—my time in Europe and the shows I had done. He had heard about the film and what had happened with that, and even said he thought it didn't sound much like me to get up and walk away from hard work.

At the time, he was looking for a new tenant for one of his places in the 600 block of Indiana Avenue. Until he found one, he said, I could use the storefront for my school. Not only that, but Mr. Jacobs said that when he did eventually find a paying tenant, he would let me counter their offer, if I so desired.

Mr. Abbott advertised my new school in the classifieds and, as an olive branch, he sent a reporter to do a profile on me along with a hearty sidebar on my storefront school, which I had named Coleman Aeronautics. At the same time, my family helped me put up flyers all over town. We papered the busses and post offices, the barber shops and coffee shops. I was invited to speak at Pilgrim Baptist Church, and right away, I started attending church regularly and inviting congregants to "come and experience the miracle of flight." It was a bit premature, but I made arrangements to buy flight time from David Behncke, who was a part owner of Checkerboard Field, and who was good enough to warn me that he was planning to sell his stake and move to Minneapolis, where he had found a wealthy investor who wanted him to start an air service there.

I only had two students at first, which didn't come close to keeping the school afloat. Despite all of our efforts, it was tough just to keep the lights on. A number of people dropped in, but only a few stayed on once they learned of the costs and intensity of study. But on one particularly grim day when I wasn't sure it was going to be worth carrying on,

Luther Ramsay pushed open the glass storefront door and strolled into my school. Luther, clearly a businessman of some kind, handled himself well. His countenance suggested a worldly man. He was a quick learner and a good sport, and of all my students, only Luther stayed current in his tuition payments.

Only two months later, Mr. Jacobs had found his paying tenant, a druggist who wanted to occupy his Indiana storefront. I wasn't making enough money to counter the druggist's offer, not to mention justify keeping the school open. It broke my heart to have to tell my students that I could not go on any longer. I felt as if I had let both them and myself down. All I could think to do was to leave them with a parting gift, so I took each of them out to Checkerboard for the flight of their lives. They all promised to return, should I re-open the school.

On the day I took Luther out to Checkerboard to fly him around, he never stopped grinning. "Wow! Bee's knees, Bessie! That was better than all the jack in the world!" Luther exclaimed. "Let me take you out to celebrate that fabulous ride," he beamed.

In his early forties, coffee-brown skinned, short and powerful, with big eyes set far apart, Luther turned out to be a delight. He was full of energy and imagination, and at a booth we shared in the Dreamland Café, I became his captive audience while he told me about his life and his plans. Luther was living in Chicago, but his employer, Coast Tire and Rubber Company, was based in Oakland, California.

"I've wanted to fly ever since I was a boy and watched those American propaganda newsreels of the Air Service pilots fighting the Germans," he said, pushing his empty roast beef plate off to the side. "And it was just as fantastic as in the picture shows!"

I smiled, thinking back to little Gage, the boy I had met in Memphis. I was happy that I was able to give Luther this pleasure and hoped I had planted a seed in Gage to fly as well.

"Listen, I have an idea," he said wiggling his gin fizz in my direction. "And it's a good one. A big one."

"What's on your mind?" I said, intrigued.

"California is a whole new scene." Luther vibrated. "There are movie stars everywhere, and every single one of 'em owns automobiles that need tires. A lot of the famous people there have sponsors—you know, companies who pay movie stars a lotta dough to represent their products. Lucky for you, my company sells the most durable tires on the market."

I looked at him in silence, wondering where he was going with all this.

"You, Miss Coleman offer more than just a pretty face. You've got skills, and you could use them to advertise for my company in a whole new way! You could distribute leaflets from your aeroplane! Why, you could even have Coast Tires on your landing gear," he said, beaming.

I felt my pulse quicken and my palms begin to sweat. No one had ever proposed such an idea to me before, but I could picture it instantly. Just as with Norma's scarves, I could sprinkle anything I liked from my position in the sky. And if I took Luther up on this offer, that's exactly where I'd be—back in the sky. We talked for two more hours about how we pictured the plan going forward, and at the end of the evening, Luther walked me to my door and promised to be in touch when he next traveled to Oakland. I was ecstatic!

Just as the dead of winter gripped Chicago and the cruel wind that blew off the lake took on a nasty bite, a note in Luther's dark block print arrived. Thankfully, Norma was at my place when it arrived. I was too nervous to open it myself, and so she took it from my shaking fingers.

"What if that company says Luther is full of horse feathers?" I paced back and forth as Norma tortured me by opening the envelope ever so slowly. Then she read it silently to herself, folded it back into thirds, and placed it in the front pocket of her apron.

"Well," she said, "Luther may be full of horse feathers, but you'd better dust off your stompers 'cause they want you in California in three weeks!"

I threw myself into Norma's arms, and we jumped up and down, hollering as if we were little girls.

"I'm going to fly again, Norma!" I whooped. "I can't believe it!"

"Yes, you sure are, Bessie, and I never had a doubt in my mind that you would," Norma said proudly.

"Warm blue sky awaits you in far-away California, honey," Norma mused before I boarded the California Zephyr from Chicago to Oakland. "You be careful and be happy, okay? And write as soon as you get settled in."

The platform and everyone on it grew small as my train pulled away. Soon I could no longer see Norma, nor Walter, nor Mama. Once again, I was heading off to some unknown place and leaving everyone I loved behind. I fell asleep to the rocking motion of the train. The first time I stirred, we had traveled out of snowy Illinois and were crossing the great gray winter of Iowa. The land seemed to stretch on forever. Every thirty minutes or so a barn, silo, or church steeple floated by, but other than that, there was only land. Neighborhoods I had just left behind in Chicago were full to bursting, and yet here there was all the space in the world.

When we had passed Omaha and about a thousand miles of wheat fields, the Platte River carved a girthy path into the plains. I recognized the word Platte, because of its literal French translation—the root plat meant flat. It snaked through the land, flowing east and slicing ruggedly through snow-crusted sandbars. On its banks a herd of bison gathered, their giant black faces accented by twin horns. Cranes, eagles, and pheasants flocked and squabbled, whether on the land or in the sky.

One hundred miles after that, a rickety bridge was the only way across rampaging rapids, and the train began a slow, steady climb up an unpromising-looking trestle scaffolding. Precariously, we swayed from side to side as we ascended. Rattling above the Platte, the bridge groaned until the last wheel had crossed. We steamed westward, arriving in Denver where the city rose a mile high into the sky and was shrouded behind a curtain of frozen fog. The Rocky Mountains loomed, their breathtaking, frosty peaks rising another two miles higher into the sky.

The conductor announced that we were crossing the Continental Divide, explaining that this imaginary longitudinal line running down through the middle of the Americas, stretched from the top of Canada to the tip of the South American continent. From here, rivers and waterways will drain toward the east or the west, as every drop of water relentlessly pushes its way west to the Pacific or drags itself one thousand, five-hundred miles east to the Atlantic. The Great Divide is marked by deep, mesmerizing gorges and by palisades of cliffs, where light travels in, becomes absorbed in the throat of canyons, and never shines again.

More than eight hours past the canyons of Colorado, and glistening along the shores of a huge blue opal, lay Salt Lake City. Six hundred miles later, sagebrush and bristle cones dotted the tracks, as we chugged through Carson City, Nevada, where the hitching posts in front of storefronts looked like giant cardboard cutouts. No-nonsense and precise, bold signs lined marquis row—BARBER, DRY GOODS & MERCANTILE, U.S. POST, SALOON, BATH HOUSE, LIVESTOCK, BLACKSMITH, FUR & BOOTS, TARTS, PHINEAS TOMBSTONES, COFFINS & GRAVEDIGGER, STOVES & LIDS, MORGUE.

Finally, we crossed the Sierra Nevadas—a dramatic escarpment between California and the rest of the country. Beyond, lay the land of a thousand sandy shores—California. Nearly three days after leaving Chicago, our huge locomotive wheezed into Oakland. I had made it.

There was so much industry and opportunity in town. The auto manufacturers that had fled the frigid Midwest and discovered Oakland, dubbed it the "Detroit of the West," with Durant Motors, Fageol Motors, and the giant of them all, General Motors, all opening plants here. Jobs were plentiful and almost every average family owned an automobile. And they all needed TIRES! Why, I reckoned I was going to mint my own gold mine, only I would be raking in greenbacks by selling rubber.

California felt so exciting, so new. I longed to fly all over that great state and see it from above, the way a bird does. I had only one day before meeting the folks at Coast Tires, and since it didn't take long to put my things away in a rented room in a small Oakland rooming house, I had time to case out the town. I found Oakland Harbor and bought a round-trip ticket for the paddleboat that crossed the neck of San Francisco Bay at its narrowest point. The boat looked out of place, more like something that should have been steaming its way across the muddy Mississippi than bobbing along the choppy blue surf of the San Francisco Bay. The enormous steamboat wove its way through the whitecaps, paddling by the ominous military prison called Alcatraz that loomed atop a craggy outcrop. Guards with binoculars scanned the island and the sea from a watchtower, and I was unnerved to think that they could see me up close, but I couldn't see them. When the fifty-cent ride was over, I was glad.

The next morning, I hurried off to Coast Tires where a chipper white man named Joe Reagan met me. About my own age, Joe shook my hand with such vigor I thought he had injured my wrist. He flashed what I had come to appreciate as a sunny California smile and said he was happy that I had arrived. We then went on to meet with the president, a dapper, blonde man named Paul Sachs, whose California-bronzed skin was darker than my own Chicago sun-deprived pastiness.

A man called Riderman thrust a stubby well-manicured hand my way. "Well now, I suppose I am meeting the loveliest flying starlet that there ever was," he said with what seemed to be genuine enthusiasm.

I had not known what to expect, but it definitely was not such a big group of friendly white men. I hadn't anticipated so much, well … damned happiness. And although together their sunny dispositions made quite a show of making me feel at home, every instinct I had was on high alert.

After much smiling and chitchatting, Luther finally appeared. He entered his boss's office wearing a wide smile of his own, greeting his colleagues with handshakes, and lavishing a familiar grin and a genuine hug on me.

"Luther, have you let the cat out of the bag, yet?" Paul asked him after we had had a chance to say our hellos.

"Why, no, sir, I thought it would please you to tell Miss Coleman our splendid news. I don't think we should make her wait another moment, though." Luther was all teeth.

With great exaggeration, the boss cleared his throat. "Miss Coleman, we'd like to offer you an aeroplane as part of your compensation."

I was sure I had not heard him correctly.

"I know we have contract details to work out, but before we get to all that, I want you to have your own aeroplane." He raised his hands up to the sky and went on, "'Coast Tire and Rubber' will run along its side, but the wings and wheels will be yours," he said, looking back at me. "And since no one else around here can fly 'em, no one else can borrow 'em!"

There was a whole lot of chuckling all around at the boss's joke. Paul and Joe laughed and laughed. Luther clapped Joe on the back and then clapped my back, too. And then Paul stopped laughing. In an instant he was serious.

"I want you to teach me, the way you taught Luther," he said.

"It would be my pleasure," I said; although the sudden mood change put me back on alert.

There was, however, no warning strong enough to keep me from rejoicing in what I had just heard. My own aeroplane! My own aeroplane! I could hear myself shouting for joy inside my own head, and it was all I could do to not let that whoop and a holler fall right out of my mouth.

PART THREE

CHAPTER 38

L uther came to pick me up in a brand-new company-owned General Motors Chevrolet. The Coast tires on the car were also brand new, and it was a good thing, because we were headed five hundred miles south to Coronado Island, a military depot outside of San Diego, where Luther would help me pick out "my" new aeroplane. I felt as if my bag of luck was full to overflowing.

Luther and I made swell traveling companions. "Swell"—a new word I had picked up since arriving in California. Everything there, the buildings, automobiles, people—they were all sunny and "swell." Not even a February rain shower seemed able to dampen anybody's spirits. And as we drove south, the wide blue sky opened up, and nothing but clear sunshine greeted us. The fact that I was here rather than trying to eke out a shivering living of winter flying in Chicago made me relax with relief.

We talked and laughed easily, Luther and I, and I learned still more about him. He had been so busy carving his way through the world and making his way in business that he had never married and so had no wife or family. What he did have was story after story about his cross-country travels and adventures, and while I was not attracted to him, I found his ability to see opportunities where others could not—as well as his general enthusiasm for living—enormously appealing.

Like me, Luther was a risk-taker, and he had the ability to make things happen, such as convincing white men that a Negro woman could fly an aeroplane and represent their company! I had never met anyone else who thought as big as he did. Luther had earned his stripes as a man of business so prominently that now white men sought his counsel. He understood that Coast Tire and Rubber executives were interested in one color, and that color was green. And while some Negroes in Chicago were able to buy a home—thanks to Jesse—many more were shut out of home-ownership completely, so instead of houses they bought cars, the biggest, fanciest ones they could finance. That trend was not lost on Coast Tire executives. Luther earned the mid-western sales rep position by selling twice as many tires in densely populated Chicago and Ford's hometown of Detroit than all the East Coast and southern reps combined.

We made our way down the California coast and then hurried along to catch a ferry to the island depot. Buzzing through the busy harbor, I considered for the hundredth time that I still had no contract for this deal. It didn't seem to bother Paul Sachs or Luther that we still had details to work out, so I decided that I wouldn't let it bother me, either. I concentrated instead on my own ideas about what would come next. I figured that with my own plane, I could drop leaflets every day, in different towns, making my way up and down the California coastline. Perhaps I could even skywrite the name of Coast Tires over the heads of sun worshippers on every Pacific beach. The sky was clear enough for that, for sure.

A couple of perfect Boeing models graced the front of the depot's yard. The aeroplanes were shiny, but their price tags were blinding. Beauties like these cost thousands, and my budget was only five hundred dollars. Undeterred, I looked around eagerly for whatever other aero-planes were available for sale.

My expectations were so high that I could not have foreseen the disappointment I would feel when we discovered the rest of the armory. Stocked with a few dozen beat-up Curtiss Jennys, it was loaded with left-overs from the War, which were already six years old, but still in their original crates. The engines would surely have suffered from internal corrosion by now. Their undercarriages would be pitted, their bearings rusted, and the camshaft would look like Swiss cheese.

"You look mighty troubled," Luther said. I had gone from happy-go-lucky to despondent, chatty to silent, and he had noticed.

I kicked a rotted exhaust pipe along my path and then inspected the crates to see which had suffered the least water damage.

"Some of these planes are older and scruffier than a barnyard dog," I said. "The material on the wings will be full of dry rot. Who knows how much rain and salt damage has corroded the engine? Look here," I pointed, "rodents have made a snack out of these wires! You can't leave an aeroplane sitting around. It's like a racehorse, and these have been rode hard and put away wet!" I was talking to Luther now as much as I was to myself. One of the crates had 1914 stamped on it. "That's nine years old!" The Boeings out front are gorgeous, but the rest of this place is just a dusty old boneyard!"

Luther disappeared. Within minutes he returned with a yardman who claimed that wooden crate #506 contained the best aeroplane left on the field in our price range. Coast Tire wired the five hundred, and we had #506 shipped off to Santa Monica, where the Coronado supervisor had recommended that we could find the best assemblers.

Meanwhile, I tried to keep myself busy and free from the worries that plagued me about flying some broken-down old plane. I heard Mama's warnings in my head and, in an effort to distract myself, decided to pay a visit to the offices of *The California Eagle*. The paper was the Los Angeles newspaper that rivaled *The Chicago Defender* in its tireless advocacy of Negro causes, and I was curious to see how similar it would be. All the same troubles that plagued Negroes in Chicago and New York plagued our people here, too. Living wages, good schools, and decent housing were all hurdles for my people in the West. Other than the weather, everything else was the same.

The newspaper was run by Mrs. Charlotta Bass, and Luther was her biggest fan. Like Mr. Abbott, Mrs. Bass had been born in the South, in a town called Sumter, South Carolina. She had escaped up north and made a home in Rhode Island, but poor health had forced her to seek the California sunshine.

Arriving in 1910, Mrs. Bass's first job was selling advertisements for a paper called *The California Owl*. Her strong work ethic and good head for business led her to climb the ranks quickly, and when the paper's founder, John Neimore, was dying, he made her promise to take over. Take it over she did and, with that, Mrs. Bass became the first woman in the country to own and publish a major Negro newspaper. She not only gave the paper a new fierce name, *The California Eagle*, she also transformed it into a must-read for every Negro in Los Angeles. At forty-nine, Mrs. Bass looked like a sweet grandma, and she fooled many who underestimated her barbed-pen, as she used it to champion causes close to her heart—the suffrage battle, migrant abuse, poor schools, and inadequate housing.

Yet, she went one step further. She was able to articulate a grand vision for the future of aviation. As if she, too, had been plotting with Fokker, she forecast that "bigger planes will one day fly people all over this great country, and the aeroplane will revolutionize travel." Not only that, she included me in that future. "Bessie, you will be a beacon to light the way for Negroes to this new technology."

Putting real action behind those words, she convinced the new owners of a five-hundred-acre former sugar-beet farm, who had just converted their land into public fairgrounds, that my airshow would be a major attraction for their new venue. They were eager for new acts, and we were convinced this would be the perfect opportunity to showcase my new tire sponsor and to introduce the public to the notion of a flying school for Negroes.

For weeks I had been trying in vain to arrange an airshow at Roger's Field in Los Angeles, where Amelia Earhart had taken her first aeroplane ride at about the same time that I was in France taking my FAI exam. In the years since, she had made a big name for herself. Because they were the only keeper of worldwide aviation records, Earhart was also issued an FAI license in 1923, but she didn't have to learn French and study in France to earn it. I coveted her ability to fly, not to mention own, new, reliable equipment, and it didn't hurt that the camera always caught her looking carefree. What I had was the satisfaction of knowing that I had led the way for nearly two years.

So, Amelia had Roger's Field and I had Palomar Park, and my own newly assembled team was busy. Luther arranged for me to stay at the YWCA for Colored Girls in Santa Monica, where I could supervise the mechanics every day until my aeroplane was finally assembled. Meanwhile, Mrs. Bass completed arrangements for the show, recruiting event workers and drumming up the more than twenty thousand people who were expected to attend over the course of three days. It was a larger audience than I could ever have dreamed of.

The only hitch in these plans was that in order to drop leaflets from the sky, I had to go and fetch them since mimeographed copies would not do. I had to make the thousand-mile round-trip to and from Oakland. Where I should have been, was working with the mechanics in Santa Monica while they finished putting everything together that had been taken out of crate #506. But by the time I returned, the last wingnut was already in place. All that remained was the payment. I assured them that Coast Tire would come through, and I crossed my fingers as I said it. The truth was, Coast had promised to buy an aeroplane, but they had not openly agreed to additional costs—costs like the unexpected assembly fee involved in building an entire aeroplane.

"Do we send the assembly invoice to Mr. Riderman?" asked the head mechanic.

"Why, yes. I believe so," I chirped reassuringly. "He is expecting it."

The job was completed the night before I would fly the short forty-five-mile flight to Palomar Park. The workers packed up the maintenance logs containing their entries and signatures. Then they helped me secure the four heavy rucksacks of Coast leaflets, latching them beside me so that in the morning, I would be ready to go. With everything in order, I examined the older aeroplane. It wasn't as fast and sleek as the brand-new Fokker I had flown, nor was it as sturdy as Robert's Albatros. It wasn't even agile and graceful like Caudrons and Nieuports, but it was mine, mine to use as I saw fit. And at that moment, that was enough. Forecasts promised high barometric pressure, excellent visibility, and gentle winds—conditions were what we called CAVU—clear and visibility unlimited.

But that glorious day feels like a lifetime ago.

PART FOUR

COMEBACK

CHAPTER 39

Three months and eight days have passed since that ghastly cast was sawed off my leg. All of the pins, spikes, linkages, and skewers were finally carved away, and the terminal ends of a half-dozen pins were sliced off at the boundary of my skin. The quarter-inch pegs remain buried deep within my bone.

These steel pins and ivory pegs will remain knit into my femur for the rest of my days. "Pins and pegs," I heard a doctor quip, describing the plate of armor welded to my bone. However medieval the remedy, I have healed well enough to support my weight with the help of a gooseneck cane.

I walk, but I limp.

Gone is all of the black and blue, but a full body stretch or even a hearty yawn or unexpected cough can cause my rib cage to rattle. A tic-tac-toe scar floats beneath my jaw, along with a stubborn zigzag saw line below my left eye. And although the scars will fade, they are a constant reminder of the primary lesson that *Monsieur* Caudron tried so hard to impress upon me long ago, that "it" can happen to you.

It did.

The danger in this game is a real and constant threat. My vulnerability persists—needing to make enough money to feed myself, to buy a safe machine, to protect myself from unsavory managers, and to find a love who holds me up when the chips are down. Dear God, I can't dwell here—sinking into a deep well of regret; its sides are greased with Vaseline. I can't crawl out because of the endless backward slides. I have to gather my strength and fly. It's the only way out for me.

I was not well enough to travel for another month. So I took the nuns up on their generous offer to move into their convent—which housed the orphanage—and there I continued to convalesce. The convent was only steps away from the hospital, and the nuns who ran the orphanage lived in its small stucco cottages, caring for the children and for me. Life here was simple, basic, wholesome.

One morning, as I sat at my bare, oak desk writing a letter to Norma, my thoughts were interrupted by a deep female voice that seemed to coil around the spare furnishings of my room.

"Do you remember me?"

Christ's words, *This do in remembrance of me*, fluttered somewhere deep inside my brain when I heard the question. Without turning to look at who spoke the words and cast the shadow across my small room, I nodded yes. The nun who ran to my rescue in the strawberry field was at my threshold. Behind me stood the woman who had drugged me, who had run to fetch a bone saw and who, despite her own misgivings, had undoubtedly helped deliver me, with my still-attached leg, to safety.

She somehow remained disturbingly sinister and I feared her.

"It's been months. We have been waiting for you," she breathed.

I turned to look into the face that unnerved me so.

"When I heard that you had arrived, I wanted to see your progress for myself. My name is Sister Agnes Eve. I spend my time in Mexican border towns where the children of the poor need me, and I leave for there again tomorrow," she said and managed what I thought might have been her version of a smile.

"Thank you for saving my life," I mustered.

"It was God's will," she said softly and turned on her heel, taking away with her the long shadow she cast.

I imagined that Sister Agnes Eve fit in where she wandered, ministering to the ragged poor along the Mexican border. Her stern dedication to the call of duty seemed out of place with those she had rescued here, though, for the children I met at the orphanage were light-hearted, cheerful, and warm. But Sister Agnes Eve was a dedicated crusader, bred to save souls and, when need be, sacrifice a limb to save a body. She led a valiant crusade against demon spirits who sought to snatch away life in the fields and the poor settlements of northern Mexico. I suppose what frightened me most about her was the sense that her strength might be able to hold death at bay or, should she deem it wise, invite it in. She was possessed with a supernatural aura that was tinged, as it seemed to me, with a want of feeling. In my case, it was she who was able to choose whether I died in a strawberry patch or spent the rest of my life either with one leg or two. Her own recognition of the unchecked power she wielded seemed to swirl around her robes like an admonition.

Yet, the children possessed none of this complexity. They were all light and goodness, for the nuns at the orphanage had created a loving household of siblings for them. Schoolwork, games, lots of time outside in the sunshine, and plenty of grub that children fancy—Kellogg's Corn Flakes with milk and sugar for breakfast and peanut butter and jelly sandwiches for lunch—created structure, normalcy, and consistency.

The children loved for me to put on my pilot's uniform and tell them about flying. Boys and girls took turns bringing me the paper aeroplanes that they had fashioned out of reused paper. Some even brought fresh-picked strawberries from the field where I had crash-landed. Simple were their gifts, but profound their desire to express thanksgiving for the story they had been told—that I had glided my aeroplane above them and past them, landing in a mangled heap to avoid crushing them under the force of my machine. After dinner each night, I donned my French uniform and showed them the Pathé News film from Potsdam. Over and over again, they begged to watch the grainy image of me mounting the plane and soaring through the sky. They had so little, yet they were so grateful for the one thing that I had plenty of to spare—my time.

I was grateful anew to Robert Thelen, as my film reels later became the centerpiece of other lectures. The nuns borrowed a film projector so that I could give talks at the YWCA. I took the reels and pictures of my exploits to all the nearby churches and auditoriums. The same audience that had condemned me when they thought I was a no-show, had been thoroughly chastised by Mrs. Bass in her newspaper, and now people turned out in droves to hear me speak. Often I would address standing-room-only crowds where some who could not get inside would listen in through open windows.

A *California Eagle* headline from a letter written by my former boss and supporter, Paul Sachs, read, "Other Race Appreciates Girl Flyer; Miss Coleman Spoken of Most Highly." Yet, while the people clapped and cheered during the film, the sight of me draped over my cane, juxta-posed against photos of my former robust self, drew compassion as well as pity. Each night I would collect about twenty dollars from ticket sales, and I squirreled away my meager earnings, suppressing my feelings of despair. Starting from scratch was dismal, and I had to will myself to push forward. The diminished luster of Luther's affections was equally disheartening, and I missed his company. I hoped desperately that he would not lose his job because of my accident, but there was no way of knowing how he fared after our friendship began to fade. Although I was forced to put most of what I earned towards my hospital bill, I knew that the one debt I could never repay was to the nuns, nurses, doctors, and the sweet children for their kindness.

I finally had to accept the reality that California held no more promise for me. It was time for me to return to Chicago. And so, on Friday, June 15, 1923, two years to the day after my triumphant FAI flight test, I slunk back home.

I was in poor spirits, even at the party Norma threw to welcome me back home. And while I tried to put on a happy face to please my family, my body and my pride ached, and I longed to end the night and go to bed. As the evening wound down, Mama came and sat down beside me.

"Here, Bessie. These came for you," she said, handing me two official looking envelopes. Both were from Columbus, Ohio—one from the city's Mayor, the other from the Governor of the state. To my surprise and delight, they had invited me to perform at the City's Labor Day festivities. It had been six months and many broken bones since I'd last flown. I was rusty. I would have to practice.

I returned to Checkerboard Field. Dave Behncke was moving on but had written to say that he would lend me one of his aeroplanes. After a thorough preflight check, I thrust my weight onto my good leg and spilled ungracefully into the cockpit. The aeroplane groaned. A rub or two and my knee was soothed, but my nerves were another matter. Could I do this again? After long weeks and hour upon hour in the cockpit, I discovered that the answer to the question was yes, I could.

I had to overcome a whole lot of anxiety at the thought of going back to Mr. Abbot again, but after a few weeks in Chicago I paid him a call. He told me that he still supported me, but I could see that his attitude toward me had cooled. While I had been off in California, Jackson had advertised heavily in *The Defender*, which meant that my fight with Jackson cost me more than I could have foreseen. To make matters worse, David Behncke was finalizing his departure. As he packed up and flew away, the rest of the long, cold winter loomed ahead, lacking any future that I could envision.

I needed a new start. I knew that once my luck turned around, supporters would emerge as they had in California, but Mr. Abbott's words echoed in my memory: "Everyone loves a winner." Well, I needed to be a winner in some place I had not yet been, and while I had been to many places, I had never considered the Deep South. It was just the kind of move Mr. Abbott would strongly disapprove of, but where else was I to turn?

Big city folk no longer had to muddy themselves traipsing out into a field to be entertained by random barnstormers who would cancel at the first sign of foul weather. Here in the city, glamour was easy to come by in the darkened nickelodeon houses. *The Mark of Zorro*, *The Three Musketeers*, and *Robin Hood* were popular features, and Douglas Fairbanks was the star of each—heroic as Zorro, swashbuckling as the musketeer D'Artagnan, and righteous as justice itself as Robin Hood. Lon Chaney thrilled and chilled, Charlie Chaplin tickled the funny bone of sophisticates, and Rudolph Valentino wooed in his daring, dashing, dreamy leading roles. Perhaps I should make a go of it where I was from, where entertainment was less readily available, and where a barnstormer could still evoke wonder and fill the grandstands up to the tippy top.

The one thing I had to do was to avoid Jackson in both Virginia and Kentucky and his associate in the Carolinas, so I planned to ask Mr. Abbott if he knew anyone in Texas who might help me make a fresh start down there. I was grateful when he threw me a bone.

"I can't believe I'm doing this, sending you back down to the godforsaken southern affliction of Texas," Mr. Abbott shook his head with disgust, directed at what I wasn't certain—my betrayal, Texas or, more likely, both. But he went ahead and helped me anyway, telling me that he would write to a Mr. Olen P. DeWalt down in Houston. According to Mr. Abbott, Mr. DeWalt and his wife were an institution in that town, and if anyone could make things happen, DeWalt and his "stunning wife, Maud" had the connections to do it.

I packed my things.

CHAPTER 40

A decade had passed since I had last set foot in Texas. When I left Waxahachie in February of 1915, I had absolutely no intention of ever returning. My departure had been an escape. With a healthy dose of fear and trepidation I was limping back, consumed by self-doubt—that is, until I met the DeWalts.

The train wobbled into Houston's Union Station on a predictably hot and steamy Gulf day. The sky was as I remembered it—Texas big. A sea of people crowded the platform, waiting for the train's arrival that Sunday afternoon. Beads of sweat clung to every brow, and limp clothing stuck to every limb, except that is, for the two well-starched figures of Olen and Maud DeWalt. Without any need for introduction, I knew them on sight.

Olen DeWalt cut a striking figure. He stood six feet tall, handsome, dark-syrup brown in color; he wore small round spectacles that made him look wise and professorial. The heat didn't appear to bother him in the least, for he stood ramrod straight in his gray cut-away suit and formal black-and-white striped tie. His confident stance made him appear as proud as a white man.

If Olen was poised, his wife was regal. Although taller than I, Maud was delicate in stature. She was fawn colored, and her sandy undertones shimmered in that searing heat. She wore her hair in a long braid that fell to the center of her back. She, too, looked polished, as though she had waltzed off a page of the Montgomery Ward Wish Book catalogue. Her white blouse, matching sage-green, long-waisted coat and lamp-shade skirt hailed from a bygone era. The top of her jacket created a tight curve around her long neck, and her white blouse peeked outside the mandarin collar. The jacket then flowed down the entire length of her torso, where it ended mid-thigh. A slimming corset pulled in her tiny waist, and although there was nothing at all provocative about her clothing, she exuded sensuality.

If their appearance was formal, they displayed no such distance in their reception.

"Welcome, welcome," Olen waved.

"You must be tired, dear. You have traveled so far," Maud purred. They too recognized me as the peripatetic whom they had come to collect.

Olen made much ado about carrying my sad cardboard travel bags. "Come, let me take those. Our automobile is just on the other side of the tracks," he said, and led the way.

Mr. Abbott had not said how the DeWalts had earned their fortune, and I didn't ask. I knew that they owned land but Olen didn't look like a farmer, and Maud was very clearly no farmer's wife. They were the cat's meow, exuding style and grace. Their brand-new Fleetwood matched their style—forest green, crank-less, clean, and sleek.

We traveled in luxury through the city to their home in Independence Heights, an all-Negro town that remained separate by choice. It was an island of prosperous Negroes—Negro mayor, town council, school-teachers, lawyers, doctors, and merchants. With its cozy bungalows, also built by Negroes, neat yards, and identical driveways, the town was indistinguishable from any other Texas outpost. Yet, what remained atypical was the homeowners' collective defiance, for this Negro enclave flourished in, of all places, Houston, Texas.

Why had Mr. Abbott kept this neighborhood, and others like it, a secret? I had been born and raised in Texas, yet I hadn't even known that this quiet community of strivers was flourishing right here in the very same state. Here were people dedicated to carving out a collective life of land ownership and education, to overcoming scarcity, and to protecting their own against lynching. These people didn't shutter schools when it came time to harvest cane and cotton; they kept their children in the classroom and hired itinerant workers to weed and pick.

Mr. Abbott knew that these fragile collectives existed, but maybe to him these towns were no more than shimmering oases. Stamps, Arkansas; Eatonville, Florida; and here, Independence Heights, Texas, were all towns that were vulnerable, teetering on the verge of extinction. Yet, they persisted and thrived. How long could the Heights's picket fences stave off hate, oppression, or a massacre the likes of Greenwood? There was no way of knowing.

Just five hundred miles north of Houston, and two short years earlier, the town of Greenwood, which was nestled inside of Tulsa, Oklahoma, was razed to the ground in a riot that *The Defender* called "Damnable and Inexcusable." Hundreds of Negroes were murdered; more than eight thousand were left homeless from fires. The charred bodies of the town's murdered citizens were tossed in the Arkansas River or dumped into mass graves. Greenwood, which Booker T. Washington had dubbed "Negro Wall Street," had been leveled after an accusation of sexual assault against a young Negro brought seventy-five armed Negro Great War veterans to the courthouse to protect a suspect whom they feared would be lynched. The seventy-five vets, men who had once fought for their county, were met by a bloodthirsty white mob of fifteen hundred. The odds were three hundred to one. Greenwood fell.

Building an independent existence was indeed a militant act, and the good people of Greenwood had paid for their independence with their lives. Not every Negro could, or wanted, to go north—the DeWalts and others like them believed that they had earned the right to live wherever they pleased, even if it happened to be in Texas. It had been the labor of Negros that had physically built that state, and they felt that every hardscrabble grain of earth upon which they stood belonged to them.

"Education is our only chance for true emancipation," Olen liked to say. "That's why teaching a slave to read and write was a crime. In this town, we do not close our schools to pick anything," he said, describing the town's separate elementary, middle, and high school. "After high school, we pour our children into my alma mater, Prairie View. It's just down the road a-piece. We want our young people to go get their independence so that they can return to keep all of us independent."

I thought of my own mother and father's illiteracy and of my one-room-schoolhouse experience. The Heights had the highest concentration of Negro college graduates that I had ever encountered. They were an example of what collective passion and fortitude could create, and to me they were a model for what our people could attain.

The DeWalts lived well. Their home was not as modest as the cottages that made up the rest of the town, but their relative wealth was not showy, either. Rather it was a reflection of how they lived—a Texas-style ranch, complete with cattle, horses, and a spring-fed pond—a classic country spot, right down to the pies that sat cooling on the windowsill. Maud put me up in a quaint, wallpapered bedroom just off the kitchen. The bedspread, the curtains, even the throw rug were flowery and peachy, as if the DeWalt's entire home existed in perpetual springtime.

Olen and Maud lived in harmony, and a deep love and respect for one another reigned. "I think my wife is the most beautiful creature that God ever made," Olen said after our first dinner. "She is a great cook, she has delicious lips, and I am quite sure that the good Lord made her especially for me."

Maud's delicate coloring blushed candy apple as she scolded him, "Hush now, Olen DeWalt." She turned to his surname when she was vexed or pleased. "Miss Coleman does not want to hear all that." She got up and disappeared through a heavy swinging oak door into the country kitchen. A few minutes later she returned, carrying a wild blueberry pie.

The DeWalt home was always a beehive. Some guests came for Maud's tasty baked goods, others came to talk politics, and still others came seeking Olen's business advice or his blessing on entrepreneurial endeavors. Before Olen had started his business, Negroes could only attend segregated midnight screenings of the movies that came through town. With his historic purchase of the Lincoln Theater, which was the only movie palace around for miles, Negroes were able to be entertained without fear, and in a place that afforded them respect. Olen was by then the most prosperous man, Negro or white, that I had ever known in Texas. But the DeWalts didn't hold on to their money and simply work towards making more, they used their influence and prosperity for the good of everyone in the Heights, launching both an NAACP chapter as well as the National Urban League in the town. Leading up to the airshow which Maud and Olen organized, I gave several talks to the new membership at the theater.

Olen announced that if we could find a plane, my show would take place on June 19, which meant that my flying free through Texas skies took on profound significance. Otherwise known as Juneteenth, it was the day synonymous with the actual emancipation of Texas slaves, who had had to wait two years longer than slaves in the rest of the country to lose their shackles, because the news of their emancipation was willfully kept from them. I told my Lincoln audience that this date was meaningful to me for another reason. "My own beloved mother was born into slavery in this very state. Mama was freed here too, although two years later than she should have been. Sometimes I wonder what it must have taken to keep the truth from so many people, don't you? But my Mama is tough. She's resilient. She's been by my side through my own journey because she knows that every generation moves its children forward as best as it can. And now it's your turn, and you all are doing that, too." The audience at the Lincoln got to their feet and applauded.

"Bessie, that speech made people weep," Olen said. "It inspired them. You need to do more talks. We need to spread your story of success to more of our people." I agreed to more lectures, and he packed the house with Freemasons, church groups, and fraternities. I added photos and the film reels, and word got around that I had something to say. Olen had pledged Omega Psi Phi, and with quite a bit of ribbing, he hosted, and roasted, the other local fraternities, Alpha Phi Alpha, Kappa Alpha Psi, and Phi Beta Sigma. "You guys are not as sophisticated as the men of Omega, but we will let Bessie speak to you anyway," he said to a room full of Omegas, Kappas, and Alphas. The Omegas laughed, the Alphas and Kappas booed good-naturedly, and in the end, all fraternity rivalry aside, everyone cheered.

Meanwhile, Maud booked me with ladies' groups, social clubs, and sororities. The women of Alpha Kappa Alpha, Delta Sigma Theta, Zeta Phi Beta, and Sigma Gamma Rho were as fashionable as she was and keen on supporting any efforts that the DeWalts endorsed. I loved speaking to the sororities and fraternities. It had been more than a decade since my college days at Langston, and in that time, these women and men had added to their ranks and created new fraternal associations, the members of which had sworn their allegiance to one another, promising themselves that they would educate our people and make a difference with their commitment to service. Their mission seemed relevant and steeped in the loyalty that was needed to work together to improve our collective lot. Both Olen and Maud were at home with their peers and took every opportunity to deliver their message of economic independence. My flying and my desire to open a school were threaded into every introduction, as my past exploits and goals for the future were yet another example of the ways in which a Negro might succeed in a white world.

One day, Maud lent me the Caddy to fetch her list of supplies from the tack and feed store in town—half chaps, field boots, a repaired saddle, new farrier rasps, and nippers. While the groom loaded the trunk, I wandered around the store. On a board loaded with tacked up advertisements, a green scrap of paper caught my eye.

> *Only two pennies a mile!*
> *Nuisance on the ground, whack it from the air!*
> *Grayson's Crop Duster at your service!*

The address, which turned out to be a grass strip by his old barn, was close, and I had fun stretching the Fleetwood's straight-eight cylinders down the long flat Texas dirt road to where the owner of the crop duster, Mr. Grayson, lived. I found him dragging a wheelbarrow out in front of his house. I introduced myself and was thrilled when he suggested that we barter—he'd lend me his bumblebee-yellow Curtiss Jenny, if I'd agree to teach him some fancy stunts. Even though he had carefully removed the giant spreader, the slender bar of metal along the bottom wing had become a gray shadow from the lead-arsenic dustings that still stained the plane's belly and trailing edge.

Olen had found a giant tract of flat, grassy land close to the Heights, and it came with its own barn, which could double as a hangar. Upon my instruction, he ordered workers to carve two closely mowed strips that formed a letter T, one heading north-south, the other east-west. I began rehearsals. Getting to know the plane and becoming familiar with the landscape consumed my attention, as did making sure the air strips were ready for unpredictable Gulf winds. It didn't take long before I felt comfortable and let Olen know we were a go. With notices put up at Prairie View, at the Lincoln, and at churches everywhere, the Juneteenth Celebration starring me and my daredevil stunts was set.

The DeWalts rallied two thousand people, mostly church folk who showed up in their Sunday best. Their children slurped ice-cold lemonade by the bucketful, as the sweltering heat radiated in oily snake waves all around us. Maud had even asked the minister of their church, a Pastor

Gumphree Stormfellow, to pray over me before my flight. He blessed the plane and my mission, lending a somber, but no doubt necessary, tone to the festivities. A fair-skinned man, covered in freckles, the pastor had an apple-round face and wore a black clerical robe. A mound of riney-red hair sat high upon his head, as though it had been shaped from a cone.

The pastor used my portable stepladder near the plane as his pulpit, and as he mounted it, he lifted his arms skyward and bent his head in prayer. Blasting his message to God through a red bullhorn, he thundered, "Lord, please watch over this woman, as she is fixin' to show us what we are capable of. If this flying lady had her way, we would all be little black birds—or in my case, a cardinal."

The crowd let out a collective snicker. "Miss Coleman will perform death-defying acts and prove to each of us that we, too, can do what our passion calls us to do! Brothers and Sisters, I look forward to telling my grandchildren what I witnessed on this day!" And then, with mounting volume, he opened his eyes and called out, "Without further ado, I present to you Miss Bessie Coleman, Queen Bess!"

The crowd responded with hallelujahs and amens.

Unlike my first surplus Jenny that had rusted in crate #506 for years on end, Farmer Grayson used his Jenny daily and took meticulous care of it. After thoroughly checking it over, I determined that it was finally show time. Grateful for a clear day with calm winds, I took off and flew west until what I hoped people saw was nothing more than a yellow speck on the horizon. Rushing back and swooping above their heads, I pulled up and roared away in the opposite direction. Then I returned and looped myself silly. The stick felt good and the plane was easy to handle, so I spun, flew a figure eight, and followed with a Max Immelmann turn. Then I circled and dead sticked a landing right in front of the crowd.

The people rose to their feet with cries of delight, and for the remainder of that day, I gave every congregant who wanted one a buzz in the Jenny. Most paid the dollar fee, but I discreetly accepted passengers who had no money to offer at all. As dusk fell, I finally packed up and got ready to go. Olen was off politicking, so Maud drove us back to the ranch. She had a heavy foot, but I somehow managed to fall fast asleep and only awoke when she hauled the Cadillac down the long, winding driveway that led to the ranch.

"Well," she said, as we walked across the lawn through the soft evening air, "it's the end of a long day. But it seems to me that it's also the beginning of your fresh start."

CHAPTER 41

A fter that, I did a heap of other shows and lectures, rambling throughout Texas all during the summer of 1925. I was back in the game! I was healing well, limping a lot less, and much less tired than I had been. I was also left with very little time to write home about my adventures in letters to Norma, Mama, or Walter that summer, as I was too busy off living them. I did make time, however, to clip articles and advertisements about my shows, and I added the most recent ones to my growing scrapbook. On July 12, 1925, *The Houston Chronicle* snuck in a tiny ad on the bottom of the left side of page four. "TODAY, FLYING CIRCUS Featuring BESSIE COLEMAN (Colored Aviatrix) and Ulysses Stallings (Parachute Jumper)." Olen had thought of everything, as the bottom of the ad promised, "If a shower should come up there will be plenty of room for shelter in the hangar."

Below an article entitled, "The Latest News from Sport's Wide Range," on page eighteen in the sports section of *The Houston Chronicle* and buried beneath both an ad for Newbro's herpicide and the results of the National and the American Leagues' baseball standings, there was an ad for my Flying Circus. I liked this title because the "Flying Circus" was evocative of the Red Baron and his dogfighters, and that was just the tone I wanted to strike.

"According to the number of tickets being sold there will be a record-breaking crowd. White persons who wish to attend the Circus will occupy a special reserved section at the field," read the Chronicle. While I was confident that Olen added the "special reserved section" in order to attract a wider audience, I wasn't crazy about the appeal. In my opinion, every spectator was special. And after all, *The Houston Chronicle* was a white newspaper, so why advertise there in the first place if you weren't trying to appeal to its audience?

Before long we had added more lectures and shows in Galveston and San Antonio, and I sought to add excitement and new elements to my air shows. As I had done in Houston, I decided to feature a wing walker and a parachute jumper again. I considered hiring Ulysses Stallings again. He was an eager student and an athletic man who courageously learned the jump techniques I showed him. But he was also a Negro man, and I knew that if I could hire a pretty white woman to fill the role, I'd attract a bigger, more affluent audience to fill that "special" section of Olen's.

In between the lectures, I interviewed a dozen white women who responded to the one-line ad I had stuck on the wall in the San Antonio YWCA. I intentionally had the candidates respond to B. Coleman, so it was no surprise to me that my applicants were shocked to find that I was the flyer as well as the employer. As I watched their expressions change when they came to terms with this discovery, I couldn't tell which was more distasteful to them: the fact that I was a Negro or that I was a woman. Even other women had trouble with it. It was hard to separate myself from the shock, and in some cases disgust, they felt, as most of the applicants did not try to hide either reaction. Not a single one of them wanted to accept the fact that I would be in charge. While white and Negro spectators were equally represented in the crowds, I guessed that watching a Negro woman perform was one thing, but working for one was quite another.

At long last, Mattie Diamond walked into the place. Her name sounded Negro, but she was anything but. Mattie was a pretty blonde and looked like a paper-doll cutout and, just as importantly, she was wafer thin. Weight is critical in flying—the less, the better. Without a moment's hesitation, she agreed to perform the parachute jump and to take instruction on wing walking. When I asked Mattie why she agreed to the job, she answered, "I needs the money and I'm guess'n you won't kill me. Will you?"

"No, Mattie, we will be together, you and I. I am not going to let anything happen to you or to me," I tried not to condescend.

An airshow in a new town meant mowing the field, setting up concessions, advertising, and practice to knock the rust off my flying skills. We scheduled a practice flight for a mere two weeks before the show and agreed that she would wing walk on a first flight, followed by a parachute jump on the second. The two busy weeks passed quickly, with the first practice being, as it always was, the hardest.

We began by harnessing Mattie to the top of the aeroplane. She had to sprawl across giant king struts that could support the weight of a wing walker. I tried not to spook her and so maneuvered her into position as gingerly as I could. Like a cat, Mattie clutched the upper wing for dear life, and I was surprised when she said she was ready for take off. I didn't dream of doing any stunts with her on this first flight—just nice and easy. The first time that cold rush of air hits you full in the face while your ankles are clamped to the wing, it's all you can do to hold yourself together. Ulysses, whom I had not hired this time, had had fun with this part. Ulysses was a natural. Mattie was not. Halfway through our first session, I smelled rain, so we quit before we had a chance to complete even one trial jump. A few more bad-weather days followed, and before I knew it, the show had crept up on us, and we hadn't had time to practice the parachute jump.

I hoped to convince Mattie that if she could get through the wing walking, the jump would be easy, since she would already have done the hard part. Being a hood ornament on a moving aeroplane was a lot more frightening, I told her, because she wasn't in control. As a jumper, however, she could say when. She was in charge of pulling the ripcord.

On the morning of the flight, Mattie stormed toward me, I could see the determination in her double-time steps.

"Miss Coleman, I am not doing this!" she said, shoving something into my hand. "Here's your ten-dollar deposit back." The plan had been for her to collect the other half once the jump was completed. "I only came back here to give you your money and your outfit back," she continued. "I may be a lot of things, but I ain't no thief and I ain't no cheat."

"Look, hold on to your money," I said, shoving the bill deep into the top pocket of the old army-green flight suit that I had lent her. Made of thick cargo canvas, it was designed to block the wind at altitude, so it was awkward and heavy. She held out my flight suit to me while we engaged in a stare down, and when her reedy bicep began to tremble, I saw an opening and took advantage. I went to get the rucksack-style parachute and then returned in a flash.

"Mattie, since you will require this piece of equipment, I want to show you how a parachute is constructed. Lay the flight suit down and take this end. I will take the other."

I started working quickly, detaching the buckle that held the ruck-sack parachute together, and I began to unfurl the yards and yards of ivory-colored silk that had been tucked inside. While she gripped her end, I took mine and ran as fast as I could, extending the 'chute as far as it would unfold. She stood there looking helpless.

We had already advertised the jump and people were expecting it. Besides, who else could I employ at this eleventh hour? Palomar Park was a lesson learned—not carrying through on an advertised promise equaled a disappointed audience, and I could not have that again. My comeback had been the result of a lot of hard work and orchestration. I was not about to let Mattie, or anything else, spoil things now.

Mattie eyed me suspiciously. Sensing vague interest in my dramatics, I shouted "Parachute," as I skirted the outside of the giant silk sail on the field, "is a French word." I waited until I had run closer to her, so I would not have to yell. "It comes from two words, really," I said, favoring my right leg as I trotted toward her, trying not to let my desperation show. "*Para* and *chute*. *Para* means protection against and *chute* means fall. You will be using my parachute; I will be using my spare," I said. "The word may be French, but it is the Germans who made this contraption a standard. They wouldn't fly a mission in the Great War without one, and neither will you here, now." Although I was desperate to convince Mattie, I allowed myself a moment of indulgence as my thoughts lingered for a few seconds on Robert. He had taught me this. Mattie was focused on every word I said to her, and her hesitation betrayed her. I had gotten her to reconsider.

"I never fly aerobatics without a 'chute," I said.

"Well, that's just it, isn't?" Mattie answered.

"What do you mean?" I questioned.

"Never fly without a 'chute —you will be doing the flying, while I will be doing the jumping!"

"Listen, if you are not up to it, I will find someone else," I lied. "But this would be great for you—an easy gig, a little cash, an opportunity for you to see and be seen."

Mattie stood still and blinked, clearly thinking it over. "You think

I could get thirty dollars for doing this job instead of twenty?" she finally asked.

"That can be arranged," I said, as calmly as I could. Heck, I would have forked over fifty if she had asked for it.

"By the way," Mattie said, her business not yet concluded. "My eldest boy, Thomas, is eighteen. If I don't make it back in one piece, Thomas will come to collect my wages, you hear? I got two other young ones, and I'm doing these jobs to keep Papa's farm. My entire family is depending on me."

"You are going to save your Papa's farm, and you are going watch Thomas's children grow up there," I said. "Everything is going to be just fine."

Mattie smiled as she plucked the crisp ten-dollar bill from the flight suit's pocket and tucked it into her bosom. "You don't think it will fall out on the way down, do you?" she said slyly. We laughed and, winking at her, I flicked her a fiver. She shoved that down deep, too.

I still had a lot of work to do. I had to repack the parachute, fuel the plane, and check in with Olen's local people. When I was ready, I had Mattie climb along the leading edge of the lower wing. It had a sturdy wooden spar, and from there, she hopped up to the top wing, this time with the agility of a young cat. Special cables with clamps like lobster claws at the ends held each of her wiry legs in place so that she stood in the shape of a triangle.

"First we just fly with you on top, no stunts, nothing fancy," I said.

"Okay. What comes next?"

"We land. Then we make the second flight. On that one, we climb high enough for you to jump. I will slow down, and within a minute of the time your thumbs go up, I want you to release your seat belt, climb onto the outer rim of your seat, swing your legs over the side and, when you are ready, dive away from the plane."

"Oh, dear Jesus," she whispered.

"Honest, it will be easy," I said, patting her shoulder. "You are going to dive right over the side. Then, you are going to count to five. You are NOT going to pull your 'chute cord until you are five seconds away from the aeroplane. Understood? You told me that you are quite a swimmer, right?" She nodded her head affirmatively.

"Good. Because all you are going to do is dive right off the side of the plane into a giant pool of sky," I smiled. Mattie's smile grew wide, too.

I didn't give her time to back out. I strapped her in, and got the show started. We made it through the first flight, and she did just fine. Upon landing, she even added a little flair to her performance when she dramatically flung off the bulky jumpsuit, revealing her bright yellow dress that matched Farmer Grayson's aeroplane and her sunshine hair.

I taxied around to our staging area behind the barn. Once away from the crowds, Mattie ditched her plastered-on smile. She looked both scared and windblown, and I worked quickly to buckle her in tightly before she could turn and run.

We took off for the second time into a gentle west wind and climbed in countless circles above the field in the same way that McVey had done with Julian. This time, I made sure the crowd never lost sight of us. With our nose pointed toward heaven, we finally reached ten thousand feet.

At two miles above the earth the air begins to thin. It's cold and sometimes it's hard to breathe. The compass wobbles as it adjusts to the lower pressure and as the alcohol inside it leaks. The higher the altitude, the better for jumping, but climb too high and you might pierce into an atmosphere that has too little oxygen. Too little oxygen causes lightheadedness, so I stopped the climb and prayed that Mattie wouldn't experience any symptoms. I needed her to jump, not pass out!

I had asked Olen to have a theater's orchestra pit musicians show up at the field and work up a twenty-minute routine to entertain the crowd as I climbed. A drummer called Sticks led the ensemble as the musicians played *Old Saloon Rag*, *The Charleston*, and *Rhapsody in Blue*, my favorite Gershwin tune. Like a snake charmer, that long oboe note could hypnotize, and I followed the note, climbing to the tip of its spiral column of air. The majesty ended abruptly, for when Mattie was ready, instead of a thumbs-up, which had been the ready-sign we had agreed on, that God-fearing woman with a cross hanging from her neck saluted me instead with her middle finger.

Despite the insult, I held the aeroplane as steady as could be. Mattie fiddled with her seat belt and, once free, she crept up to the top of the airframe, crouching there, appearing to balance herself. I thought that she might have been calming her nerves, but just then and out of nowhere, a stiff gust of wind hit her so hard that she lost her balance and like upset pudding, she slid back into the seat, plop! I was pretty sure that I had just witnessed the end of Mattie's skydiving career.

Although I did take a moment to consider climbing from my own seat and pushing her out, I figured finally I should just head back. I had just begun to conjure up the explanations that I might make to the crowd and to the DeWalts when, to my surprise, Mattie once again crept to the top of the airframe. We glided through a column of smooth air, and then Mattie, her flight suit flapping, spread her arms like a condor and jumped.

I watched her go and then counted … one, one thousand, two, two thousand, three … four … I turned the aeroplane around.

I didn't see Mattie.

Five … I could feel my palms begin to sweat on the stick.

I couldn't live with myself if Mattie became a bloody red puddle right in front of her children …

Six, six thousand.

She must have been coming real close to the ground, real fast …

Just then, a red-tailed hawk knifed in front of me. Normally, I would dive to avoid a bird, but I couldn't descend with Mattie somewhere below me, so I pulled the nose of the aeroplane up hard to avoid smashing the bird or chopping Mattie to bits. The plane stalled as airflow separated over my wings. The whole craft felt like sponge cake in my hands, and the stick was lifeless. Mattie had jumped off the right, so I sliced left. I had lost count at six. Where in the world was Mattie?

Then, like a Houdini trick, Mattie reappeared. A flash of white against the green field caught my eye. The magic of drag held Mattie beneath its bubble as she wafted gracefully towards earth, floating toward her children, and her daddy's family farm. With her descent assured, I slowly bled off altitude. I flew a loop, glided through a figure eight, and landed. A few hundred feet away from the landing strip, I spotted the sunshine yellow of Mattie's dress fluttering in the breeze.

People flocked to the aeroplane. They snapped photos and asked for my autograph, and Mattie's as well. The smiles, the waves, all moved extra slowly in my mind. The cameras clicked, but there was an abnormal delay before the sound of the shutter snapped inside my ear. I realized I had been shaken by what had almost happened. I hadn't had a drink in ages, but that experience was hearty encouragement to take the liberty of a spirit or two. Had Mattie jumped to her death, I would have had to live with a lot more than my own guilt. Her death would not just have meant the end of her own family and its livelihood, it would have been the end of everything I had worked for. If I, a Negro flyer, had caused an accident that killed a white woman, I would have landed in prison for the rest of my life.

I was still shaking off the fear of what had just only almost happened when Mattie and three of her children approached. I handed her the money I owed her and forced up the best smile I could manage.

"You sure are a fine flyer!" her littlest son blurted out. He was three feet tall and a towhead who looked just like his mom.

"Well, thank you very much," I said. "Your Mama is one bona fide brave lady."

"You only owe me fifteen, there's twenty-five here," Mattie interrupted, counting her bills for the second time.

"It's a tip," I said. "Thank you for being courageous."

She squealed and so did her little ones. Mattie gave each of them a few coins to squander at the fair and, like billiards, they scattered off in every direction. Then Mattie and Thomas, his gangly arm around his mother's shoulder, slipped happily into the crowd.

Ignorance is bliss, I thought to myself. None of them would ever know how close they had come to a full eclipse of Mattie's sunshine.

CHAPTER 42

Farmer Grayson had told me that the best planes to be bought were at Dallas Love Field so, with his blessings, I had flown his aeroplane there to look for myself. Four hours of flying, with a fuel stop midway, put me at Dallas Love Field at dusk, so I spent the night in the yellow Jenny. I wanted to be able to troll the armory at first light.

As the sun rose, I began wandering about the field. A couple dozen Curtiss JN-4s, still packaged in their original crates were the first thing I saw, and I walked right by those dry-rotted cases. I wanted nothing to do with that experience again. The place was still abandoned, but I slipped inside a hangar after glimpsing a door ajar, hoping I would find a salesman.

"How'd ya' get in 'yere?" a tall, thin, blonde man startled me from the shadows, standing so close that I could feel his breath on my neck.

"Good m-morning," I stammered. "I was looking for help with an aeroplane."

"How'd ya' get in 'yere?" he demanded again, more forcefully this time.

"That door over there was open."

"Well, you should leaves the same ways you come in 'yere," he advised.

"I didn't mean to trespass. I hoped to buy an aeroplane."

"Who's the aeroplane for?" he snapped, "Couldn't be for you, so why is you in 'yere?"

A stocky, red-headed cohort appeared. He held a giant monkey wrench in one hand like a weapon. "I don't reckon colored gals know nothin' 'bout aeroplanes."

"Look," I said, backing towards the door. "I heard that this field had lots of models to choose from, and I am in the market for a solid plane at a fair price. That's all."

"One thing's fo' sho', Al," the fat one said. "She sho' is mighty pretty for a colored girl."

Fear slid down my spine. There I was, in a darkened hangar, standing face to face with two redneck Texans. This was a bad situation, and I could feel it growing worse by the second. I had become so comfortable with my own charms that I had allowed myself to become bait. Somewhere along this road I had stopped listening to Mama's voice in my head, and there was a good chance I was about to pay for it.

I kept backing up, knowing full well that behind me there were snares all over the cluttered hangar. The path outside was an obstacle course, too—littered with planes, thousands of small parts, spare engines, propellers, and a few dozen abandoned old jalopy automobiles.

I spun on my heel and broke into a sprint.

"Wait, gal! You gots us all wrong!" the skinny one yelled. "We ain't gonna hurt cha!" But no matter how much my thigh ached, and no matter what that man called after me, there was nothing that could make me stop running.

From behind the wide wing of an old model Wright biplane, a woman stepped forward and blocked my path. She must have been there all along, but in my terror, I had not taken note of her. Scrawny, with mousy blonde hair, she cackled, "Where is you headed?"

A sleeping infant was draped over her right shoulder. The boy was shoeless, sunburned, and completely motionless; not even the sound of his mother's twangy voice echoing inside of the metal hangar was enough to rouse him.

"That there is Jimmy," she said with a quick nod toward the short, fat redhead. "He's my husband. And that there," she continued, extending a bony finger, "is Billy Dean. He, my brother."

She did little to calm me and I kept up a backwards creep.

"Listen here," she said, seeing what I was doing. "Don't be scart. Now you jis ignore those ign'ant boys. They just not used to seein' you people doing nothing but mendin' 'n' cleanin'.'"

I had made it to the mouth of the hangar, where I could see the sunshine and smell the outside air. I began to breathe again, as she went on.

"Daddy bought most of these planes after the Great War, but we got a few new ones too, and we needs to sell 'em. And money ain't colored nor white. It's green. If you fly, we sell. You wanna buy?" She giggled at her own wit with words. I smiled, as best I could. "I'm Luella, and you is?" She said to me, extending her left hand, since the right one belonged to her baby.

I mumbled my name and then stepping into the light, I again braved my request. "I am looking for a dependable, sturdy aeroplane that I will not have to struggle to find parts for. I would like a JN-4, with an OX-5 engine, just like the yellow plane over there," I gestured toward Grayson's Jenny.

"That yellow bird belong to you?" she asked.

"No," I explained. "It's borrowed. I just flew it here. I am in the market for one of my own."

"Well, you come to the right place," Luella said brightly. "We'll fix ya' up real good."

As the morning wore on, other buyers arrived, and although I got a lot of curious looks, the other customers let me be, busy as they were bargain-hunting for themselves. And there truly was something there for everyone—French Spads, Voisins, and Farmers, British Sopwith Camels, and two German Fokker Eindeckers.

When I had looked over every aeroplane at least twice, I told Luella that I would be back in the morning. I wanted to think about my choices and budget. Luella knew that this was more than an empty promise and that I would have to return, as the yellow crop duster would need to be parked here overnight. In an effort to close the sale, she kindly offered to throw in a free fueling tomorrow morning.

But as the sun set, I had demons to wrestle that had nothing to do with aeroplanes. The hangar in which I stood was very close, only about thirty miles, from Waxahachie, where I intended to spend the night. And the whole time I was looking at Jennys, I was also thinking about that little house on Palmer Road—the place where my Daddy had left us, where my Mama struggled to provide for us, and where I became Mama's stand-in, rearing my three younger sisters when I was just barely out of adolescence myself. Returning to that house, if only for a glimpse, meant wrestling with the ghosts that floated about in the firmament that I called home.

CHAPTER 43

Olen had told me that the farther I strayed from Houston, the less influence he had. If I were going to hold more events across Texas, I would have to find other producers, and the only place I knew anyone at all was Waxahachie. A little digging there turned up two of my old school-mates, who were producing amateur fairs throughout central Texas for Negro audiences hungry for entertainment. I remembered them well—bright boys, but indolent students. Between September first and fifteenth, during every year that God sent, the doors of our schools were shuttered, so that we children could pick cotton with the adults. And while many of us wanted nothing more than to return to the consistency of our school-house lives, these two boys were always glad to be done with books and slates in order to scrape up a pittance for themselves. Even as a child, I could never understand how anyone could be more excited over a few coins made from picking cotton than they were about what you could learn in school. Still, I did what I had to do to track down these two who now had a set of skills I needed.

The best part of returning to Waxahachie that evening was my stay with Mrs. Liston, my former grammar school teacher. When I first left Waxahachie, Mrs. Liston and I had written to each other faithfully for years, but as time went on and I moved from place to place, we had lost touch. I knocked on her familiar door, heard her footsteps cross the wooden floor, and a flash recollection stirred in me. I pictured for the first time in many years the dirt floor of our own shotgun house. In the kind of childhood I had had, a wooden floor was a luxury. Before I could think any more about such things, Mrs. Liston appeared in the doorway. We hugged and wept together for a long moment. In the decade since I had last seen her, her face had aged little, but her hair had turned completely silver. We picked up right where we had left off, chatting over tea until the wee hours of the morning. She told me news of our neighbors, and I told her about my travels and training.

We discussed Garland Acorn and Ben Tuskins, the two who would be responsible for putting on my air show. According to Mrs. Liston, Garland had somehow grown shorter and fatter, while Ben was his polar opposite. He had elongated into a tall string bean of a man.

"Don't allow yourself to get swindled," she cautioned. "It would not surprise me at all if those two tried to cheat you."

I assured her that I would make sure to collect my due, and that I had dealt with crooked managers before.

Garland and Ben agreed to produce the show. Ben said he'd take charge of preparing the site, while Garland would be my main publicity help. I demanded half of my money up front and the other half on the day of, and just prior to, the performance. The two objected. They preferred, they said, to pay me everything at the end.

"Listen, gents, I am staying at Mrs. Liston's. You can get in touch with me there," I said, standing up to leave the church basement, which had been the site of our impromptu meeting.

Garland touched my arm to stop me, and the contact from his skin made my own crawl. I hadn't planned it, but the reaction was instant and real, and I flashed him a snarl. He removed his hand as if I had burned his fingers. Singed, but intact, he dug into his pocket, the seam of which was badly frayed, and pulled out a blank check. He began patting his right breast pocket for, I supposed, something with which to write.

"Don't bother searching," I said, "I only take cash."

"Why, my checks are good all over Texas," Garland said in response.

"So is cash," I quipped. "Let me know when … "

"Here, here," he said, digging deeper into his fringed pocket and then poking his partner on the shoulder. Between the two of them, they scrounged together fifty dollars and assured me that I would get the other fifty before the show on the following week.

With some cash in my pocket, I made daily trips to the depot, where Luella and I were coming to an agreement on a plane. I intended to use Farmer Grayson's aeroplane for this Waxahachie show, but I knew I had to return it soon, as he needed it for crop-dusting work, so selecting a vintage JN-4 took on new urgency. There were newer planes, but they cost more—about six hundred and fifty dollars.

My goal had been to get a good deal on a vintage plane that had been flown frequently, similar to the crop duster, but with a newer engine. Luella promised to work on it and to bring my intended aeroplane up to par. This time I intended to check on every detail of the work.

I folded the paper I had been reading, and when the train arrived in Waxahachie on my second trip, I stormed off to meet Garland and Ben. Their unofficial office was at Brown's Barber Shop on Wyatt Street, which was nothing more than one of three shops in a block-long red brick building—a grocery, barber shop, and beauty parlor.

Ben was missing but Garland was inside, hanging out near the back of the shop with some friends.

"Excuse me," I called, a bit more shrilly than I had intended. "Garland, can I see you outside?"

"Oooh, you's in trouble now," one of the men ribbed Garland.

Laughter broke out around us, and Garland followed me into the street, shutting the door hard on the men's snickering. Cowbells clattered on the doorknob as he did so.

Back in Chicago, female manicurists were preferred. A pretty woman in the window perch was good for business, a lure to draw men into the shop. But not at Brown's. There was no manicurist and women were absolutely NOT welcomed in the all-male world of the southern barbershop. It was yet another reminder of how I had outgrown Waxahachie.

"Hi, ya, Bessie. You all ready for the show?" he said cheerfully, trying to avert the storm that he saw coming. The barbers and their customers crowded the window to see what was going on between us. Garland positioned his back to the window, so they could not see his face.

"Yep, I'm ready, but you're not," I said, "Not with this announcement," I unfolded the paper and pointed to the article.

"What's wrong?" he asked, genuinely mystified.

"What's wrong?" I repeated. My outrage grew along with his confusion. "What's wrong is that you have allowed these white folks to con you into two separate gates for the show. I know that the Ellis County Rodeo Fairgrounds are owned by the Clacksmans and that they're rich and powerful, but I don't want our people to be forced to enter through the south gate. Workers dump raw sewage and dung over there. You have to fix this," I demanded.

"How do you reckon' I do that?" he asked me sincerely.

"You tell old man Clacksman that I want everyone to enter through the front gate," I said. "He can sit them where he wants once they are inside, but having two entrances, especially one with animal dung all over the ground, is unacceptable. Do you want your own Mama to trudge through shit on her way in? That may be okay with you, but it's not okay with me!" I wasn't bluffing when I added, "I won't do the show till you fix this!"

"Bessie, wait," he said, but I was already walking away. "What if I can't ... " Fear rang in his words.

I kept walking.

My last glimpse of the barbershop was of all the men heckling Garland. No doubt they would tease him about a woman pushing him around, but I could not have cared less. I did not want to return to Waxahachie as a compromised conqueror. This separate gate business was wrong. I had been all over Texas, and that my hometown would do such a thing was an insult too far.

I brought Mrs. Liston up to date on the day's events.

"Bessie, since you left, many things have changed, but many more things have remained the same," she sighed. "I'm just glad that that stubborn little girl inside you is still fighting."

"To be honest, Mrs. Liston, I don't know how much more fight I got left," I said. "People want to wring it out of me every step of the way. There's always so much fear and prejudice, envy and poverty in my path. It gets harder and harder to just ... fly."

I must have looked as wan as the faded florets on the sofa where we were sitting because Mrs. Liston took my hand and said softly, "coming home is hard, Bessie."

"It took so much for me to get this little bit of learning and I have traveled so far so others wouldn't have to. I just want to share what I've learned with our people, but it sure can wear a person down." I

366

instinctively ran my hand along the side of my mended leg.

"You just stick to your guns and remember this; you are the show. Without you, there's only lemonade and popcorn," Mrs. Liston smiled. "You will prevail."

First thing the next morning, I went to see Garland.

"Mr. Clacksman won't budge," he reported before I'd even had a chance to ask him.

I wasn't convinced that Garland had mustered the courage to even approach Clacksman because I knew for a fact that he was mighty scared of white folks. I had sworn to myself that when this show was over, I would move on, but he had to continue living next to these people whom he'd known, and in many cases feared, for his entire life.

"Listen, Garland, if you aren't able to convince Clacksman, then I will have to help you be more persuasive," I said. "Tell him I want one gate. If it doesn't happen, then the air show that has already been advertised won't happen either, because I won't fly."

We stared at one another. He blinked. He could tell I was not bluffing.

"All right, Bessie. I will tell Clacksman, but I think what will help is if the aeroplane that you are fixin' to fly is parked right here. Can you set it in the middle of the field, where he can't miss it?"

"It's an inconvenience," I sighed, "but consider it done."

I made my return trip to Love Field, put a one hundred dollar deposit down on the secondhand JN-4, and ordered a rebuilt OX-5 engine. With the receipt in hand, I flew back to the rodeo grounds and parked the crop duster where everyone could see it. They must have been expecting me because this time a crowd of men was gathered when I arrived at Brown's. I didn't even have to go to the door. Garland and Ben hurried out front to meet me.

"You wasn't kidding, it's bumblebee yellow alright," Garland grinned, trying to put both of us at ease.

"Well?" I asked him, not interested in small talk. I was prepared to do battle.

"Listen, Bessie," Garland said. "This is not Chicago. You back home now. I got Clacksman to agree to one gate, but once inside, coloreds will be on one side of the grandstand, and whites will be on the other."

The same gate but segregated grandstands was a battle compromise, but I had won the war.

"Well?" he asked.

"I'll see you tomorrow," I said.

This was progress ... Texas-style.

CHAPTER 44

The wind was gentle. Light gusts from the west made the tree-tops sway and the leaves whistle. I sought out Garland for my money before the show, and he gave me the fifty dollars in a tattered and worn jumble of ones and fives. As the morning grew late, the smell of popcorn filled the air. Many, including Mrs. Jones, who had given us that magical hand-me-down doll castle that had inspired my fantasies so long ago, made it a point to come over and wish me a safe flight. The stands were filled with people I used to know.

An announcer's voice over one of those brand-new public address systems echoed all around us, sounding like a man in a tin-can funnel, floating above the more than fifteen hundred people who had gathered below. "The fine governor of our Lone Star state has made us an unexpected visit. She, that's right, I said, *she*, people ... Ma Ferguson has stopped by to see our special show today."

All the politicians I knew about had an agenda—garnering votes, collecting taxes, getting the trains to stop in their little one-horse towns. And owing to the controversy swirling around my protest of the separate gates, I was surprised that the Governor would bring attention to herself by coming to my show. What could this woman's agenda be? Whatever her reason, she at once became a bona fide rebel in my mind for braving my critics and maybe even making more of her own.

The Governor made her way to the podium and spoke into the

announcer's microphone.

"Good citizens of Waxahachie," she began, "it's great to be here on this fine day. The people of my state enjoy simple pleasures—good bar-b-cue, fair weather, and loyalty. But more than that, we support our own! That's why I am here, to support one of our own!"

Even though her language was folksy, the way she squared her shoulders and carried herself led me to believe that she came from well-bred stock. The people clapped as she extended a white gloved hand in my direction.

"And now," the announcer's voice echoed again, "As our Governor said, one of our own has traveled the world and brought this fine yella aeroplane home to do some stunts and tricks for us. Without further ado, ado, ado," his voice echoing, "I present Miss Bessie Coleman, man, man … "

I climbed up on the wing mount and waved, to robust applause. I did my usual routine, loops, spins, turns, a figure eight, and a real low flyover. Then I used my platform in the sky to deliver a message. Taking a case of Castrol Oil, I drizzled it over the hot manifold. Sky writing was difficult. Like writing on a mirror, you had to write backwards and upside down. But I had practiced this by walking out my message in the dirt before flying it. I had it straight now.

BE BRAVE. NEVER CRAWL. FLY.

Many in Waxahachie were still illiterate, but there were bound to be enough readers scattered throughout the crowd to spread my gospel. Thunderous applause erupted from the Colored section as my message was slowly revealed. Then, with my signature low flyover, I sprinkled Norma's scarves over the side. They floated through the air and people dove and howled, catching streamers right out of the air. I looped and dead sticked the landing. In the end, stretched across twenty miles of sky, my defiant phrase hung there just as I had pictured it. Every time one of those bigots looked up into the sky to gauge the weather before planting a single cotton seed, I wanted them to remember me. And every time a child had to pick cotton in those same fields, I wanted that child to think about what they could someday become.

"Hometown girl leaves, makes good, returns," brought with it reunions, trials, and encounters of the familiar and the sublime. I had struggled so hard to escape all that I feared and hated about this place that I had turned running away into a way of life. I thought I was strong enough to face coming back, but the oppression, illiteracy, poverty, and hunger that my people still suffered in my birthplace was crushing. I found it hard to breathe the air that was once the only sustenance my lungs had known.

The Governor and her four-man security escort approached, with the proud-looking lady, clutching her oval pocketbook, leading the way. Her gray-and-black hair was piled high on top of her head in a topknot, and her clothes were expensive but not stylish. I could see why they called her Ma. She looked less like a calculating politician and more like a sturdy schoolmarm. But judging from her countenance, I suspected it would be unwise to cross her and a mistake to underestimate her.

I learned later that the "Ma" came from her initials M. A., which stood for Miriam Amanda. Her husband had been Governor before her and now bore the companion sobriquet, Pa Ferguson. Pa had been impeached and removed from office, and sixteen years later Ma snatched the reins of the governorship to restore the family's name.

"I make it my business to get out of the Capitol and see all parts of our fair state," she said, looking me square in the eyes and smiling brightly. Gone was the formality of the glove, as she thrust a well-manicured hand my way. "I heard about the sand you kicked up over the entry gates. You were right to do so. Not to mention courageous."

I was both stunned and ill-prepared. Her guards had slowly, but smoothly, moved people away from us, which made me nervous. I was guessing that she could force her agenda through the legislature with a smile and a plate full of homemade cookies, but what on earth could she want from me?

Leaning in to create the feeling of an intimate conspiracy between us, she whispered, "You and I are two of a rare kind. We are alike because we are both so different from others."

My hackles went up, different? I had heard this line before. Putting me in a separate category that really meant "successful," made it seem as if other Negroes hadn't been working just as hard to get where they were going, to be truly successful in their own lives. If other Negros were given the chance, if they were not held back, if they had no boot on their necks, maybe I wouldn't seem so damn different.

"I would love to meet with you, away from the crowds. I'd like to get your thoughts on a couple of subjects on which I have very little insight. Would you be willing to meet me at the Governor's mansion for dinner next week, say, Tuesday evening?"

"Why, certainly," I heard myself chirp. Her solicitation was at once baffling, flattering, and unnerving.

"Good! Shall we say six o'clock, then?" she asked not waiting for a reply, and with her guards flanking, she glided away, disappearing into a crowd of her constituents.

For the rest of the day, I shoved all thoughts of the Governor out of my mind and gave rides to my friends and neighbors. By the time my fuel was spent, dusk was beginning to fall, so I parked the crop duster and headed back to town. The two-and-a-half mile walk down Wyatt to Palmer should have cleared my head, but I met so many people along the way that the walk turned into a passage through a long gauntlet down memory lane.

From a block away, the house looked smaller. Mama was living now in Chicago, but she still owned it and was renting it to the Carson family, perhaps imagining that someday she would return. It was not the childhood house I remembered. The yellow roses, of which my mother had once been so proud, had long since died off, and only thorny bristles clung to the buckling picket fence that was in desperate need of whitewashing. Like missing front teeth, pieces of clapboard on the face of the house were also long gone—an offense my daddy would have never allowed. Everywhere the paint curled like pork rinds.

I moved as if in a dream. Slowly, floating, I pushed the gate open, and the hinges greeted me with a wail. I walked up the path of weed-ringed flagstones and crossed the narrow porch. After a few long breaths, I rapped my knuckles on the front door.

Mrs. Carson was eight years my senior. She had ten children and she looked as weathered as the structure that was once my home. Unsteady knees supported what appeared to be painful hips, and she awkwardly rocked her weight from side to side in order to propel herself forward. Whatever discomfort she felt, it did not impede the warm welcome she gave me or dull the pleasure in the offer to join her in a jelly jar full of sweet tea. I sat in the big white wicker chair, sun-bleached now, that had once been my Mama's prized possession. We drank syrupy sweet liquid and hashed over old times. Eventually, even the long, Texas summer day came to an end, and it began to grow dark. I thanked her for the hospitality and said goodbye.

I crossed the dusty dirt road that was Palmer. Slowly creeping away from my memories and my suffering and, once again, like Lot's wife I could not resist one last look back. Truly, I should have kept going, for the parting vision broke my heart.

I had been given a second chance.

It was time to say my goodbyes and heal as many wounds from the past as I could. But I knew that this goodbye, like so many others in my life, would be final, and that I had to make peace with the little girl who had grown up in this place. Her unrest was the reason I had wandered two continents trying to fix what had been so irreparably broken inside that beat down old shack.

CHAPTER 45

I arrived at the stately Governor's mansion and stepped onto the bright red brick pavers that led up to the massive white colonnade before me. Shadows from the twenty-five-foot Ionic columns spilled all around me, and a huge marble staircase led to a glossy white, paneled front door. There were floor-to-ceiling windows on the first and second floors that were protected by black shutters that waited, wide open against the building's stark and imposing white façade.

I had been to more ancient, more impressive monuments in Paris—the Louvre, the Eiffel Tower, the National Palace, and the Arc de Triomphe—but I'd never been this close to splendor in my own country, let alone to a monument that was inhabited by a woman. I paused, not so much out of trepidation, but rather to take in the gravity of the moment, which weighed heavily upon me. My legs moved as if weights were attached to my ankles. I was about to enter the Texas Governor's mansion, and not by the back door, either. I was preparing to waltz through the front door, and as an invited supper guest. But I was under no illusions. No matter how welcome I might be on this day, this mansion had been built by slaves for white folk.

I climbed the stairs with increasingly heavy footsteps. I was wearing my flight uniform. Was that a mistake? There was no door knocker, but there was a bell. Before I could ring it, a handsome Negro man in his fifties swept the door open to me.

"Good evenin'," rang out in a rehearsed voice. It seemed to me that he nearly giggled at the sight of me, and I warmed to him immediately. His laugh was a private greeting that Negroes reserved for one another when whites were not watching, and I was glad that he was glad that I had come to dine.

"You come right on in, Miss Coleman. My, you are even prettier than your picture in the papers," he whispered.

"You are very kind. Sometimes the camera is not," I whispered, and although it was becoming faint as a pencil mark, I was self-conscious about the scar beneath my eye, and I raised my hand to touch it.

"Best get you settled," he advised, ushering me into a gracious parlor filled with Victorian chairs and what appeared to be priceless antiques. "My name is Philbert. Anything you require during your stay, I am at your service." As if on cue, the Governor appeared, and Philbert vanished.

"Well, how-do, Miss Coleman. Thank you very much for coming," she smiled brightly.

"Thank you for inviting me, Madame Governor," I returned, shaking her warm extended hand.

"Come," she commanded. "I'll show you around."

The mansion was a place of great beauty, and we walked from one room to the next, admiring the high ceilings, shimmering chandeliers, and colorful walls. The details of each room were sumptuous. Our tour ended with the Governor leading me into a huge Wedgewood-blue dining room. Although the table could accommodate as many as eighteen, it was set for two.

Philbert slipped from behind me, as if by magic, and pulled out the Governor's chair. She sat at the head of the table, facing one of the two fireplaces. He then helped me into the chair to her right.

"I have been Governor for less than a year, but I have been a Texan for my entire life," she began. "And I can tell you that one of the greatest problems we face is that of the racial situation."

She got right to the heart of things. I listened but did not speak.

"You are in a unique position, Miss Coleman," the Governor said to me as Philbert filled our crystal water goblets. "You have managed to remove yourself from our grand state, yet you have returned from your worldwide travel, and therefore you bring a perspective that few here are able to offer," she continued, opening her napkin and laying it across her lap.

I placed my own perfectly ironed napkin on my thighs and didn't touch it again. The reason for my invitation to dinner was no longer a mystery. I was meant to provide some sort of insight into our troubled race relations.

"I am a Democrat, but I am often somewhat out of step with my party. I am on the verge of passing a very controversial piece of legislation. I plan to outlaw the wearing of masks in public," she said. As if in keeping with the weightiness of the topic at hand, Philbert poured her a stiff one over ice. The brown syrupy liquid trickled gently from a cut-glass decanter.

"Care for one?" she asked, gesturing to her drink.

"No, thank you," I said.

"May I get you something else?" Philbert asked.

"Just more water would be fine. Thank you," I smiled in return.

"The mask law," she went on, "is a way of getting at the Klan, of course. Individuals who violate my mask law will be arrested and heavily fined. Hitting people in the wallet is sometimes the only punishment they understand," she said.

"My politics are convenient," she went on. "The Klan, thank heavens, has begun to diminish in popularity, but the members who remain are among the most vicious and vocal. They threaten good relations in our state, not to mention lives." Before I had a chance to reply, she added, "I don't drink this stuff."

She held up the glass of whiskey. It had begun to sweat. "I would like to sell it and tax it. So, you see, I am against the Klan and against Prohibition. I want to sell alcohol but only if I can tax it. I also happen to support pardoning some of our less violent criminals—they occupy space in prison and cost us money, but then, that's another matter entirely." The Governor waved her hand as if to dismiss the third, more complicated topic.

A slender dark-skinned woman about my mother's age entered the dining room. She carried two bowls of soup on a silver tray. I caught her eye and smiled at her. She nodded in response.

"Thank you," I said as her gloved hand placed the soup before me. I waited for the Governor to lift her spoon. Once she did, I picked my own up by its exquisite silver handle.

"I do hope you like asparagus," the Governor said.

"Oh, I do," I lied. I really was not fond of it prepared the way it was, creamed and murky, but I didn't want to be rude, so I lifted a spoonful to my lips.

"How could I possibly be of help?" I said in part to distract myself from the taste of it.

"Bessie," she said moving the small silver pitcher of flowers between us off to the side, our intimacy tightening, "I am a woman in a man's job. You are familiar with how lonely that can be. The last time I lived in this mansion, I was the First Lady. But now I am the Governor. I'm a realist, but I need to make real changes."

As if on cue, Philbert arrived carrying a stack of newspapers on a silver tray. "MA FERGUSON ROUTS KLAN IN TEXAS," read one. "Ma Ferguson expects 125,000 Majority; KNIGHTS MAKE LAST EFFORT. NO MA FOR ME," another read. And then, "10,000 Applaud Her Last Appearance in Battle with Texas Klan, SUPPORTERS CONFIDENT." These articles were from the *New York Times*!

"I have very few Negroes upon whom I can call to discuss such issues, and yet I am coming to realize that our futures, those of the Negro and of the whites, are inextricably linked. I require your counsel," she said, pushing the papers I had read aside.

What the Governor required was our vote, and she wanted me to help her get it. I wanted so badly to remind her that she was surrounded by voting Negroes, all of whom had opinions and might be helpful to her cause. Hadn't Philbert just delivered her newspapers on a silver platter? And hadn't another woman just served us a similarly supported meal? Surely someone who was as radical a thinker as the Governor would have realized that her butler and maid traversed both worlds, Negro and white, and would therefore offer some value other than serving her. Hell, they—the cook and three other Negroes—were at that very moment staring at us through the servant's peekaboo window, crowding around the tiny square, trying to read our lips! I thought of my brother Walter moving through his work as a Pullman Porter—as good as invisible as he cleared the dining car's tables, shined shoes, or carried bags. His labor was needed but his point of view was unwelcome. The fact that he had one was not even a consideration.

"I don't know that I am much of an authority on anything other than flying aeroplanes," I said wearily. Although I realized that this was not an opportunity to be squandered, I suddenly felt inadequate to explain the burden of an entire people, and I was painfully aware that I had to think of a way to enlighten, yet not insult.

"Oh, I saw the crowds watching you," she said eagerly. "The children look up to you, the men hold you in high esteem, and the women want to be like you. Not only that, you took a stand on how people would be treated at your air show, which means you are able to define the challenges of your people from a unique point of view and to demand respect. Tell me what I need to know about the New Negro in Texas that is not obvious to me?"

New Negro! Had I heard her correctly?

She knew the code! I was silent for a long moment while I thought. Although the temptation to speak upon an open stage can be irresistible, Mama had taught me that it is better to think before you utter a word.

"Forgive my silence as I gather my thoughts," I said.

"I knew I had asked the right person," the Governor said, pleased.

"Your term is a total of two years, is that right?" I asked.

"It is," she responded.

"You have little more than a year left. A year is not enough time to right centuries of wrong," I began.

We were served steak, mashed potatoes, and peas, as well as biscuits that reminded me of my mother's. Oh, yes, the cook was a Negro. They were flaky and hot and had taken someone a long time to prepare, knead, and bake. Biscuits like these were the work of great patience.

"I think you have already made great strides. The mask law aimed at snaring the Klan is genius. Taxing alcohol instead of treating adults like naughty children and punishing them through Prohibition, is a mature decision and will make you a leader that others will want to follow. More Negro men are incarcerated for minor infractions or on trumped-up charges than any other group. But there are other widespread threats. I never want us to get used to Negro schools that shut down when it is time to harvest cotton and cane. The Klan is a scourge, but the greatest threats facing the Negro in the South are poverty, hunger and substandard education. These are conditions that guarantee more of the same."

The Governor listened respectfully, but I am confident that this was not what she wanted to hear. She wanted me to simply rubber-stamp her positions, maybe even call her transformational. Taking centuries to fester, the endemic wrongs of Jim Crow and poverty were deeply rooted in slavery, and there would be no quick fix. These ills would take longer than her time in office, or even her lifetime, to eradicate, but I felt it was my duty to raise them.

Philbert brought dessert. The Governor thanked me for my honesty, and I told her sincerely that I respected her for her bravery. We exchanged pleasantries. She said she admired my French uniform and its fine woolen fabric. I said that I cherished her hospitality, and I complimented her decorating. As I stirred my steaming coffee, I couldn't help but think about the sugar I had heaped into the fine porcelain cup. Someone like Norma or her mother had picked the cane, just as I and my mother had once picked the cotton that went into the Governor's fine damask napkins. When our dinner was over, she led me to the foyer where we said our farewells. When the large white door closed behind me, I was quite sure that I would never see the other side of it again.

CHAPTER 46

As successful as the summer had been, I needed rest if I
wanted to be ready for the next season of touring. I loved the
attention of my audiences. I lived for their palpable energy,
but it drained me, too, so that fall I went home to Chicago.

On Christmas Eve, I went to Norma's new alterations
shop where I played for hours with my newest godchild and pretended
that she was my own. They lived upstairs and had turned the downstairs
into a bigger shop. Norma was pregnant again, and she looked so beautiful, with her brown skin aglow with a ruby sheen. She joked that she
was hot and greasy.

"You smell too," I ribbed her. "Glad we're not roommates anymore."

"I think it's another girl," Norma told me, patting her small, tight belly.

"How can you tell?"

"I just feel it," she said. "Feels all girlie. Actually, the way she's kicking
and rolling all around doing loops backwards and forwards, I think she is
going to be just like you! Her Aunt Bess! Raisin' Cain already!" Norma
laughed. "I gotta get some fight in me, if I'm gonna raise one like you."

"Speaking of raising people, I am off to see Mama now. I have to
break the news to her. When I head south again, I am going to settle
down there for a good long while."

"What do you mean by settle down?" Norma asked. "Is there a Mr.
Right down there?"

"Hardly!" I said. "I'm planning to go to Florida to copy the rich white folks I know. Snowbirds, who fly South for the winter," I smiled.

Norma shook her head. I knew that my wanderlust was unsettling to her. "You have only been home for an instant and already you're planning to move on."

"That's right. Next Christmas, I am going to be decorating a palm tree." I smiled.

"Hate to spoil your surprise, but I can save you the trip to Mama's. She is due here any minute." Norma laughed when the bell rang. Mama was right on cue.

"Merry Christmas!" Mama called out.

She bustled through the door lugging a heavy bag, and we dusted the snow off of her and got her settled in a chair near the fireplace. Everyone had wanted to see Norma's new shop, so Walter, Elois, Nilus, and Georgia showed up a little later with all of my nieces and nephews in tow. The children piled their wet snow boots by the door and ran to hug Mama before scampering off to play by the Christmas tree. Once every one of her grandchildren had arrived, Mama called them back and lavished dolls, toy cars, planes, and sweets on them.

I waited until things settled down before I broke the news. No matter how festive, this occasion would be yet another bon voyage for me. When the mood seemed right, I announced my departure for Florida.

"Bessie, stay!" Mama begged. "Move in with your sisters or me. No more of this Florida ramble."

"Mama," Walter flew to my defense, "Bessie has to do this. It's what she trained for. Besides, for the next five months it will be too cold for her to fly here."

"It's too much!" Mama said. "I want you in one piece. You don't have to prove anything else. That accident back in '23 nearly killed you. I can't lose you again. Please … "

"Mama," I said, pleading with her to understand. "I am doing what I love to do. And when I don't do it, I die a different sort of death. I may keep my life, but I'd lose my heart."

But Mama's fears were crippling, and there were no words in the world that could make them go away.

Seeing that we were at an impasse, Norma came to my rescue. Digging into the pocket of her apron, which jutted out because of her baby ball, she produced two train tickets.

"Here's your present!" she announced cheerily. "Nope, not for you," she said, snatching them away from my fingertips. "They are for me," she smiled teasingly. "Walter gave them to me. We just knew you would be on the move again. So, if you must go to Florida, I will just have to come to visit! I might even climb into that aeroplane contraption of yours."

"I am so happy!" I said, hugging her and then Walter. "Thank you both so much for this and for always being so good to me."

"We'll always be here for you, Bessie," Walter said, wrapping his arm loosely around Norma's shoulders. Norma smiled, fanning those duster eyelashes at me.

"Save your charms for Moe," I laughed at her. "When will you come?"

"After you get settled. But we had better hurry," she said, pulling my hand and laying it on her firm belly. The baby fluttered. I lowered my head and gently rested my cheek where my hand had been. I was a part of Norma and she was a part of me, and through my best friend, I felt a hint of the Christmas miracle—the birth of a baby.

"We only have about six months," Norma said softly. I kissed her belly. Life grew in her. Hope soared in me.

PART FOUR

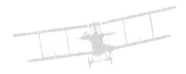

CHAPTER 47

The DeWalts had introduced me to The Reverend and Mrs. Hezekiah Hill, who lived in the all-Negro section of Orlando called Callahan, and the Hills had agreed to put me up. Callahan was my kind of town. Like Langston, Oklahoma and Independence Heights in Texas, Callahan boasted proud, supportive, open-minded Negroes determined to carve out an existence of their own.

Like the DeWalts, The Reverend and Mrs. Hill were a stabilizing force in their Central Florida neighborhood. Reverend Hill pastored the Calvary Baptist Church, which was the beating heart of Callahan. In their early fifties, he and his wife looked as if they belonged on the front of a church bulletin—a vision of what a calm life in Christ would yield. They may not have been steamy like the DeWalts, but their neat, peaceful appearance was more active than any ceremonial brochure could suggest; through the church they saved souls, fed the hungry, and found work for people, including me.

Their red-roofed bungalow was located on a street lined with magnificent palm trees, which lent shade and swaying shadows to my bedroom. The house, only a block away from their church, had a white-and-yellow tiled bathroom and a bright eat-in kitchen with a round oak table that doubled as the town meeting hall.

As I had done in Texas, I crisscrossed the state of Florida, giving lectures to sold-out crowds in Tampa and St. Petersburg, and then shooting across the state to West Palm. So many people tried to buy tickets to my talk at the Liberty Center in St. Petersburg that I had to return for second and third lectures. And while the theater was not as grand as Olen DeWalt's, it was packed to the gills each time. The balcony was so crowded that I began to worry that audience members might fall off like ants from a branch. People kept on piling in until they were forced to nearly sit upon each other.

When I first started giving lectures, I had miscalculated my audiences. I took myself too seriously. In Baltimore, for example, the people there wanted more than just a story, they needed humor. I'd thought I had them in the palm of my hand, but then I beat them over the head with the notion that we needed more aviators. It was a good lesson for me—not everyone was as interested in flying as I was. Some people just needed to hear some really good news and to laugh a little.

"Thank goodness flying a plane is easier than walking across a darkened stage," I said one night, as I walked the narrow path across the stage while being blinded at the same time by the spotlight cast upon me. When I heard the laughter, I knew I would pull out of the stall. "Phew, if I'd fallen, that would have been embarrassing!" I said in my best Texas drawl, and the crowd laughed louder. I went on to deliver my fifteen-minute lecture, ending with the Pathé reels of film of me flying in Germany.

There were many air shows in Florida, and while I was on the lecture circuit, I liked going to watch other barnstormers. Sometimes the Reverend and Mrs. Hill would go with me. They particularly enjoyed the show in Valdosta, Georgia where the Great War veterans thrilled the crowd with loops and spins. When we slipped into the crowd at the end of the day, the Reverend shooed us quickly towards the car, not wanting to get caught riding through Georgia once it turned dark. As we made our way through the parking lot, I overheard a white man insisting to his companion, "It is! It's that colored aviatrix! I am sure of it!"

The sixtyish, stout man was training his index finger right on me. I could see his hazel eyes were softened by age, and when he noticed me looking, he said, "It is so rude to point. Forgive me. My name is Harry Leland Beeman and I am an aviator. At least in my own head, I am," he said with a smile. I noticed he had the polite manners of a southerner, but the plain flat speech of a mid-westerner.

"Nice to meet you, Mr. Beeman," I said, hoping that my own smile was not too artificial. "But I'm afraid we really have to be going." I looped my arm through Mrs. Hills's and kept walking.

We were three Negroes in a sea of white spectators, and I had already dragged the Hills into enough uncomfortable situations such as this. Night was falling, and the cheap brew had been flowing all afternoon. We all felt danger lurking.

"Listen," Mr. Beeman said, aware of my discomfort, "I would love to talk aeroplanes with you. Are you visiting long or are you returning to Chicago soon? I live in Orlando, but I'm a displaced boy from Ohio," he explained. While he couldn't have known that I was relocating to Florida, he did know that I hailed from Chicago, which meant that he truly did know who I was. "I am a real fan of all you fancy flyers. Wish it were me, to tell the truth," he went on quickly.

A group of curiosity seekers was starting to swell, and Mrs. Hill started tugging hard at my elbow.

"Oh, how nice. Well, we really do have to start getting back. Long trip and all," I said.

"Of course. I understand completely," he said, reaching into the inside breast pocket of his suit jacket. "Here's my card." He handed me a fine ivory linen card:

Harry Leland Beeman, Proprietor
San Juan Hotel—ORLANDO

"Thank you again, Mr. Beeman," I said as we continued toward the car. "It was a pleasure meeting you."

"Hope I hear from you soon!" Mr. Beeman called after us.

"What in the world was all that about?" Mrs. Hill asked me once we had retreated.

"He asked whether you'd fly with him and I told him you would," I teased.

"You did what?" Mrs. Hill swatted me.

"Bessie, you are quite the jokester. Now let's get out of redneck Georgia so that we can live to laugh about this another day," Reverend Hill said, practically shoving us through the split-rail fencing to their waiting Model T.

We sped out of the parking lot, with Reverend Hill driving like a bandit who'd stolen something. And although it was considered rude to blind motorists with a cloud of dust, we kicked up a whole storm that rose up in our tracks.

Reverend Hill knew exactly who Mr. Beeman was, and on the way back home, he told me all about him. Beeman had evidently poured money into an orange grove on the outskirts of Orlando. Heir to his father's chewing-gum fortune, the younger Beeman had a Midas touch of his own, for he purchased the swank downtown hotel, too.

"He is from one of the Citrus Baron families," The Reverend said. "They buy out small farmers who don't survive the winter freezes. But he thinks differently and does things his own way," he concluded. "Beeman hires Negroes for a decent wage and he gives away much of what he earns."

No wonder it hadn't seemed to matter to Mr. Beeman that he was seen talking with a Negro female at the air show. Now his interest in me seemed much less menacing. He may just have wanted to talk aviation. I felt badly about how quickly I had rushed off, so I decided to visit Mr. Beeman at his hotel the following week.

Heads swiveled when I entered the opulent lobby of the San Juan Hotel. All the other Negroes in a hotel that fancy were the housekeeping staff, and they were expected to enter by the rear service door and in uniform. But I did not use side doors and hoped that some day no one else would have to either. I marched right over to the concierge.

He pretended not to notice me even though I stood directly in front of him, and he took a few minutes to shift around the papers on the counter before him. I was to wait. But that was fine with me. The entire time I stood there staring at the concierge, I could see his discomfort grow, as more and more guests began to gawk. Finally, and without a word, I produced Mr. Beeman's business card and slid it silently across the counter in his direction. If I were going to leave, it would have to be because Mr. Beeman himself threw me out, and I had a feeling that would not be part of his plan.

The card stunt worked. After what felt like minutes, the concierge headed off in the direction of what I assumed were offices. In what felt like hours, Harry Beeman finally appeared. Despite being short and rotund, Mr. Beeman looked regal in his dapper navy-blue suit and starched white shirt. He wore giant gold cufflinks that matched the brass buttons on his jacket and caught the sunlight shining through the hotel's floor-to-ceiling windows.

I apologized for stopping by without notice, and I told him that I could easily return at a later date, but I could tell I had him when I said offhandedly, "I just thought maybe we could jaw about flying ... "

"Oh, no, no. Please don't leave!" he cajoled.

He was very grand with his gestures as he ushered me away from the greedy eyes of clerks to a secluded salon off the main lobby. The room had emerald-green wallpaper with flocked palm trees that matched the various potted plants placed between the velvet settees and antique armchairs. The effect of the print and the greenery made the place look like an island paradise. I'm not sure why, but it was just then that I began to refer to him as Harry and not Mr. Beeman in my head. Somehow, I knew that we would be friends, he and I. He offered me one of a twin pair of plum-colored velvet chairs. The tufted backs were high and curved into the shape of a heart at the top. I eased myself up to the chair's stiffer front ledge and stretched my bad leg out in front of me.

I got right down to business, "I'll give you as many lessons as you desire. There's just one ... hurdle."

"Hurdle? What on earth could be a hurdle?" Harry questioned, immediately interested, his face plastered into a quizzical grin.

"Well, I need to finish payment on the plane that is being put together for me in Dallas."

"How much do you owe?" he asked. He, too, liked to get right to the point. I was relieved that he had matched my direct approach with a straightforwardness of his own.

"I owe two hundred and fifty dollars."

Although I was stating a fact and did not consider myself to be begging, I had to resist the urge to look away. It was just the act of having to ask that hurt my pride. He gave no indication that I should give my request a moment's thought.

"Come," Harry said, giving me a wink and springing from his velvet chair.

I trailed him back to the grand lobby. Even though Harry wobbled from side to side, he covered a lot of ground at a surprisingly rapid clip. We passed beneath an exquisite chandelier, an octopus of prisms with dangling shards of crystal that threw saw-toothed splashes of light and shade across the marble floor. Disapproving eyes followed our every step.

"Doesn't all this attention on us bother you?" I whispered.

"Pay those folks no mind whatsoever!" he beamed a devilish smile. "They are not enlightened the way we are. Just thinking about flying aeroplanes makes me giddy! These poor folks have no idea what they're missing out on!"

We spilled into his sumptuous office, which was richly decorated and dominated by a lush, beet-red Persian rug with swirls around a ruby marquis and terminating in ivory fringe along both ends of the whole affair. The rug was as much a piece of art as it was furnishing. Floating in the creamy border, was a repeating scene—brown men were hunting. Each hunter trained a bow and arrow on his own satyr. The red center was a sea of blood. I was so drawn in by the pattern, that I tripped over my own feet trying to get a better look.

A barrel-backed chair behind a giant mahogany desk sat waiting. Harry seemed somehow bigger as he mounted his throne. A rectangular, brass, open box with the single word INBOX lay before us. Nothing else polluted the glossy surface.

"Please sit down."

He motioned for me to sit in one of the two matching red tufted-leather chairs in front of his desk, and it occurred to me as I did so, that the fine carpet and luxury furnishings cost multiples of the amount I had asked him for.

"What was the name of the outfit in Dallas, the place fixing up the aeroplane for you?"

Harry pulled open a drawer in his desk and brought out a giant leather-bound notebook. A second drawer provided a golden pen, and in a grand sweeping motion he scrawled his name into the book.

"Dallas Love Field Aeroplane Sales and Maintenance," I replied.

The book's perforated edges let me know that a check—a promissory note on my future—lay suspended between his fingertips. When I took it from his hand, something other than paper transferred between us. As my eager fingers grasped the tender, I felt live current pass from him to me. He had money and access; I had skill and desire.

"Listen, Mr. Harry, I want you to come to see my next air show so you can see what all the fuss is about. It's scheduled for May Day. Why don't we make that your first lesson? In fact, we can fly until Jacksonville runs out of gas," I tried to smile coyly.

"Is that where the show will be? In Jacksonville?"

"Yep. My air show is the centerpiece of the Negro Welfare League's

May Day celebration."

He stiffened. Parading around his own hotel lobby was one thing, but a white man surrounded by thousands of Negroes, well … that was quite another.

"Negro Welfare League?" he said slowly.

"Listen, you won't be waving any banners or anything; you and I are going to be flying. Come on. It really is a happy affair. Lots of lemonade and popcorn. It's wholesome. Just a whole lot of decent, regular people. Please."

"Hmmm. Well, I do have some business in Jacksonville toward the end of April," he said. I heard the whisper glide of his desk drawer. This time he fished out his calendar.

"I can't believe it," he declared, looking up in surprise.

"What's that?"

"I will be in Jacksonville on Friday, April 30!"

"Well then, it's settled. You will be my honored guest," I said, encouraged by how things were shaping up.

"All right, Miss Bessie. I will be there. I can't wait to drill holes in the sky with you," he said. "I just hope nobody sees me making a fool of myself."

"There's never anything foolish about flying," I said. "It's a deal then, Harry. I will see you in Jacksonville."

I leapt up and we shook hands across a shining yard of polished mahogany. I floated over the Persian rug and skipped through the lobby, this time not caring who stared at me. The tune from *Shuffle Along* warbled through my head and I was powerless to stop humming and skipping. "I'm just wild about Harry!" I sang out loud.

Ha! I was back in business.

CHAPTER 48

Thanks to Harry, I had enough money to make this show a reality, and I sent word to Luella that I was ready for my aeroplane. She sent a reply that the plane wouldn't be ready until April 26, which was cutting things close for the Jacksonville show scheduled for the first of May. I had been in plenty of tight squeezes before, but I couldn't afford to have egg all over my face, not with Harry coming.

Luella wrote that I need only wire her the final payment, and for a small additional fee a pilot named William Wills, who was also a mechanic, would fly the aeroplane directly to me in Jacksonville. The trip from Dallas to Jacksonville was a thousand miles of long, hard flying, which made a door-to-door delivery an attractive prospect. Harry's check had cleared, but I was nervous about wiring Luella the final payment. How could I know that she wouldn't take my money and not deliver? Rather than a payment, I sent her a telegram.

DALLAS WESTERN UNION HOLDING FINAL PAYMENT.
STOP. WILL RELEASE UPON RECEIPT OF AEROPLANE ON
APRIL 26 AS PROMISED. STOP. BC

I held on tightly to my receipt and wrote back instructing her to have the mechanic fly my aeroplane to me in Jacksonville. If the plane could fly that far, it had to be in good working order. Right? The seventy-five dollar delivery fee cut into my savings, but I knew I could ask Mr. Beeman for this amount as well. It was chicken feed to him, but I planned to ask him for bigger investments later, and I didn't want to start begging him for a dime today and a nickel tomorrow.

With the aeroplane details on simmer, I was able to think about other things. Norma was making good on her promise and would be arriving the following week. Norma's coming really was going to be like Christmas all over again!

"You look like you swallowed a watermelon," I laughed as she lumbered off of the train.

"This one is ripe alright!" Norma hugged me as closely as her belly would allow.

Once we got home, I introduced her to the Hills, and they hugged, too. "I have heard so much about you and your hospitality, Reverend and Mrs. Hill," Norma cooed.

"Likewise," Mrs. Hill returned. "Welcome to Jacksonville and to our humble home."

"Thank you. I am honored," Norma said graciously.

I caught Norma up on the happenings. I told her that Mr. Abbott was nearby, having come to town to visit his aging mother. While he had successfully urged millions to move up north, his own mother had yet to leave Georgia—a familiar pattern, as young people set out for broader horizons while their older loved ones chose to stay back and continue on with the world as they knew it.

Mr. Abbott had grumbled but promised to travel a little further south to see my show. In addition, Mr. Richard Norman of the famous Norman Studios, right there in Jacksonville, had also promised to attend. Norman, a white man who made films featuring all-Negro casts of full, rich characters like cowboys and war heroes, wanted to film me in action! Perhaps he made his films to cash in on the Negro audiences who were starving for positive stories about themselves, but most people I knew didn't question Mr. Norman's motives, and it didn't matter anyway, because the entertainment was positively jake with me. I, like many others, was just grateful to go to the cinema and not see those Uncle Tom characters looking back at us.

As for my own motives, they were entirely out in the open. Mr. Norman and I had been exchanging letters for weeks. I had been as up front with him as I had been with Harry, and I told him in my second letter that I wanted to turn my journal and scrapbooks into a moving picture about my life. He loved the idea.

On the 26th I got up at five and dressed.

At the field, I paced and paced until seven, walking the full length of the grass that ran between Edgewood and Broadway. By eight, I had collapsed on a bench. By nine, I had begun to pace again. When Wills hadn't shown by noon, I was in a fever of anxiety. My palms began their telltale sweating, and I could hear my own breathing.

"Where on earth could he be?" I questioned Norma and the Hills when they joined me at Paxon Field.

"Now, now. He's on his way, child," Reverend Hill said calmingly. Seeing me furiously wringing my fingers he placed his hand over mine. "Don't worry. Everything is in God's hands."

"Relax," Norma said easily. "Just like you said, the man's expecting his payday. He'll show."

But I couldn't relax. My imagination and anxiety were working me into a frenzy.

Then, around three o'clock, when I was nearly spent from the hours of worry, I heard the JN-4's distinctive whir. A dark speck far off in the distance headed due east accompanied the whine of its rotary engine. But it sounded weary, as if it were struggling to maintain a steady pace. I almost hoped, from the sound of it, that this was, in fact, not my aeroplane. The engine coughed and choked, sputtered and wheezed its way on a long straight-in.

The organizers had given the field a fresh cut, having a tractor mow a giant swath of lawn a mile long and fifty feet wide. Even if he was bone weary, William Wills would be able to find us from the air. And he did. He set it down roughly and the plane bumped and bucked to a stop.

I ran toward the ailing ship, and the others followed, although I hadn't even told them what to do as we neared the spinning propeller. Some kind of instructor I was going to be! I stopped dead in my tracks and everyone bumped into one another behind me.

"Grab the hanging metal bars," I yelled, pointing to the axe handles along the bottom of either wing. "Whatever you do, stay behind the propeller at all times, or it will chop you to bits!"

The instruction wasn't needed, though. By the time we got halfway there, the plane sputtered out and rolled to a stop on its own. The engine backfired, and the prop rocked back and forth and came to a rigid, dispirited standstill.

The mechanic looked like a fifteen-year-old boy. As he hauled himself out of the cockpit, I first noticed his platinum crew cut was not shielded, as he wore no helmet. He had pushed up his goggles, and they sprouted from his forehead, leaving behind bruised tracks in a sunburned face.

Reverend Hill bent over with his hands on his knees, wheezing from our all-out sprint. Norma had her eyes screwed shut and was holding her belly, completely winded.

"Hello," I finally managed. "You must be William Wills."

"Yup," he answered. "I would like to make your proper acquaintance, ma'am, but I really do needs to relieve myself. I been in this plane an awful long time," he said, more than a hint of desperation in his voice.

"Oh, by all means, please!" I said, motioning to a clump of weeds. Modesty made the others turn their heads. I went straight to the plane to inspect it.

"I am disappointed," I said to Wills when he returned. "I was hoping that the aeroplane would be in better condition."

He maneuvered his way between me and my new, decrepit possession. Friendlier now, he offered a hand to shake. When I saw that it had drops of moisture, I hesitated before shaking it.

"Before this trip, I reckon, I would'a told you she was an oldie but a goodie. But this was a heck of a long ride," Wills said. "I planned three fuel stops, but I had to make five stops instead—three for fuel and two for 'mergencies. That's why I got here so late."

I studied his face.

"What happened?" I asked, trying to keep any accusation from my voice, but I felt as if we were breathing my distrust instead of air.

"Well, one time the engine just plain quit, so I landed next to a farmer's cane field north of Hattiesburg. Made it out of Mississippi, but then she sputtered out, and I set her down a second time 'fore I had to cross a squiggly mess of rivers outside Mobile. S'pose to get 'bout ninety horsepower, but I was lucky if she was makin' half that."

"This hunk of junk!" I burst out, no longer able to keep my anger and disappointment inside. "I should have known not to trust that Luella!"

"You got every right to be upset," said Wills, looking sheepish. "And you can always go after 'em later. But as I understands it, you needs this 'yere aeroplane in a show on Satadee. That's four days from t'day."

"You don't need to remind me," I snapped.

Undeterred, he said, "I think I know what's wrong wit' her. I mean, after all, I flew this bucket-a-bolts a thousand miles. If I can borrow a few tools, I might be able to make this thang hum again."

I desperately wanted to believe, or at least to borrow, his youthful confidence. And I was grateful for his offer. We might not have been what the other expected, but as of that moment, he and I were in this together. "Oh, before I forget." I handed him an envelope. Inside were three twenty-dollar bills, along with two sawbucks, four dog-eared dollars and, clanking from corner to corner along the fold, four quarters.

"It's not your fault the plane is junk," I said, hoping to change the tone. "What do you think the main problem is?"

"I thinks she's starved for a little love and care," Wills said, shoving his envelope into a deep pocket in his tattered, oily flight suit. "Listen, ma'am. After I eats, I wanna get to work on this 'yere ship. We can have her whistling *Dixie* by Satadee, but right now, I'm starving."

"*Dixie?*" I snapped.

"You know, speedy-like."

"Yeah, I know … "

"I don't mean to offend … " he continued.

"I am sure you don't," I replied.

"No, ma'am, I don't," Wills said. "We can have her humming whatever tune you please."

"Come on then," I said, "let's get you fed."

Norma, the Hills, and I were scheduled to meet Mr. Abbott, who was coincidentally in town to visit his aging mother, for supper at a juke joint in the Negro section of Jacksonville. I figured that we might as well drag Wills along.

"Look, I came here to see you fly, not die!" Norma grabbed my arm and pulled me into a tight curl away from the others. "This thing is junk! You said so yourself. We can postpone this May Day shindig. I'll stand right in front of that plane if I have to, and you know I mean it," Norma hissed. "Don't you dare throw your life away. I am convinced I am here to tell you not to do this."

"I can't call it off now, Norma. Look, we have four days. Let's see what the mechanic can do. After all, he did make it here in one piece," I said.

"Barely," Norma spat.

I felt as if I had sent out wedding invitations and that all the guests were already seated. This show had to go on.

CHAPTER 49

I strode into the juke joint. Norma, Reverend and Mrs. Hill behind me. Wills followed.

A Scott Joplin look-a-like was pounding out *Maple Leaf Rag* on a tinny old upright. But when he spotted Wills, the music stopped abruptly. Everyone stopped talking and chewing. The joint was so quiet, I could hear the sawdust crunch beneath my boots as I made my way across the oak planks that led to Mr. Abbott's table.

"Who is that?" Mr. Abbott demanded loudly, jerking his head in Wills's direction. "Did he come in here with you?" His question was an accusation.

"Why, this is William Wills," I offered with a tight smile. "He ferried my plane here from Dallas. He is also my mechanic." I said it loudly enough so that everyone who was staring at us could hear.

"Bessie," Mr. Abbott cut me off. "I don't like the looks of that redneck."

He made no attempt to lower his voice and just zeroed in on Wills, whose neck was indeed growing redder by the moment, and who had crimson cow splotches spreading across his cheeks and forehead.

"What on earth are you thinking, bringing that white boy in here?" Mr. Abbott demanded.

"This restaurant is an institution. I didn't think you, of all people, would need an explanation." I glanced around us at the tables loaded with mounds of fried chicken, vats of collards, big fat juicy burgers, and jelly jars full of prohibition hooch. "These regulars shed their skin at the door. They come here to be among their own people! They don't want any white man in here!" Mr. Abbott shouted.

"William flew all day yesterday, slept in a field, and then flew all day today to get me my plane on time. He's hungry and tired, and when he is fed and rested, he's going to fix the heap of junk that the depot in Dallas sold me," I said. "Please. I have to do this show."

We had a stare down. I hadn't intended to be belligerent in front of an audience, but Mr. Abbott forced the showdown. I knew I had won, when he waved to the pianist, "go on and keep playing, son."

Flexing his long fingers exaggeratedly, the piano player pecked out a few notes of *Evil Plan*, and its chords of danger broke the tension and made everyone laugh. With the heat now turned down, most people returned to their drinks and eats and ignored us completely for the rest of our stay.

Mr. Abbott didn't ask us to sit down. "I don't like the looks of that man, or should I say boy? You sure are heaping a lot of faith and trust on somebody you just met."

"I know he's young, but he's all I have right now," I whispered desperately through clenched teeth. "Now, can we please join you at your table, or should we sit at the only other table available which, I might add, is right next to yours?"

A tense moment lasted for what felt like forever. The Hills stared in horrified silence, Norma held her belly and shot daggers with her eyes at the back of Mr. Abbott's head, and Wills stood there looking splotchy and helpless.

I raised Mr. Abbott's hand to my lips and kissed it the way the faithful kiss the pontiff's ring. I looked into his eyes for any sign of give. They were neither warm nor inviting but, at long last, he flicked his fingers and extended his hand in a reluctant gesture of invitation.

"Thank you," I breathed.

I thanked God for Norma who was a peacemaker and who slid right in next to Mr. Abbott. She chatted and soothed until he relaxed a bit in his seat. Before long, he and the Hills were engaged in a lively debate about living in the South versus the North. Mr. Abbott argued that eventually, the North would yield so much more for those who migrated north. Reverend Hill declared that he had made peace with life in central Florida, and Mrs. Hill promised that if I were to settle there, she would get me an audience with Mary McLeod Bethune.

"Mrs. Bethune's college is a center of excellence for young women here in the South. Bessie will fit in with the strong, bold women here," she said.

"She surely will," agreed the Reverend.

"Reverend Hill, you are fortunate to have found the treasure of a wise spouse," Mr. Abbott said, smiling at Mrs. Hill. "I must say that Mary McLeod Bethune is an undoubted a luminary."

For his part, Wills was respectfully silent. There was no way of knowing whether he was listening to the discussion, because all he did was eat and eat and eat. He gorged in the way that only skinny people can—with abandon, gobbling down wings and gravy, biscuits, grits, pole beans, mashed potatoes, and corn-meal-fried pogies. And when he was done with that, he shoveled down four pieces of lemon meringue pie and drowned it all with strong coffee, flooded with heavy cream and about a cup of cane sugar.

When Mr. Abbott had finished his meal, he excused himself and went off to the front of the restaurant where I watched him ask for the bill. He paid for everyone, including Wills, which was particularly kind, considering his feelings about him. After chatting for a few moments with one of the waitresses, Mr. Abbott returned to the table and gathered up his hat and newspapers. He said his farewells to the Hills, gave a big hug to Norma, and did not even give Wills the time of day. He just walked right past him.

"I will see you on Saturday," Mr. Abbott said matter-of-factly as he turned to leave. Wills tried to stifle a belch, but moist vapor escaped, carrying with it the odor of fish, grits, and pie. Disgusted anew, Mr. Abbott rolled his eyes then shoved off. I ran after him to thank him.

"I know how much you hate the South, so I want you to know how much it means to me that you came to support me," I said when we reached the parking lot.

His driver scurried to open the rear door, and Mr. Abbott advised, "Remember this: many other newspapers follow *The Defender*'s lead, Bessie. I did my best to discourage them from writing stories about you after your accident. You were broken; you needed to heal. I waited until you were better before I reported on you. And look at you now—healthier than ever. I only wanted to help manage your comeback. That is why I am here. I have never left you, and I never will. I will always have your back." He stepped firmly onto the Ford's running board, making the car sink under his weight. "Now you get ready for the show. Fix your plane, get some rest, and I will see you there."

Gravel crunched under the tires as the chauffeur guided the black Ford away down the shady lane beneath the mangrove trees. As I watched it go, I felt a mixture of both melancholy and gratitude. I had judged him harshly, assuming that he no longer supported me, and in the process, may have made him think I no longer gave him my full trust. I watched until his motor disappeared, and then I returned to my best friend, my newly adopted family, and my new mechanic.

At eight the next morning, carrying all the things that Wills had requested, I arrived at the hangar and found that he was already there, inspecting the aeroplane. It was dark and smelled of livestock and hay inside the old barn that Reverend Hill had secured for us. It seemed fitting that my sad old clunker had spent the night in the company of milk cows and a broke-down mule. I handed Wills the satchel full of tools that Reverend Hill had helped me scrounge together from the auto shop of one of his parishioners.

"How bad is it?" I asked, as I bent down onto my haunches, out of breath after lugging the tool bag.

"I think we got our work cut out for us," Wills said, looking concerned.

As he worked, I followed his lead. Other than his occasional requests to pass him this or that, we worked in silence. A tray to hold milk bottles was commandeered for a soaking pan, and Wills had me fill it with gasoline. He carefully withdrew each of the OX-5's foot-long cylinders and passed the heavy rods to me, one at a time. He nodded toward the gasoline bath, where the fuel would act as a solvent. Within minutes, the pistons inside each cylinder loosened and the gasoline bath became fouled with black oil slicks and rust flakes.

"I think we got two main problems," Wills concluded after about thirty minutes. "These cylinders was clogged up. Probably 'cause they was flown, never cleant, then abandoned till I got in and flew her a thousand miles. Kind of like when you ride a horse hard and put 'im away wet."

"What's the second problem?" I asked.

"Seems like we done sprung a oil leak somewhere. We gotta find that, 'cause she's leakin' and smokin' and heatin' up like a steer in May."

"I get it."

"Oh, sorry, Miss," he smiled sheepishly, revealing a missing tooth. I thought I had seen that the day before, but then I hadn't seen Wills smile fully until now.

He might be new to flying, but Wills was a natural mechanic. Like a watchmaker, he could take things apart and put them back together again deftly. He moved his practiced hands over the parts as if he had been working on them for decades, which was remarkable for someone who seemed to have so few decades under his belt.

"They tell me you are one heck of a stunt fly'r, Miss Coleman. I don't have much to pay for lessons, but I can fix the plane for ya', and maybe iffin' we barter, you can teach me some fancy trick flyin'," he said as he fiddled with some part I couldn't see.

"How about we work something out once the show is done?" I suggested.

"That sounds fair to me. I sure can't wait to see you fly," Wills beamed.

About an hour later, he handed me a wood shingle, which he'd turned into a shopping list of items that he needed to complete the repairs. I left in a hurry. Trying my luck at another auto mechanic's shop, I found the hoses, clamps, and motor oil that Wills requested then rushed back to Paxon Field. It was past noon by the time I returned. I gave William the lunch that Mrs. Hill had packed for me—two ham biscuits, a cold jug of water, and a huge chunk of buttery pound cake.

"How old are you?" I asked as he devoured the biscuits, each in a single bite. I looked closely; he even seemed to suffer from a case of pimples.

"I'm twenty-four—well, soon to be," he admitted. "I look younger, don't I?"

"Like a baby," I muttered.

Wills shoved the hunk of pound cake into his mouth. He ate every crumb, including one that fell from his thin lip, bounced off of his knee, and landed a-top of his worn, dusty work boot.

"This here is a fine, little socket wrench," Wills admired. His brow knotted as he stumbled through the foreign engraving. *Hergestellt in Deutschland*, was stamped on the handle.

"It means Fabricated in Germany," I said.

"Lucky guess?" he asked.

"Wasn't a guess. I studied advanced aerobatics in Germany. I can't speak much German, but I can read it, and I can understand a lot. I know all the curse words, that's for sure. My instructor made use of them often."

Thoughts of Robert's sputtering guttural expletives made me smile.

"Well, suh, you really is something, ain't you?" Wills said, gazing at me.

My smile turned thin, as Wills had awakened suspicions in me that had so provoked Mr. Abbott. I had allowed my love of aeroplanes, and what I hoped was a passion that Wills and I shared, to make me put aside any fears I'd had. But given the poor condition of my aeroplane, the looming show date, and the slim choices of mechanics, keeping Wills was my only choice.

"I'll put the pistons back, connect the hoses, and tight'n the clamps. That oughtta get us through," Wills smiled.

The solution sounded simple, but I knew we still had hours of work ahead of us. We kept finding new small things that had to be addressed along the way. When I wasn't his assistant, I buffed and polished the lacquered muslin wings. They, too, were in need of attention. Bugs and sap threatened to interrupt the smooth flow of air over the wings. Like it was a baby's skin, I cleaned the plane, shining it gently, with clean rags. By early evening, Wills declared that he thought the problems of the leaking engine and the troublesome clogged cylinders had been solved.

We were putting the engine back together when we heard that the wing walker I had found declared she was too ill to perform. The pretty young brunette sent word by way of a messenger who greeted us in the twilight in Paxon Field, thrust a note at me, and turned and ran.

Dear Miss Coleman,
I can't make the jump. I am sick with fever.
Yours trooly, Dellphelia Pettycoat

"Here we go again!" I shouted.

"What's wrong?" Wills asked, genuine concern ringing in his voice.

"I keep hiring wing walkers who get cold feet and blame it on a fever!" Concern knotted his eyebrows and plagued his slender face. "Listen," I said to Wills, "would you mind flying for me while I do the jump?"

"Sure, no problem," he agreed. "It'd be an honor! I'll fly for you any day!" he smiled that missing-tooth grin again. "You sure you don't want me to do the jump?" he asked.

I paused. It was tempting, but I knew that first-timers needed thorough training, and I didn't want the threat of another disaster on my conscience. A hasty explanation was inadequate. Mattie had taught me that. We had no time. Since Wills could both fix and fly, we would be better off if I just did the jump.

The crowd wanted to see a pretty woman, whether Negro or white, in a smart flapper dress, fringe and tassels blowing in the wind. What would a man do upon touching down? Rip off his flight suit and show off what? Denim overalls? Hairy legs?

"No, I will need you to fly while I parachute near the crowd. In order to reuse my parachute, I will have to make adjustments to the rigging. I'll have to figure that out ... how to use it, stow it quickly, then use it again," I mused out loud. "Anyway, while they are still thinking about the jump, you bring the plane back around behind the barn. This is the last time that I will ever promise a jumper, and this is the last time that I will ever jump out of a perfectly good aeroplane!"

Although I had initially had my suspicions, after working together all day, I felt a genuine connection with William Wills. If he had come, as Mr. Abbott suggested, to do me harm, none of his actions today indicated any such malevolence. His mechanical work meant that I now had a working plane, and his willingness to fly meant the show really would go on.

At the end of the long day, Norma borrowed Reverend Hill's auto so she could come and fetch me.

"I don't know much about the upkeep of these contraptions," she admitted as she walked around the plane, holding her belly. "It looks better, I guess. It is clean, anyway, but I have just one question for you, Bess, would you put me into this thing? Or if not me, how about your namesake that I'm carrying?"

"S'cuse me, Miss Coleman," Wills interrupted, "I think I found the solution. I need to ask you to hold this clamp for me before you go," Wills called.

So as to lend Wills a hand, I quickly slipped away from Norma, without ever giving her an answer.

PART FOUR

CHAPTER 50

Jacksonville, Florida
April 30, 1926

When I first came to live with the Hills, they listened to my life's story and my lengthy explanation for why I had journeyed to Florida. When I had finished, Reverend Hill gave me the greatest words of wisdom I had ever received. His voice was a deep baritone, and just listening to him inspired a confidence deep within me. It felt as if I had been sent to him to receive this spirit.

"Bessie, you have lived a remarkable life in a short amount of time. I want you to celebrate every little victory. Celebrate all progress, regardless of how small it seems. This," he said, and he paused, "triggers hope."

Until I met Reverend Hill, success, in my mind, had been a yardstick measured only by accomplishments. I pictured success as a flight school that would proudly bear my name, or a shining fleet of aeroplanes painted identically, like the ones I'd seen at Fokker's factory, glistening in the sun. But that's not how Reverend Hill defined it.

"Achievement in your case is not limited to a hangar, or a mechanic in a spiffy uniform. Real accomplishment is your footprint left deep in the soil. It is a footprint that makes the path easier to tread for those who will follow—a chance for someone else to smooth the path that you have cut rough. Perhaps your life, by the example that you set, will convince another Race woman that she can do what she believes in. And it will be that much easier for her to step forward towards her dream. Success wears your face and bears your name, and it will carve your life upon history's page. Some milestones cannot be measured by anything but faith," he continued. "God has already ordained your victory."

And then, without the benefit of text, he recited from the first chapter of the book of Joshua.

Be strong and of a good courage: for unto this people shalt thou divide for an inheritance the land, which I sware unto their fathers to give them.

Only be thou strong and very courageous, that thou mayest observe to do according to all the law, which Moses my servant commanded thee: turn not from it to the right hand or to the left, that thou mayest prosper whithersoever thou goest.

Have not I commanded thee? Be strong and of a good courage; be not afraid, neither be thou dismayed: for the Lord thy God is with thee whithersoever thou goest.

This chapter and verse I knew well. Mrs. Bass had quoted this same scripture to me after my accident, and I had spent weeks taking it into my heart. It reinforced the belief that I have always held firmly—that you do not live once; you only die once. And so, I have tried to live every day to its fullest, to fly every flight with gusto, as if it were both my first and my last.

I dreamed of a school because I believe that life's best teachers are often the students who have struggled the most. They are burnished by their struggles—their lessons are the evidence of the life they have lived and not some ivory tower presupposition of what flying or, for that matter, life should be. I can look back on some of my darkest days and see now that it is at those very junctures that the most talented teachers emerged in my life. Without struggle, I may not have been able to absorb the lessons that they had to teach me. It was that fight, those constant jabs that made my spirit porous enough to let learning, and humility, seep inside. I have pursued my passion for flying and I have worked hard, never believing that I was a victim of circumstance. I have worked even harder to have a cheery disposition throughout my journey, and I have learned that you must never, ever, ever give up and that you must never take no for an answer. You must keep going no matter what obstacles are put in your path.

And in the end, I am a link in a chain, one single soul in a long line of people whose only job it has been to light a torch and pass it to the next person. I clawed my way to the sky so others could fly and soar beside me, and I hope and pray that they in turn, will look behind them to pull up those who are still waiting.

It's three in the morning. I want to sleep but I cannot. Despite my best efforts to convince my friends not to be fearful, I am truly worried about that hunk of junk that William and I cobbled together. And no, I would not allow Norma in it. Not yet. But I know I have already flown through plenty of challenges, and tomorrow will be one more. Whatever the new day brings, I am grateful to the Lord God for giving me his bounty.

I have an insatiable need to write down my thoughts on this, the eve of the Jacksonville flight, but in order to fly well, I will need to rest. In my sleep, I will conjure up a full-color dream, complete with Vivaldi's *Storm*, blaring, thunderous, and majestic. I will chase a rainbow that stains the clouds and makes an arc so gigantic that zooming under and over it makes me drunk and dizzy from the chase. The pungent exhaust of spent petrol will flood my nostrils, the racket of a beastly engine drowning out everything other than the straining violins. And in that rushing frenzy of air and sound, I will feel the others marching in behind me.

AFTERWORD

Bessie Coleman died early the next morning on Friday, April 30, 1926, at thirty-four years old. She was not at the controls.

As always, Bessie wanted to thrill her audience, and so working out the details on the day before the show was part of her methodical preparation for the Jacksonville Negro Welfare League's May Day performance. So that she could determine the best location for her parachute jump, William D. Wills flew while Coleman looked over the side of the plane. Just after she had unlatched her seatbelt in order to raise her torso above the deep well of the fuselage to see below her, her Curtiss Jenny JN-4 aeroplane lurched forward and went into a nose-dive. She was thrown from the plane and to her death.

At the time, many wondered if Wills had tried to murder Coleman, intentionally tossing her from her own plane. And although speculation thrived for decades, the facts do not bear that story out. Minutes after Bessie was killed, Wills crash-landed. He was gravely injured but still alive upon impact, dying only when a rescuer lit a cigarette and tossed the match, igniting the wreck and burning Wills alive.

A subsequent investigation revealed that it was an engine failure that caused Wills to lose control of the plane. A small wrench that had not been discovered before takeoff had become lodged in the JN-4's timing gears.

Bessie Coleman's death was a national tragedy. Three funerals were held, one in Jacksonville, one in Orlando and, finally, the last in Chicago, where she was laid to rest. It was reported that the Pullman porters began singing *My Country 'Tis of Thee* as they carried her flag-draped casket onto the train for her body's final journey home. Across the country, sorrowful memorials befitting a head of state took place, and heartfelt tributes were followed by services attended by thousands of mourners, some of whom had witnessed her flying, and some who never had the chance. In Chicago, thousands more braved a cold spring rain at the service held at Pilgrim Baptist Church, where civil rights crusader, Ida B. Wells, and boxing great, Jack Johnson, participated in her funeral. After her death, the legendary Tuskegee Airmen adopted Coleman their archetype mother figure.

Bessie Coleman travelled north during the dawn of the Great Migration and, once there, propelled herself straight into the dawn of aviation. It is the indefatigable spirit of this one woman that forced these two distinct but parallel phenomena that came to define America— ingenuity and racial intolerance—to intersect. Her skill as a pilot, her courage and fortitude in the face of what appeared to be insurmountable odds, and her relentless pursuit of her dream to fly, inspired and continue to inspire others, including this author, to do the same.

PHOTOGRAPHS

F. H. McCullough, Photograph of African American Aviators Bessie Coleman and Hubert F. Julian. James Weldon Johnson Collection in the Yale Collection of American Literature, Beinecke Rare Book and Manuscript Library.

.BESSIE COLEMAN

Bessie Coleman. First licensed African American female pilot.
National Air and Space Museum, Smithsonian Institution.

Bessie Coleman's pilot's license.
National Air and Space Museum, Smithsonian Institution.

General view of a group of flight students at the École d'Aviation des Frères Caudron at Le Crotoy, France, standing beside a Caudron Type G3. Bessie Coleman is shown sitting on the rear elevator.
National Air and Space Museum, Smithsonian Institution.

ACKNOWLEDGEMENTS

As a woman who loves flight, people who fly, and machines that soar and skip through time zones, I am ashamed to admit that I did not learn who Bessie Coleman was until I was thirty-four years old. Coleman was not in any history book or journal that I had ever read in high school, college, or even graduate school, but ever since learning who she was, I have wanted to write about her remarkable accomplishments. Her story was revealed to me by Captain Jenny Beatty, who gave me two gifts—a coffee mug with Bessie's image on it and friendship, mentorship, and sister-hood—all of which has spanned two decades.

The knowledge that Bessie Coleman did what she did in 1921 made me realize that I had the power to accomplish my own goals. I saw a woman who, over one hundred years ago, willed herself into a world where she became a *first*—and all without any of the modern conveniences that I had at my fingertips. If I had any doubts before, I was now convinced that I could go to flight school and pursue my dreams of becoming an airline pilot. That was more than twenty years ago. During that time, dozens of people have helped me turn my dream of becoming an airline pilot into a reality. Many of these same people have also helped me breathe life into Bessie's story.

I tried for days and days to list everyone I could think of who has played a part in my journey. But I realized eventually that I would inevitably forget someone, and since I couldn't live with that, I decided instead to thank groups of people rather than individuals. I would like to begin by saying thank you to the key organizations that have supported and encouraged me along the way. The Organization of Black Aerospace Professionals (OBAP) and everyone in the trenches with me, have been pivotal in my development, both as an aviator and a mentor. I would be nowhere without them.

Carol Gentry was the heartbeat of OBAP. She was administrator and peacekeeper; she was our soul. During a break from my first SIM session at Expressjet, I went to the ladies' room. (There were so few women,

I called the bathroom "my office.") I looked at the six calls from OBAP Chair Karl Minter and phoned him back immediately. He informed me that Carol had passed away in her sleep. I fell to my knees. Carol and I shared a name, a love of aviation, a passion for OBAP, and we shared the same birthdate, too. One of my mentees phoned. Her voice was wobbly and she was crying. "I called you first," Gabby Hewitt said. "I didn't know which one of my Carol(e) mothers was gone." Carol and I shared a love for her brother, FedEx Captain Albert Glenn. Albert is my mentor and remains one of my dearest friends.

I'd also like to thank the following institutions and organizations: Columbia University Graduate School of Journalism, The University of Virginia, College of Arts & Sciences, St. Louis University in Madrid, Rutgers University, B. Coleman Aviation, Aircraft Owners and Pilots Association, Air Line Pilots Association, International, American Flyers, American Institute of Aeronautics and Astronautics, Atlas Obscura, ICL, LLC, General Atomics, Guardy's Pharmacy, Intentional Talk Radio Network, Los Angeles Unified School District, Latino Pilots Association, Lt. Col. Luke Weathers Flight Academy (OBAP), MacDan Aeronautics, National Aeronautics and Space Administration, National Black Coalition of Federal Aviation Employees, National Business Aviation Association, Professional Asian Pilots Association, National Gay Pilots Association, Professional Pilots of Tomorrow, Sisters of the Skies (OBAP), Solarius Aviation, The National Association of Black Journalists, The Caudron Brothers Museum in Le Crotoy, France, The DuSable Museum of African American History, The Schomburg Center for Research in Black Culture, Smithsonian National Museum of African American History & Culture, Smithsonian National Museum of Air and Space, Vaughn College, The Greater Philadelphia Chapter of Tuskegee Airmen, Inc., Teens of Color Abroad, Tuskegee NEXT, Women in Aviation, The Philadelphia Inquirer, The Bergen Record, The National Football League, Foot Locker, USA, L'Oreal Cosmetics, and Expressjet Airlines.

The following journals and newspapers have added to my research: *Aerial Age Weekly*, *The Baltimore Afro-American*, *Bakersfield Morning Echo*, *The Broad Ax*, *The California Eagle*, *The Chicago Tribune*, *The Crisis Magazine*, The *Dallas Morning News*, *Houston Chronicle*, *Leslie's Weekly*, *Los Angeles Times*, *New York Times*, The *New York Herald*, *San Francisco Examiner*, and of course, *The Chicago Defender*, which chronicled Bessie's career. Newspapers were the social media of Bessie's day, and *The Defender* headlines, along with

Bessie's accomplishments, led thousands of African Americans from the South to the North. The Great Migration was encouraged by *The Defender*'s publisher, Robert Sengstack Abbott—in every ad for a cold-water flat and in each classified that heralded jobs, jobs, jobs.

My research involved going to almost every place that Bessie traveled and reading everything I could get my hands on about her time. Among the many books that I hold dear, five stand out. *The Warmth of Other Suns*, by Isabel Wilkerson; *Stick and Rudder*, by Wolfgang Langewiesche; *Binga: The Rise and Fall of Chicago's First Black Banker*, by Don Hayner; and *Shadow and Sunshine* by Eliza Suggs. The roadmap of Bessie's life was written by Smithsonian biographer Doris L. Rich, who researched and wrote *Queen Bess: Daredevil Aviator*. My hat goes off to Doris Rich, and I treasure the work that she did to chronicle Bessie Coleman's life.

I would also like to offer my most heartfelt thanks to United Airlines. I chose United because many of the people who work for this organization were like family to me before I ever joined the company. I love United Airlines and all the men and women who have chosen to bleed blue. I love everything about United, from its theme song, the iconic George Gershwin 1924 anthem *Rhapsody in Blue*, to the dedication of aviators and professionals in every discipline—communications, human resources, customer service, IT, and inflight. We work through holidays, weather events, and global challenges—and we do it together. We share travel tips—charcoal tablets for an upset stomach, the best brand of compression socks, and we often share the contents of our lunch boxes. United Airlines is a truly unique organization. It is a place where the most senior executives walk the airport corridors and are interested in every aspect of our work and family lives. For an extremely short, but intense, period of time we work and live with our colleagues. The best crews I have worked with de-escalate conflict, soothe the traveling public, support one another, and are empathetic to our customers and to one another, which is evident in our *United We Care* 501c.3 organization, which provides confidential, timely, short-term financial relief for those in the United Family needing assistance as a result of a crisis. I am honored to be on the Board of this extraordinary cross-functional team that does so much good for our colleagues.

Before becoming a pilot, I worked in media, entertainment, and corporate roles—but the airlines are different. In most jobs, one prepares for that first day of work only once—the initial meet-and-greet of colleagues, the right suit, haircut, a practiced conversation, the rehearsed handshake. But in our case, we meet and greet a new set of colleagues on each one-day, two-day, three-day, or four-day trip. I love that aspect of my job, and I live for the staccato pace of our work.

I have had editors along this journey and a remarkable agent in Marie Brown. My editor, Jessie Williams Burns at Tursulowe Press was extraordinary, with a strong wit with the stamina to get things right. I love her for taking on this project. Our skillful designer, Ute Kraidy brought our vision to life. Candace Williams-Brown has been my right hand this last year. We met while I hosted an OBAP program entitled Courageous Conversations. It was a dialogue with industry, union, affinity groups, and military and college students that was the brainchild of my mentor, Vanessa Blacknall-Jamison, who was at the time Chairwoman of OBAP. One day we will tell our children about how the world slept during the pandemic and how we were then catapulted from our sleep as we watched in horror while a black man named George Floyd was murdered by a white police officer in the street outside a Minneapolis bodega. A nation, and people all over the world, could sleep no more. Candace and I came together to host five conversations—a first in the aerospace industry. Candid, wrenching, and at times raw conversation defined our work together and made me realize that I needed her help to finish the mission I had started. She is honest, intellectual, and talented.

Bessie Coleman's great niece and nephew, Gigi Coleman and Arthur Freeman, have been extremely generous with their time and historical resources. They, too, have become family over the course of my work on this project.

More than anyone, I would like to offer my love and thanks to my own family: My grandparents, my mother's mother Emily Hamilton and my father's parents Lorene and Earle Jackson created the generational support that was necessary for me to grow into the confident woman I am. My mother and father, Carole and John Cary, poured every resource they had into making sure that my sister and I had a great education, because they knew that nothing was more important to our success. They left West Philadelphia and moved to a suburb called Yeadon, where they planted roots in order that we could flourish. My best friend Roslyn Russell lived two doors away and was the true inspiration for Norma in this book. My Sister, Lorene Cary, is an award-winning, best-selling author who helped me develop as a writer. She is my closest friend in this world. Lorene and her husband Bob have two beautiful daughters, Laura and Zoe. My nieces are my gems. Like Bessie, I am also a great-aunt—Laura has two daughters whom I adore. My two cousins, Dana Ridley and Kimberly Miller, are as close as sisters to me. (Kim's mom was also named Norma.) I loved her, and my mother's two sisters completely—Evelyn Campbell and Emily Ridley were identical twins and eighteen months younger than Mom. Together that trio was naughty, funny, gorgeous, hardscrabble, and full of moxie and talent. In high school I had another cherished Norma, my best friend, Norma Velazquez. I would be remiss if I did not thank Teresa Cruz, who came into our life when my children were small. My boys know her as Grandma Teresa, and she helped me manage home and hearth as I was working as a flight instructor and writing this book. Finally, my mother-in-law Shirley Hopson read an early draft of my manuscript. I loved her for her honest and helpful feedback. She and husband Wendell produced my husband. I will always love them, for they raised three remarkable individuals—Kathy Wesley, Christopher Hopson, and Michael Hopson.

And so it is that my greatest thanks go to my husband Michael Hopson. Michael has always believed in this project and, more importantly, in me. He read countless drafts and provided the steam for me to power through challenges. He gave me the gift of my first flight lesson and supported me through each and every lesson thereafter. Our two sons, Joshua and Coleman, are the fruit and joy of my life. Coleman used to climb the stairs in the dark to our third-floor office as I wrote throughout the night so that he could fall asleep in my lap as I typed. Joshua, when he was ten, and after a particularly long day, snuggled beneath the covers and said sleepily that he thought *A Pair of Wings* should be the title of my book. My children are my muse and inspiration, and I could not love them more.

I am grateful to God for the enormous blessings he has given me, of which there are too many to count. And I am grateful that Bessie Coleman walked this earth before me and forged a path for me so that I in turn could forge a path for others. All those who follow her are the granddaughters of her dream.

Author photo by Mr. Derrick Davis

CAROLE HOPSON

Carole flies the Boeing 737 for United Airlines as a First Officer,
based in Newark, New Jersey. After a twenty-year career as a journalist and then a
corporate executive, she followed her dream to become a pilot, working as a flight
instructor while raising her family. Walking away from executive-level positions and at
the peak of her corporate accomplishments, she went to flight school and completed
training in spite of having taken a circuitous path. *A Pair of Wings
A Novel Inspired by Pioneer Aviatrix Bessie Coleman* is Hopson's debut novel.

A PAIR OF WINGS

A Pair of Wings is a novel based on the life of pioneer aviatrix Bessie Coleman.
When no one in the United States will teach a Black woman to fly, Coleman travels
to France where she learns from the most illustrious flyers of the Great War. As
aviation and the Great Migration progress, Coleman becomes the only woman in the
world to contribute to both. Not only did she overcome racial, economic, and social
obstacles to learn to fly, she worked to inspire others to do the same. A century later,
Coleman's story, as well as her mission, is brought to life by author and pilot Carole
Hopson who has created the 100 Pairs of Wings Project, which aims to send one
hundred Black women to flight school by 2035; twenty percent of the proceeds from
the sale of each book will support this cause.

CPSIA information can be obtained
at www.ICGtesting.com
Printed in the USA
LVHW050134041121
702426LV00001B/189

9 781735 511160